APPOINTED

*Re*GENERATIONS
AFRICAN AMERICAN LITERATURE AND CULTURE

Also in this series:

SERIES EDITORS

John Ernest, Professor and Chair of English, University of Delaware

Joycelyn K. Moody, Sue E. Denman Distinguished Chair in American Literature, University of Texas at San Antonio

WILLIAM H. ANDERSON

WALTER H. STOWERS

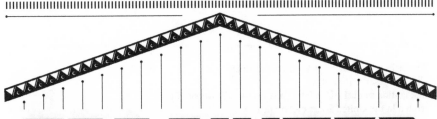

APPOINTED

AN AMERICAN NOVEL

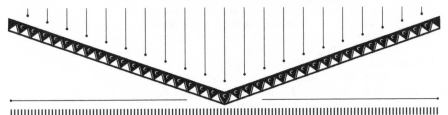

EDITED BY

ERIC GARDNER

AND

BRYAN SINCHE

· WEST VIRGINIA UNIVERSITY PRESS · MORGANTOWN 2019 ·

ISBN
Cloth 978-1-946684-39-4
Paper 978-1-949199-00-0
Ebook 978-1-949199-01-7

Library of Congress Cataloging-in-Publication Data
Names: Stowers, Walter H., 1859–1932, author. | Anderson, William H.,
        1857–1916, author. | Gardner, Eric, editor. | Sinche, Bryan, editor.
Title: Appointed : an American novel / by William H. Anderson and
        Walter H. Stowers ; edited by Eric Gardner and Bryan Sinche.
Description: First edition. | Morgantown : West Virginia University Press,
        2019. | Series: Regenerations | Includes bibliographical references.
Identifiers: LCCN 2019010276| ISBN 9781946684394 (cloth) | ISBN
        9781949199000 (paperback) | ISBN 9781949199017 (ebook)
Subjects: LCSH: United States–Race relations–History–19th century–
        Fiction. | Racism–Southern States–History–19th century–Fiction.
Classification: LCC PS2959.S23 A86 2019 | DDC 813/.4–dc23
LC record available at https://lccn.loc.gov/2019010276

Book and cover design by Than Saffel / WVU Press

CONTENTS

ACKNOWLEDGMENTS

The editors would like to thank Joycelyn Moody and John Ernest not only for their support of this volume and their broader efforts surrounding the Regenerations series but also for their embodiment of what it means to be scholar-citizens and their deep commitment to sharing and studying a richer range of African American literature. They have taught us much. West Virginia University Press has shown tremendous support for these ideals throughout the process too. Derek Krissoff especially offered valuable assistance as we worked, including soliciting very useful feedback from an anonymous peer reader. Sara Georgi managed the copyediting process with grace and efficiency. Thanks also to Charlotte Vester, Abby Freeland, and everyone else at West Virginia University Press who helped to produce this edition.

This edition would not have been possible without the aid of numerous libraries, including the Library of Congress, the Harvard University Library, the University of Michigan Library, the Bentley Historical Library, the William Clements Library, the Beinecke Library, and the Harrison Library at the University of Hartford. Among the myriad scholars who have shaped our thinking and paved the way for this volume, we would like to highlight William L. Andrews, P. Gabrielle Foreman, Frances Smith Foster, Henry Louis Gates Jr., Koritha Mitchell, and Carla Peterson.

The incomparable Nina Baym was on Eric Gardner's mind often during the preparation of this edition, and he dedicates his work here to her memory.

Dr. Gardner also wishes to thank Bryan Sinche for leading the work on this project and for his collegiality, Saginaw Valley State University for its ongoing support, his students past and present for always asking tough questions, and his family—teachers and readers all.

Dr. Sinche began working on *Appointed* during his year as a W. E. B. Du Bois Fellow at the Hutchins Center at Harvard University. For support both then and now, he thanks Skip Gates, Krishna Lewis, and Abby Wolf. He also thanks Belle K. Ribicoff for her extraordinary generosity, the University of Hartford faculty senate for awarding him the Coffin Grant that supported this work, and his students for making him a more careful and thoughtful scholar. Among many colleagues who have assisted him in ways both great and small, he would especially like to thank Eric Gardner for his scholarly commitment and generosity and Bill Major for his careful criticism, guidance, and friendship.

Dr. Sinche is pleased to share this book—and everything else—with Charles, Henry, and Melanie, and he wishes to dedicate his work on this edition to his parents, Charlie and Sheryl Sinche, whose love and support remain a source of inspiration.

Introduction

"SANDA" AND "JOHN SAUNDERS"

William Anderson (1857–1916) and Walter Haslip Stowers (1859–1932)—collectively "Sanda," the pseudonym listed on the title page of *Appointed: An American Novel*—may never have known a figure like the main character of their 1894 novel. Late in the text after growing more and more awake to the racism woven into the very fibers of the United States, the white Seth Stanley is named—by his dying African American friend John Saunders—the "appointed" to help lead the fight against white supremacy. Stanley pledges himself to battle "to aid in clearing our country from its false ideas" and to work for broad civil rights (235). Imperfect though he is, Stanley would have nonetheless been an immense rarity in the 1890s.

But John Saunders embodied facets not only of many of Anderson and Stowers's friends and acquaintances but also of the authors themselves.[1] Like Saunders, both Anderson and Stowers had family roots in the South. Passing through Kentucky on a train, Saunders tells Stanley that the "tenderness and pleasure" at seeing where his parents were born is an act "mingled with . . . horror and sorrow" at the "remorseless curse" of slavery and ongoing racism (154). Anderson's parents—Richard and Mary Lott Anderson—were similar to many African Americans in the Midwest. Anderson's mother's family had lived in Indiana for at least two generations, but his father had been born in Kentucky. (Anderson himself had been born and raised in Sandusky, Ohio, before moving to Detroit as a teenager.) Stowers's family history looks more like Saunders's. Different sources place his birth in Kentucky, Ontario, or Michigan, in part because his Kentucky-born parents (Jesse and Hester Stowers) fled from the racist South and slave power to Ontario and then eventually settled in Detroit.

Like Saunders, both Anderson and Stowers were graduates of Detroit's city high school (classes of 1875 and 1879, respectively). Like Saunders, Anderson worked in a department store (Newcomb, Endicott, and Company) after graduating, initially as a porter and eventually as a bookkeeper. Stowers spent seven years after high school as a clerk with Charles Root's dry goods store. And like Saunders, Anderson and Stowers were "strivers"—part of a small but growing group of urban African Americans fighting to enter the middle class via education, business, and community engagement.

For Anderson and Stowers, that identity was masculinist, and it marked heterosexual marriage and family as crucial to community uplift. As much as Saunders describes his deep love for his fiancée Edith Darrow, she is also represented as a logical match, a true complement to Saunders. While he calls her "pretty"—and, in the sometimes-strange rhetoric of a pro-Black novel, light-skinned enough to pass "for a brunette" in a white family—he especially highlights the fact that "she is as refined and intelligent as anyone you have ever met and more accomplished than the majority" (139). She comes from one of Detroit's "most prominent Afro-American families," each member of which had proven themselves "energetic and unusually successful"; while her father began in the trades as a mason and contractor "by dint of economy and thrift," he had "amassed considerable property" (143). Saunders's impending marriage to Edith Darrow thus represents not only the culmination of a romantic love story but also, perhaps primarily, what Anderson and Stowers would characterize as a sensible alliance for the "good of the race"—one that would increase educational attainment (through their children) and property in Black Detroit. (Notably, Saunders tells Stanley that he has already purchased a lot and drawn plans for a house that he hopes to have completed before they wed.)

Anderson and Stowers were further down this path than their character, in part because they conceptualized Saunders as a bit younger and in part because they had moved more quickly into the world of work than Saunders did. In September 1885, Anderson married Lucy J. Bowdre (ca. 1861–1961), the daughter of George Washington and Ann Fox Bowdre,[2] Georgia-born African Americans who had settled on a farm in Jefferson, Ohio. Like her husband, Lucy Bowdre Anderson worked for several years as a bookkeeper at Newcomb-Endicott, and, while the couple did not have children, was deeply active in Detroit community work at the end of the nineteenth century. Stowers married Susan F. Wallace (1859–1936, often listed as "Susie"), on February 23, 1886, in Lorain County, Ohio. Records on Wallace are much more scant, but most agree that she was born in Oberlin, Ohio, to parents from Virginia; her mother was likely Eliza Wallace, who was listed as Eliza Bell in Oberlin in 1870 (after marrying Walter Bell). Walter and Susie Stowers had two children, Marjorie (born in 1889) and Walter J. (born in 1895). Both the Anderson and Stowers families settled in Detroit's Third Ward on Division Street, where they were next-door neighbors (50 Division and 44 Division, respectively) for more than a decade before prosperity and the gradual opening of housing possibilities—something Stowers would fight especially hard for later in his life—gave them broader options.

These differences in work, marital, and familial status between Anderson and Stowers highlight another key difference from John Saunders. While the fictional Saunders attended and graduated from the University of Michigan, only Stowers would attend college—initially a commercial college focused on book-keeping and business practice, Mayhew's Business University—before eventually attending the Detroit College of Law and becoming one of that school's first Black graduates.[3] In Michigan in the 1880s, even that course was the exception for young African American men. African American students at the state's flag-ship university were even more rare: while Samuel Codes Watson broke the color barrier to enroll in the medical department from 1853 to 1855, for example, it was not until John Summerfield Davidson and Gabriel Franklin Hargo enrolled in 1868 that the college saw more African American students. The first Black woman, Mary Henrietta Graham, was admitted in 1876, and only at the turn of the century did numbers reach levels high enough to see Black organizations on campus. In short, Anderson and Stowers gave their character John Saunders significant educational advantages, but must have keenly felt that, even with such advantages, many African Americans *still* faced decided barriers when trying to enter the professions.[4] Thus, Saunders's department store clerking is, in part, the result of the failure of white Detroit entities to allow him to practice in his field—civil engineering. As much as he embodies the rare gains made by a small group of African Americans in higher education at the end of the nineteenth century, Saunders also marks the continuing discrimination of the world of work, discrimination Anderson and Stowers knew well.

Nonetheless, like Saunders, Anderson and Stowers continued their educa-tions outside of formal channels too. Both read widely and deeply and learned from a supportive Black community around them.[5] That learning brought them quickly into an exciting moment in Black print culture. It was a moment when select Black newspapers like the African Methodist Episcopal Church *Christian Recorder* and more secular titles like the San Francisco *Elevator* had established both multiyear publication histories and significant Black audiences.[6] It was a moment, as well, when African Americans were able to expand the slim points of entry into the print trades a bit more.[7] And it was a moment when a grow-ing Black reading public looked—sometimes desperately—for print material that spoke to their diverse experiences. Thus, Anderson and especially Stowers grew interested when, in 1879, Robert Pelham Jr. (1859–1943) and his brother Benjamin (1862–1948), both apprentice typesetters at the white-run *Detroit Post-Tribune* (where Benjamin had begun as a newsboy when the paper was the *Detroit Post*), began what can be best described in the tradition of late nineteenth-century amateur newspapers, an eight-page offering called the *Venture*. That paper, generally a monthly, was published somewhat spottily until 1882.

Joined by Byron G. Redmond (1860–1932), the Pelham brothers, Anderson, and Stowers formed a group of five, later christened the "Plaindealer Boys." The five young men, all of whom had grown up in the midst of the Civil War and Reconstruction, keenly felt both the hopes of and the threats to African Americans in the mid-nineteenth century; they felt, as well, a deep sense of responsibility to their fellows. Recognizing education and participation in American print culture as central goals, in May 1883, they audaciously started their own weekly newspaper, the *Plaindealer*—a newspaper written and run by African Americans that was first and foremost for African Americans.[8] They initially negotiated with the *Post-Tribune*[9] to print the *Plaindealer* in their facilities, and later gained their own equipment and offices. While we know comparatively little about the paper's initial years because issues published before 1889 have not been located, the paper quickly became a force. Plugging into the long Black convention movement, which had powerful roots in the antebellum "Colored Conventions,"[10] the paper advocated strongly for the February 1884 Colored Men's State Convention held at Battle Creek, and this work highlighted the editors' increased presence in Republican party politics in both Detroit and the larger state. (Anderson would become a key player in the National Afro-American League, especially in the 1890s, and Stowers would later garner appointments as deputy sheriff of Wayne County and deputy county clerk.)

The paper expanded in size (at one point running twenty pages), garnered praise from the likes of Frederick Douglass, became a go-to source for white newspapers reporting on Black Detroit, gained a readership well beyond Detroit's then-small Black community, and at times thought of itself as a regional paper with a national reach rather than just a city paper—including articles on and from, for example, the small Black community in East Saginaw, Michigan, a hundred miles to the north, as well as work from a regular correspondent in Washington, DC. The paper even had what was essentially a Cincinnati branch for a year in 1892, and ran, for a time, what it called a "monthly novel supplement" that reprinted popular novels of the period. The *Plaindealer* managed to survive for eleven years in a print landscape littered with failed periodical ventures, and the extensive extant run of issues between 1889 and 1893 begs for fuller study. Writing in his landmark 1891 *The Afro-American Press and Its Editors*, I. Garland Penn said the *Plaindealer* demonstrated that "with the proper business capacity and editorial ability," Black periodicals "can be made most emphatically a success"; Penn called the editors "men of push and men of the hour."[11] Penn concluded that the paper was always "full of news," with columns "teeming with bright editorials," and so "will always be a welcome visitor to the home of every Afro-American."[12]

When the paper finally folded, its editors had strong local and, among African Americans, national reputations. While financial difficulties certainly played a part in closing the paper, the Pelham brothers and Stowers became even more active in both local politics and civil service—endeavors that, like Anderson's work with the National Afro-American League, took much time and energy.[13] *Appointed* was published in the midst of this transitional moment.

APPOINTED IN CONTEXT

Unfortunately, key documents surrounding *Appointed*—a manuscript of the novel, correspondence about (or first-person accounts of) its composition, materials relating to publication—have not yet come to light. This means that we cannot yet trace what seems both an exciting and comparatively rare phenomenon: the creative collaboration of two young African American men at the end of the nineteenth century to produce a novel.

We can say that the networks that Anderson and Stowers established during this period were essential to *Appointed*. The novel regularly quotes from (and even offers footnotes citing) both white and African American periodicals of the period. Such texts would have been readily available via the *Plaindealer's* participation in the nineteenth-century practice of periodical exchange, in which a newspaper would send out copies of each issue to several other newspapers and, in turn, receive copies of those newspapers. Internal evidence strongly suggests that Anderson and Stowers may have been drafting the novel as early as the mid-1880s. Many of the stories and statistics that the novel includes appeared in newspapers between 1885 and 1890. Moreover, the novel mentions the massacre "last fall" of African Americans at Thibodaux, Louisiana, which happened in November 1887, and shows great interest in the 1888 presidential election (166).[14] At the very least, Anderson and Stowers were using either a back file of periodicals they had created or perhaps a kind of scrapbook of clippings from such periodicals.

And it is crystal clear that the novel was a collaborative effort. While the novel's title page carried the pseudonym "Sanda"—visually close to "Saunders," but also a plausible condensation and joining of Stowers and Anderson— Anderson and Stowers were listed jointly on the book's copyright page, ads referred potential buyers to Anderson by name, and contemporary notices listed both men as authors.[15]

Anderson and Stowers could not tap into a burgeoning market for African American novels or poetry in book form. When they wrote *Appointed*, there were comparatively few belletristic books by African Americans that had been published by major (or even minor) publishing houses, even though the Black press had begun publishing select serial novels by African American writers in the 1860s and had long been a central outlet for Black poetry.[16] In the white-dominated world of bound books, the bestselling fictions about African Americans were those authored by white men writing in the deep racism of the "plantation tradition." Thomas Nelson Page's *In Ole Virginia* (1887) and Joel Chandler Harris's *Uncle Remus: His Songs and His Sayings* (1880) circulated widely and attracted favorable reviews from white readers in the North and the South. If Anderson and Stowers wanted to publish their novel serially, they had a ready vehicle, but most of the serialized fiction printed by the *Plaindealer* was also authored by white men and women.[17] Some African American authors looking to publish bound books chose to self-publish, a course pursued by the poets Albery A. Whitman and Islay Walden and the fiction writer James H. W. Howard.[18]

Anderson and Stowers chose this approach, but their version of self-/subsidized publication was especially interesting. The title page carries what looks like a publisher's imprint: "Detroit: Detroit Law Printing Co., 47 Griswold St., 1894." WorldCat lists no other imprints from this firm, and no directory we have examined includes it. Instead, 47 Griswold was, for several years prior to and after the publication of *Appointed*, the print shop of Joseph A. Topping. Topping was essentially a jobber—a printer of texts ranging from Charles Richmond Henderson's 1890 pamphlet *The Ascension of Christ* and Lee McCollester's 1892 sermon *The American Citizen* to the 1892 commemorative pamphlet for the *Reunion [of] Battery I, 1st Michigan Light Artillery* and the Detroit High School Scholarship Committee's 1903 *Twelve Years of Detroit High School Scholarship*. In short, Anderson and Stowers seem to have created the "Detroit Law Printing Co." specifically for the purpose of publishing *Appointed*, giving the novel what perhaps read as a boutique publishing imprint, one that notably carried the weight of "law" in its name—something especially fascinating, given the book's attention to lynching and "lynch law." Of course, "Detroit Law" carried a much more personal connection for Stowers, who was completing his course of study at the relatively young Detroit College of Law; Stowers might well have seen this as a stamp of his aspirations, as his practice of law would include significant civil rights work in Detroit fighting for causes noted in the novel.

Anderson and Stowers may also have wanted to join the number of texts of the 1880s and 1890s that treated the "color line."[19] They certainly seem to have thought that they could leverage personal, political, and press contacts in order to find buyers and readers. And, for the most part, what readers the men did find seemed impressed with the book. Even the New York–based *Churchman*, founded by white Episcopalian clergyman and entrepreneur George S. Mallory, which found it "all manifestly amateur work" and submitted that "author, printer, and publishers are evidently alike new at book-making," noted "an earnestness in it and an honest desire to better an undoubtedly shameful condition of things."[20]

The reviewer for the *Cleveland Gazette* was far more enthusiastic; he classed the book with "Judge [Albion] Tourgee's splendid works" and appended a lengthy review from Tourgee himself that praised the book and urged its purchase by commanding readers to consider the words of "the calmest, most hopeful and self-respecting of the people we are insisting upon thrusting to one side and giving only the crumbs that fall from the table of civilization."[21] Writing in the *Indianapolis Freeman*, a reviewer noted Tourgee's praise for *Appointed* and insisted that "T. Thomas Fortune . . . pronounced it the best book issued in 1894 by members of the race."[22] As quoted in an advertisement for the novel, Frederick Douglass called *Appointed* "a very good and timely book," and the authors' friend David Augustus Straker deemed it the "complement to *Uncle Tom's Cabin*."[23] The novel also merited mention or more in the *Leavenworth* (KS) *Herald, Parsons* (KS) *Weekly Blade, New York Independent, Richmond Planet,* and *Detroit News-Tribune,* among others. Cleveland's most famous Black author, Charles Chesnutt, probably read about the novel in his hometown *Gazette*; in 1896, he mentioned it to a correspondent as an example of "commendable efforts" in the "direction" of literature.[24] Chesnutt's perhaps tepid praise aside, the endorsements from Black newspapers and from Douglass, Tourgee, and Fortune situate *Appointed* at the very center of late nineteenth-century African American literary culture, and praise from such "leading men" suggests that they viewed *Appointed* as a meaningful contribution to the aesthetic and political goals of the moment.

It was published at a time when "the novel became an instrument of choice" in what Daylanne K. English calls a "literary-political struggle," and it met that call.[25] The novel focuses almost entirely on the Black middle class and the injustices that flow from a failure to recognize the equality of those Du Bois would call "the talented tenth"—the 10 percent of Black men who were, to Du Bois, "exceptional."[26] As one might expect given this focus, *Appointed* directs readers to hope for assimilation rather than revolution—and so is very different from Frances Ellen Watkins Harper's novel *Iola Leroy* (1892). As Anderson and Stowers probe the potential for assimilation, they offer a window into relationships between Black and white people in the post–Civil War period and use that window to argue for changes running from the personal to the social to the political. And, like *Iola Leroy*, Charles Chesnutt's *The House Behind the Cedars* (1900), Pauline Elizabeth Hopkins's *Contending Forces* (1900), and James Weldon Johnson's *The Autobiography of an Ex-Colored Man* (1912), *Appointed* uses romantic relationships between individuals to mirror the relationships between Black and white Americans, just as the authors later did in their short story "A Strange Freak of Fate," which was published in the *A. M. E. Church Review* in 1897.[27]

Appointed is also notable both for its depiction of a white protagonist and his circle and for the ways it foregrounds the role of the African American press.[28] By reworking the romance plot, Anderson and Stowers developed a new way to understand love, duty, and obligation in relation to race. Within that romantic framework, the authors mined the rich legacy of African American newspaper reporting to show the struggles and indignities attending Black life in the post-Reconstruction United States. Through a combination of romance and reportage, Anderson and Stowers created something unique and uniquely upsetting: a novel that illuminates the chasm between white ideals and Black experiences and, ultimately, underscores the sacrifices Black people make so white Americans can maintain their ideals. While assimilation may be the goal for Black characters in *Appointed*, the authors insist it is the national body into which those characters might be assimilated that is in dire need of rehabilitation.

READING *APPOINTED*

Experienced readers of nineteenth-century fiction will feel themselves on familiar ground when they begin *Appointed*, for the plot of the novel rhymes with those of popular sentimental tales. As Book I opens, the white Seth Stanley sits aboard his father's yacht in the Detroit River planning a pleasure trip with his friends. Seth is the son of a wealthy widower whose business success stems from "constant energy, good luck, and the natural increase in land valuations," but the younger Stanley does not share his father's industriousness (4). Seth is an affable college dropout whose fondness for the idle pleasures of youth (boating, smoking, card playing, etc.) has kept him from taking his place at the head of the family. Though Seth is far from irredeemable, he is still awaiting the "transition from the careless, thoughtless youth, to the thoughtful man of great purposes and lofty ideals" (10). The primary force in helping him make that transition, it turns out, is a churchgoing young white woman named Marjorie Stone. As the novel progresses, Marjorie comes to occupy Seth's thoughts and his attentions, and, when he proposes marriage, he insists that their relationship has "transformed the young madcap of many fancies into an earnest, thinking and loving man, whose dearest thought is to win and love [her]" (79). Despite his eloquent plea, Marjorie cannot accept Seth; she worries that his years of pleasure-seeking hint at a fundamental lack of seriousness that will make him a poor husband. Thus, "love and distrust are mated in [her] mind" (82). To ensure that Seth's transformation from "madcap" to man is indeed complete, she proposes that she and Seth separate for a year to test the permanence of his transformation and the endurance of their mutual affections. When she declines his offer of marriage, Marjorie *believes* that Seth is a changed man, but she does not *know* that this is the case; evidence is wanting.

Over the first third of the novel, Anderson and Stowers establish the two problems that must be solved before the novel can reach its expected conclusion. First, Seth must become a man by learning to dedicate himself to something greater than his own pleasures. Second, Seth must give positive evidence of this transformation to win Marjorie's trust and affection. The nature of the evidence that Marjorie desires is quite clear, too, for she evinces "courage . . . patience, [and] fortitude" and expects the same from Seth. As such, she demands that they "pass through" a "vale of self-sacrifice" before contemplating a future together (94, 95). Marjorie's insistence looks like that of characters such as the eponymous antihero of William Dean Howells's later "Editha" (1905), who expects heroic action by her beau prior to marriage and, as a result, sends him off to die in the Spanish American War. True, the kind of demonstration Marjorie desires is markedly different from the foolhardy enlistment Editha demands of her lover, but this comparison reminds us of the ultimate stakes of Marjorie's plan. And whereas Editha's lover George meets his own death, Seth Stanley's "self-sacrifice" turns out, instead, to involve much greater sacrifices by the novel's Black characters.

Left with no choice but to follow Marjorie's prescribed course and sacrifice himself in service of an ideal, Seth decides to embrace his opportunity to grow. He throws himself into learning his father's business, and he outlines a program of reading and study that will help him gain the knowledge he lacks. All that is wanting as he begins this work is a "trusted friend in whom he could repose confidence, and perhaps, receive comfort" (102). That friend proves to be John Saunders, a Black clerk in the Stanley family store. Anderson and Stowers seem to understand that a deep and abiding cross-racial friendship like the one between Stanley and Saunders could only emerge from a unique set of circumstances, and a god in the form of a machine arranges those circumstances nicely. At the very moment when Stanley is shedding old friends and looking for new ones to help him make the transition into adulthood, he suffers a head injury in an elevator accident and is confined to his room. While convalescing, he falls ill with malaria and is temporarily rendered an invalid; all the while, John Saunders fills the roles of "nurse and entertainer" for a patient broken in body and mind (106). As the weeks go by, Saunders and Stanley grow to like and trust one another, and Book I ends with their friendship in full flower.

Indeed, the transition from Book I to Book II marks the novel's transition from the first love story—between Seth and Marjorie—to something like a second. For Seth, winning Marjorie remains a goal to strive for, but he has agreed to avoid her for a full year, and his injuries mean that he cannot return to work. Therefore, his program of personal development must take place within the confines of his relationship with John Saunders, the companion whose status as a civil engineering graduate of the University of Michigan contrasts deeply with Seth's as a profligate dropout. Despite this inequality, Stanley offers condescending compliments like, "If you were a white man I could make a companion of you that would stand me well in hand for a year at least" (116). When confronted with this sort of language, or with Stanley's insistence that "there is a better day coming for the colored people," Saunders rejects the flawed premises on which Stanley's words are based (117). Put in a position where he can speak frankly and confidentially to a white man, Saunders does not play the accommodationist. Instead, Saunders shows Stanley the error of his own ways; Saunders shows Stanley that—like other progressive white people—Stanley erroneously assumes that racism and inequality should be dismantled by its victims rather than its perpetrators.

The catalyst that transforms the nascent Stanley-Saunders friendship into a political relationship is, appropriately enough, a story in a news magazine. While the two men are lounging and reading at Seth's lake house, Seth comes upon the incendiary "Race Antagonism in the South," a real article by Senator James B. Eustis of Louisiana published in the October 1888 issue of the *Forum*.[29] In his essay, Eustis explains that the "condition of inequality between the Negro and the white race, which has always existed and will always exist in this country, springs from a consciousness of superiority in the white man, and from a consciousness of inferiority in the Negro, enabling the former to claim and enforce superior rights and privileges, and compelling the latter to recognize and acquiesce in the superiority of the white race." This imagined superiority leads Eustis to argue that the "Negro can live, can prosper, and can be happy under a white man's government, but a white man can never and will never do either under a Negro government."[30]

Discussion of the Eustis essay and the ensuing debate between Seth and John take up most of chapter 5 in Book II, and the debate offers grounds for disagreement and conflict between Seth and John, the working out of which propels the action for the rest of the novel. Crucially, the article positions that disagreement within a textual (rather than personal) context: each man makes reference to the claims therein numerous times during their discussion, and while they are not united in their opinions, they are willing to discuss those opinions rationally and dispassionately. In fact, as the two men discuss the falsehoods and misrepresentations in Eustis's essay, Seth exclaims, "I have half made up my mind to go South, as I have never been there, and see if these things are true, and to judge for myself" (137). As was true for his beloved Marjorie Stone, Seth questions his beliefs and demands *evidence*. Ultimately for Seth, any refutation of the Eustis essay requires the evidence and reportage that emerges not only from eyewitness accounts but also from the collective endeavors of journalists and editors. Rather than believe Eustis, Seth (perhaps like some readers of the novel itself) is called to believe the testimony of writers who are best positioned to understand the true nature of the "Negro Problem."

When John responds to Seth's questions about the South, he draws on an extensive report from the 1886 *Cleveland Gazette* to highlight the expanding influence of Black entrepreneurship and the significance of Black property ownership. He notes, for example, that African Americans paid taxes on over thirty million dollars of income and property in Louisiana and, at the same time, bemoans that this money was not used to support education.[31] As the two men continue to discuss education in the South and the problem of separate and unequal schools, Saunders offers a raft of statistics, some of which are backed up by footnotes from the conservative white New Orleans *Times-Democrat*. Saunders also celebrates the successes of historically Black southern colleges like Tougaloo and Tuskegee, using statistics and information that were gathered from the white-edited *Memphis Appeal*.[32] Finally, when it comes time to address the issues of labor in the South, especially in the wake of the Thibodaux massacre of 1887, Saunders turns to information he has gleaned from the *New York Freeman*.[33]

When Seth chides John for sounding like an "encyclopedia," John explains, "There are so many misstatements made about [African Americans] that [they] have to go around armed with facts to contradict them" (135). As one might expect, Saunders draws upon the work of the press—as a collective—to offer alternative testimony and thereby correct the "false representations" that emerge from the South (191). Saunders also uses decidedly unsympathetic news sources in order to show that the evidence itself is beyond question. The facts, the authors seem to say, are available North and South, to and in black and white, but as John Saunders's father later explains, "the trouble is that one-half the world is trying to devise means to escape facts" (195). The careful reader—the person who can separate factual evidence from emotional appeals—can divine the true state of affairs. Part of Saunders's mission, then, is to help Seth learn to see more clearly and to read more skeptically, something Anderson and Stowers had probably learned through years of reading newspaper clippings from southern papers.

Interestingly, even though citations from newspaper articles make up a significant portion of select chapters of Book II, none of the articles that the authors cite come from the *Plaindealer*. This is especially surprising since the authors mention, tongue in cheek, that their newspaper was "Saunders's favorite journal" (166). Still, what emerges is a sense of the importance of newspapers as a collective endeavor. Given this, what is even more surprising is the disjunction between the date of the novel's composition (perhaps as early as 1888) versus the moment of the novel's appearance (1894)—a break that seems particularly important given that the novel is rooted in *news*. Even though so much of what we read in the second half of *Appointed* is characterized by its temporalities, the novel's publication date in some ways made it old news or even, more simply, not news at all, but history.

Ultimately, that history is a tragic one. Despite the fact (indeed, in the racist logic of the period, perhaps *because* of the fact) that Saunders behaves with stunning grace and dignity throughout his southern journey—not only continuing to educate and convince the often thick-headed Seth but even helping save women and children on board a burning steamboat—none of that matters in the end.[34] Near the end of their visit to the South, Saunders and Stanley take a walk through a Birmingham park. Saunders accidentally bumps into an aging unreconstructed Confederate, Colonel Grub, and tries to apologize only to be insulted and then struck by Grub, finally striking back after Grub assaults him with his cane.[35] From there, the story proceeds along a predictable course: despite Stanley's desperate efforts to save his friend, Saunders (along with another anonymous Black man caught up in the violence) is murdered by a lynch mob.

In writing about the horror of lynching and the pettiness, jealousy, insecurity, and fear that motivated white extralegal violence against Blacks, Anderson and Stowers joined a chorus of African American voices that decried the scourge of racist attacks during the Jim Crow era. *Appointed* appeared contemporaneously with Ida B. Wells's *Southern Horrors* (1892) and *A Red Record* (1895), both of which draw on white newspaper reports of lynchings to document the white-authored violence that decimated African American lives and communities. Wells was particularly insistent on dispelling the notion of the "Black beast" whose supposed sexual desire for white women led southern white men to protect the "honor" of threatened women by murdering Black men. Much like Wells's work and "The Coming of John" in Du Bois's *The Souls of Black Folk* (1903), the story of John Saunders calls out the lie, the sexual mythology, that whites used to justify their violence.[36] Like Du Bois's John, Saunders is a college-educated, mild-mannered individual whose intelligence and self-regard is intolerable to the "howling, roaring, senseless, hating mob" that attacks him (221).

There is another way in which Anderson and Stowers's treatment of Saunders's death and its aftermath cuts against the grain of white supremacist depictions of lynching and lynching victims. As Koritha Mitchell explains in *Living with Lynching: African American Lynching Plays, Performance, and Citizenship, 1890–1930*, white attacks on Black victims were often commemorated in photographs taken from the attackers' point of view, photographs that focus on the death of a Black man and the violence done to his body. In those depictions, Mitchell insists, we see an "acknowledgment of black bodies and even black bodily pain," but not "the community's more enduring losses, including psychological, emotional, and financial suffering."[37]

While Anderson and Stowers describe the violence done to Saunders in graphic detail and position his death at the climax of the novel, his body does not pass into the hands of his attackers, nor is his body treated as disposable. Seth Stanley remains with Saunders's body in Alabama and returns it to Saunders's family in Detroit. Before he leaves Birmingham, Seth thinks again and again about that family and imagines "John's father, his brother, sisters, and his sweetheart Edith, all demanding of him an account for the life of the murdered man" (240). Seth knows—as readers know—that Saunders's life had meaning beyond either his friendship with Seth or his symbolic end. Indeed, by highlighting the effect that Saunders's murder had on his father and his betrothed, the authors show that lynch mobs "targeted valued community members, not isolated brutes."[38] In other words, Anderson and Stowers insist that readers consider the meanings of Saunders's life rather than just his death.

The meaning of that life is certainly clear to Seth as well, since Saunders insists with his dying breaths that Seth has been "appointed" to hasten the advent of racial equality. Upon returning to Detroit, though, Seth can only provide "a handsome monolith" to mark Saunders's grave and, thereafter, ensure that the Stanley family business would make room for "two or three bright

Afro-American youths" who would be given "every opportunity to rise" (248). Through these actions, Seth believes that he might begin to destroy "false teachings" and contribute to the "present cycle of . . . National growth" (248).

The horrifying end of the novel accomplishes the political and social message that Anderson and Stowers hoped to communicate: only when white men and women purge themselves of racism and commit themselves to the work of equality will "National growth" be possible. At the same time, that message only emerges at the end of a novel that concludes in the happy home of Seth and Marjorie Stanley. This ending—in which Marjorie and Seth get to enjoy a lifetime of self-satisfied happiness—engenders a number of questions: Why, finally, does John Saunders have to die to make Seth Stanley a better man and an advocate for racial equality? Why do the Stanleys get to enjoy a lifetime of domestic bliss while Saunders's fiancée accepts a future of grief?

One answer takes us back to the problem of evidence that the authors foreground throughout the novel. Before Saunders's death, Stanley seems a good listener and a willing learner; he accepts facts that were previously unknown to him and modifies his opinions of the South accordingly. When he is about to depart for the South, Saunders tells his fiancée that he wants Stanley to have "a favorable opportunity of seeing the South as I have represented it, and not as the Southerners he may meet with, will show it to him" (150). Like Marjorie Stone, John Saunders seems to favor a particular kind of evidence, and he knows that the only way Stanley can truly learn about the South is by seeing it with a Black man. Since Stanley maintains a strong belief in meritocracy for most of the novel, he has no understanding of a true caste system until he sees it up close. Added to this, Seth later finds accounts of John's lynching so "garbled" that his good and gentle friend seemed like the "aggressor." Indeed, "thinking that the Associated Press report might be likewise garbled," Stanley writes a letter to Marjorie in which "he gave a clear concise record of the events that finally cost the life of his friend" (242). Only when Stanley recognizes both the injustice of Saunders's murder *and* the injustice of its representation in the southern press, does he fully realize what he must do. By testifying to what *he* has seen, Stanley will try to change the minds of his white friends and (presumably) his white readers.

Through his southern sojourn, Stanley learns and confirms that the evidence of the collective Black press merits belief. But at what cost? After John Saunders's death, his father dies from grief and can say nothing to Seth Stanley; Saunders's fiancée moves to Alabama to teach African American children and is never heard from again. For the white characters, a romantic ending is still possible. This is a particularly vexing aspect of the conjunction of the romance plot of Book I with the social realism of Book II. Whereas an author like Howells showcases romantic ideals only to reveal their inadequacy in the world of war and struggle, *Appointed* uses the realistic mode to ennoble the romantic white character. Seth is willing to fight for Black economic justice and civil rights, but he only begins to understand the true stakes of that fight after "two souls had been sent into eternity" at the hands of a Birmingham lynch mob (239). Dickson Bruce thus argues that Saunders's "contribution to racial justice" is "more passive than active."[39] Perhaps. The danger in this construction is that it also demands a Black martyr. The best a character like Saunders seems to be able to do, given the raw force of white power, is to die to prove a point. White Seth Stanley is "appointed" to the work, but if we follow the logic of the novel to its grisly conclusion, Seth's work is incomparably lighter than that of John Saunders and his family. And who will be left to realize the benefits of that work? Perhaps it will be the three young men working at Stanley's shop, men who will "have every opportunity to rise accorded to their fellow laborers" (248). But even if, by arguing for equality of opportunity and the possibility of Black economic success, the authors hint at more radical long-term possibilities, they strike a distinctly assimilationist note at the end of a novel that, confined within a story of white romantic fulfillment and domestic bliss, indicates that real white sacrifice is not a precondition for true equality.

That said, perhaps we might see the very lack of white sacrifice in *Appointed* as a testament to the possibilities for a united response to political and economic inequality and a recognition that white folks are responsible for white racist behavior—that it is on them to change. And while it is true that Seth Stanley does not have to give his own life or fortune to transform the civic landscape, he does take concrete steps that men and women of good will might make: reshaping hiring practices and supporting talented Black employees, engaging in social relationships with Black men and women, and reading Black newspapers to learn the true state of affairs in both the North and the South. Ultimately, like Seth, who imagines himself "an instrument in the hands of God," white readers might accept that they are also "appointed" to remedy what was so often called the "Negro problem" but is and has always been a white problem (248). As Anderson and Stowers make clear, people like John Saunders have done their part over and over again. Now, the authors insist, it is Seth Stanley who must begin the work of trying to solve that problem. And Seth knows that he cannot simply announce a commitment to certain solutions; instead, he will have to produce evidence of his deeply held beliefs and the changes they have wrought.

There is a fascinating moment toward the end of the novel that suggests even more layers of possibility. On his deathbed, Saunders tells Stanley, "Don't blame yourself for this. You could not foresee the incidents of this terrible day. ... [B]lame the customs and prejudices of this people under which they have been raised" (234). Perhaps this moment is designed to absolve Stanley from individual blame, even though his privileged ignorance of these very "customs and prejudices" has been a key contributing factor in putting and keeping Saunders at risk (including Stanley's sense that "friendly" white locals may be able to save Saunders from being lynched). However, the fact that Saunders makes this statement and that Anderson and Stowers decided to *have* him make it suggest that some readers might find plenty of blame for Stanley—and a lesson in the dangers of oversimplifying the act of being an ally. Read this way, it is frighteningly, ironically, bitingly good that Anderson and Stowers may never have met a Seth Stanley or may have, at least, kept their distance from his "awakening."

Anderson and Stowers's later lives mark a different path. While both engaged with white people, especially through Republican Party politics, they charted courses that emphasized local action within Black communities. Though Anderson died of Bright's disease in 1916—not yet sixty years old—he continued to work with Michigan's African Americans, serving, for example, as one of the honorary vice presidents of the Freedmen's Progress Commission, a group nominally charged with preparing material for an upcoming exposition in Chicago but that produced a much broader range of materials on Michigan's Black history. Stowers, who lived until 1932, paired his work in county and city politics with active litigation—some of which moved up to the Michigan Supreme Court—fighting against, among other things, restrictive covenants and housing discrimination.[40] He also set up one of Michigan's earliest and most important Black law firms, Barnes and Stowers. In all of this work, Anderson and Stowers perhaps embody both what John Saunders could have been and a recognition that the systems that killed Saunders continued to place powerful limits on Black lives and actions.

NOTE ON THE TEXT

This volume is based on the first edition of *Appointed* published in 1894 by the authors themselves and printed at the Detroit Law Printing Company. The materials printed in the appendices are based on digitized copies of original documents.

Throughout this volume, we have regularized punctuation of contractions and hyphenated terms and have silently corrected misspellings and obvious typographical errors. The editors' notes and the authors' original notes are interspersed and consecutively numbered. Original notes are indicated by the bracketed statement *[Authors' note]*.

APPOINTED.

AN

AMERICAN NOVEL.

BY

SANDA.

DETROIT:
DETROIT LAW PRINTING CO., 47 GRISWOLD ST.
1894.

BOOK I.

Seth Stanley.

CHAPTER I.

The summer of 188– was remarkable for its intense heat during a continuous period of several weeks. It was not only warm, but very dry, and the little breeze that was astir was so laden with the heat, reflected by the parched earth, that it seemed like a breath from an oven. Instead of allaying discomfort it added to it. When this was especially noticeable, one afternoon in midsummer, and work doubly laborious, and the confinement of an office a burden, there lay in the slip at the foot of —— avenue, the pleasure yacht Sylvia, gently moving with the small ripples, that were caused by the passing of larger boats and by the hot land breeze. The intense heat of the sun had caused the streets of the beautiful City of the Straits to be deserted, save by those whose business required them to be abroad. At the foremast of the Sylvia was a bright new American flag, whose folds lazily yielded to the breeze. Obedient to the motion of the yacht, and as if proud of its flag, the mast swayed gently to and fro, as if paying obeisance to the clear sparkling waters beneath.

On deck, lounging in easy attitudes and protected from the rays of the sun by its new awning, were four young men, apparently overwhelmed with ennui and heat. Lost in the day dreams of their own imagery, not one of them felt communicative enough to break the silence. Meanwhile the captain, steward and cook, who with the engineer, constituted the crew, were engaged in preparation for a trip up the lakes—the Mecca of the tourists and home of the enervated, with its inviting innovations to the business man, and others who seek rest and pleasure from the activities of a busy life, and an escape from the stifling air of stores and offices.

The Sylvia was the property of George Stanley, a prominent business man, who lavished all that ingenuity could devise upon his only son—Seth, who was

3

then on board the yacht, the life of the party. George Stanley had risen to his present position of wealth from the ranks of the people, by dint of constant energy, good luck and the natural increase in land valuations. Schooled in the hardships of money-getting, he had become a devotee at the shrine of wealth, and gave but little time to leisure or enjoyment, so exacting was his business. Notwithstanding his busy life and rigorous habits, he lapsed into a very sunshine of tenderness when the interests of Seth or his daughter Imogene were brought to his attention. Success had always attended his ventures, but if failure had met him, his strong will and great energy would never have allowed him to acknowledge it. He was rather tall and angular, with iron grey hair and beard, restless black eyes piercing through shaggy lashes, a face somewhat wrinkled, but exhibiting that restless energy which characterized his every act. He dressed plainly but becomingly to one of his years and station. He acted quickly and with precision, and was generally right in his apparently hasty yet well formed conclusions.

As the young men lay, each apparently absorbed in his particular thoughts, Seth Stanley who had been quietly watching the crowded ferry boats passing to and fro, grew weary of this, and looking for something else to attract his attention, for continued lounging becomes irksome, observed the shadows of the masts dancing on the waters that sparkled under the rays of the sun. Being possessed of a vivid imagination, these shadows suggested images of graces which he at once clothed in the habiliments of personified life, peculiar to his surroundings.

"Look boys!" he exclaimed, "do you see the shadows of the masts reaching to and fro over the waters. What do they remind you of?"

The others, as if they had been waiting for some one to break the monotony of lounging, instantly cast all lethargy aside, and looked in the direction indicated by Stanley.

"It seems to me to suggest the idea of beauty bowing to purity," he continued without waiting for a reply to his question.

"A very appropriate simile," said Charley Parker, who was then standing next to Stanley, "for all things bow to virtue and purity, and if nature in her moods perform what we recognize as our ideal of the true gallantry of action it confirms us in our beliefs."

"Another instance of the conscious waters," replied Stanley.

"Rather the conscious masthead," said Parker facetiously.

"Why not say the conscious creative imagination, shaking off the lethargy the body has entailed upon it, makes grotesque figures or fairy images to suit its moods," answered Stanley.

"That seems about all that there is left in us that we can exercise without sweating and puffing. Yet I can find energy enough to admire our river—it seems like a flowing blessing."

Fred Morgan, who had stood silently by, interested in the conversation, now spoke up, "No wonder that the poets of all ages were moved to such inspirations when contemplating nature. They discover beauties that we dullards would never have dreamed of, and when we read their thoughts in the meter of their lines, we wonder why we had not seen it in that light before. They see speech and song in every sound, in every movement grace and beauty, in every shape symmetry, and eloquent expression in the mute inanimate. We see the object; they the intention of the Creator in that which the object ministers unto man. Not his bodily wants alone but his mental conceptions of beauty, grace and fitness."

"Eloquent! eloquent! but is it not the same in scientific discoveries?" said Parker, "Great truths lie right under our noses, but we heed them not until some one has gained distinction by calling attention to them, and by utilizing the forces of nature. Then we wonder why we had not discovered the same thing before and taken advantage of it. But we don't, for the majority of us are wedded to prevailing ideas."

Paul Fox then spoke for the first time. "Then the earth does contain truths as well as wealth that the inventive genius and philosophy of man has not yet dreamed of."

"I think," said Stanley, "that if the ability, time and energy which is now spent in trying to rob men of their faith were given to the scientific researches that contribute to man's material welfare, there would be many more revelations unearthed from Nature's store house."

"Such reasoning and speculation pleases a large number of people," observed Fox, "although we believe it so much mental energy wasted. Nevertheless I believe that the things eternal are not to be arrived at by finite reasoning. Beside the peasant with his faith is happier than the philosopher who creates for himself a religion."

"A discussion like this is fit ending for such a dissipated day," put in Parker. "Religion, science, and philosophy." His remark, however, did not stop the thread of the conversation, as no one paid much attention to his attempted diversion.

Their conversation became animated and in it they forgot the time so swiftly passing away, until the low descending sun warned them that it was time to hurry ashore and bid friends and folk adieu, as they intended to pass the night on board the yacht. A thin line of fleecy clouds girded the western horizon, extending upwards toward the zenith. Upon these the rays of the setting sun falling, formed a gorgeous golden tinted sunset reflecting all hues and tints from a deep red to a light orange. It was a magnificent sight, and one which would have made the reputation of any artist, could he have successfully reproduced it on canvass. The scene was not without its effect upon the party, for they admired beauty in all its forms, and it elicited considerable admiration.

"Such a sunset," remarked Stanley, as they prepared to go ashore, "if made the theme of a master poet, would make Italy jealous of her laurels."

"You have seen both and ought to know, but I have always believed that Italy's clear azure skies are very much overrated," said Fox, "and that it is largely due to the English tourist, fresh from the fogs and mists of London. Besides, being aided by the mystery of romance which hangs over her, her reputation has sustained the wear of years. But I doubt if ever Italy saw a more beautiful sunset."

"As I never saw a sunset in Italy, I can't say," said Parker, "but I know that a little romance transfers the ordinary dull vulgar things of life into those of interest."

"If we stand here admiring the sunset we shall have but little time for adieus. It is already late," broke in Morgan, disturbing their sentiments. "When we are once off we can revel in the beauties of nature until we become satiated."

"I believe," rejoined Parker, "if we were admiring the New Jerusalem with its symmetrical dimensions, streets of gold, sea of glass and river of life, you would remember some earthly obligation and advise the people to wait until they were there before they went into ecstasies."

"I would invite some to wait a long time if I did."

"I suppose that would depend on what creed your disciples adhered to," said Fox, "whether their doctrine was of the universal character or of the select."

"Something is breeding contention in this crowd," said Stanley. "If we keep on we will have hatched a new faith ere we return. Fred can't wait to see the varying shades of the setting sun making glorious the West, but he could spend another hour in discussion and not miss the time."

"Men and mules are contentious by nature," sagely remarked Parker.

By this time they were on shore and had turned their steps hurriedly homeward, and the excitement attending upon the novelty of their proposed trip, with the eagerness to return to the yacht, lent unusual vigor to their walk.

CHAPTER II.

————————

Fox and Morgan soon separated from the others as their homes lay in different directions. Fox was a recent graduate of Ann Arbor, and had the tall thin frame and slight stoop of the shoulders peculiar to close scholars.[1] His high forehead, Roman nose, dark brown hair, gray eyes and peaked features, gave him a rather classical look. Indeed the adaptation of his taste and habits marked him as one beyond his years. On the contrary, his friend and close companion, who in the fall would enter the senior class in the Michigan Military Academy at Orchard Lake, had light hair, dark brown eyes, broad square shoulders, was stoutly built, of a good medium height, and his every movement reflected the precision and grace of strict military training.[2] Although opposite in taste and temperament, each found in the other elements that bound and knit them closely together. Fox could have passed for a hard working, studious young minister, while Morgan looked like an amateur athlete.

"Didn't Seth's action and conversation strike you as rather peculiar?" asked Fox, after a few moments. "He seemed so thoughtful for one of his activity and lightheartedness. He really talked soberly this afternoon about beauty and purity. I'll wager it is the first sensible thing, that didn't savor of frivolity, he has uttered since leaving college. You know he left it in his Freshman's year after convincing his father that confinement and study was telling on his health. Since then he has done nothing but hunt, fish, and travel around the country. Now he has struck this yacht scheme and I don't suppose this mania will last him long, as nothing satisfies him after he has attained it, although, before in the possession of an object he sees the consummation of complete happiness. He is a good fellow though, with a kind heart, and deep in his soul there exist qualities which, if called forth and permitted to grow would change his whole life, and make him one of nature's noblemen. Everybody seems to like him."

"I wonder if Seth has fallen in love," said Morgan meditatively. "It would be too funny. He never seemed to care for anyone in particular, although by reason of his popularity and his wealth, he could have his choice from many, besides his very indifference serves as an attraction. Seth in love! How ridiculous!"

Both laughed heartily.

"But as you say," continued Morgan, "I noticed his thoughtfulness, but attributed it to the langour caused by this sultry weather. However we shall be able to tell before we get back. If anything is in the wind it will out in some way on the trip."

Meanwhile Seth Stanley and Charley Parker had proceeded on their way, and had gone but a little distance when Parker, who lived near Stanley, left him to attend to a few matters, promising however to call by for him on his way to the yacht. Parker was dudishly inclined, wearing the latest styles and was fastidiously neat.[3] His form was slight, hair light and eyes a deep blue. Notwithstanding his tastes he had ready wit and considerable tact, which together with his natural good humor, that showed itself on all occasions, made him companionable as an associate. He was quite a ladies' man, and was seldom overlooked by his wide range of acquaintances when anything of a social nature was on the tapis.

Stanley went on his way alone, his head held slightly forward as if engaged in thought. It was something new for him to be serious. His nearest approach to it heretofore was in his imperious manner. He inherited the determined nature of his father, and when once resolved upon a thing, followed it to its conclusion despite opposition. In devising means for pleasure he was an enthusiast. The pleasure attained, however, he longed and sought for new ones. Yet he had a kind nature and under noble impulses had done many a kindly deed and given aid to many a poor fellow in hard circumstances. At the time of our story he was in his twenty-seventh year, was rather tall and muscular with broad shoulders and a deep chest, and of the dark complexion of his father. He had a rather good-looking face, unfurrowed by care or serious purpose but marked somewhat by the dissipation of late hours. His hair and luxuriant mustache were black, and his black piercing eyes that sparkled in merriment, and which were formidable in anger, his young sister, Imogene, doted upon.

Fox and Morgan were not far wrong, for if Stanley was not actually in love he had a very peculiar liking for a certain young lady that he was too unwilling and too proud to call love. One evening, a few weeks back, he had been pressed to attend a church entertainment. He only went for the novelty of it, for hitherto he had resisted the persuasions of father and sister to attend church. Not since his mother died five years ago had he entered one.

One of the numbers on the program was a solo by Miss Marjorie Stone.

As she appeared upon the stage, neatly and plainly dressed, something about her attracted his attention. She was not what some people would call beautiful, yet she had a very pleasing and attractive appearance. Her face was round and her features regular. Her form was of middle height, slender and graceful. What constituted her chief attraction was the pure noble soul that seemed to look out of her expressive blue eyes. This and the modest grace of her bearing attracted Seth Stanley. Her song was of a semi-religious nature, and when her voice, which was remarkably pure and sweet, rose full and rich with melody and expression, he sat like one entranced. The words turned his thoughts back to the teachings of his youth, and for a moment he felt a twinge of conscience. Then reverting back to the singer he became enraptured with her voice, bearing and expressive face, and for the rest of the evening he thought of her considerably and joined heartily with the others in giving her hearty applause for an encore.

After the concert was over he sought out his friend Fox, as he was desirous of meeting her, and whom he found was an intimate acquaintance of hers. He was presented and was somewhat surprised that she exhibited no sign of gratification as others had done, on meeting him. She had often seen him in passing up and down the street and had admired his gentlemanly bearing, and had often wondered why a young man of his ability and opportunity had so wasted them.

Her unassuming manner attracted him more than if she had used all the finesse of the coquette to the same end. As he sauntered home that evening thoughts of her constantly flitted through his mind, but why he could hardly understand, "for," said he, trying to analyze his thoughts, "she is not beautiful, though decidedly comely, and her retiring modesty amuses me, so different is it from that of most of the young ladies I have met with, and her rich voice certainly thrilled me. I must see more of her."

He was pleased with Miss Stone from the fact that he recognized that she, being an exceptional character, would be able to amuse him, and for that object he resolved to cultivate her acquaintance; in fact it could be well doubted if he was at that moment actuated by any motive outside of what he experienced when determining upon a trip, or carrying out any plan in which he expected to derive some great pleasure. Some will perhaps be shocked at him, but then consider his training, the child of an immensely rich father, gratified in every whim, sought after by the mammas of marriageable daughters, a petted spoiled child, surfeited with pleasure and fastidious to a high degree, one who thought that with money all things could be purchased. Was he so much different from the rest of the world in this? How many noble souls and great characters have sunk into insignificance? How many giant minds have become dwarfed in intellect through the wealth of the world and the lavish praise of the flatterer heaped upon them? How many young men of exceptional opportunity and parentage are the sons of their fathers only? Is it to be wondered at that so many of the sons of the rich never obtain pre-eminence in learning, statesmanship, or literature, or that they rise above mediocrity, so enervating is the power of wealth among the majority that possess it? Some of us learn too late that happiness and contentment are more to be desired than money, and that money cannot buy them. Stanley found this out, but at what a cost of mental torture and anguish. Considering his fastidious tastes and his training, his resolve as to the extended acquaintance with Miss Stone must be considered in the light of a compliment to her qualities that, even without effort she exerted so great an influence over him. At any rate the next Sunday found him at church in company with Imogene, an attentive listener to the minister, but a still more attentive one to the choir, situated directly back and above the pulpit. He had learned that she was a member of it, and he could distinguish her voice above the others. He found his good opinion of her increasing. As he listened he was unable to tell which interested him most, voice or girl. He stared at her a great deal, and once or twice, when she caught him, he flushed slightly, and with some confusion looked quickly away.

Two or three weeks of the same routine followed. He becoming a constant attendant at church; thus serving a good end, for the words of the preacher awakened in him many old memories which caused him to reflect. From that time he had a double purpose in attending church. This was the beginning of his transition from the careless, thoughtless youth, to the thoughtful man of great purposes and lofty ideals. His mother was a good Christian and had endeavored to teach her child aright, but he found such teachings at variance with his inclinations and the practices of certain companions, and he had quietly lain them aside. Since that time he had sturdily refused to be upbraided for his shortcomings by any one except his father, who once in a while bluffly, but curtly, asked if he ever intended to be a man and settle down to business. In this case, once in the church, circumstances compelled him to listen. Listening aroused thoughts which brought in vivid contrast his own loose life, with the one of sacrifice now reflected by his new surroundings and teachings. Sometimes an incident in a man's life changes the whole course of his nature, while all other efforts in that direction have proved futile. As his mind reverted to his mother a spark of tenderness lit up his soul as no other thought could. He was in the humor for such thoughts, feeling depressed and remorseful.

The change was growing, he was fast becoming serious, more of a man. Thinking less of pleasure and more of the responsibility of manhood. His former boon companions he began to shake for the more profitable companionship of the young men we have seen him with.

He desired more than ever to become better acquainted with Miss Stone. He succeeded and it came about in this way.

CHAPTER III.

_____

At the solicitation of Imogene he called with her upon Mrs. Charles Durham, who had been an intimate friend of his mother's. As they entered the richly furnished parlors, where hung many a costly work of art, luxuriant drapings, and which were filled with costly bric-a-brac, Stanley's heart gave a great thump as he noticed a young lady at the piano whose form seemed familiar. While wondering who she was, she turned around and he recognized Miss Stone. Bowing gracefully, he approached her, and was about to make some remark when Mrs. Durham, a matronly lady, appeared with as many fluffs and ornaments as she made courtesies.

"I am so glad to see you, my dears," she said, as she kissed Imogene. "Let me introduce you to Miss Stone. I hope you will become great friends. You are acquainted with her, are you not?" turning to Stanley.

"Yes, I met her once at a church entertainment," he replied hesitatingly.

Mrs. Durham arched her eye-brows as she replied, "Now that's a surprise for me. We old people are way behind the times. You young people get around and acquainted so fast."

She then set about making the young people better acquainted, and to judge from the clatter of tongues and the sounds of laughter succeeded admirably.

"You must stay to tea," she said shortly, and out she went bustling without waiting for a reply to have the necessary preparation made.

Stanley noticed in Miss Stone the same indifferent, yet pleasing manner she exhibited at their first meeting. At first it annoyed him, finally it amused and entertained him. Finding that he must lead in the conversation if it continued as sprightly as before, he chose to speak of the concert where he had first met her.

"Miss Stone, as I have not had the opportunity before, I must compliment you at this late hour on your success at the concert. Without flattery I can say your voice and rendition were superb, far superior to some who make professional pretentions."

"Yes, indeed," chimed in Imogene, "your solo was lovely."

"I disclaim all pretensions to merit," replied Miss Stone, "and only filled in the program for lack of some one to complete it, and the concert was given for a laudable purpose."

"May I ask what that purpose was?"

"Certainly. Our sexton had been quite ill. His family having no other means of support were in sad want. They have three little children, and had scarcely food and fire enough for comfort. I visited them myself, and could hardly believe that there were people so wretched. But one never knows what he can bear until he has been called to undergo the scourge. We cleared over one hundred dollars, and you should have seen the tears of gratitude in that woman's eyes when we gave it to her. Even the children, in a shy way, clinging to their mother's skirts, looked their thanks. We felt amply repaid."

Marjorie told her story in a simple, earnest manner and there was the slight suspicion of a tear in her eye as she closed.

"Oh! It's a good thing to help the poor when you're certain they are needy, but there are so many impostors," said Stanley uncharitably, for he seldom gave any thought except of late, to anything not conducive to his own pleasure or to those whom he dubbed, "poor unfortunate fellows," who had drunk the cup of folly to its very dregs to find the bitter potion at the bottom. For these he had a fellow feeling, and they were the first to touch the dormant tenderness of what might have been a charitable nature.

"It may have seemed to you that people living in such want wouldn't care to live at all, but more than two-thirds of the suicides are those who were once above want, but have either ruined their own prospects, or have had them ruined by adverse circumstances."

"Perhaps you are right. Those who know only poverty and strife expect but little, and never consider their lot in the same light with those who have fallen from a position of wealth and affluence."

"It is brooding over one's difficulties and prospects that drive men to despair. They find themselves on the verge of financial or social ruin, and rather than trust themselves to the consequences, they fling themselves into the uncertainties of the eternal beyond."

Before she could reply, Mr. Durham came in, but Stanley's speech concerning the deserving poor disturbed her a little. Mr. Durham was small in stature, rather fat, and like most fat men, jovial, good natured and fond of a joke at some one else's expense. Marjorie was his niece, and the Durham's having no children, made much of her.

"Good evening," said he, on entering the room. Then catching sight of

Stanley and his sister, remarked as a twinkle lit up his eye. "Are young ladies so scarce that you have to use your sister for company?"

"No, not at all. Is it surprising that a young man should be seen out in company with his sister?"

"Only it is an exception," rejoined Mr. Durham laughing.

"I enjoy being an exception in this case."

Just then in came Mrs. Durham. "Why, Charles, what made you so late to tea? Come right out now, everything is ready. Seth will you please escort Marjorie, and you Charles, Imogene."

"Mr. Stanley has just said he enjoyed being an exception, in the fact that his sister is quite entertaining society, therefore he prefers her above his lady friends. You have broken in upon his enjoyment and made him give his sister 'the shake' already, to use the parlance of the street."

"It won't be many years before Imogene will have all the beaux around her ears that she desires and they won't be such bald-headed badgers as you either," replied Mrs. Durham.

"The lucky one soon will be if he takes after me," and he patted his semi-bald pate in conscious glee, at having floored Mrs. Durham in the first bout.

Mrs. Durham was very much pleased to have Stanley and Miss Stone meet at her home, for while she had been away at school studying music, Mrs. Durham had been very lavish in her praises. She had a warm place in her heart for the young man for his mother's sake and she believed that beneath the exterior of his careless life there might lay dormant, excellent qualities, which only needed some spark to set them alive. He looked so much like his mother that he couldn't be inherently bad. But Mrs. Durham was very susceptible in her opinions, and was easily led away after strange doctrines and beliefs concerning persons. Her simplicity and credulity made her an easy prey to representations.

Marjorie was a frequent visitor, but Stanley's life of pleasure and roving, since her return from school, accounted for their not having met before.

Mr. Durham sat at the head of the table while on either side sat Imogene and Marjorie. Stanley sat next to her, while Mrs. Durham sat at the foot of the table. During tea he had abundant opportunity to study the young lady. Although Mr. Durham engaged her attention more than was satisfactory to his taste, yet he had sufficient conversation with her to know that she was his intellectual superior. She talked more readily and clearly on all subjects than he could, even politics, and proved a worthy opponent to the caustic arguments of Mr. Durham, who prided himself on his ability to worst an enemy in debate.

During one of their heated discussions on Universalism, which was Mr. Durham's hobby, Stanley had time to reflect on his general ignorance, for though he had nearly finished a year at college, he had failed to follow up the information gained from his text books, by general reading and study.[4] He realized that he was sadly deficient in general information and in deductions, as compared with these two. Mrs. Durham tried to entertain Imogene but she was so engrossed in the arguments of the others that she proved only a passive listener. Once or twice Stanley essayed to engage in the argument siding with Miss Stone, but he gave a sigh of relief when the conversation drifted to the commonplace topics of society and music. He then had opportunity to engage her attention and to keep it awhile from Mr. Durham, of whom he had actually began to feel jealous. Supper over, they were again in the drawing room and Imogene suggested that they have some music.

"Won't you please sing for us Miss Stone, Seth admires your voice very much?"

He crimsoned a little at his sister's remark, he termed it a bad break, but joined in her request, "Yes, do, Miss Stone, for music you know hath charms to sooth the civilized, as well as the savage breast."

"Shall we consider that as an acknowledgment that yours is troubled?" piquantly asked Mr. Durham.

"Not at all, only I am passionately fond of music. When I was in Europe last summer nothing attracted me more than the opera at Bayreuth."[5]

"Then you must be something of a musician," said Marjorie, who was now interested. "For we generally practice that which pleases us most. Perhaps you are a connoisseur and my singing may disappoint you."

"Allow me to assure you to the contrary. I have heard your voice and have placed it on my list of attractions, of course with your permission always."

It was Marjorie's turn to blush, but before she could reply as she would have liked, Mrs. Durham who had planned while at table that she should sing, threw her weight into the scale by saying, "I have it. You can sing my favorite, 'Oh Restless Sea,' Charles can sing the tenor, and Seth, whom Imogene has just told me, has studied some at Munich, will sing the bass."

"Only a smattering," protested Stanley. "It seems to me that my life has been a series of smatterings. In culture I am like what Richard III was in physical appearance, only half made up."[6]

"Self-deprecation," said Marjorie, "is the first step towards wisdom. One cannot be wise until he can comprehend what wisdom is and what must be done to attain it."

"Philosopher as well as musician. May I become one of your pupils? I assure you I shall be attentive and an enthusiast."

"You might be both and yet despise my doctrine. You would hardly go around the world to find your Socrates or Plato in an obscure girl who knows little of philosophy and less of the world. Your remarks savor of flattery, but of course you were jesting."

"Neither jest or flattery, I protest, upon honor. The knowledge of the world teaches arrogance, while the philosophy of to-day is a medley of fact and speculation, contradiction and assertion. A man may be skilled in these and yet need to learn simplicity and humility."

"Have you not learned either e're this?"

"Don't put your scholar to the test of examination until you have given him lessons."

By this time the music was found and Imogene had seated herself at the piano to act as accompanist, so further conversation was cut off. In the duet, between the tenor and bass, Stanley's voice, which was rich with melody, rose so full and pure, so strong and sure, and free from the harsh rasping tone of the amateur, that Marjorie was both surprised and pleased, while Mrs. Durham, who sat in a large easy chair, rubbed her hands in delight during the whole song. It was finely rendered.

"Bravo," cried the accompanist when the song was finished. "Bravo," echoed Mrs. Durham from the depths of her easy chair, and insisted upon a repetition of it, but Mr. Durham claimed he was at a disadvantage in company with two professionals and refused to sing, which caused Mrs. Durham to scowl.

Marjorie and Stanley at once began to enter their protestations: "Why, the idea, uncle," exclaimed Marjorie, "of you leading Mr. Stanley to believe me a professional."

"Allow me to say," said Stanley, who had been trying to speak, "that you have presented my grievance exactly."

Mr. Durham saw that he had put his foot in it and called their attention to a painting he had recently purchased. From that their attention wandered to other paintings and Stanley found himself talking as loquaciously as a village pastor, in blending events of travel with his knowledge of the masters. He surprised himself and talked so long that the time for their departure arrived altogether too soon.

The Stones lived on a side street not far from the Stanleys, and Stanley and Imogene saw Marjorie safely home. Before bidding them good night, she had graciously invited both to call upon her. They promised, Stanley rather eagerly, for he was very much pleased with her.

CHAPTER IV.

As Stanley and his sister, after leaving Miss Stone at her door, continued on their way home, he felt as if there was something lacking. "What can it be?" ran in his thoughts. "I surely am not in love with her. The idea is ridiculous. I have never known care, or sought after that which did not minister to my pleasure. I have never taken time to consider one girl above another, and only this year father has tried to persuade me to enter the store, become better acquainted with the business, settle down and marry." So absorbed was he that Imogene wondered at his unusual silence. She tried to rally him from his reverie, but she was unsuccessful. All at once the idea struck her that perhaps her brother had fallen in love with Miss Stone. Then her brother's actions since that church concert, his church going, rhapsodies over Miss Stone's voice and his moments of quiet thoughtfulness, all occurred to her and convinced her that it was the solution of his changed manner. She was still thinking of it that night when she went to bed. When she rose in the morning she felt convinced of it, and in her impulsiveness communicated her suspicions to her father. He welcomed her intelligence gladly, for he was grieved at his son's thoughtless mode of life, and anxiously looking forward to the time when he would be able to relieve him of some of the cares of business. He thought also if Imogene's surmises were correct, and his son could win Miss Stone, he would find an intelligent, worthy, helpmate. The fact that her parents were not rich was nothing to him, for coming from the ranks of the people he knew the value of conscious worth whenever and wherever he saw it.

Imogene could hardly restrain herself, so pleased was she with her thoughts. If she had dared she would have told her brother. She would also liked to have told Miss Stone, for, with her short acquaintance, she imagined that Marjorie would make a nice sister-in-law. She was curious to find out if her brother's love was returned, and for that purpose called on Miss Stone before he had the opportunity to do so, and was disappointed at not being able to discover anything.

As for Stanley, in vain he protested to himself that he was not in love, and that he only sought and desired her company for the mere purpose of being amused. When he retired that evening he was still deeply absorbed in his thoughts, planning and dispelling, building and destroying, yet still protesting that he was not in love. Poor fellow, he did not know then as he afterwards learned that the very fact of his protestations against this new sensation was proof that Cupid had not vainly directed his dart at him. That it was the beginning of the passion of his life. That it was the beginning of sorrow and struggle that eventually destroyed his old notions of the power and influence of wealth to attain all things; which clarified his soul for the future happiness in store for it, and made it all the sweeter for having been delayed by the stirring scenes, incidents and perils through which he had passed.

The following Sunday found him again on his way to church, and he met her just as she came out of her street to take the main thoroughfare. He was surprised and delighted nevertheless.

She greeted him with a smile and they went the rest of the way together. Very quiet was the young man and somewhat abstracted. She noticing it asked, "Why, Mr. Stanley, you seem very thoughtful this morning. Are you oppressed with the extraordinary heat, or preoccupied with the services?"

"Neither, I was thinking how recreant I had been. Going to church is a new custom with me."

She was somewhat surprised at this remark, but remembering what he had said at Mrs. Durham's, concerning himself, after a pause, she said: "Noble resolves, like other virtues, come better late than never."

"I have thought," he replied, "that I could not tie myself to any one object. If I were a Christian today, tomorrow, from mere restlessness, I would be a sinner. Ever since I left college, I have flitted from one thing to another, epicurean-like, and like them, I have less pleasure in the realization of desires than in their pursuit. I have about reached the conclusion that all men of my stamp eventually reach the vanity of vanities."[7]

She was shocked now, and afterwards remembered this little speech and compared it with what people said about him. However, she protested against applying the standard of earthly, to celestial things. Said she:

"You cannot compare heavenly things by earthly standards. When all things else fail, the earnest Christian is buoyed up and strengthened through his faith. It is quite lamentable that so many people never look for the comfort and blessings to be attained by the acceptance of Christ, except when their days of usefulness are past, or when in great distress, but so seldom when in prosperity."

"I should be glad to discuss this subject further with you," said Stanley, as they parted at the church door, "and at some future time we will."

The sermon of the Rev. Mr. Elliot might have been as interesting as usual, and he as earnest as ever in the enunciation of the truths embodied, but Stanley's mind was far away and he began to realize that he was either in love or that some other inexplicable mental ailment had seized him. He immediately began to plan some diversion by which he could overcome the feeling, thinking that this new born sensation, the plaything of a day, could be laid aside at will, as easily as he could lay aside one pleasure to take up another. A trip up the lakes suggested itself and all that afternoon and evening he thought of it, and finally consummated a plan. Parker came over in the evening, and as they sat smoking together, he unfolded the plan to him, and he was delighted with it. In fact he had been in a quandary as to how, and where he would spend his summer vacation. During the week Fox and Morgan were made aware of it and they became enthusiastic over it. He acquainted his father with his intention, and he, after giving his son a lecture upon the necessity of soon giving his strict attention to business, gave his assent, and placed the pretty little steam yacht Sylvia at his disposal. Seth immediately began his preparations. He had promised to call on Miss Stone, and he hardly knew whether to do so before or after their trip. He began to reason with himself. "If I go before I will have redeemed my promise, and when I return my mind will be occupied with other things. I shall then keep out of her way and so drown this sudden impulse of sentiment, for it can be nothing else. I could not settle down to household cares now, (In his conceit he thought he had only to offer himself to be accepted) and give my devoted attention to a woman. The romance and the newness of the passion would soon wear off and I should long to be free again, to come and go with the boys as I have been wont. I'll pay the visit first." By this conclusion it might be rightly assumed that he was not a little afraid of the effects Miss Stone's qualities might have upon him. Accordingly about a couple evenings before they were to go on their trip, with the most fastidious care, he dressed himself and started to pay his promised call.

CHAPTER V.

Not until he had mounted the steps and rang the bell, did he fully realize what he was doing, so abstracted had he been. A feeling of extreme diffidence came over him and he felt that he would like to retreat, but too late, for Miss Stone herself answered the bell and greeted him cordially. Something in her smile overcame his diffident feeling, for there was in it, he thought, a something which seemed to indicate that he was expected and welcome.

Upon entering the parlor he was somewhat surprised to find that a rather thin, dudish looking chap had preceded him. He was dressed in the very latest styles, his exceedingly light hair was parted in the middle, and to cap it all he wore eye-glasses.

Miss Stone was not long in making the two acquainted, and each instinctively felt that he had a rival in the other. Stanley advanced and extended his hand while the other, half rising, received it languidly and then dropped back into his easy position.

"Aw, Mr. Stanley," said Mr. Maxwell, "I have heard of you before. I believe that you, with some friends, are soon to take a pleasure trip up the lake."

"Yes, that is my plan at present, and I have called upon Miss Stone to pay my adieus before going," replied Stanley turning to her.

"Aw, very kind of you," said Maxwell, and he stared at her, as if waiting for her approbation.

Stanley thought he felt a feeling of dislike for the man rising up within him which he could attribute to no particular reason except his dudish manners, and that he promised to be a bore.

As Maxwell continued to look inquisitively at her, as if he deemed it necessary she should say something, she replied: "Yes, Mr. Stanley recently offered himself as a pupil, promised to be attentive, and now he is plotting to rid himself of me entirely."

"Perhaps he is only taking his vacation preparatory to assuming his new duties," said Maxwell.

"You have stated it better than I, Mr. Maxwell, accept my thanks. I go but I return again. I suppose by that time there will be a class of us as devoted as Hypatia's pupils."[8]

"If you go much further, Mr. Stanley, I shall accuse you of being a coquette."

"Then I'm as dumb as an hoyster," turning to see what effect his remark would have upon Maxwell.[9] But in that vacant countenance he could discern nothing.

Marjorie Stone appeared lovely to Stanley that evening. She was dressed plainly in a light fabric, no ornaments save a bunch of violets that lay upon her bosom. Her round mobile face, bright red lips, expressive eyes, high forehead, from which the hair rose and fell in seeming disorder, and coiled in a neat knot behind, formed a picture that completely entranced him, and he could not conceal the look of admiration and pleasure it gave him. She saw the look, flushed slightly and made haste to re-open the conversation. They were talking of his proposed trip and the places of interest he intended to stop at, when Mrs. Stone entered the room. She was of medium height, rather stout, very well preserved for her age, and was dressed as neatly and as plainly as her daughter. Stanley immediately noticed the likeness of person, and the similitude of manners between mother and daughter. After being formally introduced she entered into the conversation with the same gusto of one just entering life, and to whom plans for its enjoyment were always welcome.

The evening passed merrily, for at times the conversation became lively. Mrs. Stone recalled many incidents connected with Stanley's mother and her anxieties concerning him, and he almost felt his heart leap as she touched on this topic, for fear she would refer to his waywardness. Not that he was yet fully ashamed of his past, but he did not want it discussed in Marjorie's presence, as he had recently been in the habit of calling her in his thoughts. But much to his relief Mrs. Stone dwelt solely on the bright side of matters, and his eyes looked the thanks he felt.

"Before you go," said she to Stanley, "I should like to have you and Marjorie sing for me, for she told me that you have an excellent voice."

"Ah! just the idea," put in Maxwell, "I'm very fond of singing, doncher know."

He had been conspicuously quiet, but that was his way, and it made him an enigma to Stanley who could not have listlessly sat through an animated discussion without taking some part in it.

"I fear that Miss Stone has given my voice a reputation then, to which it is not entitled."

"We are not severe critics Mr. Stanley, and if your voice pleases Marjorie it will certainly please me."

Stanley, however, did desire to sing, for her voice had a great attraction for him. He proposed a selection from "The Gypsy Baron," as he thought that one so proficient and so interested in music as Marjorie was, would certainly have it.[10] Their voices blended so well as to elicit complimentary remarks from even Maxwell. As he stood by her he felt the influences that she seemed to exert over him unconsciously strengthen. He could feel that, in her presence, the wild caprices that governed his whole life's actions were being negatived by her quiet, gentle manners, strong character and purposes. He felt then as if he could never again enter into the wild excesses into which he had too often plunged, at other times and places, either of speech or of the imagination. He felt that his thoughts were growing purer, his purposes nobler, and he half resolved to possess her for his wife. Afterward at her request he sang alone. He chose "True to the Last," and acted as his own accompanist.[11] He put great feeling into his song and sung as if to her alone, for he felt then that despite his restless nature he could be true to her, and would not desire to be free again to long after new joys or new pleasures. Such deep fervor did he put into it that both Mrs. Stone and Maxwell looked apprehensively at Marjorie, but she was listening only to the song and admiring the voice, and speculating upon the effect it would produce were it brought to perfection. Shortly after Stanley prepared to go, leaving Maxwell in almost the same position in which he found him. She accompanied him to the door, and moved by his feeling, he broke up the object for which the pleasure trip was planned and riveted the chains more firmly than he desired to break by asking: "May I have the pleasure of dropping you an account of our outing?"

She hardly expected such a proffer, and it took her rather unawares, but she said in what he thought was a delightfully bewitching manner, "I should be pleased to know of it, but mind," she added naively, "you must tell me all."

"That is a part of the bargain," he replied gaily, and lifting his hat, bid her good-bye in high spirits.

Between that time and the hour of his departure his mind was at sea. At times he abused himself soundly for his soft-heartedness, at others he was half inclined to let his feelings have full sway. Between these conflicting emotions, at the time this story opens, he had arrived at no fixed conclusions as to his future purposes. Of her he was thinking when Parker left him to see after a few matters that needed his attention. It was of her he was thinking on arriving home. He went directly to his room to make some preparations and was kept busy until it was about time for Parker to arrive. He lit a cigar and smoked awhile in silence. He did not have to wait very long, for Parker soon came and was in buoyant spirits. Stanley exhibited his impatience to be off for he at once made ready to go.

He bid his father good-bye, embraced Imogene, who was somewhat disappointed that he should go away so soon, for it looked as if her surmises were not correct after all. In consequence she was nervous, and she said to Parker, "Take good care of my brother."

"Don't bother about me," said Stanley impatiently, as he rather hurriedly unclasped her hands, "Women are always imagining something is going to happen."

Parker, however, assured her that he would look after him, and the two then started for the yacht. Paul Fox and Fred Morgan had preceded them and were sitting on deck smoking, exchanging stories, and enjoying the cool breezes of the evening.

CHAPTER VI.

The Sylvia was a beautiful steam yacht of a decidedly rakish appearance, that had been built and fitted up under Mr. Stanley's directions, for pleasure purposes. Her cabin, which was finished in hard wood and furnished completely throughout, was divided into three apartments, dining room, drawing-room and the sleeping apartments. The kitchen and engine-room were below. The decks were fitted around with seats, and overhead was suspended an awning to protect her guests from the rays of the sun. The deck's surface was polished so smoothly that it reflected the objects upon it. Everything had been put in readiness and tastefully arranged by John Saunders, who acted for this occasion as steward and cabin-boy. Saunders was an Afro-American,[12] but his complexion was fair and his features regular. He was slender of form and of a medium height; his hair, slightly curling, was raven black, and his eyes were of the same hue. He had been a class-mate of Stanley in the High School at Detroit, and entered college at the same time at Ann Arbor taking the course of civil engineer. Stanley had always taken an interest in him, because of his close application to his studies, and the sacrifices he had made to remain at school. After his graduation, being unable to obtain work in his chosen avocation Stanley had secured a place for him in his father's store, where he became assistant bookkeeper. He was, however, always subject to his call when he thought he needed a valet to accompany him on his rambling trips. Stanley not only found him reliable, but an agreeable and instructive companion. In fact, if it had not been for the circumstance of color, and the adverse criticism he feared would be heaped upon him by society, he would have made a friend and confidant of him.

It was the intention of the party to make the trip by daylight, and as they expected to be off at dawn retired early. Saunders was strictly charged to be up with the lark and arouse the others early. All slept soundly and when Saunders awoke them, just as the sun began to peep over the trees on Belle Isle, the active busy life of the day had commenced along the wharves, and the ferry boats had began to ply between Detroit and Windsor, they turned out with many a stretch and yawn.[13]

"It doesn't seem to me as if I've slept two hours," said Parker in a gaping voice.

"I know I slept very soundly," added Morgan. "I didn't wake once. No wonder sailors are so healthy. Such refreshing air, restful sleep and keen appetite. I feel as if I could eat right away."

"The way of the laggard," remarked Paul Fox.

"You are a nice one to say laggard," replied Morgan, "when you sit rubbing your eyes and too lazy to dress."

"My stomach is not more active than my limbs, at any rate," retorted Fox. "I can wait until breakfast is ready."

"This river air must have sharpened your wits as well as appetites," said Parker, who was standing in the middle of the room going through the dumb bell practice with closed fists.

"I suppose you wanted to be odd and thought you would whet your muscle," said Morgan, looking up. "You need it, however, for its precious little exercise you get outside the gymnasium."

"Don't think Orchard Lake is the only place where people exercise. We kick football, row and put on the gloves here, if we are not so straight up and down that people think our backs and shoulders are moulded instead of having grown to that shape."

"I wish we had brought a pair of gloves," said Stanley, who had remained silent.

"I'd give Parker a lesson in the manly art if we had," said Morgan.

"You mean we would probably give each other a lesson," replied Parker, still swinging his arms.

"I didn't know I was in a nest of gladiators," said Fox, who was far from muscular. "I guess I'll go up and wrestle with the breakfast table."

"That's right in your line," said Morgan, who had been waiting for an opportunity to get even with Fox.

All now hurried on deck, and while the cook was preparing breakfast they helped the Captain and Saunders to get the boat under way. All of them were eager to be off for their minds were stored with the fun and pleasure they expected to get out of the trip. On their left lay Detroit, with the curling smoke and steam of its various manufactories contrasting with the clear blue sky and light fleecy clouds which were beginning to disappear under the heat of the sun. Detroit is the most beautiful city of America, handsomely adorned by nature and man; with fine churches whose immense spires serve as the index finger of the mind of its inhabitants; palatial residences of the rich and the neat artistic cottages of the laborers; with its handsome business blocks, broad paved streets, shady promenades, and numerous little parks to be found almost everywhere, offering rest for the tired pedestrians. Pointing above them was the island park, Belle Isle, carved out of the sparkling waters that form the gate-way to the great lakes, and around them the plying wheels of a commerce that represented the greatest inland traffic of the world.[14] They took their course up the Canadian channel, and were near the upper end of Belle Isle when the cook sang out breakfast. What a rush they made for the dining-room, and with what a zest they "fell to."

The Sylvia seemed to fairly glide through the water, and as her well formed rakish hull rushed through and cleft it at its bow, they thought it glorious.

"Let Byron have his solitudes of ocean," said Fox, "and her ceaseless breathing with the tide of time, give me the lakes and their outlets, then lend me his vivid imagination and I would immortalize these waters."[15]

"It is curious that people go into ecstasies about scenery and romance far away, while right under their nose can be found some of the grandest natural pictures the eye ever beheld," said Stanley. "True we have no Rip Van Winkle legends like those which surround the Catskills, nor have such deeds been enacted here as have characterized Greece to inspire our poets with epics of conquest; but if we desire to commune with nature and be inspired by her wondrous works, where could we ask for better opportunity than in the verdure laden banks of the river we have just come through, contrasted with its bright waters which leads into the broad expanse where those same trees seem but a fringe on the edge of space."

"You forgot Hull's surrender, and Pontiac's Conspiracy, when you said Detroit had no history," said Morgan.[16]

"There goes our military genius again," said Fox.

"Are not beautiful poems with their pleasing phrases regulated by moods and surroundings?" asked Parker. "We read them, give our fancy full play, and say, 'surely this is a fine picture,' and we ask ourselves why we had not seen it in that way before. The fact is, these things are a part of ourselves, and we look to far away things for beauty and pleasure. The poet will find a psalm of praise in the hum of machinery, while the laborer, whose business keeps him with it daily finds it prosy. Possibly if Lowell were with us he might find something in this rarely beautiful morning that would make him go into rhapsodies over 'a day in July.'"[17]

"Right you are," replied Stanley. "We feel that which we cannot express yet cannot all conceal, but let me warn you, don't let your spirits overflow before we are fairly under way, or before we return it may grow monotonous."

"Sufficient unto the day is the evil thereof," interposed Fox.[18]

"Saith the preacher," chimed in Morgan.

This created a laugh at Fox's expense, for he was ministerial looking.

They did not hurry any with this early morning meal, but mid jest and laughter prolonged the double repast of food and wit for some time. By this time the Sylvia was well out in Lake St. Clair, and books, magazines, papers and sketching utensils were brought out and each busied himself with his particular book or engaged in his favorite pastime, until the government canal with its made banks supported and lined by willows, the club houses and private residences of the "Flats" came in view.[19]

Stanley had picked up a copy of the *Century*, but did not read much, for as the needle is attracted and turns to the magnet, so his thoughts went out to Marjorie Stone.[20] He thought it would have been pleasanter had there been ladies and music on board. The boys were good company, and they were having a good time, but something appeared to be lacking. Remembering his offer of writing to her he wondered how he was going to do it without the other fellows finding it out. This was succeeded by another, a companion thought. If he had the opportunity how would he write, what would he say, how should he say it? He had many correspondents, all gentlemen, but no ladies, and he wanted to create a favorable impression. "I shall not write until we get to Mackinac," he said almost aloud.[21] "She has been around here probably a dozen times or more, and what I might say about it would be dull and commonplace."

Morgan, who was on the alert to find out what troubled him, had been quietly observing him. He noticed that since the conversation dropped he had not read a page in his magazine, and was apparently absorbed in dreams, so leaning over toward Fox he said, "I say, Paul, I guess our conjecture was right after all. Seth is in another mood."

"Don't be in too big a hurry to judge, Fred. He may be brooding over some irritating circumstance."

"Say, boys, don't you think it is time for lunch," exclaimed Parker, who had also been unable to settle down to anything. "This trip will make a glutton of me."

"I don't mind if we do," answered Stanley. "Say, John, prepare a lunch for us, please."

"All right, Mr. Stanley."

Saunders had been quietly and busily engaged at something on the forward deck and had hitherto escaped their notice. He quickly laid down his materials and started for the kitchen to have the lunch made ready. Stanley, who was somewhat familiar with his character and had often been astonished at his versatility, then quietly strolled over, out of mere curiosity, to where Saunders had been sitting. Much to his surprise he found that he had been sketching the Grosse Point Light House, and its surroundings.

"Look here, Paul!" he shouted. "John has been trespassing on your field. Here is the first sketch of the trip."

The young men at once hastened to Stanley's side and seeing the sketch had to recognize the ability of the artist.

"What sort of a colored man is that, Seth?" asked Parker, "a prodigy? I was surprised this morning at his manner of speech, he seemed so intelligent."

"And he is intelligent," replied Stanley, "and I confess that he is far better informed than I am. I often think it's a pity he isn't white." Then in a few words he gave them a concise account of Saunders' history, as he knew it. "That he had been unfortunate after leaving college, for though well-equipped as a civil engineer and for other kinds of work, he could not find employment, so I secured him a place at the store and he is getting along finely."

"There was a young colored man in my class at college," said Fox, "and he was as smart as a whip, but I don't consider a man a prodigy because he is learned above the ordinary. With the volume and cheapness of literature there is no excuse for ignorance in the most humble home. However, I must get my material out after luncheon and make a few sketches of the club houses and scenery along the Flats that look like a miniature Venice."

"A Venice in the fact that it sits in the water that is all," replied Stanley.

Saunders and his art after this was given some attention. He and Fox made several sketches and gave to the others as souvenirs of the trip, and he afterward copied some for Stanley who thought it might be just the thing to accompany his first letter to her.

CHAPTER VII.

Sunset rubies glistened in the western sky when the yacht Sylvia arrived at Sand Beach. The next morning, bright and early, they were under way again. At Mackinac they intended to stop two or three days then go to Sault Ste. de Marie, which was then in the beginning of its real estate boom, via the Detour Pass.[22] Returning by almost the same route and stopping wherever their fancy struck them, for a day or two. Meanwhile Stanley had found the time to write the letter. He had thought of Miss Stone continually, and he began to feel by this time that while one may run away from the object of one's affections, the impressions made on the heart cannot be eliminated at will. With him the impression had deepened, and every recurring thought seemed to add to its strength. He surmised that the others suspected his attachment, for Parker had had the boldness to speak of it once. In his own mind he concluded that he was really in love and decided to let his affections have full sway. Whether it was pure and lasting or merely ephemeral, the future would tell, and he would be sure of its character first, before he made it known to her. It should be no heartless flirtation, or toying conquest to be ruthlessly thrown aside should his present notion forsake him, she seemed too confiding in the simplicity of her manners for that. He would be sure himself, then muster every energy to prove his sincerity.

He wrote to her in detail about the trip, and asked for a reply on the plea, that he would be glad to hear from home. When he had finished he gave the letter to Saunders at Alpena, secretly, to post for him.

All were on deck as they approached Mackinac Island, which rose like "a greenhouse from out a silvery plane." Fort Mackinac with its white-washed walls and approaches had the appearance of a feudal castle.

The Sylvia soon landed them at the wharf and they were not long in making arrangements and getting ashore. After inspecting Old Curiosity shop, they proceeded to find the most romantic and suitable spot in which to pitch their tent. As they walked along the hard graveled walk, under thick foliage, past meadow, orchard and fields of grain gently waving in the breeze, they all agreed in thinking the island the most beautiful and romantic. Once on the crest of a hill, that commanded the view for quite a distance, they could see the beauties of this little natural world unfold itself like a panorama. On one hill side a reaper plied its course around a field of wheat gradually narrowing as the grain toppled on the receiving board and was pushed off for the binder. Over and over went the combing rakes gently inclining the stalks of wheat to the blade. In the valley stood the growing corn, tall and straight, just putting forth its silk tasseling, looking like the serried ranks of soldiers returning home with the fruits of conquest. Across the valley, lazily feeding in the shade of the orchard was the faithful milch cow, filling herself from the abundance of clover that carpeted the fields. In the distance nestled a farm house among the trees rich with fruit, waiting for the autumnal ripening. Absorbed in the beauty of nature, for these young men loved the beautiful and the romantic, they were silent until Fox broke the stillness by saying: "Wealth and ease form a glamor which may be the rewards of city life; but the riches of nature shaped by the hand of God is the inheritance of the farmer. Here are fields unalloyed by the hands of man, save to tickle it for the harvest. The flowers that toil not neither do they spin, (Stanley started, for the words used by Fox, reminded him of that evening when he first saw her in the concert and of the song she sung), and yet their beauty in their natural arrangement exceeds all that the ingenuity of man had attempted by reproduction."

"I have thought," said Stanley, "that it must be a siren that tempts the countryman from his home to the squalid scenes of city life where employment is so uncertain, and articles of food and fuel stand for so many bills of Uncle Sam's 'promises to pay.'"

"But everyone doesn't stop to reason it out, in that way," protested Morgan. "Here we are with our minds open and directed towards just the impression we are receiving. The question of an early rising and an all day's work under a beaming sun or in a heavy rain has not entered into our calculation. This is why finely woven theories are accepted as truths by those who have no experience We know that the best theorizer is a man with the least experience in the matter he has to deal with."

"Enough of that," cried Parker, "I came on this trip for unalloyed pleasure, and I don't want you to paint for me the dark side of life at this time."

"I was only knocking out the foundation of the air castles Paul and Seth were building."

"When a man gets beyond the point where castle building ceases to be a pleasure, if not a profitable pastime, because he believes it breeds discontent; he must close the gates of Paradise, for there, some believe, that the wish supplies the want."

"But your castles," remonstrated Morgan, "were to fit other men's ideas. If they builded for themselves, it might be different in every particular from what you have pictured it."

"You talk like a philosopher," said Parker, "Let us get the points of the compass and see which side of the island we are on."

"Top side," said Fox, "sun's at zenith."

"Facetious," grunted Parker. "But that's better than Fred's harangue about human misery. If one wanted to contemplate that, he should have remained in the city."

This was a corker, and drew out a round of "Ohs!" followed by silence.

Mackinac Island, which is rock girt, is a delightful summer resort and one of the most beautiful natural parks to be found anywhere. It is within easy access of all the attractions of Northern Michigan, and the few days spent here, and in its vicinity by the young men, teemed with incident and pleasure. Fishing in the lake, whose waters around the island are so clear that the eye can see the bottom at a great depth; lying in the shade reading, sketching from picturesque rocks that line the islands of the northern shore, or in taking brief trips to St. Ignace, Cheboygan, Petoskey, and other resorts.[23] One of the most interesting, novel and romantic trips that can be found anywhere, is the island route to Petoskey. You go upon crooked rivers and through lovely lakes, encircled by hills covered with dense foliage, that form a ruggedness of outline decidedly picturesque; and over the bosom of the water is a sheen peculiar to inland lakes that casts a dreamy haze over all. You go among logs and booms, past saw mills and through locks, where after many turns, twists, scrapes, backs, stops, and pushes, and a day of excitement you are landed at Oden, from where you are conveyed by a dummy to Petoskey. They felt amply repaid for taking this trip, for not only is Petoskey a healthful summer resort, but is justly celebrated for the hunting and fishing in its vicinity, and for the excellence of its views. It is situated on the west side of Little Traverse Bay, alongside a high bluff which is often used for camping purposes. Behind, and overtopping it, rises an eminence upon which many a villa can be seen, and from whose tops, thanks to the pure atmosphere one can get an excellent view of the bay, which is in shape a half circle. He also has a fine view of the white pebbly beach made prominent by its green background, and the ridge of hills, five miles distant, that sweep in symmetrical curves along the farther shore, terminating in high cliffs.

Much time, too, was spent in exploring the caves with which Mackinac abounds, and listening to the quaint legends of Indian lore. In climbing rocks and cliffs, and visiting scenes of historical interest and places of rare and rugged beauty.

One morning bright and early before sunrise, they seldom saw the sun rise at home, they went to Plummer's Lookout, one of the eminences on the island. The air was laden with the perfume of flowers. Grass and shrubbery glistened with dew. The birds were holding high carnival, and the air was fresh and bracing. They were in jubilant spirits and soon arrived at the summit where the view that met their eyes repaid them for their early rising, so glorious did it appear. In the east where the sun was about to rise the sky was a golden red. In the heavens above the line between the grey of the early morning and the rosy light of the sunrise was distinctly visible, and with a delight mingled with awe and wonder, they watched the line of purple, red and gold speed across the heavens driving before it the shadow of the night, until the sun, like a great yellow ball, appeared from out Lake Huron and caused lake and forest to glisten under its rays. In the distance lay the Les Cheneaux Islands; while to the south, a mere speck upon the horizon, was a steamer from whose stack the smoke rose in curls and floated like black clouds toward the east. Turning their eyes to nearer objects the beauties of the island opened to them in all their loveliness. Beneath, the valley with its woods, its farmhouses, its fields of grain; a little to the south, Sugar Loaf Rock rose up like a sentinel in his line of duty. Here and there a solitary pedestrian could be seen, who like themselves was seeking the bracing air of the morning, and field hands going to their work. From yonder farmhouse rose a thin blue curl of smoke; still further south they could see the white-washed walls of the Fort. Again looking eastward could be seen Arch Rock, a natural bridge, and nearby Cliffs and Robinson's Folly.[24]

"I do not wonder that the Indians thought this island to be the home of Manitou, or that Longfellow should choose it with its wild Indian legends and their heroes, and be able to weave them into verses so romantic as to charm the world with their beauty and simplicity. Inspiration to do or accomplish something more than the ordinary seems to be in the air we breathe," said Paul Fox, breaking the silence.[25]

"I feel like doing something in the ordinary," said Parker, "let us eat. Whether this appetite of mine is due to the air we breathe or this early morning walk is a conundrum that doesn't detract from my desire to do."

"I have noticed," said Stanley, not heeding Parker's loquacity, "that the air here is never sultry and oppressive, and that it is always cool and refreshing.

Under such conditions it is not surprising that one feels able to do more than ordinary."

"There are no land breezes here," said Morgan, "and therein lies the beauty of it. The breeze from Lake Huron no sooner stops, than one sets in from Lake Michigan; both failing, Lake Superior supplies the deficiency."

"Let us eat," again said Parker, "for in this climate where one seems spurred on to do something, and one's spirits keep so buoyant, digestion being good, one has a keen appetite. This feasting with one's eyes upon the beauty of our surroundings and the contemplation of the causes that render this air invigorating does not satisfy the innerself. Come, let us go and eat."

His logic and invitation were irresistible. They went.

CHAPTER VIII.

One afternoon during their stay at the Island, Stanley, who was unable to banish Marjorie Stone from his thoughts, left the others and went on board the Sylvia to write to her. In his letter he said that he often wished that she was one of the party so that she might participate in their enjoyment. He gave a minute account of their pleasures, their trips to places of interest, and dilated upon the excellence of the climate, claiming that its reputation as a health resort had not been overrated. "In a day or two," he added, "the rest of the party might determine they would go on to the 'Soo' and then return."

Two nights before their departure to the Soo the others, being tired from the day's tramp, turned in early. Stanley, unable to sleep because of the many thoughts that ran riot in his brain, went out for a walk. In the course of his walk he found himself near Arch Rock. This was a favorite spot of his. It was decidedly romantic, and afforded an excellent view of the lake. It is inexplicable, yet true, that in our hours of unconsciousness of our surroundings, the mind and even the steps revert to things we love best, nor do they need a guide other than an intuition that might be denominated one of the senses. The moon was at its full at the time and cast a soft silvery light, which falling upon the dancing ripples beneath, created a coruscating splendor. The rippling waters breaking like soft cadences upon the beach had a soothing effect upon him, while the ceaseless beating upon the shore reminded him a great deal of the steady current of thought going on in his own mind in regard to "her." Even as those waters, now so quietly splashing upon the beach, dash when aroused, wave after wave, in impetuous and angry fury upon the shore, so to, at times in his mind, was his love aroused, and thoughts tumultuous would rush through his brain of doubt, fear and anger. Of anger for the past, of fear and doubt whether the past would rise up to cheat him of her. Now his thoughts were attuned to the gentle flow beneath and the romance and quiet of his surroundings affected him, and made his thoughts flow in a calm and easy stream, as he analyzed his love for "her" and considered his own unworthiness.

"I love her! I love her!" he repeated to himself, "and this separation from her and her influences only tells me how deep and fervent my love is, and how unworthy I am of her. She is so pure and innocent, while I—I have been a rioter after pleasures, not with my own, but my father's earnings. Not one penny that I enjoy is rightfully the result of my own exertion. The days of youthful preparation for usefulness, and the opportunities I have had to make a man of myself, I have slighted or neglected. I am neither good, learned or capable, and yet I love and would be loved. These qualities I know are not essential to love, still for a man in my position of life they are essential to perfect manhood. Whether love be a child of the head or heart, I feel it awakening my energies to satisfy the longing it creates. Since I have felt it, for the first time I have been animated to action, and surely with one so noble to cherish, it should change the whole course of my nature. I feel the change. I will try to win her, and shall make that one of my special objects when I return home. Were it not that the boys were my guests, and it would be too bad to spoil their pleasure by cutting the trip short, I would start for Detroit to-morrow."

Love had worked a great change in Stanley. From seeking the society of a young lady, solely because she pleased him and gratified his desire for pleasure, as other pleasures had done, he now finds that society to be an actual necessity. Love, too, was changing him for the better. It was beginning to ennoble and uplift him. For, instead of seeking after vain pleasures, he suddenly became aware of the responsibilities of manhood and was eager to prepare himself for such a life as an alliance with a pure and lofty-minded young woman would demand. There is a great deal of truth in the saying that love either uplifts or debases, according to the character of the object it sets its affections upon. Many through its influences have been lifted up, and many worthy people, it has caused to wallow in infamy.

Is not life, after all, a game of chance? Ought we, or our surroundings, be responsible if our game be lost, and as a result, instead of pursuing honorable lives, we become infamous?

Five days had passed in Mackinac and its vicinity before they were ready to proceed on their way to the "Soo." These days had passed too slowly for Stanley who was anxious to return home, yet, in all their pleasures he was the life of the party. He recognized that to cut the time and trip short without some good excuse would not only be discourteous, but attract attention to himself in a way that he did not desire. So betwixt a smile and a sigh he ordered preparations for an early start in the morning, on the evening before.

Early next morning, the fires ready, Capt. Lake gave the word. The anchor was weighed. The engine started. The screw wheel fairly churned and lashed the water, slowly at first, then like a thing of life, the Sylvia sped on her journey. When the young men came on deck, Mackinac in the rear, was hardly visible, and abreast of them were the Les Cheneaux Islands. Speeding at the rate of sixteen miles per hour, it was not long before the Sylvia entered St. Mary's river through the Detour Pass. There are numerous little islands in the river many of which are utilized by fishing and hunting clubs. Along its course there are also many popular summer resorts. As they proceeded up the river they were surprised at the number of broad straits and little lakes through which they passed. Along the banks on either side, rising from the water's edge were high cliffs which shut in the river and lent to the scenery a rugged beauty. Fox and Saunders got out their sketching utensils, and busied themselves in endeavoring to depict some of its views, while the others gathered around them, watched their progress, and commented on the different phases of scenery.

The channel of the river is narrow, crooked and shallow, and the trip is usually made by daylight. Capt. Lake, however, was an old sailor, and knew all the crooks and turns, the ins and outs, the most attractive spots and the prettiest islands, and in his bluff, hearty way took pleasure in pointing out the places of interest, and stopping when they wanted to explore any particular spot. He further told them, as their time was limited, at some future time he would like to take them on a trip to the pictured rocks off the up-channel course.

After a pleasant day's ride, they arrived at the "Soo." They spent the whole of the following day there and in its vicinity visiting Fort Brady, the government canal, and the new bridge which was nearing completion. The "Soo" was enjoying a great boom. The water-way convention met there that summer. Real estate was advancing rapidly, and several roads were making their way to that point.

The government canal here is one of the chief attractions. Owing to the rapids above the town which have a fall of twenty-two feet, and which forms the natural channel connecting Lake Superior with the St. Mary's river, the channel is an absolute necessity. It is mostly hewn out of solid rock; the lock is 650 feet long, 80 feet wide and has a lift of 18 feet. When in the canal an excellent view is had of the American and Canadian towns below and of the fall of the rapids. Desirous of experiencing the sensation of being lifted up and passing through the canal to Lake Superior and returning, at Stanley's suggestion, Captain Lake gratified them.

Homeward bound: What a world of meaning that meant for Stanley. It meant that he would see Marjorie again, and she was now to him the sum of existence. Did he plan anything? She was never left out, and the number of little excursions, picnics and boat rides he conceived with her as a companion, were legion. Did he promise himself that he would earnestly enter the actualities of life? He did so that he might meet her on equal ground. He did not dream of such a thing as his plans miscarrying for he loved her. He was wealthy and a desirable catch. His ideas of wealth and its power to acquire happiness had not changed like his feelings for her, that was to come later. For the present, an all-absorbing love, which absence served only to strengthen permeated his whole being, yet on that yacht, there was not a soul more joyous, no person more active and buoyant in spirit than he, when the little vessel turned its prow homeward, none were more agreeable or bristled with more humor.

Speed little bark, and cleave the water rapidly in your onward rush. Engineer keep your fires going, the boilers full, the engine well oiled, the throttle open. Rapidly the Sylvia glided through the water, and Stanley with pleasure noted its speed. At Alpena he received a letter from Marjorie. It was not lengthy, a mere acknowledgment of his own, and the sketches he had sent, and expressing the hope that he was having a splendid time. It was not much, but it transported him with happiness, and he fairly bubbled over with humor and reminiscences of former trips; of persons he had met and things he had seen. Is it strange that he was thus moved? What lover has not been thrilled with the first lines he has received from his lady-love? What ecstasy lies in every word the fair hand has traced? How often has it been re-read and how often kissed?

CHAPTER IX.

While Stanley and his friends were enjoying their outing, Marjorie heard of many stories concerning him that would have rendered him uneasy had he known of it.

Her uncle, Mr. Durham, had told her many episodes of his past life, not that he wished to create in her mind an unfavorable opinion, but as a mere matter of having an interesting tale to tell, interspersed with reminiscences of his own boyish pranks. He little suspected what an interesting listener he had. Once when relating a little story where his goodness of heart was made manifest, Mrs. Durham said, "Yes, he is a good hearted boy, but he has been wild. I remember his conduct used to so worry his mother, and he never seemed to imagine he was doing wrong. It could not be said that he was mean or wilful, but he was certainly wayward and fickle. He never seemed to care for anything longer than to know what it was. His experience in business has been the same."

"But, Auntie, do you not think Mr. Stanley has changed a great deal," interrupted Marjorie.

"He seemed very different the evening he took tea with us, but I hardly think he is through sowing his wild oats yet," said Mrs. Durham.

"When he is through he will be all the better for it," said Mr. Durham.

"That is the way you men look at it," retorted Mrs. Durham.

When she said this, she had not the least suspicion of the reason that actuated Marjorie's question, for she thought that because of Maxwell's persistent and constant attentions, he would be her accepted suitor. She did not know that Marjorie did everything she could, without being rude, to discourage his attentions. His effeminate and dudish ways seemed to overlap and cover up, his good qualities. She had contrasted Stanley and Maxwell the evening they had met at her own home, and Stanley's sinewy form, easy manners, and enthusiasm, that seemed to show that his soul was in all that he did, contrasted favorably with anything she had been able to discern in Maxwell.

After a moment's reflection upon Mrs. Durham's opinion, she said, "Gossip is not as charitable as law; for law gives man the benefit of a doubt, while gossip seeks a doubt to establish the truth of its reports."

"Girl like, girl like," said Mr. Durham, rubbing his fat hands together. "They won't allow their gallant knights to be abused, guilty or not guilty."

"I am not passing on his guilt or innocence," retorted Marjorie, "I was speaking of the uncharitableness of gossip. Men outgrow youthful follies as they outgrow other childish things."

"To him that is pure all things are pure," said Mr. Durham somewhat absent mindedly. "Shall I say you are fortunate or unfortunate in that you have two such extremes for beaux as Stanley and Maxwell?"

"Say I am both and you about have the truth of it. Could I cement their two characters together and blend them harmoniously, I should have a man of my liking."

"It is too bad that men are not made to order, so as to save the women the trouble of remodeling them as soon as they get them. Why, Mrs. Durham isn't through with me yet." And Mr. Durham cast a side glance at his wife and chuckled.

"I am not quite satisfied with my work on Mr. Durham," said Mrs. Durham with a sigh, "but gossip has nothing to do with Seth's case, for many of his shortcomings have come directly under the observations of many. Yet possibly under pressure he may develop what good there is in him."

Marjorie said no more on this subject as she did not want to appear too interested. She had dispatched a letter to Stanley, and had invited him to call on his return. From his actions she had noticed that he had at least a regard for her which she reciprocated. She was not satisfied with Mrs. Durham's remarks about him. She knew, however, that despite them Mrs. Durham had a warm corner in her heart for him for his mother's sake, and that liking Marjorie wished to fan into a stronger feeling, or it might be necessary for her friendship with him to come to a standstill. Until late that night she thought over what she had heard, resolving to inquire further. Call it hypnotism or what you may, we often tempt fate inviting knowledge that we know will bring suffering and pain, while we rebel at the narration of it.

Marjorie's father was a traveling agent, consequently away from home much of the time, but she resolved to find if possible her mother's views on the subject. On the first convenient occasion she mentioned him in connection with his trip, and showed her the sketches he had sent. From that she skillfully led the conversation until she had her mother's estimate of him and his character. She was agreeably surprised to find that her mother, while she deprecated the past, was disposed to do him justice, and admit that his chances to retrieve the past were good. She cited many instances of men, who, to her knowledge had been reckless in their youth, yet had developed into men of strong characters. Mrs. Stone's great aim in life was to try to be just, and, while she deplored evil, she covered a great deal with the mantle of charity. While she did not condone or excuse it, she reasoned that under better and more favorable circumstances the result might have been different. These principles she had carefully instilled into her daughter, and as we have seen, with success.

"Isn't it the exception instead of the rule," said Marjorie, bending her earnest eyes intently on her mother, "that a man who has spent his early years in riotous living turns out to be sober and steady?"

"I would not say that," replied Mrs. Stone, looking at Marjorie in return, who flushed a little under her gaze. "It depends largely on circumstances. I must admit the chances are against a man who has wealth, and has been pampered and flattered even in his vices. This heedless way in which people go into ecstacies over position for favors and recognition, spoil more lives than it helps."

"Do you think Mr. Stanley has acquired such vices, and that they are so deep seated as to be always a part of him?" asked Marjorie.

"Oh, no! I was only speaking generally, but you know that our animal, or what is ordinarily termed our natural inclinations, tend to make us like the brute, it is our cultivated faculties that lift us above these inclinations. Character is like a tender precious plant, the weeds should be kept down when it is growing or it is liable to be dwarfed."

Marjorie sat musing over this last proposition, and her mother letting the conversation drop, busied herself with her crocheting. The relation between mother and daughter were those of confidants; hence their lives seemed to be centered in each other, and their thoughts, from their associations ran in almost the same groove. The daughter had never been called upon to exercise her judgment in matters of much moment, for she had always relied upon her mother's judgment. The mother in her turn constantly consulted her daughter, more frequently than she probably would have done owing to Mr. Stone's absence. It did not at first occur to Mrs. Stone that there was anything more than a passing commentary on events, things and persons in her daughter's questioning. But when Marjorie continued them, it aroused her suspicions, and intuition led her mind back to the evening when Stanley had called, and the interest Marjorie had shown in him. The intent of the inquiry was revealed to her, but her inherent love of justice made her deal as fairly with him afterward, as she could. She did not desire that Marjorie should become strongly attached to Stanley, until he had shown that he was worthy of her. Above all things she desired her happiness, and she knew to a great degree there was that in his manner, and enthusiastic action that would captivate a girl of her daughter's temperament, and that he had qualities, now dormant, that would contribute to her happiness, if the interest between the two should develop into love. Unlike Mrs. Durham, she knew that the bond between Maxwell and her daughter was not strong, owing to the vast difference in temperaments.

Mrs. Stone possessed a great deal of tact and did not reveal the thoughts that passed through her mind to Marjorie. Neither was she at all anxious as to the outcome of the relation between Stanley and Marjorie, because she had faith in Marjorie's strength of purpose and character, and knew that she would not contract an alliance with an unworthy person, though she loved them dearly, and suffered in consequence of refusal.

Marjorie felt some doubt in her mind in consequence of her talks with Mrs. Durham and her mother as to her future relations with Stanley. Though she was pleased with him, certain expressions he had made use of when in her company she did not like. What did he mean by being half made up in character? Was it the consciousness of what he had lost or a bold confession of his weakness? In her experience she had met foolhardy braggadocios who prided themselves in certain shortcomings, rather than being ashamed of them. Which was it in Seth's case?

In this frame of mind she busied herself with church matters, for she was a prominent active factor in all the ladies aids and charitable societies connected with their church. As is usually the case, the burden of the work in all such societies falls upon a few, while the others are content to look on, to criticise the failures, and to applaud and demand a share in the successes. Experience and willingness had developed in her a tact for such work. This with her general reading and music, had occupied her time profitably. Little thought being given to beaux, except when in company with other young ladies they fell to discussing them.

. . . .

Maxwell, as if alarmed at the sudden appearance of Stanley as a rival, and the interest he saw that Marjorie exhibited in him had been paying assiduous attention to her in his peculiar way. Despite his tendency toward the genus dude he had some attractions which commended him to the graces of the fair sex. With strangers he was quiet and unobstrusive, but he was one of those characters that improve on acquaintance. He read a great deal, was well informed on many

subjects, and when interested he surprised a great many by his extensive knowledge and clear thought; because they did not expect such things to emanate
from one of his appearance. He was also a fairly successful business man, had
no disgusting habits, and a character that was above reproach. These qualities
accounted for his being so intimate a friend, and so frequent a caller upon the
Stones, and his company endured by a young lady of Marjorie's attainments. The
frequency of his calls and the knack he had of outstaying the other young men
gave the impression, which Mrs. Durham possessed, that Marjorie and he were
engaged. With his other qualities had he possessed the vivacity and earnestness of
Stanley, he would have so inserted himself into her good graces that the wooing
that Stanley had determined upon, would be in vain. In his attitude toward her
now, while redoubling his attentions, he was backward and shy. While loving, he
was too timid to express it in action or words sufficiently strong to attract her attention. While by his sighs and uneasy postures, the upward glancing and rolling
of his eyes gave her the impression that he was unwell. He endeavored to interest
himself more in her charitable work, read up on the foibles of the day that were
attractive to the gentler sex, bought expensive works on pottery, which was then
in its craze, and became an authority in discussing Palissys Severes, tiles, etc.[26]
He studied the language of the flowers and often sent her bouquets significant of
his love for her. His dress was scrupulously neat, his eye glass always glistened,
hats in the latest styles, and his canes the envy of all the dudes. Sometimes he and
Marjorie would go out for a stroll in the evening, and under pale Luna's influence
he would become inexpressibly tender in manner, but the words of affection
hesitated upon his lips.

Once, when engaged in looking over a work on pottery he had sent her,
their hands touched and a thrill went through him like an electric shock. All his
passions were aroused, his tender regard and deep feeling. His fingers and lips
twitched convulsively in his great effort to muster his courage and find his voice.
His story was nearly told. "Marjorie," he said, ready to drop upon his knees. She
turned, surprised at the tone of his voice, and with a look of wonder in her eyes.
The story remained untold, the words died upon his lips, the calm passionless
face that turned on him such surprise, was too much for him. His wits did not,
however, desert him and he feigned a sudden illness. Marjorie was anxious and
interested at once, for while she did not love she did esteem him, and she would
have gone immediately for some simple remedy to afford him relief. He would
not however, permit her and claimed that he felt better. In his excuses, she was as
desirous as he that he should think her ignorant of the real cause of his manner.

That evening he left her presence much earlier than usual. On his way home

he did what many another man has done under far less embarrassing circumstances. He felt like dashing his head against a stone wall, or having some one
kick him for letting the bright eyes of the girl he loved turn him from his purpose. To think that he lacked the words and sentiment when most needed that
now so freely rushed through his mind, to tell his love and plead for a return of
affection was heart rending. He berated himself soundly for his timidity, and he
wondered if she when she looked at him thought he was the consummate idiot
he then believed himself to be, or whether she believed in his faintness. If she
did believe in that, and the interest was real that she manifested, the thought
was intoxicating, and he at once began to plan what to say and do the next time.
Only when the time came to find all his thoughts and plans forgotten and himself
completely routed, and no more able to declare his love than before. Still he
continued his visits, planned and devised means for her pleasure, and hoped.

CHAPTER X.

———————

Marjorie Stone's easy and graceful manners, her many accomplishments and affability, had won for her many friends and admirers. Many gentlemen were only restrained from being pointed in their addresses, because of the supposed relation between her and that "dude" Maxwell. They commiserated her in their conversation with each other on her preference, and thought it a shame that all her accomplishments should be wasted on that mute, inanimate thing. A quiet unostentatious young man does not take well among the ordinary swells. But Maxwell was peculiar to a degree, effeminate and quiet. Young Harper, who was rapidly forcing his way to the front at the bar, had passed many a pleasant evening in her company, and was delighted with her breadth of thought, and the ease with which she analyzed and judged things, of which only the masculine mind is thought to be proficient. He had often been heard to declare if he was not already engaged he would sail in and cut that fellow out, and those who knew the honest, open-hearted young fellow did not doubt him.

Among her many young lady friends there were none in whom she reposed more confidence and liked better than Flora Aikman. "Flo.," as all her friends called her, was an old school mate, and the friendship formed then had ripened in the years that had lapsed. They had been correspondents while Marjorie had been studying music at Boston, and through her she was kept well informed of the principal events happening in her absence. Miss Aikman, who was lively and vivacious, but not at all silly, formed quite a contrast to Marjorie, whose manner was more dignified and thoughtful. She was one of those girls that seemed to invite confidences, was pleasant and agreeable, to all, and always willing to do some one a favor. As a consequence most of her gentlemen friends were half in love with her, and all held themselves in readiness to obey her slightest mandates. It was a rare thing that on a pleasant evening, not that her friends were fair weather's only, her parlors did not contain more than one gentleman caller. She was rather pretty, not any taller than Marjorie, but a little heavier in build.

One warm afternoon about a couple of days before the return of the Sylvia,

Marjorie, desiring to spend the afternoon on the river, called by for "Flo." to see if she would not go with her. She readily complied and thither they wended their way. They were soon comfortably seated on one of the ferries that ply their way to and from the Island Park, and enjoying all the ease and comfort, these little trips afford on a hot summer day. In their conversation they encompassed nearly every subject that ladies like to talk about, of the last Kettle drum given by Mrs. Raleigh; or the reception to be given by Mrs. Manton to Governor and Mrs. Fast; of toilet, of what they were going to wear, of the latest most fashionable fabrics displayed by the merchants on the avenue over their counters; of Marjorie's progress in music, of the latest fads, patchwork and of the latest novels.

"Have you read *Ben Hur* yet, Margy?"[27]

"Yes, I just finished it last week."

"How did you like it?"

"Ever so much. I was deeply interested in it. Ben Hur's wanderings, hair breadth escapes and thrilling adventures with their numerous perils, and the incidents in the life of Christ, and the crucifixion are so graphically pictured."

"While the strange meeting of the Egyptian, Hindoo and Greek, the strange story they tell in their search for the truth, the invisible Supreme God, the command given to each in a dream to follow the guiding star to the scene of the incarnation are full of interest. While their arrival at Bethlehem, then thronged with people going up to Jerusalem, the incidents in the khan, the strange, mystical light that lit up the vicinity and hovered over one of the outhouses, that so excited, alarmed and awed the early morning worshippers, but which revealed to the travelers the place where our Lord was born, are events so well told that while they may not add anything new to what is chronicled in the gospels, yet certainly clothe them in a novel and attractive garb. It also gives one an idea of the customs of that time, and makes to me, at least, that event clearer."

"Yes," added Marjorie, "books like *Ben Hur*, that are based on historical events are certainly great helps in the study of history, for they invest dull facts with the pleasing dress of romance, and many become acquainted with them who would not otherwise pore over dusty details. But, by the way, what was the opinion of the club in regard to our American novelists, Howell and James. You know that I was unable to be present at the meeting."[28]

"Well, it was rather unsatisfactory, although it was generally conceded that they were the greatest of our novelists. Some were of the opinion that James was too analytical, and others that Howell was too prosy; yet while most of them thought that their novels were models of realism, they did not think that their style would meet the acceptation of the masses. For in action and love, their characters were tame, every-day sort of people, and but served as a glass in which one sees himself reflected. They said that people read novels because they desire something out of the ordinary life."

"Then they thought feeling one thing, and action another. The heroic age has passed in fact, but not in ideal. Passions, ambitions and sorrows are just as strong now as ever except in those who have made listlessness a life cultivation, or are incapable of being moved. Now, a person who raves about all that they feel, would be considered a bore, and dubbed a crank. One's manner, in these days of propriety, is no index to their souls."

"Propriety is good in its place. It often acts as a brake on one's passions," replied Flora, "when the first crude and ill considered thoughts rush to the mind. First thoughts are not always wise, for they seldom spring from reason. However, taking my limited observation and experience as a criterion, I believe people who possess the finer senses live beyond that which they exhibit to their fellows."

"That is very true," said Marjorie, "for life itself is a succession of struggles and aspirations for something just beyond our reach, and life generally ends with it just beyond. Our ambitions prompt us to do something better than our neighbors; and to surpass some one else in some particular vocation. There is a desire to be loved better, or a wish to be regarded as brighter, shrewder, abler and more intelligent than our fellows. For myself, if I should have a husband, I should like one whose love would not be tame, but fervid and glowing, deep and all pervading. In this respect I fear I am like those who fail to appreciate the realistic novel."

"Then Maxwell would not suit you."

"No! But he is misjudged, poor fellow. Under the countenance so blank, except to his friends, and that dudish exterior, are hidden excellent qualities and a mind that is well trained and well informed."

The sacred passions of men were not to be made light of by Marjorie, and she refrained from telling her most intimate friend of Maxwell's attempt at proposing to her.

"What do you think of young Harper?"

"The incarnation of frankness, an excellent friend, who as you know is engaged to Carrie Lambert."

Flora then went over a list of eligible men of their acquaintance, but all failed in some respects to satisfy Marjorie's ideal, at length she asked her to describe him.

"Before I do so," replied Marjorie, "I must say that I think this catechism is all on one side. Let me ask your opinion of Walter Bogers and the relation he bears to your ideal."

It was a palpable hit, but Flora was equal to the occasion. "He is a fine fellow, but then you know my relation to the young men. They like me, some half adore me but seldom get above that. It would seem that I have but little chance for the fulfillment of my ideal. You see they get too confident, and tell me all their little troubles, looking for advice. In fact they regard me in a platonic relation only. I am a confirmed old maid." (Flora was only twenty-three). "Now, for your ideal."

"Well, I guess that would be rather difficult to describe. In his personal appearance I should like him to be handsome above the ordinary, tall, courteous and refined in his manners, and of course gallant; earnest and enthusiastic in what he undertakes, and of strong individuality. In temper I should like him to be firm, yet gentle, a man of great purposes, and noble. I should like him to be well educated, well informed, and have a well-balanced mind. I should like him to be an appreciator of nature, and one who could look from nature to nature's God."

"Anything else?" remarked Flora, who had been listening intently and thinking.

"Oh, yes! I should like him to be well up in music, for you know I am devoted to it, and should like to keep up the study, and I think it would be so much easier to keep up the study if he possessed a love for it."

"I don't suppose an angel would be out of place, if he was only affable and dealt with terrestrial subjects," laughed Flora. "These goody-goody fellows were never made to be husbands to mortals. They smile sparingly, think it a sin to laugh aloud and are always out of tune with everybody and everything. You are laying plans to be an old maid too," and Flora marked her last words off with her index finger as if to give them emphasis.

Marjorie laughed and replied, "that does not necessarily follow. Now, really, haven't you known people who came almost up to your ideal?"

Flora had to acknowledge that she had, then after thinking a moment said: "Lately I have seen Mr. Seth Stanley occasionally in your company."

"Yes, I met him for the first time at the concert given for the sexton's family, and afterwards at Uncle Durham's."

"Do you like him?"

"As a man, yes," replied Marjorie simply; "for he is so earnest, enthusiastic and courteous, that I could not help doing so. He is fond of music, too, and has an excellent voice."

"Then he has some of the essentials of your ideal, but have you not thought that this liking him as a man might develop into something stronger?"

"Why, Flo., you know the reputation he has, don't you?"

"Reputation!" said Flora, contemptuously "Reputation. What is it? Nothing of any consequence to a man, but everything to a woman. A man may wallow in the mire, reform and afterwards become conspicuous in society and be honored and respected. Circumstances are not rare where men with worse reputations than Stanley's have become as active in pursuing honorable lives as they formerly did dishonorable ones. Besides, his recklessness, I have heard some friends say, is due more to his thoughtlessness than to malicious instincts, and that his offenses against society have grown in proportion as gossip has repeated them. He is said by some to be kind, generous and courteous to a high degree, and they cannot believe that one who watches as carefully over his young sister is utterly devoid of good moral principles. A change they say has been noticeable in him, and for the past two months society has had no fresh escapade of his to talk about. I know that Fox, Morgan and Parker would not be so intimate with him were he as bad as represented. They are up the lakes now."

"I know it," said Marjorie. "I have received a letter from him, and copies of some views sketched by his steward."

"Oh!" said Flora, with a look of surprise, then added quickly, "you were sketching from real life then when you enumerated so glibly some of the very qualities he possessed. What say you, my lady?"

"He has some, it is true," replied Marjorie after a pause.

"He only lacks some great incentive to possess them all," said Flora vigorously, "and I predict that that incentive will soon be found if he continues to seek your society. But come, let us go, it grows late."

"You think you have guessed it exactly now, don't you? So you are willing to close the conversation and seal the seals thereof. You are wrong nevertheless. One or two visits do not make a match any more than one swallow makes a spring."

"That is all right, the one swallow only precedes the others, likewise the visits."

Marjorie then remembered her invitation for him to call and she felt her color rising.

"Don't blush, Margy. Honest love is legitimate, and we all do it, although we ever deny it. Another of the conventionalities or proprieties. I believe it is one of the old fellow's agencies of sin."

The club, of which the young ladies talked about in relation to novels and novelists, was one of young ladies, called the "Nineteenth Century Club." They met fortnightly, and one of their special purposes was to familiarize themselves with authors and their works. They were quite thorough in their work. They did not disdain the events of the day, for another of their features was the discussion of home and foreign news, and some of them, without doubt, were much better informed of the trend of events and the causes which led up to them than many men who pride themselves on their general intelligence and information. On the birthdays of certain authors, they had, what might be called memorial days and their work was chiefly confined to the author and his productions. On such occasions their meeting was a social one, and their gentlemen friends were invited. They had also a question box, and whenever anyone desired information on any particular subject, she put her question in writing and placed it in a box provided for the purpose. These questions were taken out and read, and if the information was not at once forthcoming, all members made a special effort to secure the desired information. It was about the affairs of this club, the future work that had been laid out for it, that busily occupied the attention of the young ladies until they reached home. Marjorie was rather ill at ease that night. She had received another letter from Stanley, and this with her conversation with her friend rendered the attitude she ought to assume toward him more uncertain. If anything the conversation of the afternoon had increased his chances, and she was disposed to regard much of the gossip about him as the invention of imaginative minds. However, she would watch and wait. Only a day or two would elapse before the return of the Sylvia, and he had written that he would embrace the first opportunity to call upon her, and she looked forward to that time with considerable pleasure. How true Pope read human nature when he said that "deformities lose their hideousness by contemplation."[29]

CHAPTER XI.

To again return to the boys, whom we left speeding homeward, we find them lying at anchor, while they spent a day fishing in the marshes and about the "Flats." The sport was not at all satisfactory, for the fish did not bite rapidly enough to make it interesting, and they lay around rather listlessly looking about for something to attract their attention. But ennui does not tarry long with youth and health, for life and pleasure are their complements. They who have youth and not life, who seek not after pleasure, or who have not something more serious to attract their minds are troubled with some bodily or mental ailment. True enjoyment of spontaneous pleasure, growing out of a healthy nature, seems to have become in our day a lost art. Our present age is a sieve into which health and youth are poured and drained until only the husk of precociousness, and a false idea of a life is left. The present generation lives too fast. At twelve we have children who are breathing eternal constancy. At twenty their characters are formed. At twenty-five they are in the prime of life. At thirty they are like old men and women, who have tasted and pursued all the pleasures and have become satiated with them. They have grown cynical, when they should be enjoying and appreciating all the pleasures and beauties of life. Our young men while they had health and youth had not altogether escaped the tendency of the age, though as has been seen, they were full of spirit, enjoyed pleasure, and appreciated the natural beauties of life. While waiting between "bites," for the first time their personal appearances attracted their attention. Excellent air, vigorous appetites, and a broiling sun had all done eminent work. All were well tanned and looked the picture of health, while each had added several pounds to his weight. Fox with his stooped shoulders seemed to have acquired a greater breadth of chest, and his naturally serious look was missing. The appearance of the others seemed to have struck a comical vein in each, for they commenced to chaff one another.

"Give Seth a buckskin suit and a few feathers," said Parker, "and he would look like an Indian fresh from a reservation."

"Well then," replied Stanley, "what I escaped as a boy I am receiving now—a little tanning."

"Smart! aren't you?" said Morgan. "Some new influence has taken possession of you these last two days, for before at times you have seemed as dreamy as a poet. What potent power has worked the change?"

"The most potent power I know of," interrupted Fox, "is a good appetite, a clear conscience and healthful sleep. Seth has two, at least, of these essentials."

"While the third naturally follows as the result of the other two," said Stanley. "Besides to judge from appearances all have succumbed to some magic influence, for you seem ruddier, brighter, wittier, and look more healthy than when we left home."

"Flatterer, a new way to turn a joke," said Morgan, as if reading a definition from Webster.

"You are a jocose lad," said Parker.

"Humph! after that we had better go ashore. Perhaps there may be found metal more attractive for your display of wit."

"A witless task we may find it," said Fox.

"But, hello!" Parker exclaimed, "here comes the Idlewild through the canal. There may be some friends aboard, some ladies. That would be metal more attractive."

"A few more fish suppers would make you unbearable," said Fox. "For such a bare assertion, thanks."

There was a quick movement of an arm over the surface of the water, a scoop and a handful or more flew directly at the punster, which he dodged only by a quicker movement and the water struck Morgan, who was busily engaged in watching the steamer, back of his neck and ran down his back in a manner that caused him almost to jump out of the boat. His caperings made the others shriek with laughter.

"What are you idiots laughing about? There is no fun in a lot of water running down a fellow's back," growled Morgan.

"I am, ha! ha! ha! laughing at the, ha! ha! ha! Warm and startled reception you, ha! ha! ha! gave the water," shrieked Parker, between bursts of laughter.

"Seeing that you like it so well have some," said Morgan, as he directed a handful at Parker that flew into the latter's face and open mouth, ran down his throat, and catching him unprepared almost choked him, and changed his peals of laughter to a fit of coughing.

"Who laughs last laughs best," said Morgan. He was satisfied and chuckled to himself all the way as they rowed to the landing. None of their friends happened to be aboard the steamer, which was another disappointment, so they went on board the Sylvia in order to reach home early, and Capt. Lake gave the orders that sent the Sylvia again homeward.

"A fellow can't expect the earth and four dollars all at once," commented Parker, partly to himself and partly to the others. "We have had a good time if we haven't seen the dear creatures for nearly a month."

"I am glad to see you extract some comfort out of the situation like a true philosopher, particularly so after your attempt to swallow the river. You may catch a mermaid before we get home," said Fox.

"No! He will catch the mere maid after he gets home," replied Morgan.

The others, as Fox afterward put it, sunk down in despair until Morgan should sober up.

Stanley recovering from the transports of happiness into which the receival of Marjorie's letter had thrown him began again an eager scrutiny of the same to see if he could not find some word, thought or phrase that would indicate to him a line of action by which he might hope to win her, but in vain. The calm demeanor, the earnest sensible talk that characterized her when in his presence seemed stamped upon the written page. Thus left to his own resources for the rest of the trip he began to form and reform plans which he proposed to inaugurate in pushing forward his suit.

Reaching Detroit, hurried orders were given to Capt. Lake concerning the Sylvia, and to John Saunders as to their luggage. Then they hastened ashore and to their several homes.

Imogene, who had been expecting her brother for the past two or three days, was watching for him. She heard his steps and rushed to the door.

"Oh, Seth!" she exclaimed, "I am awful glad you have come back. It has been very lonesome here without you. I have had no one to go out with, and have only had Kitsey and Jack (the names of her cat and pug), to spend the evenings with." "My!" she continued, as she took his hat and had a clearer view of his face in the bright gas light, "how tanned you are."

"And how tickled you are."

"You mean fellow, to talk like that when you have been gone so long, and I have been so lonesome."

Stanley placed one hand upon her head, another under her chin, then kissed the upturned face and lips. Then handing her a satchel said: "Here, Puss! You will find something in this to pay you for past loneliness."

He had been very attentive to his sister of late. He could see her budding into womanhood without the influence of a mother to guide and direct her, and with a father so occupied with business cares that he gave but little time to her, so he had become her confidant and adviser. Since his acquaintance with Marjorie Stone, his care and love for his sister had become more marked. He would have liked her to be as much as possible like that young lady, and he so tried to direct and influence her thoughts. He perhaps made a better mentor from the fact that he had led a life that was a little reckless and knew what temptation lay in the way of a young girl, and how she could best be protected.

While Stanley went to his room, Imogene opened up the satchel and found the duplicate sketches that he had had Saunders prepare, together with a number of Indian relics and curiosities he had purchased at Mackinac Island.

When she had examined them she took them to Mrs. Burwell, an elderly and refined lady who had served them for a number of years as housekeeper, to show them to her.

After Mrs. Burwell had adjusted her spectacles and had examined them for a while, Imogene asked: "Don't you think they are nice? Seth had John Saunders, the book keeper at the store, to draw them for me."

"I didn't know that he could do such nice work. These sketches show considerable skill. I suppose Mr. Seth is quite tired."

"I guess he is. You would hardly know him. He must have gained at least ten pounds, and he is almost as dark as John. When he comes down stairs he is going to tell me all about it," and she tripped out of the room with a light heart and a light step as she thought of the pleasure she would have in having her brother at home again for an evening, and listening to his tale of pleasure and fun, told as only he could tell it. She was very proud of that brother of hers. Shortly after Stanley came down, and while she sat down on a low stool at his feet devouring him with her eyes, he narrated the chief incidents of the trip, and described some of the beautiful scenery they had witnessed, she all the while busy plying him with questions. During their conversation, their father came in, and after greeting him, said, "Well Seth, you are back. I suppose you have enjoyed yourself."

"Yes, father, I certainly did, and now I am ready to try to settle down to business and give you a chance to rest yourself, for you certainly need it."

"I was thinking of going down east for a few days after a while, and since you have expressed a desire to settle down, I will put you in harness at once so I can turn affairs over to you when I go."

They talked away, these three, until bed time, Stanley enthusiastically over the trip up the lakes, and afterwards patiently listening to his father when he read him a lecture upon the necessity of settling down. He also mentioned during their conversation, several matters he desired that Seth should give immediate attention to. While now and then Imogene would break in upon their talk by asking a question, and declaring that next time she must go "as she didn't intend that the boys should have all the fun."

On the following day he commenced his duties at the store, trying to master all the details in a day, and between the labor and the heat of the day he was quite tired in the evening. However he had made the resolution, and had shut his teeth down hard upon it. Many of his father's clerks he found were far more proficient than he, but he thought what they had mastered, he could, and consequently stuck close to his duty during the entire day and for several succeeding days.

CHAPTER XII.

That evening he disappointed his sister, who had been calculating on again enjoying her big brother's company, by spending the evening away from home. During the day he had made up his mind to call on Miss Stone, and thither he went. On his way he could not help wondering whether he would be successful in his wooing, or whether she was pledged to another. As he mounted the steps of the Stone residence and rang the bell he nerved himself, for like a skillful general, he intended first to reconnoiter, to send out skirmishers to find the weak points of the enemy and to take advantage of them. The servant who answered the bell ushered him into the parlor, where much to his surprise and annoyance, sat Maxwell like a fixture. He began to suspect that he, like himself, was also a suitor, and he wondered if he would ever be able to find her alone. Marjorie, however, seemed pleased to see him, shook hands with him, and thanked him for his kindness in so remembering her, as to send her the sketches. Her welcome set him instantly at ease and they plunged into an animated conversation, while Mr. Stone, who was present, tried to entertain Maxwell, as far as his reserved manners would permit, with some of his experiences on the road.

"Those sketches you sent me were certainly fine," said Marjorie.

"I am glad that you like them. They are the work of Paul Fox and John Saunders, a colored clerk at the store, who accompanied us in the capacity of general handy man."

"I should like to see them," said Mr. Stone rising and joining in their conversation. "I heard Fred Douglass lecture while I was East and I consider him a prodigy, for he is certainly the equal of any white man I have ever heard lecture.[30] He is one of the few old style impassioned orators that are left us, whose elegant and rounded periods used to so thrill the people. If you have discovered another prodigy among the race I would like to see him or some of his work."

Marjorie handed him the sketches, and while he was carefully examining them, the general conversation flowed on, on different subjects. When he had finished he asked, "Is this a mere gift the fellow possesses, or is his general intelligence in keeping with his work in this line?"

"He is an old school and college mate of mine," answered Stanley, "but he finished his course while I did not. I think him exceptionally learned and intelligent, besides having a large stock of common sense to draw from."

"Has tact as well as talent," said Mr. Stone.

"Why, papa," said Marjorie. "You must remember that our public schools are making many intelligent and refined colored boys and girls. I suppose it was different when you were a school boy. One of my classmates, a colored girl, once loaned me a volume of poems written by a black girl named Phyllis Wheatley, who lived in the time of Washington. It contained a translation of Homer's Odyssey, with a personal note from the Father of his country, congratulating her on its merits."[31]

Mr. Stone said no more, but laid the sketches aside, to again entertain Maxwell. Maxwell's father was a jeweler, and he was a partner in the firm. Mr. Stone being a traveling man they commenced to talk business and trade while the others conversed on society, music and travels.

So pleasant did the time speed away that Stanley was scarcely conscious of it, and with a feeling akin to dismay he saw on glancing at the clock that stood on the mantle that he had made his call as long as possible, without having had the opportunity to listen to that divine voice. Maxwell as usual outstayed him. And as usual he remained but for a few moments after the other had left. This peculiarity had often vexed Marjorie and had caused her parents to smile.

"Maxwell, as usual is bound to have the last word," laughed her father. In the solitude of their own chamber Mr. Stone said to his wife, "I do not like the idea of young Stanley being on intimate terms with Marjorie. He is given too much to pleasure seeking, and his reputation is none of the best. There is contamination in the society of the vicious."

"Do not fear for her," replied his wife. "Marjorie's principles of right and wrong are rooted, and influence all with whom she comes in contact."

"I don't rely so much on well-formed principles," said Mr. Stone, "when there is love in the case. You know the old story, of how it paints only the best side."

"How absurd you talk," said Mrs. Stone impatiently, "Marjorie is surely not head over heels in love with that fellow yet."

"You can't tell how soon she will be, he is comely, fairly educated, good prospects and devilish winning. I must acknowledge. You could see the difference between him and Maxwell at a glance, and one would not be long in saying Stanley was the more preferable."

"Marjorie is acquainted with his career and I have no doubt but that she has her eyes open, and I don't want you to bother her with your apprehensions until you have occasion."

Mr. Stone gave a surprised whistle which he turned into a "Mikado" air to the tune of "Here's a Pretty Mess," and said no more.[32]

Stanley on his way home, tried to figure out Maxwell's relations to Marjorie, and in that light to figure out his own chances for success, but he could arrive at no satisfactory conclusion. "He is a confounded bore at any rate," he muttered to himself rather savagely. "He seems to be there every night in the week and sits like a bump on a log. If this is to be a contest, I'll make him show his colors, if such a thing is possible." Then he again fell to speculating on his chances, and rapidly his mind ran over all the conversation, and the different phases it assumed, to find some loop hole that would give him a clue. He could find none. She hadn't exhibited anything in her manner that she would not have shown to anyone who had a pleasant tale to tell. He was in a quandary over more than one question, and like all men of his temperament, who are truly in love, he was somewhat chagrined. The object to be gained had become precious in his sight, while the attainment was not at all sure; but it awakened in him a determination to overcome if possible all difficulties that lay between him and its accomplishment. Obstacles only serve to whet the ambitions of some men and spur them to greater action. In many instances before, his wealth and prospective position in life, had brought around him many flippant flatterers, a number of whom possessed more wealth than Marjorie was heir to. His father had humored him, his sister made him her ideal, and young men of his age had courted him because of his means and tact in improvising plans for pleasure. Hence it is not at all surprising, that despite his determination to try to win he was at the same time disappointed at what he thought was slow progress. In that respect he was an overgrown child spoiled by his surroundings, intoxicated by his successes, and just beginning to sober up on experience. The most costly and precious things in life that come easy are not valued as highly as the mere commonplaces that cost thought and anxiety. Stanley was realizing this to its full capacity. Wealth, luxury and ease had come to him without thought. Now he found himself the slave of a sentimental passion that summoned every mental force. If he had had the power, however, to look into the mind and heart of the object of his love, he would have found that her regard for him was warm, and the basis of it was the good she had discovered in him, and not for his wealth or position in life.

With Parker a few evenings later he called on Miss Mabel Downing, a young lady on —— street, that he had often seen with his companion. She was tall, stately and quite beautiful, not very long a resident of the city, and he at once began to contrast her with Marjorie Stone. She was a woman of fashion, bright, vivacious and very often witty. Just the qualities that met Parker's approbation. She loved to dwell on fashionable topics, the delights of splendor and the achievements of men. Although handsomer than Marjorie, he thought she was not near so desirable. Marjorie possessed qualities and purposes, while Miss Downing, liking and seeking ideals, proposed to shine only in society, and was somewhat frivolous. Parker, however, was delighted with her, for the glamour, which she shed around her was in harmony with his own disposition. When he and Parker had parted on his way home he commented in this manner: "She and I would make a great pair with like temperaments and tendencies," then he laughed at himself to think that he was planning love conquests with the same zest he once planned pleasure trips, parties or suppers. "If I am jilted or refused I suppose my next role will be that of a misanthrope, and if I play the last as well as I have the first two roles, the earth will soon contain no virtue or purity for me." How easily the sensible, reasoning and logical man plays the jumping-jack to the grimaces and smirks of fortune. How he makes for himself conditions, by stifling reason, which he calls fate, and then rants at them.

He applied himself at the store diligently, and the zeal and earnestness with which he took up the work was creditable. He determined to master all the details of the business, and whereas he had gained a reputation for profligacy and instability, he now desired to gain one for diligence, and perseverance. For a few days all went well then he found that all at once he could not overcome the habit of years, and possess the requisite energy necessary for the requirements of an active business life without a struggle. However, he had calculated the task and tried to quell his rebellious longings with work. Despite his effort the desire to be free and roaming would often arise and make him exceedingly nervous. "Create desires at pleasure, and they will make their demands at leisure," was a little couplet his mother had often quoted to him, and which had great significance now.

He did not visit the club as often now as formerly, and the fellows noticed it, and his changed manners. Some were bold enough to twit him with trying to be religious, some said he was in love, others that there had been reverses in business which affected him. Generally he responded with a laughing repartee, and although he felt their sarcasms, it served only to make firmer his resolutions. Going home one evening, after being twitted his thoughts ran as follows in a soliloquy which of late he was becoming addicted to: "I know now what warnings against keeping bad company means. Every form of association has its demands upon us, and sooner or later we find ourselves yielding until we become the creature of our surroundings. Those whose position oft calls them into other fields of life find a demand there also but one different from what they have been accustomed to. Our better natures tell us at once what appeals to the man and what to the animal, and our inclinations tell us and others, under what master we have served. Habits of character are like habits of taste. Their march is slow and insidious, but sure, and before one is aware he is in their clutches. Often one does not realize his true position until a desire is born to reform and to cast off the old habits and associations. It was easy for me to gratify every desire for pleasure to the very extreme of voluptuous imagining, now it is very hard for me to shake off these desires of habit. Could I start life anew, shorn of these detracting influences that beset me, and form a part of me, I could probably approach near to what I desire to be. Twenty-seven years of life lost to me save in the recollection of many things I would fain forget. Yet not altogether lost if I can profit by their lesson. Ah, that regrets cannot undo the past." Then as his thoughts turned towards Marjorie, "But she can help me to atone and to forget and she must. She has lived and moved in other spheres than mine, she has breathed purer air and been moved by nobler impulses. The uneven places of my life and character she can help fill in; its jagged excesses, smooth, and so restore to itself a character not wholly bad nor devoid of generous impulses. If I must testify to my own good qualities and be guilty of self praise. What would life without her be to me? She is already the incentive that has pushed me on to overcome the past, forget its follies and to live and act more soberly. Will the past, with its oft repeated tales step between us? For they too, like little streams gather as they run and grow. If I have not been painted to her ten times as bad as I am, gossip has lost its inventive imagination."

The self accusation of a penitent mind is often more scrutinizing and severe than the harshest outside criticism. Small facts are magnified when they seem to stand between one and the accomplishment of results. It was so in Stanley's case. "If they should separate us," he would not pursue the subject further, for the idea cast a chill over him and he shuddered, and tried to turn his attention to more pleasing topics such as planning a ride or a jaunt in which he could derive the benefit of her company.

He had almost decided to give up the club as it told on his resolutions. His companionable associates, Parker, Fox and Morgan often visited him and he them. His room where they chatted, smoked or played cards was about all the club he wanted under the circumstances. Then Imogene claimed her share of his time, and generally received it ere he had peace. Once she had bluntly told him that "Marjorie Stone shouldn't receive all his attentions."

"Little sister," he had replied, "you are getting jealous, and you are too young for that."

"If you want her then, why don't you quit fooling, and marry her?"

"Hush! hush! Who said anything about marrying? Don't you ever mention that to anyone."

"Oh! I didn't know it was a secret."

"You don't suppose she cares for me, do you?" He had lain particular stress on the "me."

"She's foolish if she don't. I do, and she's no better than I am." She had her way of looking at things and didn't want him to be fooling away his time. In this respect she was like her father.

CHAPTER XIII.

The commendations won by Stanley from his father, concerning his business qualities, were very pleasing to the young man. He was consulted on all occasions when any important innovation was considered. This had the effect of increasing his confidence in his own abilities, and increasing a love for business, that he did not dream a few months back, he was capable of feeling.

He had become a constant church attendant, partly because of Marjorie, partly because of his new conceptions of life. It was also because it was a relief from his restless hours at home alone, when images of sport and travel asserted a place in his mind to confuse and bewilder him. Some of the money that he had been wont to spend in pleasure, now served to render little acts of charity. His constant association with Marjorie had broadened his views, and at the same time threw him into the society of men and women of greater depth of thought and better purposes in life than he had formerly been accustomed to. In this sphere he felt his horizon expanding, and in the effort to keep pace with his new acquaintances, he began to acquire a vast fund of knowledge and information. He took Marjorie to concerts, operas and receptions, where his sparkling humor was shown to advantage. And as the summer days merged into autumn they took many a pleasant drive to places of interest in and around the city. There are no mountains or very high hills in Lower Michigan, yet there are places where hill and lake alternate with the general undulation of the country, and make pleasing natural pictures. During the summer season the shores of these lakes are transformed into villages by those seeking change and rest from the cities. Summer cottages fringe their borders. Here and there a hotel is located to accommodate the surplus of visitors coming to these resorts. Around Detroit, however, the country flattens out and the highest elevation for some miles around, hardly rises above the dignity of an ordinary ridge. The city was redeemed from the swamps, and around what was intended as a military post, because of its superior position as a shipping point, for the great inland traffic that traverses the lakes, has grown a large and thriving metropolis. Its growth has, to a great extent followed the river's course, upon whose banks are situated the majority of its large manufactures, thus leaving the resident part remarkably free from the smoke and soot that hovers over most of the large manufacturing cities. Notwithstanding the number of factories that line the river's bank, there are few driveways surpassing that out Jefferson Avenue to Grosse Pointe, with its almost unbroken line of handsome residences and princely villas along the lake and river fronts. The drive out Woodward avenue is no less attractive, and is almost a boulevard with its fine residences and spacious grounds. Different groups of these are called after the English style of parks and courts. One passes these on the way to Senator Palmer's far famed Log Cabin Farm, which is regarded as a marvel in its section.[33] The log cabin is only named from its outside appearance, within one might think it an antique museum of some old family in which all its heirlooms are kept. A deer's antler overhangs the door, on either side of which is tacked a coon skin. Within suspended from the ceiling are strings of corn and dried apples. Old fashioned clocks, stand in the corners, and in the rooms are beds, arm chairs, and a cradle, all older than the nation. The surroundings of the cabin are in keeping with its inner furnishings. Two artificial lakes, connected by a single stream are fed by an artesian well. The earth removed to form these lakes have been made into a hill which is covered with ferns and plants. Here Stanley sometimes came with Marjorie, and together they would admire the scores of Percheron horses and Jersey cattle, or at other times, make an entomological collection and gather the fast turning leaves.

"All beauty in nature or man depends upon the condition of one's mind," he thought one day in mid-autumn as they drove along, past wood and field, which, obedient to the season's call, had put off Nature's gay garb for the winter, then preparing, which would lull them to sleep with its storms. "Two years ago this same scene was too commonplace to attract my attention, today with love permeating my being, and inspiring my vision, all these things seem beautiful. What would they appear to one overwhelmed in sorrow, but a mockery setting his own condition all the more boldly in relief? What to the weary plodder, burdened with toil and the thought of tomorrow's bread, but mere trees, woods or fields occupying so much space that must be cleared, cultivated, to yield a given amount of produce! What to the thinker, but the revelation that only to man is committed care."

Wrapped in these thoughts he had forgotten all else, and Marjorie who had spoken to him and received no answer, began to watch him. As her gaze was steady, intuition, or some other power of the mind which makes one aware that another is watching him, made him aware of her gaze, and he became somewhat confused. Why, he knew not, but as he turned quickly and caught her staring, a crimson glow mounted to her cheek and she stammered out, "I didn't know you could be so serious, Mr. Stanley."

"I am not serious. I happened to be thinking of something that interested me, which our surroundings suggested, and I unconsciously dropped into a brown study. I beg a thousand pardons. But do you think me incapable of seriousness?"

"You are freely forgiven, but I would not judge your qualities, or whether you could be serious or not. But I have heard that you had no cares, if you had, you succeeded in keeping them from your associates."

"It is hard for a man to escape his past reputation," he said bitterly. "Be it good or bad, and my reputation is one of carelessness and frivolity, I know. Still if we could read each other's minds, how different our conjectures might be, we might find a change going on, and thoughts dwelling there perhaps that were not in harmony with one's past actions or reputation. Things are not always what they seem in either the mental or material world. Good thoughts may dwell behind actions considered unworthy, and evil behind those considered good. An incident in a man's life may change his nature and yet the world would still continue to judge by the past."

"Isn't it a good saying that by their fruits, or records, which is the same thing, ye shall know them?"[34]

"It is, as a rule, but like all rules there are exceptions, even if it were not so, could the same old standard be applied to me as formally. Have I not changed my associations?"

"But how are we to know the exceptions, Mr. Stanley?" replied Marjorie, paying no heed to his question. "I grant the motives, even the lives of many are judged by one single act, but when we have an accumulation of circumstances, doesn't reason, unswerved by sympathy, decide with the preponderance of evidence?"

"Your mental law with its modifications, is generally correct, but sympathy often sways reason, and in that the mischief lies. From now on I shall try to be serious, and make a new record to be judged by."

"I hate, if you will excuse the expression, appearances or forced manners. Let us be ourselves at whatever cost."

"This is what I mean to be, and always have been, too much so, I fear. I could never practice deceit on myself."

"I believe that what you are, you are earnestly."

"Is that a compliment?"

"It is a quality I admire. To be frank, weather-cocks cannot be men, nor should men be weather-cocks. You might know Mr. Stanley, that I would not have the audacity to upbraid!"

"It is profitable to be able to see ourselves as others see us, if we have confidence that our faults are being criticized charitably. We are so prone to be selfish, that our best attempts to take an honest view of ourselves are liable to be biased."

"Conscience is often like a poet's muse—capricious, but we make it so by warping it out of shape to sanction our opinions."

"Do you think so? By the way I think your friend Miss Aikman quite frank, in fact she has many other admirable qualities beside that and her beauty."

"You and I agree on that point, for 'Flo.' and I chide each other like sisters, when in our best humors but that has only made our friendship closer and stronger."

"You and she are confidants, I suppose?"

"We are and we are not. Somewhat of a paradox isn't it?"

"It seems like one. Parker comes nearer being a confidant of mine than any one else; but there are some things it is not wise to tell even our best friends. In other words, as poor Richard says, 'When you keep your own counsels you know they are well kept.'[35] This is perhaps what you mean by your paradox, is it not?"

"You have hit it perfectly, Mr. Stanley. We seem to agree admirably this afternoon."

"Then we are agreeable, to compass the whole matter."

Both laughed at his attempt at wit.

"The heart, Miss Stone, is like the earth, dull and unattractive, but from it springs beauty and wealth of sentiment, and in its recesses are many hidden treasures. It needs to be penetrated by influences that separate and bring out its desirable qualities, like the flowers that bring forth pleasing colors and rich perfumes."

"Your similes are fine, Mr. Stanley. I think you would make a great poet. Only with poetic geniuses do such sentiments flow so readily."

She stopped then as if she thought she had said too much, and maintained a quiet reserve for the rest of their drive. On different occasions like these arguments were indulged in, outside of the small talk that generally accompanies conversations. He trying to impress upon her, while arguing in the abstract, that a change in his life was going on, and that an incentive for it had been found. He was pained, however, because she seemed to have joined in the general verdict against him, but to what extent it prejudiced her against him, he could not tell. He also thought, and in that he was not far wrong, that outside influences were brought to bear against him. She was always kind and gracious to him, and seemed to enjoy his society, but she was always discreet enough not to exhibit any sign by which he might predicate whether or no, his suit was favored. He could see that he was preferred above Maxwell. That individual did not call so frequently now, but when he did, he stayed as long as ever and Stanley considered him as much of a bore.

CHAPTER XIV.

"Love seldom makes good business men," said Mr. Stanley, "but in your case, my boy, the rule has been reversed."

Seth and his father were in the office quietly talking over business affairs, the volume of trade, the estimated profits for the season, and what new ventures should be made in the Spring. Afterward the father naturally referred to the active interest taken by his son in the business, and ended with the above remark.

"Why do you say that?" asked Seth, turning quickly and coloring, although he surmised that his father had guessed the secret of his interest, but, wishing to find how his choice was regarded, thought it best to push the matter and get his father's opinion. He said again, "Why do you say that, father?"

"Do you think me blind?" replied his father. "Why even a blind man could see that you were in love with Marjorie Stone. When before, did the pursuit of an object ever work such a change in you, even for a week? Church, hard work, and a struggle with yourself for mastery over the pursuits of fleeting pleasure, deserting your club rooms and drives, and a constant attendance upon one whom I fancy reciprocates your affections. I have seen it creeping out in your manner, when with her, in a hundred different ways. My boy, your choice meets my full approval, for I think her a very practicable, businesslike and intelligent woman. Just the one for such a harum-scarum fellow as you have been, and if she thoroughly tames you I shall certainly count her a worthy daughter. I was quite wild once Seth, I can remember when I used to go courting your mother down in New York, what wild pranks we boys used to indulge in. We lived on farms then, on the beautiful sloping plateaus to the south of the Adirondacks, through which ran many little streams that fed the Mohawk.[36] Our folks owned adjoining farms. We married and came West, with little else but hope and determination. Your mother nobly seconded my efforts, and what I am, what I have acquired, is due as much to her as to any effort of mine. Miss Stone's actions and temperaments are very much like hers, and I would advise you to go in and win."

66

He was standing over Stanley as he finished, and as if to give his injunction emphasis, gave him a resounding slap across the shoulders.

"I suppose I may as well own up since you have guessed my attachment, but I have not declared my love to her, and I am not so sure I will be accepted when I do."

"Tut! tut! no sensible girl is going to stand against her best interests. You have money and position. The two form a power not to be despised. My motto has ever been to conquer all obstacles that I may meet. As society is now organized an ounce of cheek is worth a pound of merit, very often."

"I have at times proceeded on that basis, and find it does well among the unthinking ones. It might even win a wife, but does wealth always win love? I believe Marjorie Stone would consider wealth among the least of my attainments, and I think you misjudge her."

"Such a heart as yours was made for a chicken, but never mind it will grow with experience," so saying Stanley *pere* returned to his desk, leaving his son to think over what had been said.

"It must be a game chicken then," commented Stanley to himself after a little reflection, "for I have pushed my suit with all the vigor and earnestness that I can muster, and I mean to follow up whatever advantage I have gained. Father has no idea how original and firm she is in her convictions, her likes and dislikes, I could not explain the situation to him, though I am satisfied with my present position. If I win I shall win in my own way."

With this determination he continued his visits. He went out with her often, played at love, without making it boldly, until he grew in her affections unawares. If he did not come on the usual evenings she was disappointed. If he missed in his attendance at church she upbraided him as her pupil. Thus the Autumn merged into Winter and the time passed rapidly. At Christmas he gave her a necklace of pearls, because pearls represented purity. It was the first present he had offered her during their acquaintance and she accepted it. By this time the friends of both had come to the conclusion that they were engaged. Their more intimate ones, except Flora Stedman, declared that this attachment of Stanley's was only another infatuation for something to gratify his pleasure and ambition. That his attachment was only ephemeral and after a few months of married life she would be left to repent the folly of marrying a good-looking and good-natured young man, who was too unstable in character to apply himself to anything for any length of time. Among these was an old lady, Mrs. Brooks, who admired Miss Stone very much. When she heard of this reported engagement, she determined to call on Mrs. Stone and let her know what a wild life young Stanley had led. Some, jealously inclined, declared she was going to marry him for his money, and said that it would serve her right if he had tired of her, and would leave her and go off to Europe in a week. If you want to enlist the active interest of your friends, just let it be noised about that you are about to marry, and if you will allow it, you will instantly find yourself overburdened with advice and find yourself the theme on nearly every tongue. Speculation, not always good natured, but more frequently tinged with envy, and spiced with ill-natured remarks, becomes rife, even among those who are only casual acquaintances. Conservative people who do not mean to be followers of Madame Grundy, have, many times, when such subjects are introduced and started, fallen into the general rut and said more than they would like to father in more serious moments.[37]

Mrs. Brooks, to whom we have referred, was a widow living with her brother's family. She had passed the time of marriageable probabilities and having a comfortable income had nothing else to do but visit, gossip and read novels. She was quite conversant with all the small talk of the neighborhood, was an inveterate reader and prided herself on her general information of current topics. She was noted for her loquacity and for the concessions people made to her hobbies, age and respectability. Language emanating from her passed unnoticed, that coming from others would have been considered impertinent, and at once challenged. She chose a stormy afternoon shortly after the holidays, in which to make the visit to Mrs. Stone to inform her of Stanley's character, because she thought she would more surely find her at home. As she stood in the hallway shaking off the snow from her fascinator and wrap, Mrs. Stone came down the stairway, and with a look of surprise she asked:

"Why Mrs. Brooks, what has induced you to come out on such a day as this?"

"I don't mind the weather. Nothing daunts me, when I make up my mind. I wanted to see you and I thought I would run over for a few minutes. You know I am not of those delicate makeups that sneeze every time the wind blows, or hurries off to the doctor for every pain." Mrs. Brooks' portly form seemed to attest the truthfulness of her statements. "I only consult my feelings when I want to do anything, and snap my fingers at outside circumstances. Where is Marjorie?"

"She has gone to the matinee of the American Opera Company with Mr. Stanley. They are so fond of music that they have braved the storm. But come into the sitting room."

This was the opening Mrs. Brooks desired, and she gladly availed herself of it. When they were comfortably seated, she approached the subject as naturally and glibly as she would have done in dispensing with some choice bit of gossip, or talking of the weather. "Mr. Stanley has been very attentive to her of late," she said. "I did not know he could be such a gallant."

"Yes," replied Mrs. Stone. "The young people have very many ideas and pleasures in common, and he seems to enjoy her society very much. He is becoming more of a society man and enjoys society. He chats with me almost as much as he does with her and I find him very interesting."

"But he is said to be very wild," clearing her throat.

"So I have been told. But I think his reputation has outstripped his acts. I have been unable to discover any objectionable feature in his character. He is a constant church-goer, but to what influence it should be attributed, is more than I know."

"But he'll not stand the restraint, Mrs. Stone. It isn't his nature to be quiet. A more restless young man one seldom sees."

"Don't you think that he realizes the folly of his restlessness, and has made up his mind to conquer it, and assume the business of his father?"

"I can hardly say that I do. He may have resolved to do so, but I should want several years of his reform to convince me that he is sincere. I should not be so hard though, for I hear that he and Marjorie are engaged."

Mrs. Stone's eyes flashed and she was about to make some angry retort, reprimanding her for meddling and circulating reports about her daughter. She realized now the object of the visit, and she choked back the half uttered words for fear it might compromise Marjorie and give to gossip fresh material, so she quietly replied, "You have been misinformed. If anything of that nature had happened she would have told me, for since she has been a child she has made me her confidant, and considers me her best friend."

"We generally keep our own confidence in love affairs, Mrs. Stone. Still I am glad to hear that it hasn't gone that far, and I hope Marjorie will be firm enough not to put her head into a halter, even if it is represented by the only son of a millionaire."

"Marjorie is a sensible child, and I do not believe that she would do anything willfully that she would afterward have cause to regret. Besides, her parents are able to advise her in case they deem a warning necessary. It has always been a mystery to me why people should trouble themselves so much about other people's affairs," said Mrs. Stone with some feeling. Mrs. Brooks fearing now that further conversation on that subject would be unpleasant turned the talk into other channels, and rattled glibly on until Marjorie and Stanley returned.

She confessed to herself that in appearance, at least, they made a handsome couple, but she had taken a position as to his character, and this so warped her judgement that she would not allow it to change. She was not the only person who entertains positive notions without any reason for them. People have a belief just because, and that is their stronghold. It is easy to conjure up sufficient evidence to support one's position, if the prejudices sanction the conclusion.

Stanley with his broad shoulders and clear black eyes, which seemed to glow with a peculiar light when directed toward Marjorie, looked the picture of perfect manhood. While Marjorie with cheeks flushed to a crimson by the storm was a picture of charming simplicity. Her father had recently established a business of his own and was at home oftener. This, together with the pleasure she derived in Stanley's society, and their rides in the country, had improved her color, and strengthened her in health and spirits.

CHAPTER XV.

Mrs. Brooks addressed both in the kindliest manner, as if proud of them and of their friendly relation to each other, while Mrs. Stone looked on and could not help but think when she saw her changed demeanor that she was a she-Janus.

Stanley had rather shunned her knowing her disposition and reputation, since he had been paying court to Marjorie; but her kindly tone and pleasing manner in which she complimented them on their appearance and inquired about the opera, disarmed him of any suspicion that he had formerly entertained. In her own mind Mrs. Brooks was satisfied that they both by nature and temperament were adapted to each other. She had been or rather was a devotee of Fowler, and she believed in his theory that temperaments ranged generally with the color, and that opposites were best calculated as mates.[38] At heart she was not a malicious woman. She liked conversation and gossip, and often when discussing a person, their merits and demerits, she substituted her imaginings for facts, which caused her to go to excess in criticisms, and say what she did not really mean. Then her stubbornness made her stand by her expressed criticism.

Her comments on the probably close relation Marjorie and Stanley might bear to each other, and Mrs. Stone's remarks on the same, she repeated to many other acquaintances, and these in turn discussed it with others, and occasionally Marjorie would catch an inkling of the trend of gossip much to her confusion and discomfort.

When they were alone her mother told her what Mrs. Brooks had said more in indignation at what she termed "unwarranted interference," than as a warning to her, for she had full confidence in Marjorie's judgment.

"I wish she would mind her own business," said Marjorie petulantly. "If I had known that she had been meddling in my affairs I should have told her, too. It will soon be so that two people will not be able to keep each other company without being discussed and belied, even questioned and upbraided to their faces."

"Don't lose your temper, my dear," expostulated her mother. "You must respect her age and her inclinations. I said all that was necessary. Besides anger won't stop a tongue, in fact I have never found a remedy that would."

"I never could use such audacity, and I can't understand people who do, that's all," said Marjorie, who was nettled. "Such a person's enmity is more valuable than their friendship."

"That isn't a Christian spirit, my child."

"Christianity, mother, never calls one to give the devil an advantage. That is carrying meekness to an extreme not contemplated in the books."

"But you'll not mention it to her unless she sees fit to meddle with you."

"No, I am willing to make her a present of that much grace, but if she comes to me inquiring after my private affairs she'll find that there are more tongues in town than hers. Mr. Stanley hasn't mooted love to me, and of course I haven't to him. I enjoy his company, and he must mine or he wouldn't seek it." Marjorie had spoken in a more decided manner than ever before in her life.

Many times during the winter Stanley took Marjorie to the opera, and many pleasant evenings were spent at her home in conversation and song. She could easily see from his manner what his attentions were leading to, although not yet expressed in words. She was sure that he loved her, and she felt a strong responsive chord in her own heart, that beat in unison with every advance of his. Often at night, after vainly endeavoring to free her mind of thoughts of him, she would find them constantly recurring to him. She would find herself planning and building air castles for the future, always with him as the chief corner stone. She did not question the sincerity of his love, but she did have grave doubts and apprehensions regarding its stability. He had depreciated himself in her presence, and his own estimate of self was confirmed by those who knew him in his former unsettled state. His hints about men to whom a passing incident or some great incentive had changed the current of their thoughts and lives, she understood as applying to himself, and to her as his incentive. She was pleased at this, and the knowledge that her life and person could so transform a man of his appearance as to draw out the better side of his character, was a source of great satisfaction and happiness. His most serious fault lay in the fact, she thought, that he was always restless. Her sometimes evasive manners toward him were for the purpose of gaining time to test his last resolve to be sturdy. She would not become an easy sacrifice to a sentimental passion, but must be convinced that the passion had in it the elements of strength. If he loved her as she desired to be loved by him, the months of waiting would purify and strengthen it. For his prospective fortune she had nothing to offer but herself and love in return.

Nevertheless, born of respectable parents and of good connections, with her many accomplishments she thought the scales would be balanced. So veiled had her affections been for him, that while she charmed, he had found no opportunity to propose. Stanley meanwhile withstood the good-natured jibes of his associates and kept his own counsel. His father began to grow impatient and feared that a shock now would unfit him for business, and would have advised, had he not seen that it wouldn't be acceptable. The good-natured queries of Parker, who attributed it all to the boat ride, he met with the best of humor, but he was often bored by presuming young ladies who referred to his prospective marriage relations with provoking assurance. He felt sure that in Marjorie's estimation he ranked higher than any of her gentlemen friends, while many a little token led him to believe that he had not pressed his case in vain. His great *bete noir* was the past, and often, "the doubt, the agony, the fear," would return that the past would rise up to mar his happiness, and this caused him to waver in his eagerness and made him a little uncertain, despite his belief.[39]

One day during the first part of March when wind and fleeting snow made it exceedingly uncomfortable for pedestrians, he determined to call and have the question settled at once. At six o'clock in the evening the storm was still raging, and hurled the falling snow hither and thither. No matter which way one turned he encountered the wind and progress along the street was necessarily slow. "The weather is against me," thought he, as he trudged homeward. "Pshaw! I am not superstitious," he said aloud, and tucking his head deeper in the collar of his great coat went on his way devising ways by which he might call up the subject. Several suggested themselves, but he dismissed all as unsatisfactory. "The best laid plans of mice and men oft gang awee," and so it was with Stanley this evening.[40] He had hardly seated himself comfortably at home when Paul Fox was announced. Fox had braved the storm to come, for he thought it would be an excellent chance to catch him in and have a talk. Stanley accepted the situation with good grace and did all that he was able to make his friend comfortable and the evening pass pleasantly.

When Fox arose to go the storm had quieted considerably, and Stanley accompanied him a short distance. On the way, Fox speaking of common reports said, "Seth, I must congratulate you on your engagement. You could hardly have made a better selection in the city."

"Allow me to protest," replied Stanley, "your congratulations are not in season. I am only a friend to the young lady, nothing more."

"Come! come! now! Seth we supposed you were in love last summer, when we went on that pleasure trip to Mackinac. What puzzled us then was the object of your affection. Now you will certainly let an old friend wish you well. I suppose it isn't time to own up yet and you have availed yourself of the old chestnut."

"I thank you for your interest, but since neither denial nor affirmation will change your opinion I will neither deny or affirm its truth. There is nothing a man hugs more firm, than a delusion that is pleasant to believe true, and one of these delusions is to marry two whom gossip has joined together before the interested parties have agreed to form a contract. Those whom gossip have joined any circumstance may put asunder. Whether it does or does not the wise ones say, 'I told you so.' They hang on both sides of the fence and consider themselves right whichever way an affair turns. So you were studying me instead of our surroundings while on the trip."

"Well said for you, but right or wrong, I shall hold to my opinion and wish you well until time sets me right."

This was Fox's parting shot as he bid his friend good night, and went upon his way. Upon this subject, Stanley, knowing Parker's temperament, had once or twice silenced him, but Fox did and said everything in such a nice way that he could not "sit down on him" so easily.

Imogene also because of this attachment of his, had begun to view Miss Stone as a prospective sister-in-law, and was so pleased at the thought of having a home companion other than Mrs. Burwell, that she often made him annoyed at her questions, which he did not wish to answer. Mrs. Burwell was refined and well-educated, had been a teacher in a female seminary, but her mode of life was rigorous and her habits and tastes so settled that as a companion for Imogene, who possessed all the warm blood and imagination of youth budding into womanhood, she was not a success. Imogene kept her pretty well informed of her brother's love affairs, as far as she knew of them, and often added a little, that her ardent wishes and enthusiasm made real to her, of Marjorie's accomplishments. In consequence Mrs. Burwell looked forward to the time when perhaps her services would be no longer required, for with her usual faculty of jumping at things, Imogene assured her that Seth and his wife would live at home with them. Mrs. Burwell's perceptions were aroused and she noticed that Stanley for several days past appeared a little down hearted, and she wondered if Miss Stone was at all responsible for it. In fact he was so preoccupied with his prospects for a future success as viewed in the light of recent events, that for a time he was absent minded.

The Durhams were also on the tiptoe with expectation. They were amazed at his constant attachment, and they had several long talks about it. The change in his habits, his strict attention to business for the past few months was to Mrs. Durham a source of still greater amazement than his constant courtship of Marjorie. She was surprised to know that Marjorie and Maxwell were not engaged, and while she knew that Marjorie and Stanley were not either, their increasing attachment to each other she viewed according to her mood as favorable or unfavorable. Still even in her most favorable moods she thought a little more time was necessary to show whether Stanley's change was permanent. This idea vexed Mr. Durham, and sometimes put him out of patience, but then he was a man and men view these things differently from women. He would have let the matter drop and awaited events had Mrs. Durham not referred to it so frequently. In these conversations, she found herself siding with Maxwell and gave her husband to understand who had her sympathy, and she frequently wound up each conversation by saying, "Well, Maxwell is nice anyway, and his character is above reproach."

Disappointed in not being able to call upon Marjorie on the evening referred to, Stanley resolved to embrace the first opportunity and broach the subject. The chance did not come soon, for one hindrance after another aided by his own diffidence, when in her company, and by her shrewdness in turning the conversation when it approached near dangerous channels, that April passed before the opportunity came.

CHAPTER XVI.

_____

"In the Spring a young man's fancy
Lightly turns to thoughts of love."[41]

With the opening up of Spring and the resurrection of nature, Stanley's love seemed to grow, expand and intensify. The spring rains which made riding so unpleasant helped nature to unveil her beauty. To his eager eyes, and a soul exalted by love, nothing seemed more beautiful than the grass turning green, and budding plant and tree. After all, one has to be in love to enjoy to the full the beauties of the natural world, for not until then does nature seem to reveal to us her treasures. Love makes the senses keener, the perceptions clearer. It exalts the soul and makes for us a paradise upon earth where we live in the pictured future in which we see the fruition of our dearest hopes. They who have not loved have not enjoyed life to its best, and they are to be pitied who go down to their grave, after reaching man's estate, without ever loving or having been loved. The cynic, the scoffer, the misanthrope and all who rant against love have bodies or minds diseased, their finer senses are blunted, and they have no appreciation of the noblest passion. They are to be pitied, for love is divine.

One evening in May, Stanley found the opportunity he had been long seeking. They were alone and by degrees he tried to lead up to the momentous question. Young Harper and Carrie Lambert had recently married and they had attended the reception together. Stanley began to talk of them.

"I think that Mr. and Mrs. Harper should live happily together," said he, "they seem so well suited to each other."

"I hope so for it is bad enough to be unhappy when the chance still remains for us to alter and better our condition. That is why I have often adjured you, as a pupil, in this life to prepare for what you may expect in the next."

"Most of our unhappy marriages I think are due to mismated temperaments, especially among the wealthy, whose love is sometimes hardly more than a blind passion," not heeding her moral lesson.

"That is because they see so little of each other," said she taking advantage of the chance to give him her opinion on the subject. "Very often they do not examine themselves to see if their love is of the nature that lasts. That would yield up the entire being so that the two lives may blend into one dual existence, and make them so dependent upon each other that their joys, sorrows, and aspirations become one. Nothing short of this is true love; nothing short of it should end in matrimony,

'Two souls with but a single thought,
Two hearts that beat as one.'[42]

may be considered sentimental, it is nevertheless sense."

"Your ideal is certainly high, and I endorse it."

Marjorie interrupted him by saying, "Too many men consider their wives mere dolls, good enough for amusement and pleasure, but who are to be laid aside at their sweet will. Instead of installing them as helpmates they become the creatures of their husband's caprices."

"Only unthinking men would act in such a way," said he, surprised at her animation.

"You have already said," she continued desperately, for her woman's wit had divined the object of his conversation, which she wished to postpone as long as possible, "that sympathy often biased reason, would not love also do so. The mere thinking comes when it is of no use in mending the matter."

This remark discomfited him and he thought it best not to push the question which involved so much, but to wait for a better opportunity. For the present he was outtalked and outwitted and he changed the topic. When he departed he did not retain in his mind even a lingering suspicion of the positiveness of her manner and he chided himself for his lack of courage. It was a mystery to him too, why he, who had such a general reputation for daring should fail in his intentions at that particular moment. "I have played the coward tonight, sure," he thought. "It was not conscience but consciousness. She's a shy one and no mistake. I'll wager my chances that she divined what was uppermost in my mind. The next time she shall know from my bearing that I shall not allow her intuitions to cheat me out of my intentions. Seth, old boy, this is a bargain, and don't you ever be found lying to yourself."

A week elapsed before he called again, and he was determined to propose.

As on the former occasion, when he had been outwitted, his mind was full of the absorbing question and the answer it might call forth. The manner of dress in which it should be clothed was what troubled him most. In her presence, however, the fine spun little speech which he had put together flew he knew not where. She had been reading and still held her book in her hand after they were both seated. Noticing this he ventured a question about it. "Something interesting you are reading?"

"Yes, intensely so. I have read it before. It is *Ben Hur*, and I had just finished the series of events that led up to the chariot race as you came in."

"I am sorry if I intruded." This was a feeler.

"I never consider your visits as intrusions, for I owe so much of my enjoyment and good spirits to you for the last few months, that I certainly would prove an ingrate, did I prefer a book to your society."

This reply was all that he needed. It gave him an opportunity which he quickly embraced. While screwing up his courage to the sticking point, and gathering himself and his thoughts together, he arose from his chair, crossed the room, and took a seat beside her on the sofa, allowing his right arm to rest on the back of it.

"Marjorie," for the first time calling her by her Christian name. "Did you think when you read the Egyptian maid's narration of the creation how true to life its theory was? That the beauty, the eye beholds, the melody that the ear hears; the exhilaration the body feels of youth and strength, even all nature's beauties and manifold forms, are inadequate to satisfy the longings of man, or to awaken his noblest passions and tenderest emotions. Experience has taught me that love actuates the universe, pervades every force, times every heartbeat and sustains every aspiration. Have you not guessed, Marjorie, that I have loved you? Loved you so sincerely, with a passion so sacred and strong that I cannot longer withstand the demand, that constantly welling up in my heart, bids me speak."

As he spoke he gently dropped his arm to her waist but she arrested it in its descent, and held his hand nervously while he continued. "I have sought pleasure in nearly every fleeting fancy that flashed before me. I have been an epicure. I have climbed the rugged Alps, looked down with pride upon vast domains in our own country from Pike's Peak. I have been almost around the world, seen most of its beauty, but have met with no experience or felt no longing that has so moved the depths of my soul." He paused for a reply but she inclined her head to one side and said nothing, so great seemed the silence, that he could fancy he almost heard her heart beat. He resumed. "Marjorie, you cannot doubt I love you? Has not my every act proved it? I lay at your feet my wealth, my life, my love. You surely cannot doubt me?" dropping into a more serious tone, "Rather doubt the truths of holy writ in which you find such hope and consolation; doubt that the awakening buds start at the first approach of spring, but do not doubt that I love you or cast away, without consideration, the sum of my first pure unselfish impulses, that has transformed the young madcap of many fancies into an earnest, thinking and loving man, whose dearest thought is to win and love you." He pressed her hand gently, as it lay partly in his, as he waited anxiously for a reply.

She turned partly around, and with downcast eyes, she spoke feelingly, and there was a tremor in her voice. "Mr. Stanley, I have not been unmindful of your kind favors and attentions, nor have I been blind to the fact that the pleasure we have found in each other would lead to this. I have tried to stay it for a time, and although aware of its certain approach, I am unprepared to give you an answer. Give me a week of earnest thought and prayer and you shall have my answer."

He was embarrassed, but alive to her position he at once arose to take his leave, saying, "I commit my fate into your keeping. Do not turn me back to a life of wandering and unfixed purposes. If my actions have not been eloquent in pleading for me, my tongue cannot aid them, for I cannot formulate in speech all that I feel."

"Do not urge me now, I believe you honorable and sincere in all that you have done and said. I am overwhelmed with conflicting thoughts that I must settle alone."

She loved him, and would have consented now, for his outburst of love had so awakened her feelings, that she could scarce control her heart that beat in unison with his. If she were only sure of the depth of his love. She must not and would not give way, so she stood with downcast eyes until he turned to go. He then extended his hand and as she laid hers tremblingly in his she said: "All will be for the best, Mr. Stanley, all will be for the best."

Hastily donning his coat and hat he went out and paraded the streets for an hour or more ere he went home, thinking over the events of the evening, and trying to clear his mind from the mist which enveloped it. The quick, restless, motion of his body was more in harmony with the chaos of thought tumbling around in his brain, than it would have been sitting quietly in his room, looking over the field of his hopes, doubts and fears.

After Stanley had left the house Marjorie sat for a while motionless while her mind actively ran over the situation. She knew that she had loved him before, but that burst of uncontrolled passion and fervid eloquence had set free the dormant springs of affection and she loved as she had never thought of loving before. She longed to be his, her heart yearned for him, and when the tide of his passion was at its flood, had almost consented to become his wife, but something within her seemed to whisper, "Love sways judgment, you must take time to think calmly over this step of a lifetime." No other thought could enter her mind and over and over she revolved her position—love debating on one side, caution and reason the other.

Said Love: "Why not accept him and make both your lives happy, for nearly ten months have you known him, and watched him closely, surely he has been cured of his careless roving disposition."

Said Reason: "But then his own confession. Nothing gratified him but for the moment. Even in the hour of his proposal, his mind reverted to this propensity, a return to which he yet feared. He said, 'do not turn me back to a life of wandering.'"

Love again said: "The greater reason that you should look favorably upon his suit, for under your influence he certainly will not turn back."

But Caution answered, "still if he should turn back your life would be miserable. It will be better to take longer time to see if his reformation is deep-rooted."

Not being able to decide for herself then, she resolved to take her mother in her confidence, for she certainly must have guessed his intentions. When she was more composed on the morrow she would consult with her. She had hardly come to this conclusion when her mother came in.

"Mr. Stanley gone so soon?" She enquired, then noticing Marjorie's appearance, her motherly instincts were aroused, "Why my dear, what is the matter? Are you ill?"

"I do not feel very well and I think I had better go up to my room and rest." In an instant it dawned upon Mrs. Stone that Stanley's early disappearance had something to do with Marjorie's condition. She forbore from questioning her further, as she saw that her heart was full. So laying her hand gently on her arm, she asked. "Can I do anything for you, dear?"

"Nothing Mother," and throwing her arms around her mother's neck, she kissed her good night and left the room.

CHAPTER XVII.

―――――――

When Marjorie reached her room she burst into tears. Why, was a mystery even to herself. They were neither tears of joy nor of sorrow. Still they gave relief to a heart that was overburdened, and prepared the way for thought. At such times as this solitude is a welcome boon, and Marjorie was glad enough to be alone. She looked into the glass of her dresser and was surprised to find that her face was so pale, and that deep black rings had gathered around her eyes. No wonder, thought she, that mother thought I was ill.

Rather mechanically she began to undress herself. It was her usual custom before retiring to open her bible and read a chapter or so. As she opened it at random almost the first words that met her eye were, "Come unto me all ye that labor and are heavy laden, and I will give you rest."[43] She closed the book, got down upon her knees and tried to pray for strength and wisdom, but so heavy did her thoughts bear upon her that her mind would wander from its purpose, which wanderings she tried to check by becoming more earnest in her supplications. When she laid down she could not sleep, for her thoughts seemed to flow more rapidly, and images of her position appeared more vivid. She felt that she was no longer the gentle trusting Marjorie of yesterday, and that a day had wrought a great change in her. I have reached the age of thoughtfulness she soliloquised, why not be thoughtful. I cannot expect to go through this world with ease at every turning when others earn their bread by the sweat of their brow, to which is often added sorrow, that is at times the sweat of the very soul. Yesterday my prospects were bright, for the crisis had not come. Now that it has arrived those same prospects seem to fill me with forebodings and I doubt.

As the sun gives color to the world, so the mind gives color to life's prospects. The sun's absence darkens the world, so the absence of content, which is our sun, and the entrance of doubt darkens our life. "Why should I not trust him, and why should I?" she continued. "Man is fallible in his most exalted state. He finds in his heart to distrust the infinite God, why not I him? Before I troth the homage of a life why should I not know more of him? Yet I cannot tell him that love and distrust are mated in my mind. It might crush and humiliate him, and make him despise me." So her mind jumped from thought to thought, grasping at every suggestion that might satisfy her conscience, and yet not dwarf her love or his. She turned and tossed till her head began to ache, the room felt close to her. Then she arose and opened the window for air. Fearing that the night dampness might give her a cold she shut it again, and wrapping a blanket about her she sat gazing upon the street, and thus sitting she decided upon what line of conduct to pursue. With all her good traits Marjorie Stone was not insensible to gossip. She was a little afraid of it, and no small share of her conflict could be attributed to it. It had come to her ears that people had said she was going to marry Stanley on account of his wealth, that he would soon tire of her and she would finally rue her bargain. Gossip created in her doubts she could hardly overcome, and made her ask herself what if the prediction should prove true? How cruel the people were to speculate upon her happiness, and so she decided to test him. If he loved as truly as she did, he would be willing to make some sacrifice. The sacrifice was this: He must give up the culmination of his desires without even the assurance of a betrothal for a year. It was to prove the durability of his change of life and of his love. Mr. Stone had spent the evening out and on his return as usual he and his wife talked over the events of the day, and finally Mrs. Stone spoke of Marjorie's "indisposition."

"I expect that she and Stanley had a spat this evening. He went away unusually early, and she looked and seemed to feel so badly, that she went to her room early."

"And you didn't ask her what the trouble was?"

"No, I didn't care to worry her when I saw how pale she was, besides I knew she would tell me in the morning."

Mr. Stone was a quick-tempered man and apt to jump at conclusions. The idea that Stanley was at all responsible for his daughter's paleness made him angry and he exclaimed, "I never did think much of that young Mogul going with Marjorie. What does he care for her with all his wealth? And when he can marry nearly anyone he chooses. He wanted a little flirtation and he didn't care whose heart it broke. If I catch him around her again I'll read the riot act to him. You can bet on that."

"Come, Tom, don't be hasty," remonstrated his wife, "We don't really know what the trouble is, and until we do, it is not necessary to work yourself into a passion. You might do something, of which you afterwards may be ashamed."

"No danger, I know those fellows. I have heard them boast, sometimes over their betters, and they are about all alike."

"But we don't know how matters stand and I think Stanley is too much of a gentleman for that."

"Gentleman, bosh! Most of them are cads. It's a pity Marjorie should show him preference over Maxwell, who despite his looks is a gentleman. I shall go to Stanley tomorrow and demand an explanation. He shall apologize to me. I'll humble his proud heart or break his senseless noodle with as little compunction as he has tried to break her heart."

"Come, Tom, you are angry, calm yourself."

"Calm yourself!" he repeated, "and let people run right over you. That kind of nonsense will do to teach in Sunday Schools, but I believe in striking back, and I mean to."

Tom was growing more furious and she finding that argument was of no avail, begged him to say nothing to Marjorie at breakfast, and assured him that he should know all the next evening. Thus by the use of considerable tact in branching off into other matters, Tom forgot his anger, became interested in her remarks, and finally promised, with some reluctance, to wait.

After Marjorie had decided upon what course to adopt, her mind found some relief and she went to sleep, but it proved a restless slumber, which was so fraught with terrible dreams, that she often awoke with a start. As a result she received but very little rest. In the morning she took a cold bath and tried to put on a forced look to hide the marks of mental anguish, which the battle of the previous night had left upon her features. But her efforts were in vain, for though the spirit was willing, the thoughts of the night were too recent and too strong to be cast aside at will. When she went down to breakfast her father had gone, but her mother saw at a glance the traces of a mental struggle, and with all tenderness she applied herself to the work of pleasing her. With her own hands she set her breakfast, and then sat down to keep her company. Marjorie could not eat much for her mind and heart were full, and while she sipped her tea and munched her biscuit she was thinking how she would tell her mother. Finally she launched right into it by saying, "mother, Seth proposed last night."

You can never mince matters when a doubt is overbalanced by resolution. A sudden plunge in cold water does not give the chill or the shock that gradual wading does. So it is in the great affairs of men, a straightforward plunge into the question to be settled robs it of the many terrors that a gradual attempt to grapple with invests it. Having made her plunge she paused and looked to see what impression it had made upon her mother, but she made no sign except that there was a slightly visible arching of the eyebrows which seemed to say, "well?" Marjorie presently resumed. "I did not tell you that I expected this, but I have, and I have tried to ward it off longer to see if the love he showed in his actions had in it the elements of strength and endurance. Last evening his ardor broke forth and his soul poured forth such a torrent of eloquence, as he asked and pleaded with me to become his wife, that I could hardly resist him. But somehow, I did, and asked him for a week in which to consider." Again she paused and a tear trickled down her cheek. Mrs. Stone seemed stunned by the intelligence and sat a picture of dumb astonishment. With trembling voice Marjorie continued, "I love him more than I thought that I did and so dearly that I could give up all for him. He has always been so gentle, honorable and kind, and his actions so manly, and yet I find in my heart a mistrust of his sincerity, and this feeling almost breaks it." She broke down completely then and sobbed as if her heart would break. Her mother felt that this heart trouble was too much for her to unravel, yet she went to her daughter and tried to console her.

"Don't cry my darling. Let us talk it over. You do not think he is so mean as to tell, and live a lie, to deceive you so as to entrap you into marrying him."

"No! No! No! Not that. I do not believe that he knows himself. I fear the love he professes is not as deep-seated as he thinks it is, and as I would like it to be. I fear that after the novelty of his passion has worn off, he would tire of me and then I would become perfectly miserable. I cannot accept him now, yet how can I refuse him. I could not stand before him and say I mistrust him, yet the issue must be averted, and I cannot give the reason why. That is what makes me so sorrowful."

Then she told her mother of the occurrences of the night before; of her resolution to have him wait a year, and her mother, taking in consideration all that she had heard and remembering the opposition of friends, agreed with her in the decision she had formed. Still she tried to console her by saying that she believed that Stanley would prove himself all that he had claimed, and that at the end of the year he would come back, renew his vows, with their love purified and strengthened by the waiting. Further she said: "I have always been proud of you my child," putting her arm around Marjorie's neck, and drawing her head gently to her breast as she stroked the warm and fevered cheek, "today I am prouder still. If a mother's love will aid you, it will be given full and free."

"I know it mother, and that is a sustaining thought. That is why I came to you with my burden, I wanted to seek your advice. You agree with me and I feel better."

For the whole of that week mother and daughter were like sisters or intimate friends. They talked the matter over many times in that relation. Ah, that such mutual confidences between mother and child were more frequent. How much less misery there would be in the world, and how fewer the heartaches would be. Such relations bind and cement closer together, and makes even the ordinary life of home, more pleasant and cheerful. Marjorie, whose nerves were strained to the highest tension looked for advice, consolation and encouragement, while the mother soothed and comforted, and was hopeful. Picturing hope in bright colors, with love's happy reunion when the trial was over, as sure as the bright clear sky should take the place of the dark lowering clouds above.

Mr. Stone came home earlier that evening. He was worried over his wife's communication and was anxious to know the real cause of Marjorie's trouble the night before. He watched Marjorie's countenance closely as if trying to read her thoughts, but she had stilled her nerves and gained such control of her feelings, as to appear almost natural, so he hastily inferred that it was some little "kitten spat that would soon blow over." However at supper the usual sprightly conversation which characterized that meal, lagged, and over all there seemed a cloud of some import.

Supper over, Mr. Stone picked up his evening paper, put on his spectacles, and was soon apparently busy in its contents. Marjorie tried to interest herself in a book. Mrs. Stone busied herself with some fancy work, but the general talk such as they were accustomed to, was missing. There were several attempts at it but they were all failures. At an early hour Marjorie bid them good night and left the room. After she had gone Mr. Stone laid the paper aside, took off his spectacles, looked at his wife and said, "well?" In his tone there was a world of meaning, anxiety and curiosity. It contained all that had been pent up in him and agitating his mind the entire day. "Well?" he repeated. She had pretended not to hear him the first time.

"I told you, Tom, that you were hasty. He has not flirted with her at all, but is head over heels in love with her. He proposed to her last night, and what do you suppose she said."

He shook his head and motioned for her to go on.

"She told him that she must take a week to consider."

"What did she expect to gain by that?"

"Time to make up her mind."

"What does she intend doing?"

"Put him to a year's trial without any definite answer, to see if his love is abiding."

"The little vixen," slapping his hand on his knee. "Very few girls would let slip a chance like that."

"But she does not think it such a great chance. He has been wild and she fears that his love may weaken. She thinks that he may regret his bargain when the honeymoon is past."

"Her head does her credit I must say. Not one girl in a hundred would stop to consider that. But does she love him."

"Most ardently, and that is why she grieves and looks so bad. I believe if during the year he should prove untrue, or run after other idols, her heart would almost break."

"Does she expect that a young fellow of his chances will accept the situation and come back when the year expires?"

"That is her hope. If he does she will accept him."

"Humph! Mollie. We didn't go through with all that foolishness, did we?" She shook her head.

"But then society was not as frivolous as it is now, and I did not have the money to carry me to the extremes to which these fellows with wealthy fathers are liable to go to."

"I suppose, Tom, you will rest easier tonight, now that the boot appears to be on the other leg."

And so he did. Never had he felt so proud of their child as on that evening when her judgment had so commended itself to him, for, said he, talking the matter over with the Durhams and his wife sometime afterwards, "It is seldom that wisdom outweighs sentiments in matters of love," and to this they all agreed. Mrs. Durham's mind was at rest at last. "Marjorie has always seemed like a daughter to me, and I thought that when she and Seth met at my house that sometime their lives would be thrown together. I told Mr. Durham so, but he said it was one of my superstitions. What is to become of poor Maxwell? I have always liked him and advocated his cause, but it seems of no use now."

"Stanley routed him long ago, but he spends a silent evening with us now and then. It's a pity he has so little animation," said Mr. Stone. "But as soon as he finds that Marjorie and Stanley are out, and if Stanley is such a simpleton as to run away because she won't accept him in his way, we can depend upon it, that Maxwell will be a regular visitor again."

Mr. Stone was right for Maxwell was one of the first to know that there was a partial estrangement.

The reader is perhaps eager to hear how Stanley has fared, so we rejoin him as he paces restlessly the streets after leaving Marjorie.

CHAPTER XVIII.

In his confusion Stanley took no note of time, distance or direction. His fears began to assume large proportions, as he tried to reconcile her request for time, with the love he thought she had for him. The few scintillations of hope that penetrated through all the confusion, were quickly overcome by his doubts and fears. At times he half blamed himself for his haste in proposing, because a refusal might banish him altogether from her presence; for loving with a deep, fervid and passionate love he could not play the calm passionless role of friend.

When he finally became conscious of his surroundings he found that he was out near the bridge on Fort Street West, quite a distance from his home. As he heard the bell of an approaching locomotive coming down the track he stepped upon the bridge, for the time, as unconscious of the thoughts that had troubled him, as he was a few moments before, of the people hurrying to and fro, that had passed him. Shutting out his sorrow, he stood with elbows resting on the railing, his chin in the palms of his hands, and watched the freight train as it came thundering along, and passed under the bridge with a long line of cars freighted with merchandise—its evidence of man's ingenuity and skill in giving to inanimate substances the power of life. Falling into his usual habit of serious musing, which he had contracted during the past year, he began to consider this train in relation to his present state. "What are these things without love? What is the climax of our ambitions, our access to place and power, the triumph of our ideal, but to place it unselfishly, to the credit of those we love? And yet we are ashamed of that most holy passion and speak only of it in whispers. We bind it within our breast until it becomes so strong as to almost break its prison house and reveal itself to others despite ourselves, by an overt act or word. Its principle is divine. It is the secret agency that preserves the harmony of the universe. It moved the Creator to the sacrifice of his only begotten son, and it brings blessings upon the just and the unjust. It clothes the earth with beauty, and makes its herds, with joy to break forth into song and thanksgiving. Only man—poor fool—tries to hide it under a bushel, and chides himself should but a ray escape to attract the attention of others. That which we cherish; that which exalts, ennobles and purifies; that which makes our burdens light and tasks easy, we hide. Why? For fear of the cynic, the taunt of the envious, and the good-natured chaff of friends. Shakespeare was right in saying, 'What fools we mortals be.'"[44]

For a few moments he stood leaning upon the rail of the bridge, his thoughts taking a wide range. As he looked upon the interlacing of the tracks below, in his mood, it seemed to him that his position on the bridge was not unlike his prospects. Was he not then standing on the "Bridge of Sighs," with his hopes buried beneath?[45] Swifter than the steam messengers were his thoughts and freighted with more precious merchandise. What exceeds human hopes in value? The sound of another bell awoke him from his reverie and then with a sigh, he began to retrace his step homeward.

He had never been so much disturbed in mind before; his heart had never felt such yearning. For the week, at least, he intended to keep his own counsel. If Marjorie accepted him he would take the news to his father with joy. If she refused, then with sorrow, and prove to him how erroneous were his opinions as to the power of wealth and influence in securing love and happiness. It was quite late when he arrived at home, and as he did not desire to meet anyone he went direct to his room. Of one thing he was certain, that whatever course she would pursue, no power at his command could dissuade her from her purpose, and that he would have to accept the fiat. His acquaintance with her had shown him the truth, with her at least, of these lines:

"Where is the man who has the power and skill,
 To stem the torrent of a woman's will?"[46]

The next day Mr. Stanley detected an air of languor and care about his appearance, but the true cause of it never struck his mind. Stanley attended to his duties all that week strictly and silently.

During the week Imogene noticed that he frequently indulged in reverie, sometimes he sighed, his usual good spirits were lacking, and that only with difficulty could he interest himself in anything. She laid it all to the store and thought it mean.

Marjorie Stone and she were good friends, for Marjorie's tact in interesting her in good books, and shaping her musical tastes, won her love and respect. Becoming lonesome and worried over her brother's silence and seclusion, one afternoon during the latter part of the week, she thought she might throw off the feeling by paying Marjorie a visit. She too had a preoccupied air and appeared more thoughtful than usual. "Oh, dear," thought she, "what is the matter with the people?"

But she affectionately greeted Marjorie and said: "Everybody at our house seems to have had the blues since the first part of the week. Papa hasn't talked of anything except business and newspapers, and Seth seems to have something on his mind, that keeps his mouth shut as tight as a clam, so I thought I would come over here and see you before I caught the infection."

Marjorie would like to have known how Stanley felt about the answer she had given him. As for herself she could cheerfully wait, but she shrank from giving pain to one who had been so gallant and manly with her. She dared not inquire about him, for she was afraid the truth might fit the overdrawn picture she had formed of his suffering grief.

"We are glad you came," said Mrs. Stone. "I know it must be lonesome for you without mother or sister."

"I am going to make Marjorie my sister and then I shan't be so lonesome. Won't you be my sister?" turning to Marjorie.

"I should be glad to be, but I could not bargain to always shield you from gloomy thoughts, for they seem to be twins with experience. Yet we should not acknowledge their authority for they lead to despair, and despair too often indulged, becomes a master, with many demands."

"I'll not borrow any trouble," replied Imogene, "for Seth always says it will come in time to give us all the worry we want."

"And he is right," said Mrs. Stone, "never worry trouble, until trouble worries you." She noticed the flashes of pain that passed over Marjorie's countenance on these allusions to Stanley, and she asked Imogene how she was getting along with that new stitch she had shown her on her last visit.

"Very nicely, and I am going to make papa a pair of slippers, that is, if my studies will allow me the time. I have been trying to persuade Seth to take us with him on his next trip, and he has consented. Won't that be nice? and you will go, won't you?"

"Oh, yes," replied Marjorie. "Then you would have a chance to try me, when we are together, and see if you would like me as a sister."

"I have made up my mind already about that. I get so tired of Mrs. Burwell sometimes."

Marjorie arose and took a seat beside her as she asked, "do you think you could always love me?"

Imogene looked up with surprise at the earnestness of the question, and said with an injured air, "of course I could. I often wish I was old enough to go with you and Flora Stedman, she came to see me the other day and she is so sweet."

"Don't be in such a hurry to grow old. Why, when Flo. and I are old maids you will be enjoying yourself immensely, you'll just be in the bloom of young womanhood."

Imogene looked at her incredulously. "Mrs. Burwell must think that of me now. You know she is serious all the time, and she seems to think I am old enough to settle down and knit and nod like she does," and Imogene laughed as if pleased with the thought and the picture she had formed of the housekeeper. After spending a pleasant afternoon she arose to go, saying, "I must go now. Papa and Seth will soon be home."

Marjorie kissed her good-bye as with a light heart, and in excellent spirits she went away.

· · · ·

Imogene and Seth were sitting quietly in their sitting room that evening, he was absorbed in a book, and she was trying to study her lessons and watch him at the same time. The silence was too much for her and she broke it by saying: "Say, Seth, I was over to Marjorie's this afternoon."

"Were you?" He didn't even raise his head.

"Yes, I was feeling blue and so lonesome that I couldn't think of anything else to do, and she is so nice. I told her I was going to have her for a big sister." He pricked up his ears, and his interest was at once aroused at this. "Oh! you know it's real lonesome here sometimes Papa is away so much and you have the dumps so often. Oh, it isn't near so cheerful as you imagine (this was in answer to his look of surprise) going through the same thing every day and coming home and only have Mrs. Burwell to talk to. Then she doesn't always seem to care, and is beside prosy. It is very monotonous, (with a yawn) and so wanting a companion who would take an interest in things, who is older and charming, and as sweet as she could be, I asked Marjorie if she wouldn't be a sister."

"And what did she say to your proposal?"

"Why, she accepted, of course. Oh, I should like to live with her when you take a notion to be abroad again or get into one of your silent moods. That would be jolly."

"Well you are progressing at any rate. But don't be so disconsolate. I am not going abroad soon and if I do you shall go with me. Beside you ought to allow a fellow to be a little moody now and then. We can't always be gay," and walking over to her he patted her on the cheek and kissed her.

This restored Imogene to good humor, and she prattled away at a great rate, forgetting all about her lessons. He, becoming talkative related reminiscences of his trips abroad, described the work of the great masters he had seen, talked about the books he had been reading, of his favorite poets, and promised to take her to the Thomas concert the next week. Stanley told his stories in such an entertaining and romantic way that Imogene was always glad to get him started. This evening she looked at him open-mouthed, listening intently, and we are constrained to say, that he sometimes drew on his imagination which was vivid, just to see the round eyes open wider, and to see the look of wonder in her full, dark orbs. When he had finished he felt much better after the evening's diversion than he had any night since his proposal. Action relieves a distressed mind, but the more one broods over troubles, the more despondent and wretched he becomes.

Some months back when he first began to recognize that he was living far below his opportunities, and that he was being outstripped by many who had fewer chances to acquire intellectual advancement and general information, he commenced to give considerable time to reading. His mind was quick to grasp ideas and thoughts. It was subtle, and enabled him to easily detect sophistries. It was also capable of great expansion, and possessing an excellent memory, retained the best of what he had read.

What seemed useless to strive for in former years, had become worthy of aspiration now. His thirst for knowledge increased, as his new quest, opened up to him new fields of pleasure and thought. He laid aside one evening, while waiting for the week to go by, an interesting volume, Hugo's Les Miserables, that he had taken from his father's library.[47] He had been reading of the good Bishop Bienvenu in connection with Jean Valjean. Then he began to reflect on his own past and its neglect of high ideals, it seemed as if that subject would not down. If we could only look forward with the same ease that we can look back how different would be the course of our lives. If we could only see present opportunities as clearly as we can see past mistakes how wise we would be, and how different would be the face of the world. Regrets are useless, experience is a dear teacher, and while she often deals roughly with us, we are gainers if we try to follow her lessons in the future.

So in the study and contemplation of his inner self and in making himself agreeable to Imogene what promised to be a week of tedious waiting passed more quickly than he imagined it would. Too quickly, when his thoughts doubted a favorable answer. Too slowly, however, when his heart beat high with the hope of pleasant anticipations.

At last the appointed day came. The evening of his defeat or success, of sorrow or happiness.

CHAPTER XIX.

Not now the hour, at thy request
To seal my fate. There is a test.

Marjorie answered the bell in person and her set features, the evidences of her week of struggle, immediately attracted his attention and cast a damper upon his feelings. As he took off his light top coat and hung it on the hall tree, he said, "Let us spend the evening as usual. I will not ask you for my answer until later."

"Just as you like Mr. Stanley," she said, and she led the way into the sitting-room where her father and mother were seated. It was quite a little while before the conversation gained a natural tone, because of the tinge of embarrassment which seemed to be common to all. Mr. Stone was at first the life of the conversation, and started it by asking, "How is business now, Mr. Stanley?"

"I can't say that it is rushing just now, but it is very fair, and has been excellent. I didn't think that I would like the store as well as I do."

"A person can learn to like most any kind of work if he but accepts the situation and makes the most of it."

"So I have found out, and I find that a task is made easy by cheerfulness."

"When I was traveling it became a burden for me to go on the road, not because I disliked the business so much, but that it took me away from my family often when I wished to be at home." Stanley thought that he didn't blame Mr. Stone for wanting to be at home with such a family. His errand there was to gain the right to be there as well. Most of their talk was upon business or social matters, Mrs. Stone and Marjorie occasionally joining in. Stanley and Marjorie both sang during the evening with considerable feeling. In their voices, however, there was a vein of sadness, as if both knew and felt a premonition of what was to come. Soon after, when Mr. and Mrs. Stone left the room, Marjorie expected that Stanley would at once request an answer. But he, as if fearing an approach to the subject, talked on for over half an hour on various subjects; while she, all the time, was painfully conscious of the pain she was to inflict.

At last he said, "May I now ask you for the reply to my proposal? If you have given the subject as much concern and thought as I have, you will have arrived at a conclusion; one which I shall accept as the conscientious outgrowth of an earnest effort to be just both to yourself and to me."

"It has been continually on my mind and I have thought it over," dropping her eyes, she paused for a moment as if to consider the choice of words in which to reveal to him her decision, and to give the least pain, "and I hope you will view my reply in the same spirit in which I have arrived at it and give it to you. Your confidence in me is flattering and overwhelming. You have placed your future at my disposal. I appreciate the trust, it shall be sacred, and in return I will impose one upon you. The union which you propose is one that may blight or bless both our lives. Ought we not be sure that it would prove a blessing, and that by nature and purpose we are adapted to each other? The ceremonial rite should be more than a mere form with its promises. It should be the linking of soul to soul, so that the two would be as one in life, and not separable in death. Are we certain that these impulses move within us to bring us to such a union?"

"You have almost taken all argument out of my mouth, but I hope that my feelings will convey to you that which my lips have been unable to express. You have not yet, by words, revealed to me the feeling of your own heart toward me, whether it be love or the regard given to a friend, but my own heart and purposes lie open to you. If you can doubt the sincerity of my speech you cannot the motives of my acts, which have all conformed to the one end—to show the love I feel."

"I do not doubt you Mr. Stanley. I never have, but sometimes we misunderstand ourselves. Our feelings bear false impressions to the mind which only time dispels. Can we trust ourselves to believe that our present feeling will result in a life devotion, and that it is not a mere fancy which is to be replaced by another should the other prove stronger?"

"You shall have all the time you want," and he started to embrace her thinking the field already won, but she shrank away from him. "Let the engagement be as long as it will, but let me rest in the hope that at the end all will be well. To see purposes broken and hopes blighted may not fall so keenly upon old age, for they who have reached it have fought the battle of life and only await the summons home. Disappointment is different in youth, for theirs are the days of expectation and hope that color all future prospects. With what dull hues would they be painted when the bright tints at our command are destroyed at the outset? Only a set firmness can overcome the languor and the inaction which it invites." There was an appeal in voice and gesture, in eye and person, but she remained firm, stemmed the tide of love in her own heart, that would have rushed to and commingled with his, such as only first love can, and spoke words that chilled him to the marrow.

"We cannot be engaged now, Mr. Stanley. I do not think it best; but if in one year from now, you and I are constant in that love which desires its consummation in perfect union, the test of time will have been applied. Then we can renew these relations, having subdued self and become better fitted to assume the near relation which you would now press me to. If you love as I do the task will not seem so hard because of the end to be gained when it is finished."

This was the first confession of love that her maiden lips had ever given to lover, although from the trend of her thoughts and bearing he had discovered it despite previous efforts to hide it. Her acknowledgement did not then soften the sting of refusal. It is a peculiar feature of the mind that things which we desire most and are reasonably certain of, we are the most apprehensive of. It was so with Stanley. He was reasonably certain that she loved him, and yet the least adverse circumstance made him uncertain.

"I understand, I understand," he said in an almost inaudible tone as if speaking to himself. "Your love is mingled with distrust. You think I have not sufficiently analyzed my affections. You judge me too much by what is past, rather than by what I have been for a year. This cup of bitterness I must drink to the dregs for the past fancies in which I have indulged, though it be at the expense of my very soul. A balance sheet has been struck between what I was and what I am, in favor of the past, and you send me into exile to do penance for a year. And now out of despair I shall drink the long and bitter draught."

"No! No! No!" she cried beseechingly as she caught his hand. "Do not talk so. Is not a life of happiness worth a year of waiting, aye more? Is it not meet that we be schooled in the virtue of self-sacrifice to obtain that which we long for? Oh Seth, let us prove to each other that our love is no blind folly, but that like charity it can suffer long and be patient. If we set a reward upon our waiting by mutual promises, do we not rob ourselves of the value of its schooling?"

There was silence for a few moments. He was confused and bewildered, and she, from a supplicating attitude, had risen with her words to a bearing, that sought to instill into him the courage and patience, the fortitude and self-sacrifice which she possessed. While within, her beating heart revolted at the idea of its love being hushed by a period of self-imposed waiting. In conspicuous contrast to their silence the big clock on the mantle ticked louder than ever, as if in compassion it sought to drown the sighs and the rapid beating of their own hearts, tick! tack! tick! tack! it went disturbing the stillness. Could it but dole out to one, the year, with the rapidity it doled out the seconds or hours. Longfellow's "Old Clock" on the stairs with its,

Forever—Never!
Never—Forever![48]

flitted across his mind and seemed to whisper to him, which? He could not tell. After a few moments silence he said. "I suppose it would be worse than useless, Marjorie for me to try to change your decision, so completely absorbed do you appear in this spirit of self-sacrifice; but you have put a heavy task on me which now seems to make my future uncertain and darker than the night without. Hardships that are afar off we can often eliminate from our mind by a blind, trusting to chance, and in our conceits we even slight the inexorable scourge of the judgment. But to know that I am to wander on the verge of Elysian fields, always near yet far off, seems to overwhelm me. But I will go. I will not tempt you further. We cannot tell what this may bring forth, so if it should be our last meeting, mark my sincerity so that in after years you can refer to it with pleasant thoughts of me—one whom you could not trust."

He rose to go but she caught one of his hands in hers again, and laying the other gently upon his shoulder. She turned her face, now pale, up to his, and met his gaze unflinchingly; but through the tears glistening in her eyes and stealing down her cheek, gleamed noble resolutions and lofty inspirations, that seemed to pierce through the vista of time and which impressed and carried all before it.

"Seth," she said. "Seth you do not know what you say. I can see just beyond this vale of self-sacrifice, which I have chosen that we pass through, the brightest future, that in this hour makes me rejoice. Let us prove ourselves not unworthy of it. Let gossip be robbed of their carping criticisms, and let despair be turned into triumph. I have trusted you, and know that I trust you now so that the memory of it may sustain you, so that you do nothing rash."

Her appeal, her tears, her profound convictions and inspiration moved him greatly, and he felt a soothing influence permeating his whole being; and the woeful harbingers he had conjured up in his mind began to dissolve before her earnest persuasions as he replied. "I will try to merit your confidence and trust."

What was there then in his life—years, money, treasure, that he would not have given to have embraced her and called her his own, his wife, at that moment. How bitterly he regretted all past follies that had now returned to render him miserable. How he closed the interview he could not tell. The only thing he could remember was pressing her hand and saying goodnight, as he went out into the street; and the night, dark as it was, seemed but feebly so in comparison with the confusion and bewilderment to which his mind had now become a victim.

CHAPTER XX.

It was not ten o'clock when Stanley, whose brain was partially stunned by the queer ending of his proposal, left the Stone residence. The night was dark, and the vivid flashes of lightning which disclosed heavy scurrying and lowering clouds with ragged outlines, warned him of an approaching storm. As he proceeded on his way, he thought a great deal about Marjorie and her self-sacrifice, and tried to think what course it would be best for him to adopt for the future. Now even the hope of winning her as his wife seemed forbidden him. Her strange request, with the task it imposed upon him, as a natural sequence, shut him out entirely from her presence. Under the circumstances he considered it better so, for how could be he thrown continually in her society, without increase of pain, by awakening a passion which must slumber, for his peace of mind, until her set time had expired. As he was passing along, he heard the soft strains of an organ and the sound of voices singing a hymn, issuing from a house near by. There was something in the air and words that caused him to stop and listen. It was one he had heard often, and it was now being sung by a family that were concluding the evening devotion. It seemed in his present condition to possess a significance he had not felt before.

Again rose the voices:

"Swift to its close ebbs out life's little day;
Earth's joys grow dim, its glories pass away.
Change and decay in all around I see;
Oh thou who changest not, abide with me.
I need thy presence every passing hour,
What but thy grace can foil the tempter's power?
Who, like thyself, my guide and stay can be?
Through cloud and sunshine, Lord, abide with me.
I fear no foe with thee at hand to bless;
Ills have no weight and tears no bitterness."[49]

Then the rain began to fall, and much against his will, he was compelled to move on at a brisk rate, as he had no umbrella with him, to escape a drenching. Yet the words of the beautiful evening hymn had made a deep impression upon him, for both his mind and body, suffering from the scene he had passed through, needed solace and comfort, to serve as an antidote for the gloom and darkness which he had pictured as the result of Marjorie's test. "What comfort," he thought, "the earnest Christian must have in his simple faith. No prospects so dark, no events so full of misfortune seems to destroy his faith in God and Christ; though

'Earth's joys grow dim, its glories pass away,
Change and decay in all around he sees.'

"Still he prays for the presence of the comforter. In trying situations—accidents, reverses in business, in poverty, loss of friends and love, he seeks only for the solace which can be had through faith. The faith how simple. To possess it how easy. How different is my own situation. I distrust myself because of the vacancy in my life, because through her, I drew the inspiration that has given me strength. She has been the leaven of my existence. Will I fall back into the old life; do not I need some substitute or aid that will fill the void, left by non-association with her." Again his mind reverted to the hymn, and he seemed to hear

"I need thy presence every passing hour,
What but thy grace can foil the tempter's power?
Who like thyself, my guide and stay can be?
Through cloud and sunshine, Lord, abide with me.
I fear no foe with thee at hand to bless;
Ills have no weight and tears no bitterness."

"Even the Christian must have something to rely on, and that something is found in the Divine Presence to keep him from the temptations of evil and to act as counsellor and guide." In this way his thoughts ran a long while together with those of her. The more the words ran in his mind the more significance they seemed to possess, and the better fitted did they appear to him in his present distress. At last having unclothed himself he went down upon his knees the first time since he was a boy, and prayed for the continual presence of Him whose grace could foil the tempter's power, who would be guide and stay through cloud and sunshine, who would render his non-association with her more bearable, and enable him to make a virtue of this self-sacrifice by remaining firm, so that he might in her eyes be considered worthy to be called husband, and in the eyes of Him to be called son. When he rose from his knees he felt comforted, and lying in bed the soothing influence of the rain pattering on the roof and street, seemed to sing over again the hymn while it lulled him to sleep.

The following morning he went to work as usual and tried to keep up a brave front. He desired to let his father know the result of his proposal, but because of the views expressed by him on a former occasion he hesitated. Mr. Stanley, however, noticing that he did not appear as well as usual and that he looked a little haggard, asked him if he was out late last night.

"Not very," replied Stanley. "I was at Miss Stone's and met with a disappointment which worries me a great deal, as I was unprepared for it."

"Proposed and was refused, eh?"

"Not exactly, but it amounts to about the same thing. She did not jump at the chance as quickly as you thought she would."

"Tut, tut! You have a faint heart to let a girl outwit you and then sit down and pine over it," and without waiting for a reply Mr. Stanley turned upon his heel and walked away. He was dissatisfied with his son's failure for he had not made any allowance for it. He was rather put out too that a girl should knock out the under pins of his argument as to the power and influence of wealth. Since he could not congratulate his son he would not add to his misery by chiding him, but as he went to his desk he thought that Seth had a great deal to learn before he could take his place. Stanley knew his father was disappointed, but then his own chagrin was far greater. He alone knew the circumstances, and the feeling that now moved him could not be appreciated, perhaps, never felt again by his father. With something like a sigh he took up the large pile of communications that lay on his desk needing attention. He went at it vigorously so as to drown his thoughts, but the subject was so magnetic that it drew his mind to it despite himself. He did not esteem Marjorie Stone less because of her decision. He even admitted her superior judgment in protecting herself, although it was opposed to his most ardent wishes. To keep her company further would be but to keep his love inflamed with a constant realization of the present inexorable barrier between them. He must escape her company to escape his own feeling. Reader, if you have ever had your brightest anticipations suddenly brushed away when they seemed almost certain of consummation, you may know how Stanley felt.

The office seemed close to him. He longed to be out in the open air where he could perhaps give greater vent to his feelings, but it still rained and the streets were still muddy so he made the most of it and tried to work.

Imogene again had reason to complain of him that night, for despite her best efforts to draw him out he maintained a moody reserve. He seemed to be giving up to his feeling, and was the worse for it, while he seemed to have forgotten, for the time, that action of any kind is the best tonic for disappointments. He realized that he was not doing what was best for him, still he uplifted not a finger to help himself. To all practical purposes, he was no better off than a person in a trance, who, knowing everything that is happening around them, are powerless to act. With something like relief he heard the whirring of the call announcing some one at the door. He jumped up to answer it in person, and was surprised to see Parker and Fox.

"What brought you out such a night as this?"

"It wasn't the weather," replied Parker, "although if it keeps up it will bring the leaves out."

"Parker can't leave out his pun," said Fox, "we always come when it rains. We thought it would be an excellent chance to catch you in and have a chat, some cards and—"

"It might be a relief from so much feminine society," interrupted Parker.

"Well I certainly am glad to see you both, and I know Imogene will be too," as they entered the room he had just left. "Won't you Imogene?"

"Yes, indeed," she said, "for it's been quite lonesome and it's so hard to try to entertain one who does not wish to be."

Stanley darted a reproachful glance at her and turned to the others. "By the way, Parker, I suppose the boys at the club are discussing their summer plans. Any of them brought their yachts out?"

"No, but several are overhauling them. They expect to go out as soon as the weather gets warm enough, and take short trips to the Flats on a Saturday evening and return Sunday nights."

"I would like to go on one of those trips very much," said Imogene, "but you boys are so selfish."

"When the season is further advanced and the weather gets warmer we'll get up a party," said Parker, "but say Seth aren't you coming around anymore?"

"I can hardly tell just yet. I have been so busy at the store learning all the ropes so as to give father more recreation, and I am besides so much occupied with a course of reading that my time is pretty well taken up."

"And occupied with a young lady on — street." Stanley reddened and appeared confused. Fox, who observed everything and suspected there was a hitch somewhere, to keep Parker from pursuing a subject he saw was unpleasant to Stanley, proposed a game of pedro.[50] The young men remained with him quite a while and as they were in excellent spirits it relieved his mind of the strain upon it. After they had gone and his sister had retired he again gave way to his feelings, and like men when oppressed and downhearted he began to doubt. He doubted most everything, for the time he had lost faith in himself. It seems that distrust, doubt and selfishness are curses laying near to the surface in our mental economy, and require but a little chafing to bring them to the top. While this is a misfortune, it is fortunate for mankind that the blessings, hope, faith and charity, lie equally near and require but little effort also, to bring them into prominence. In our mental economy the good and the bad beneath the surface are so nicely adjusted that the slightest influence either way calls up its corresponding qualities. Stanley was in Doubting Castle, unaware of the near approach of Giant Despair.[51] While he was brooding he happened to lay his head down carelessly upon a paper that lay on the table beside him. He picked it up and glancing carelessly over it, without aim or purpose, for his mind was far from its contents, his attention was drawn to an article that abounded with beauty of expression and thought. He read it through and was so pleased with it that he cut it out and it formed the first article in the scrap book he started the next morning. It read thus: "It cannot be that earth is man's only abiding place. It cannot be that our life is a bubble cast up by the ocean of eternity to float a moment on its waves and sink into nothingness. Else why these high and glorious aspirations which leap like angles from our hearts forever wandering and unsatisfied? Why is it that the rainbows of the clouds come over us with a beauty that is not of earth then pass off and leave us to muse on their loveliness? Why is it that the stars that hold their festival around the midnight throne are set above the grasp of our limited faculties forever mocking us with their unapproachable glory? And finally, why is it that the bright forms of human beauty are presented to our views and taken from us leaving the thousand streams of our affections to flow back in Alpine torrents upon our hearts? We were born for a higher destiny than earth. There is a realm where the rainbow never fades, where the stars will be spread before us like islands that slumber on the ocean, and where the beautiful things that pass before us will stay forever in our presence."

The reading of the article turned his thoughts to those of the night before, and between the two he found the same longing or aspiration for higher things that seemed to make men overcome obstacles and triumph over evil habits and association. Such articles as these were now attracting his attention and were having their effect on him. When he awoke that morning the first thing that occurred to him was the blow he had received the night before, and in brooding over this he had forgotten the lesson he had derived from that evening hymn. He had now left Doubting Castle. The scales of his mental economy were again readjusted. The evil was driven back, and the good usurped its place. Now he associated the two together. He had seen the thoughts contained in the article before in reading Bulwer, now they had added force and meaning. The thousand streams of an affection, the likes of which he had never known, came flowing back now. Why at some time would not the tide change and he receive the consummation spoken of, when the things we desire shall stay forever in our sight. "Say what you will," he reasoned with himself, "night is the time for reflection. There is something in the stillness with which we are surrounded that calls out our better natures. It brings out our best selves, our thoughts are higher and resolutions nobler. Why should I, who went to sleep restful and contented, have awakened with a burden on my heart that went with me throughout the day until by chance I lighted on this article? Is it because the day brings with it the full realization of our faults and troubles? Are its influences detrimental to the good of the ordinary individual, and is it only the strong mind that can carry out the good resolves planned in the night? Am I so weak that I must give way to this heart trouble and allow its gloom to sway my better judgment? The common drunkard who vows at night that he will not touch another drop, who stops the next morning at the first saloon to gratify his appetite is no more despicable, mentally, than the man who has planned some worthy action, or to do some necessary duty neglected or postponed, and who on the morrow warps his mind against his better self. All are slaves. One to drink, one to inaction, one to neglect, while I am to a morbid feeling. I must conquer. I have a great battle to fight. Now, in the night I feel it will be easy, but on the morrow when grief and discontent rush pell-mell upon me, with the tortures of a thousand questions from interested friends, I know the fight will be stubborn. But why should it be so? Why will not the possession of the thoughts that now thrill me to triumph over self remain with me? Unless I be a slave with a mind too weak and purposes too feeble I shall carry more of them with me in the future than I did today, and if I am to be schooled in the virtue of self-sacrifice what matters it if the training be severe, I shall profit in the end."

CHAPTER XXI.

In thinking that he had a hard struggle before him, Stanley was right, and on the following morning he began to think of plans by which his future should be guided. His father owned a farm in North Lenawee County, that bordered on one of the beautiful sparkling lakes for which that region is particularly noted.[52] He thought once of going there for the summer, taking his library with him, and for a time live like a recluse—spending his time in study and meditation, with the fields, hills and lakes for his outdoor companions, and his books for his bosom friends. This idea he soon dismissed from his mind, like many other plans. He thought he had better stick to business and engage a competent tutor to help him in his evening study. He realized that he was deficient in many things, and he wanted to choose a course of study and reading that would bring him the most solid return in stored knowledge, so that the year might be one of profit in more ways than one, and that in the event of Marjorie and he being again thrown together, he would not be her mental inferior as he knew himself to be now.

However he decided not to choose at once, but to leave the matter over a week or two, in order to thoroughly canvass his situation. Despite the peace of mind he had obtained the evening before, in yielding up to noble inspirations, his mind was still so confused that he thought it unwise to act hastily. He could not fully comprehend Marjorie's position yet. She certainly had confessed that she loved him, but she also distrusted him. What such a mental combination would lead to, he could not tell. He was at times impatient, jealous and melancholy by turns, and became for a while so morose that the clerks at the store shunned him. His sister stood in awe of him, and his father watched him with a feeling akin to disgust, and actually felt ashamed that a son of his should give up to such a morbid feeling.

As the days sped by Stanley felt the need of a trusted friend in whom he could repose confidence, and perhaps, receive comfort. He shrank from making confidants of either Parker or Fox, not because they were unfitted, but because, to an extent, they had been sharers of his confidences and pleasures, when his heart was light and his purposes chiefly pleasure. To trust either to the secret of his present situation, be the outcome what it may, he could not. While Parker was naturally light hearted, he had many good points, but he was then spending much of his time with Miss Downing, with whom he was infatuated. Fox while loving pleasure, was very studious, and observed a great deal, and while Stanley appreciated him he rather dreaded his lynx eyes. He admired his learning, but to have him as a confidant—well, he wouldn't do.

Spring was now far advanced, and the evenings were pleasant, so when oppressed by his thoughts he would go up to the boat house, get out his row boat, and take a spin up the river. Sometimes when he was particularly gloomy, to drive the spell from him, he put such vim into his strokes as to make his boat fairly fly through the water. This caused some of his former friends to think that he must be getting into trim for work during the summer. Under this tension he was perhaps less careful than he ordinarily would have been, and the seeds of malaria were sown in his body that afterwards made themselves apparent, when his spirits and his strength were weakened by confinement. His casual appearance, now and then, was hailed with delight by his former acquaintances, for Stanley was well liked and a general favorite among the boys. He had also taken to novel reading, partly as a diversion, and also for further acquaintance with the standard authors. The works of Hugo, Dickens, Read, Cooper, Bulwer, Eliott and others adorned his library shelves, intermingled with some of lighter vein.[53] In resorting to novel reading he argued that by the time he had finished them, he would be in such perfect control of himself as to be ready for more solid thought, then he would be ready for a tutor. More than once when thus engaged, he had laid aside his book mechanically, and under the influence of former association and the impulse of the moment, he found himself on the familiar route to her home. Once as he passed by he caught a glimpse of her through the window but he dared not trust himself to enter. However by dint of close application he found his desire for study increasing, and his library constantly filling with the new books he saw, and thought he would like to read. What his definite course would have been had he been left to himself to decide, is not known; but an accident occurred to him, the consequence of which, opened up to him a plan of action, which ushered in the most stirring period of his life.

Events as well as years are chroniclers of time, whether we apply them to the history of nations or of individuals. History is divided into epochs, the central ideas of which are those of men who have put into being the events around which cluster all the minor events and ideas of their epoch and which control them.

The birth of the Nazarene, whom we call Christ, the son of God, unsettled all old chronologies or systems of reckoning time. We date from that event because it is considered the greatest in the world's history, and because the teachings he promulgated are made the principles of what is now called the civilized world. With individuals the merest chance or accident in their lives has had for its result the shaping of their future careers, and from it they date all preceding and subsequent events in their lives. Caesar might not have been the Caesar the world knows had not the intrigues of rivals forced him to cross the Rubicon, and begin the career that gave him an imperishable name, and ended in his becoming the head of the Roman world—the greatest of men. The falling of an apple suggested to Newton thoughts which resulted in the discovery of the laws of gravitation. Accident and chance have been great factors in the world.

One day during the latter part of May as Stanley stood near the freight elevator giving orders concerning the shipment of goods, someone from above pulled the rope and it started downward. The noise from the street coming through the open door drowned the slight noise it made in its approach. Nearer it came, and just as one of the employees with a loaded truck came near to Stanley he stepped backward to get out of the way, and in doing so unconsciously stepped under the elevator. The shipping clerk saw his danger, and had no more than time to shout a warning before Stanley was struck squarely on top of his head and knocked senseless to the floor. Anxious hands grasped the ropes and the elevator stopped just in time to save him from being crushed beneath it. He was hurriedly pulled from under it, carried out into the open air, and a doctor immediately sent for. Some one notified his father, and he, wild with excitement, came rushing down to where his son was. For once the man of inflexible will lost his nerve and was helpless. He rushed around aimlessly wringing his hands and calling for water, and ended by sending another man to the telephone to summon the family physician. The harsh words he had uttered a few days since, and his sullen demeanor to his boy rushed upon him in a flood of remorse, and he regretted that he had not been kinder to his boy in his hour of trial. How vivid the mind is in presence of danger? With what exactitude it recalls the minutest details of acts, conversations and thoughts? Mr. Stanley's conscience smote him hard as he watched, waited and hoped for some sign of returning consciousness.

Before either doctor came Stanley regained consciousness and opened his eyes. He saw the crowd around him and noticed that he was lying on a hastily made pallet, his head supported on the lap of one of the employees, his father before him stroking his dark hair in utter bewilderment and helplessness. In a rather faint voice, whose weakness startled him, he inquired what had happened and started to rise, only to find that his strength was suddenly gone. He felt a dull, aching pain in his head, a feeling of extreme lassitude all over his body, and a sharp throbbing pain where he had been struck by the elevator. Those around him, in a gentle way that was rough at its best, were doing what they could to alleviate his pain, and trying to stay the flow of blood from the wound by applying bandages. They were rewarded then with a faint smile. He realized that something must have happened to him, but how or where he had no conception, and those around him were too excited to give him an intelligent answer. Panic had seized upon them, occasioned by the dread of what the "old man" might do, if he thought the accident could be attributed to carelessness.

When Stanley smiled his father bent down and asked eagerly, "Seth, my boy, do you feel better? You are hurt badly, and must not stir."

"I feel all right, father," he replied faintly. "Take me home."

"Poor boy," said his father.

"Poor fellow," echoed a few of the clerks. "It is too bad."

"The doctor will be here in a few moments," said Mr. Stanley, still rubbing his son's hand, and paying no attention to the expressed sympathy of his employees. "He will know better what to do than we. Lay quietly for a few moments. I wonder why that confounded doctor don't hurry up," he added impatiently. "Here are fifteen minutes wasted. Here, you!" turning to a clerk who stood by looking on like a statue, "put on your hat and go find him." The clerk was off before he had finished and met the doctor at the door. Dr. Barker, the first physician sent for, at once went to work to examine the extent of the injury. He inquired as to the speed of the elevator, so as to calculate the force of the blow, the length of time he had been unconscious, and about his previous condition. He then examined Stanley's head and found a dark blue spot, from which trickled a little blood. The skin was abrased in places, and although the blow had been heavy the skull was not fractured.

"A mere scalp wound," he said, "Nothing more serious will result from it than a probable series of headaches and a little nervousness."

"Then he will be around in a few days?" asked Mr. Stanley.

"Oh yes, if his general condition is good. How has he been for the past few days?"

"Well in body, but a little downhearted. Nothing serious."

"He'll pull through all right then," said the doctor reassuringly.

A carriage was sent for and Stanley sent home, the family physician, Dr. Pillworth, arriving in time to accompany him. While he substantially agreed with Dr. Barker as to the nature of the wound, he did not take as bright a view of

Stanley's condition and quick recovery. He saw behind the bruises a disconsolate look and from his bodily weakness he feared he might be attacked with brain fever, and he took immediate steps to prevent it. He was forbidden to read and urged to be cheerful.

"You don't think his condition dangerous Doc, do you?" Mr. Stanley had known Dr. Pillworth a long time and always addressed him familiarly as "Doc."

"The wound is not dangerous, but it is the effect it may have on the mind, is what I am afraid of. Care is what he needs, and care is everything. Isn't it so doctor?" turning to Dr. Barker.

"Yes, sir, there is as much in care as there is in medicine. If his body is weak he must have it. There may be lurking in his system, the seeds of malaria. I do not say there is, but if there should be any, it will assert itself, and there is no telling what malaria will do."

Dr. Pillworth's fears were realized, he was mistaken only in the nature of the disease. Malaria was lurking in his veins as the result of his exposure, and it took advantage of his depressed condition to assert the mastery. Dr. Pillworth went about his patient with a serious countenance and to the anxious inquiries of Mr. Stanley only said, "There is no telling what malaria will do."

From the first John Saunders was detailed to act as nurse, much against Stanley's request, because he did not think he needed a nurse. But later when malaria fastened its grip upon him, Saunders became a necessity, both as nurse and entertainer. The first week of his malarial attack he was a very sick patient, sometimes he was delirious. Then his mind always dwelt on Marjorie, and he continually upbraided her and protested against her decision. But with constant care he began to mend, aided by the delightful June weather, until he was able to move about though considerably emaciated. The turning point of his sickness had been marked by an event. The event turned the tide. Before this he had been so ill that all visitors were excluded from his room.

CHAPTER XXII.

During this time, Marjorie Stone was by no means happy. When he went out from her presence, despite her confidence, she felt disturbed in mind. The great mental strain under which she labored, was telling upon her, and her resolute will now forsook her. Sitting down one day she gave full vent to her feelings in tears. She wept bitterly for some time, and began to upbraid herself. Love for him was asserting itself and punishing her for not yielding to it. Can you blame him if in the time you have imposed upon him he seeks relief, and finds it and love, in the person of another, and never comes back? This and similar queries rushed in upon her and made her restless. Her nature was devout and she sought comfort and found it in Him who has promised aid to all who call upon Him.

Since that night she had suffered a great deal, for nature cannot be outraged with impunity. She missed his frequent visits, his cheery conversations, the long drives and that contentment she felt when in his presence. Not even the companionship of Flora Stedman, and her other girl friends, or the deep sympathy of her mother could compensate for his absence. She loved, and like all persons of her temperament, she loved ardently, with her whole soul. She had miscalculated her strength and her love wrought fears. She chided herself on being too severe. She felt that he would attribute her decision to her distrust of him. Seeking for objects on which to vent blame, she blamed society and its small talk in saying that she was only going to marry Stanley for his money; she blamed herself for giving heed to it—thereby causing this great sacrifice to self, her heart qualms, and the humiliations she must have cast upon him. Would he return? The thought was parent to the wish that he would, or would he spurn her for her weakness. The pain, the misery, she was in, can be conceived only by those in like situations. Her burdens she carried to her mother who did her best to console. She tried to prevent her from being too disconsolate and from judging herself too harshly, by telling her that there was wisdom in her choice, and that if his love were genuine it would not be quenched by waiting, but grow with its hunger. At such times

Marjorie would say, "Ah! mother, but my heart aches so." There is no pain like that of love abused, other pains are perhaps more intense, sharper and more dangerous, but that continuous gnaw and ache, that tugs at our heart strings, always with us, in our sleeping and waking hours, creating misery and making us so wretched, is without equal. Is it not so, dear reader?

Marjorie would have liked to have seen the conditions of her decision broken. She would have liked to have had his society for the year without the committal, and each day found her hoping that he would come to renew their relations. In the morning she thought, "I hope he will come today." In the evening, "He will surely come tomorrow." Thus the time wore away; her cheeks began to get paler, and her form to droop. She used to sit somewhat hidden by the lace curtain in the recesses of the front bay window, when her sense of loneliness overcame her, and look up the street in the direction he was wont to come. The night that he passed the house and caught a glimpse of her, she was watching as usual. When she saw him her blood quickened in her veins, and her heart beat furiously. The innerself was in a tumult of love, fear and hope, while the outerself was calm and apparently busily engaged in a piece of work, while in fact her fingers trembled so that she lost several stitches. He must not see the glad light that shone in her eyes so she kept her head down while pride and nature struggled for the mastery. Pride won and while she was conscious that his step was hesitating as he passed the gate, she did not see the hungry look in his eyes as he passed and gazed in upon her. With downcast eyes she hoped every minute to hear his step upon the walk and the ring of the bell, and still she refused to look up with the smile, the look, that would have assured her of such a thing. Of what a mass of contradictions human nature is made. We actually suffer from the want of the food of love—a smile or a look and we refuse it when within our grasp. We see souls in torture, that we wish to comfort, the opportunity is offered, and we pass it by. The next minute we bitterly reproach ourselves for our heartlessness, and conscience pricks and stings, oh, so hard. These things Marjorie now suffered. What a hateful thing is pride. Pride, that having obtained the mastery, gloated over her pain, and mocked at her aches. Pride, the monster, that had influenced her decision, prevented the look, the smile that would have brought happiness to two hearts.

Despite the wisdom of judgment on her side, and her mother's sympathy, her heart aches were harder to bear than Stanley's, for she had not the avenues of ridding her mind of its singleness that lay in his reach. Naturally the requirements of business turned his thoughts, at times, into other channels, and relieved it, while in the quiet of home life she had to nurse her feeling.

"Man's love is with him a thing apart,
While 'tis woman's whole existence."[54]

and he who wantonly steals the love of a confiding maid and disturbs her peace of mind, by being recreant to his trust when once her confidence is bestowed upon him, is responsible for a greater crime than he imagines.

With a person of her qualities it is not to be supposed that she brooded continually, or that melancholy fed upon her cheeks, or that she pined away, in lamenting her lot. She gradually conquered her feeling, and in time she began to look at the matter in the same light as when she had decided upon the tests of his affection. Not that she loved him less, but at times cold impartial reasoning, aided by absence, gained the ascendency, for if his love could not stand the test, it was not fit to mate with hers.

The evening of the day that Stanley met with his accident in her old place in the bay window, she sat looking over an evening newspaper. Suddenly she turned pale and almost dropped the paper, for there staring her in the face, was an article of great vital interest to her, with great headlines.

NARROW ESCAPE.

SETH STANLEY SERIOUSLY INJURED.

And Almost Crushed to
Death by Freight
Elevator.

The article was lengthy and went into the particulars of the accident as far as the reporter had been able to glean the facts from the excited employees, and for the rest he drew upon his imagination. It cited the fact of Doctors Barker and Pillworth being called in and gave their opinions as being adverse to quick recovery; that there were severe fractures in the skull and that both doctors feared brain fever. Recovery was rendered uncertain because of the weakness of his body. The article concluded saying that Mr. Seth Stanley was a very popular young man, who for some years had traveled extensively and was one of the leaders of his circle in planning and devising means of enjoyment. He was an enthusiastic young athlete fond of all outdoor exercises in which he had attained great proficiency. The last year, however, he had given strict attention to business, the old familiar haunts had seen him no more, and he had been paying assiduous court to one of Detroit's belles.

Dismay struggled with confusion as she read the article through several times, and when she had fully comprehended its meaning she sank back nerveless in her chair, overwhelmed by the rush of apprehensive anxiety. All color forsook her cheek, and she looked like some inanimate statue, so pale and lifeless she seemed. In this condition her mother found her on coming into the room a few moments later. She saw at once that Marjorie had fainted, and being of a practicable turn of mind and not given to hysterics she took the necessary means to restore her. As the result of her efforts Marjorie soon recovered and went to her room. Her mother did not ask her the cause of her weakness, but waited until her daughter chose to tell her. When she returned to the room the paper still lay where it had fallen, and picking it up she afterward saw the article that had so upset her daughter. Experience had taught her that not everything that appeared in newspapers was wholly true, and that first reports were often colored by the imagination and excited feelings of the writer. Also that given a few facts the average newspaper writer of the present day can weave an interesting, thrilling and lengthy tale, which he adorns with startling and attractive headlines, whose special object is to create a sale of the paper, sometimes at the expense of the exact truth. Her experience impelled her to Marjorie in her room where she found her in tears. By considerable tact she infused into her a brighter outlook as to Stanley's condition than the paper gave.

One of Marjorie's first thoughts were to rush to his bedside, but the proprieties of society forbade such an act, and in their dominions proprieties and etiquette are tyrants. Let the heart lacerate in the agony of vanishing hopes that lie within our reach; let the soul pour itself out in longing for that which might satisfy, yet if propriety but suggests vague suspicions of prattling gossip, her voice, like the tempters, is usually heeded. Then she fell to upbraiding herself again for her test of love, and now that he lay at home seriously injured she felt doubly bitter against herself and Mother Grundy. She seemed to feel conscious that she added to the ills caused by his wounds. All her self-control, derived from her sense of duty and the knowledge that she had been but just to herself, was at once swept away by this calamity. The river of love overcame the dam of self-control, and her grief was all the more bitter for having been curbed, as a river is always more dangerous after overleaping its imposed barriers. Her mother's presence with her words of comfort checked her outburst, and she at last hoped that perhaps it was not so bad after all. She would wait patiently for later reports, and she would have her father or Uncle Durham make inquiries.

CHAPTER XXIII.

The next day the morning paper was eagerly scanned, and in it she found a reference to the article. It stated that while the wound was painful, the skull was not fractured, that his general condition was not as bad as made out by a sensational evening paper, and that barring fever, he would quickly recover, as he was a man of great constitutional strength. Marjorie felt better after this and later reports confirmed the news. A week or so later, the weather being exceptionally fine, she went out shopping and chanced to meet Imogene, whose face lighted up on seeing her.

"Oh, Marjorie, I am real glad to see you. Did you know that Seth has been hurt? Now malaria has attacked him. I tell you what, our house is busy now."

"Is he very sick?"

"I should say that he was. John Saunders has been sent up from the store to attend him. We could not. He is light-headed and delirious. Mrs. Burwell thinks he is dangerously ill."

"But the doctor, what does he say?"

"Oh, Dr. Pillworth looks wise and solemn and shakes his head when he comes out of the room, and to our inquiries he says, 'He is in a bad way,' if we ask, 'will he get better soon?' with a solemn tone he answers, 'I hope so, but you can't tell anything about malaria.'" She imitated the manner and tone of the doctor, and caused Marjorie to smile. "Won't you come and see me sometime? The house is solemn we need some one to cheer us up occasionally."

Imogene did not suspect the changed relations between her brother and Miss Stone, and her complete innocence showed in her manner, so Marjorie promised.

"You know that you promised to be like a sister to me," continued Imogene, "and I—I, well I haven't seen you for some time."

Marjorie stammered out some commonplace remark, about having been busy or indisposed.

"You look awfully pale too," prattled on the unconscious Imogene, as she noted her appearance. "I guess you need the doctor's aid also. Isn't it too bad that all the people I am most interested in seem to have the dumps, are sick or look bad at the same time? It does beat all."

All these allusions were inward stabs to Marjorie. They were all the deeper and more painful because she thought herself responsible, in part, for them. But desiring to know all, by dint of a few questions, she gleaned from Imogene the full extent of Seth's accident and sickness. Imogene possessed a great deal of her brother's art of entertaining, and having some one to talk to, she rattled away at a terrific rate, and laughed at her own little follies and conceits, while her smiles chased away some of that sad look that had settled upon Marjorie's countenance.

The remembrance of her promise to Imogene was ever in her mind, and mingled with a strong desire to see Stanley, a few days later, as she sat thinking about him the desire seemed to grow. It made her anxious and restless. If anything, she had become a trifle paler and thinner, and the blood forsaking her cheek, left the skin a marble whiteness. As she sat looking out of the window, inhaling the sweet fresh air of June, and admiring the spring garb of nature, her eyes lighted upon a bed of flowers in the yard. The thought occurred to her, why not go and take him a bouquet? The more she thought of the idea, the better she liked it, and she made up her mind to do so finally.

From plants that her own hands had nurtured, she prepared for him, a choice bouquet of pansies, roses, forget-me-nots and geraniums. In the bosom of her dress, which was of a light texture, she placed a single fine pansy and geranium leaf, and proceeded, not without some doubt and apprehension, to call on Imogene and to see him.

Imogene herself answered her call and welcomed her with many exclamations of delight as she ushered her through the large hall into the parlor, that it seemed to fully repay Marjorie for coming.

"I am real glad to see you Marjorie," said Imogene, as she put her arms about Marjorie's neck and kissed her.

"You will smother me and crush my flowers," said Marjorie smiling.

"How good of you to come and what lovely flowers you have brought."

"Do you think so? I picked them out of my garden. They are for the sick room. Is your brother any better today?"

"Not very much. Would you like to see him?"

"Yes, if he can be seen."

Instead of trusting the announcement of Marjorie's presence to a servant, Imogene herself ran up to his room with the message that made his dull eyes brighten up wonderfully. He gave an assenting answer and then told Saunders to arrange the room, and to Imogene, "you may come up in a few moments."

Saunders, who was a very neat and tasty person, soon had the room in presentable shape. He was pleased too, for he had noted the glad look in the sick man's eyes. Nothing like it had he seen since he had been acting as nurse, and he thought it augured well for the patient. Then at a word from Stanley he went down and announced, "that Mr. Stanley would be pleased to have them come up now." He accompanied them to the room and then started for the chamber that had been Stanley's until the noise of the street compelled his removal to a more quiet room, when he was called by Imogene, who had happened to think that perhaps they might prefer that there should be no witness of their meeting. Upon the pretense of giving John some order, she ushered Marjorie into the room, and asked to be excused for a few moments.

Stanley, propped up by pillows, looked pale and emaciated, but his eyes lighted up with joy as he saw her enter the room. In her simple costume, to his eager eyes, she looked far more beautiful than any poet's dream, as with moistened eyes, she came toward him holding the flowers in her hand. When she saw him so pale and emaciated she was moved to pity, and tears unbidden gathered in her eyes as with tremulous voice she said, "you will please excuse me for coming unbidden, Mr. Stanley, but I heard of your accident and subsequent illness, and was so sorry to hear of it that I have brought you these flowers as a reminder of spring, and as an expression of my deep sympathy and hope for your quick recovery. Further, I would say that my conscience is clear of any wrong toward you."

Stanley took the flowers as he said, "I thank you with all my heart Miss Stone for these flowers, and for this visit. You have done nothing to excuse. Let us forget, for the time that I was a too ardent lover. I have been convinced that in that matter you are wiser than I. I could not trust myself to continue my visits for fear that I might trespass on that which was forbidden. Your assurance, however, lightens the task which I have tried cheerfully to bear." His eyes spoke more than his lips expressed.

This ended all allusion to the past. Then Imogene came in, and they chatted merrily. The sick man, as far as he was able, joined in with them, and the improvement that was going on in him was wonderful. He kept them laughing with droll stories, while she told him of the happenings during his illness and of future events in musical circles.

They did not remain long and in parting Marjorie shook hands with him. As she did so there was such a wistful look in his dark eyes that she was deeply touched. She remained a while longer with Imogene, and when she went home she felt more at ease with herself. She was happier and lighter hearted than she had been for many a day. Stanley from the hour of her visit began to improve, slowly at first, but the pains had left his head and malaria racked his frame less. Dr. Pillworth predicted, while he wondered at the marvelous change, that he would soon be able to drive out. Mind, after all, controls more than medicine, and Marjorie's call and flowers had brightened up his mind and robbed it of its gloom and despondency. Had Marjorie known the excellent effect her visit had upon that house, and the happiness she had brought to it, her heart would have been lighter still, and all the more cheerfully would have looked forward to the time when her self-imposed task would be finished, and to its result.

BOOK II.

CHAPTER I.

———————

Stanley's improvement was rapid and he was soon able to sit up. Then Saunders selected books from the library and read to him. When tired of listening and reading they talked over what they had read. These conversations revealed to Stanley something of the extent of Saunders' information, his wide range of reading and his wonderful retentive memory. While his intelligence was a matter of never failing and increasing wonder to him.

John Saunders enjoyed this diversion. He was glad to escape from the confinement of the office these pleasant days. He was glad to have gained the measure of Stanley's confidence which he could easily discern. Besides, he had access to the library, which contained many choice and valuable works, and he made good use of his time and opportunity. He was a great reader and had spent much time in searching for the connection between the African of today, and those Egyptians and Ethiopians who played so prominent a part in ancient history.

He had read Herodotus, Plutarch, Rawlinson, Muller, Blumenbach and other writers of ancient history, for the purpose of seeing how their views of the different races of men, compare with bible history.[55] There were slaves in those days, black and white, but who, on obtaining their freedom, became mingled with the free citizens and further trace of them as men of different nationality or color was lost. This was different to the experience of his class in America and was a puzzler. He had read in Plutarch's life of Marius that this soldier in his African wars, had been very successful. He had captured many slaves and was returning home in triumph, when rivals, jealous of his success, secured a decree of banishment against him from the Roman Senate and had his command taken from him. His army espoused the cause of their leader. He promised his numerous Ethiopian slaves, if they would fight for him, freedom and the privileges of Roman citizenship. Marius fought, conquered and returned to Rome in triumph. The after fate of these new made citizens, history furnished him no inkling, nor could he find any allusion to them as a distinct class of the people.[56] Finally he came to this conclusion, that the Roman citizen did not cherish that prejudice against race so common among Americans, and Americans only.

Less than a week after Stanley was able to take a little outdoor exercise, they had taken a morning drive and in the afternoon took their usual station on the lawn. Saunders had read for some time when Stanley somewhat abruptly interrupted his reading by saying:

"Let the books go for a while, John, I want to talk to you. Do you know that I think you're a very clever fellow, and I have often thought that it was too bad that you are colored? If you were a white man I could make a companion of you that would stand me well in hand for a year at least. I owe you considerable already."

"Is my color all that causes you to think less of me?"

"Your color doesn't matter so much to me at all, but people would talk if I should take you for a companion. I do not mean any insult to you," Stanley said confusedly and apologetically, "for you are different from other colored men."

"Not one bit different from hundreds of others whom I know. I consider many of my associates just as intelligent and some, perhaps, are more so. No doubt the same thing has been said to them by white people they have come in contact with, as it is not the first time it has been said to me. Such remarks show that no race has a premium on intelligence, and that racial superiority is a sham. It also proves that under equal conditions equal results will follow."

"I would be glad," said Stanley, "if it were different. I think a colored person is as good as a white one if he behaves as well and is as intelligent."

"I can convince you differently," replied Saunders. "If tomorrow I should prove unworthy of your trust you would at once say 'all niggers are alike,' and I would be the last colored person to ever get a situation from you while a hundred of your white employees might do much worse. You would simply discharge him and hire another without thinking of his nationality. With us the many have to suffer for the sins of the one. With others the one alone suffers. Isn't that a difference?"

Stanley thought for a moment before he said, "I guess you are right about that, and it isn't right either. Still I have always treated you well, I don't take any credit for it either, for you have deserved it."

Saunders thought, "If I had been white would I have been detailed to act as nurse? Would I have had to leave my duties as I have often done to serve as a valet or do other duties not consistent with that of my position," but he said, "I thank you for the compliment, but while we are talking about these things I will call your attention to a few little every-day prejudices, practiced thoughtlessly perhaps, but they are hurtful and humiliating. I will cite you a case right here in this city. There are scores of intelligent Afro-Americans, young men and women, some graduates from the common schools, others from the high school, and still others from different universities throughout the States. How many hold places of honor and trust? You can almost count them on your fingers ends. Is it because they are unworthy, incapable or ignorant? No. Philanthropists and politicians tell us to get education and money, and the race question will settle itself. But these same philanthropists and politicians will not carry their theories into practice by giving us profitable employment. Their trees are barren. I might travel today, as many another one of us has done, this city over from store to store, with the best of references as to honesty and capability, and hardly one man in a thousand would consider my application seriously in any capacity save that of porter. We have young ladies intelligent above the ordinary, fully equal to and superior to the majority of girls that clerk in the stores. They are of pleasing address, comely in features and fair to look upon, yet the fact that their skins are dark, or that there is a slight trace of African about them shuts them out from all such situations. And the excuse is so flimsy."

"What is it?"

"That their clerks won't work with colored people. How many of your employees left when I entered your firm? Not one. Clerks do not work for sentiment but for bread and butter, and if a merchant once tells them that if they don't want to work, because he has employed a colored person or any other person, they can quit, they will work all right enough. For a sentimental prejudice will yield when it interferes with one's livelihood. I have proof of this. But candidly, can a race improve rapidly under such conditions?"

"Not as rapidly as it might otherwise. But don't be disconsolate John. There is a better day coming for the colored people and you may live to see it. Meditations on what might have been, are the dark valleys through which the soul passes, into which only gleams of hope can enter. It is better to dwell on the anticipations of the possibilities of the future, than to brood over misfortunes that are the realities of the past. He who lives and thinks only of the past, is sure to dwell on the dark side of what he has passed through. He finds only bitterness in his reflections, that influences his whole expectations of the future. Our constant hope of the blessings that lie just beyond smooths the path of life as we go. I speak from experience, but it has come as the result of my own folly. Desires gratified without cost, often so pampers a man, that he plunges into excess. Sometimes he plunges right on to ruin, and becomes a wreck, sometimes an incident reveals his folly, and he awakens to a repentance that makes memory, for a time, a gaul of bitterness."[57]

"Few men," replied Saunders, "have escaped the experiences described by a man of passion, (Burns) that when the passions are excited, conscience flees like the shadows of night before the morning sun, and that when the passions are gone, conscience comes creeping back like a sleuth hound on our track.[58] But man's chiefest manhood lies in those impulses which move him to penance. Often when in the embrace of despair, I have felt as if I would like to take off the brakes, and be what the enemies and maligners of my race say we are—unfit for association and recognition, and devoid of all manly attributes. You have a prospect to live for, but what incentive have I except that I must render unto God an account for deeds done in the flesh? That promise of the future is alone the inspiration for me to live an upright and an honorable life among men."

"Now that is where you make a mistake. A man may commit one error in youth, the effects of which will last for years, and darken his life. The same is true of races. What your race is passing through, ours has passed. We have spent our time beneath the yoke, we have been branded and disgraced. What condition could be more abject than that of the English people at the time of the Norman conquest, or what can equal the feudal system that prevailed in Europe? The time has not been so long since the masses among the Caucasians have attained liberty of action and thought, and the struggle is still on—Russia is the scene of strife. Action and thought are still enslaved. The Jew is still made a mark of opprobrium.

"The colored people are in the youth of their general development, although they have furnished conspicuous examples of men of superior ability, many of whom are widely known and respected. Even I, with my limited knowledge of affairs can point to a few men, and they are but the marks of the possibilities of the bulk of your people. Men never arrive at complete satiety in this life, for inventive want is too prolific with ideas. We often envy other men their positions, from our standpoint it seems the acme of happiness and content. When we attain like conditions we are still unsatisfied. We aspire for something higher, and when too late, we see some beauty in the life behind and sigh for the past and the might have beens. Inordinate ambition is a bane to mankind in that it swells discontent and blinds their eyes to the opportunities in their station of life. I am convinced that it is the advantage taken of apparently trivial circumstances that make grand men."

CHAPTER II.

"You talk like a philosopher," said Saunders, "and I find much inspiration and good in your ideas. But the ambition of the Afro-American to escape from the toils is not inordinate. While we are in our mother's womb we are proscribed, and when we have grown to youth and manhood on every hand and in every pursuit we meet the proscriptions placed upon us, when we were yet unborn. Without being guilty of offense we are condemned. You remember the sad story of Jean Valjean, who wandered from place to place, shunned because of what he had been, and for what he was still supposed to be. But he was conscious of his guilt; he knew that his treatment was in part a punishment for crime, though it was heartless. He knew further that he could drown his identity, and through upright living, regain the confidence of men which he had forfeited; with us it is different. Each gleam of intelligence but reveals the fact that we should mourn for the common opportunities of life that have never been ours, and may not be in this generation under the light of present prospects. What a rude and continued awakening then is our knowledge? If we look back [at] the past like a hideous, horrible nightmare, that has over-ridden and blighted our ancestors, confronts us; we turn from it to the future and aside from the apprehensions that confront all men as to success, we see over on either side of the road those threat[en]ing, unreasoning, unsparing monsters— prejudice and proscription. What wonder then that it should arouse in us desires? Desires that are denied, but which are none the less persisted in. Would you call that desire or ambition inordinate, that nerves one to action even when hope seems to be dead, to live upright; to perform something that would add luster to one's name; to soften some of the prejudices, and hence mitigate the condition of the race to which he belongs?"

"The desire to achieve such things is praiseworthy ambition, and they who are thus moved are heroes."

"It is thus that I have been moved when almost in despair, when hope had almost vanished and I could not see of what use it was to struggle against the designs of our enemies together with what seemed an inevitable fate. Then when I commenced to compare the history of races as you have done, I said, 'It is but a comparatively short time since as savages the race roamed in Africa, that but a shorter time still it was under the yoke of body and mental servitude.' Then hope again returned, I felt ambition's fire coursing rapidly through my veins, and upon the instant I became another person—one with resolves to do something for humanity."

Saunders in his earnestness had left his seat and was pacing to and fro oblivious of almost everything, save his and his race's condition. His form seemed to dilate and expand, his face was aglow with excitement and earnestness and his eyes sparkled with resolution. Stanley thought him a picture as he paced thus, of perfect manhood animated by high purposes, and he could not help but think that out of such stuff were heroes made. It takes but little to fan discontent into a raging flame which, according to circumstances, breeds dark sinister imaginings, or unveils noble inspirations. The man with a grievance is not always to be encouraged, for if you hold with him that his cause is just his grievance becomes magnified. If you agree to the full extent of his claims his cause of complaint is doubly magnified to himself. Most all of the pernicious isms of our day, so dangerous to government, are the result of commiserating spirits mutually magnifying their wrongs, until in a frenzy of excitement judgment and reason are overthrown and the passions reign. Sympathy is the bond of human fellowship. It unravels the secrets of the heart, the longings, the aspirations, but it should be used with judgment. It is worthy to use it in the interest of the oppressed struggling for light so as to get at the objects of their desires. It is noble to use it to inspire men on to noble thought and action, and to relieve the cry of the people that wells up against most unrighteous wrongs. It is grand to use it to inspire a race upon whom odium is heaped, whose ambitions are checked by environments, to struggle on to overcome the barriers. Saunders was a man with a grievance. Stanley's sympathy had called it out, the discontent was checked, and the inspiration to hope took its place. This is the proper way to treat a man with such complaints. Sympathy was rightly shown and no doubt even Stanley felt the impassioned fire that surged in Saunders' veins. He no doubt felt a few of the noble resolutions that helped him in his own battle with self, as he witnessed this man pacing to and fro depicting a race's struggle.

After pausing a while he continued: "Amidst degrading influences and the wreck of morals, despite the heat of prejudices, the slanders of enemies and the calumnies of society, while bodies were made barters of merchandise, the soul products of exchange and women means of commerce in flesh, lofty manhood and inborn courage was still preserved. The world has not seen a grander type of nobler manhood than the black African prince, who achieved Haytian independence—Touissant L'Overture.[59] They who would deny us instincts above the brute, or view us an inferior race, seem to forget that we too, fought for American independence, and for the maintenance of the Union. Our blood, in the person of Attucks, was the first to be shed for independence.[60] Our forces in the field brought down rebellion's head, while the bravery and courage of our troops at the "Crater," Fort Wagner, Olustee, Honey Hill and a hundred other battle fields, are not excelled in history.[61] Can we not justly claim, in view of our environments, that the people of the Republic are ungrateful? Not alone on the field of battle displaying courage, have we proven that in us are the same instincts, desires and ambitions that move other races. Under slavery, the many beneficial inventions emanating from the brain of the slave, became the property of the master who received all credit. Under the inspiration of freedom, inventive skill is showing itself as may be proved by the records at Washington. A Greek grammar, the product of one of our race is the text book of one of our celebrated Eastern colleges.[62] There are many who are as great and as deserving in their field as those you have mentioned. In all localities there are many who have commanded attention and honor by dint of superior ability over their fellows, and this has been won without the aid of the hypocritical politician, or the weeping philanthropists, who have only words for an answer to appeals for work. If I could find a sufficient number of men whose actions would be in comport with their words whose hearts beat as yours, I would have no cause to ever despair. But we have taken up the whole afternoon in talk, what shall we take up next?"

"The talk has been very profitable to me, and I shall make it so to you. You have made me see many things in a different light from what I have hitherto viewed them and I am constrained to believe you have a righteous complaint against your country and against society. Someday we will try to more fully discuss how it can be remedied. By the way, I intend to spend my vacation at the farm with Parker, Morgan and Fox, and you shall keep us company."

Saunders expressed his thanks and they then re-entered the house.

Seth's condition was now so much better that in a few days Mr. Stanley thought it would be better for Saunders to go back to the store, which he did thinking of the great interest father and son seemed to take in him, and his coming vacation. Stanley, however, missed the long, congenial talks, when John had gone. He had not fully recovered and was at times subject to disagreeable headaches. He made occasional visits to the store and did a little work to keep his hand in as he was far from feeling as depressed as before. Marjorie's call had relieved his mind of a great doubt, and he was more content to stand by her dictum. Besides, whenever he felt a little gloomy, he thought of Saunders, and that conversation when his inner soul had been revealed, and he compared his own burden with that of one whose ambitions were so checked, and he profited by the comparison. He turned, therefore, with more content than before the accident, to other matters. He began to study Saunders, and he found the study interesting in many ways, as well as profitable, as the reader will see hereafter.

CHAPTER III.

———————

The fabled hydra-headed serpent, slain by Hercules, was not more dangerous than that hydra-tongued creature, called gossip, and society is one of its hand-maids.[63] Gossip, through society was still agog in discussing the relations between Seth Stanley and Marjorie Stone. Now that he had apparently recovered from his sickness, and was not known to call upon her or to be seen in her company, gossip found fresh material with which to amuse itself. Rumors of a broken engagement were numerous, and it was attributed to various causes.

Since Stanley's convalescence Parker had renewed his calls. But Parker, who was a great society man, failed to extract from him any information on the matter, or to get him out in society. He, finally, by putting this and that together concluded that much of Stanley's illness was due to broken relations with Miss Stone, and without asking directly, used all the ways and means known to society to pump him. He was unsuccessful, and compelled to give up the job as useless.

"You need a little mental tonic," Parker said on one occasion. "If you will let me prescribe for you I will have you in the old spirits in no time."

"I have always been down on quackery," returned Stanley, "and I know that your tonic is the same old patent stuff. Lose yourself in gaiety for the moment to awake consciousness again. You cannot dissipate depression by dissipating the body. Many a confirmed drunkard has tried this formula of yours in the glass, to find that he was out of the frying pan into the fire."

"Oh, your trouble is of the heart then," said Parker, conscious that [he] had sent out a feeler, but avoiding Stanley's eyes for fear that he would find in them a rebuke.

"You have now changed your profession," said Stanley, shifting his position and noticing Parker's embarrassment. "You play the role of a diviner as well as that of the physician. I cannot accept you in the capacity of either."

Parker felt relieved at even this gentle rebuke and dropped the subject. Fred Morgan had returned from Orchard Lake where he had graduated with high honors. He had so thoroughly enjoyed his last summer's outing that he desired to repeat it, and he looked forward to it with greater anticipations than usual, because it would be the last before entering on a business career. He had brought home with him a school mate, Edward Burleigh, whose home was in the East. Burleigh had suggested a trip down the St. Lawrence and among the Thousand Islands.[64]

"That will be just the thing to knock the malaria out of Stanley," said Morgan, and hence he suggested the idea to him confidently. Stanley, however, had time to think the matter over, and had changed his mind as to whom he would spend the time with and where. He did not care for the companionship of his old friends because he was almost sure that some one of them would, during this vacation, take the liberty of inquiring into his present relations with Miss Stone, and he did not desire to be bored with such questions. He had about made up his mind to take Saunders and go out to the farm for a quiet time in the woods and among the little lakes. His original plan was to take a party with him, but as he had been reticent about it and communicated with no one he had no difficulty in settling upon this course. Hence he declined to go with the others despite their pleadings. His refusal caused them to be disappointed and none were more so than Burleigh. He had heard so much from Morgan as to Stanley's qualities and good fellowship that he expected to derive a great deal of pleasure out of the trip. Stanley's refusal did not prevent them from going ahead with their preparations, although they felt the disappointment sorely.

They expected to start about July 8th. In the interim, however, their efforts to induce him to accompany them were frequent and their arguments strong, but they were useless.

Once they waited on him in a body thinking that as the time drew near he would change his mind. "We have heard and we believe that in union there is strength," said Fox opening the conversation, "and united we have come to persuade you to go with us. I tell you beforehand we shall not take no for an answer."

"If I were a candidate for office," replied Stanley, "I could not feel prouder to know that my friends were bound to thrust honors upon me. I am sure though that you will take what I feel compelled to give you with regret. I appreciate your company, I assure you, and I appreciate the feeling that brings you here to ask me to go with you, but I ask the same consideration from you when I say it is impossible." Stanley's courteous and forcible answer forestalled many choice bits of argument that had been prepared for the occasion.

"I am very sorry," said Burleigh, "for Fred has been telling me what a jolly fellow you are. I suppose that malaria unfits a fellow for long jaunts."

Stanley was glad to lay his refusal at the door of malaria and there it rested.

On the day of their departure he accompanied them down to the river where they took the propeller —— for Buffalo.[65] As he did not wish them to know that he had been planning another trip while they had been urging him to go with them, he decided it best to wait until about the 15th before going to the farm, as that would be the time for Saunders' vacation. It had always been the custom of the Stanley establishment to give their employees each year a vacation of two weeks with pay.

He then said to Saunders: "You have earned a vacation where you will not have to play the part of a servant. I have written Mr. Tobin, who lives on the farm, to prepare the cottage for us. We can board at the farm house and all our time will be our own. Will you go?"

"I shall only be happy to go," said Saunders, "for as I told you before one gets all he wants of city life in the fifty weeks he spends closeted in an office. A little country life is an excellent thing, as it gives freedom to both mind and body and I thank you for the privilege."

"No thanks, I am under obligations to you for your kind treatment and excellent nursing when I was sick and I haven't forgotten it."

"Don't mention that, for I have been amply repaid for all that I did."

"For your labor, that is true, but money cannot buy such devotion as you exhibited, and because of that I am still in your debt. We will leave day after tomorrow. Please have the satchels ready and fill one with books and magazine of your own choosing. I have the *Century, Forum*, and *North American Review* for this month, and you will find them in my room."[66]

"You can depend upon everything being ready," replied Saunders. And he at once began to prepare for their departure.

On the morning of July 17th Stanley and Saunders took the early train over the Michigan Central to Ypsilanti, where they connected with the Hillsdale branch of the Lake Shore and Michigan Southern. At ten o'clock they were at Brooklyn, a small town about sixty-five miles from Detroit. Here they were met by Mr. Tobin, the manager of the farm, and taken to Sand Lake, about six miles distant, on which a part of the farm bordered. Saunders was very much impressed with the beauty of the scenery. It was novel to him. Before him lay the lake, a beautiful sheet of water glistening under the rays of the sun, about one and a half miles long and three quarters of a mile wide. Its sides, save on the north, where lay a small swamp, were dotted with summer cottages, surrounded by one continuous growth of woods. The face of the country for miles around was hilly, and hill, valley and lake, alternating with each other formed a scene decidedly picturesque and pleasing. Prospect Hill in the distance, which was the tallest in that section, loomed up like a monitor overlooking the rest, while to the southeast of it was Cedar Hill from which an excellent view could be obtained of Wampler's Lake.

They were driven at once to the cottage, on the left bank of the lake, which was somewhat isolated from the rest and about a quarter of a mile from the farm house. Everything had been recently cleaned and neatly arranged, so that it presented a cozy and home-like appearance, that called from Saunders an expression of satisfaction. Having washed and dusted themselves they donned their flannel shirts, swung a hammock in the shade and prepared to rest until the large farm-house bell rang for dinner. Meanwhile Mr. Tobin, to whom Saunders was a perfect stranger had gone on home to tell his wife and folk that young Mr. Stanley had come and brought with him a young colored man who was very rich and decidedly good looking. As to Saunders' wealth he had no real information, but he reasoned that Seth Stanley would never lower himself to take a colored man as a companion, unless he were rich, and the others agreed with him.

"Colored men be all right in their place," said Mr. Tobin, "and we allers allowed Tom to sit with us at the table jest like one of the family, but we wouldn't have gone a galavantin' round the country with him."

"I've hearn tell," spoke up his wife, "of some right peart colored men and they were rich too."

"He must be smart too, and I reckon he must come from some other state. They say that some of 'em down in Ohio have been elected to the legislatur."

"There's Fred Douglass, I've hearn tell that he's so smart that people like to be in his company. Is he good looking?"

"Fair to middlin," said Mr. Tobin, "and he's not very dark either. But he's colored, sure's I'm livin', thats what gets me."

Before they were through speculating, John Saunders had grown to be quite an important personage with them, and he was eyed a great deal when he came to dinner, and was introduced to the family. His gentlemanly appearance was such that it seemed to confirm their conjectures.

When he had gone Mrs. Tobin said, "I knew he must be somebody. He was all dressed up just like Mr. Stanley, and his hands were softer'n Daisey's."

"'Taint Fred Douglass' son anyhow," said Mr. Tobin reflectively, "cos his name is Saunders, and I never hearn tell of any Saunders afore."

"Well I reckon there's lots o' people as we never hearn tell of," replied his wife.

The news soon spread around among the neighbors until it reached the occupants of the cottages, that Seth Stanley and a rich colored man from the East had taken possession of the Stanley cottage.

"He must be somebody," they remarked to each other on hearing it, "or the Stanleys would not take him in tow."

Mystery is a telescope to the mind. It either enlarges or belittles according to the end one gets hold of. In this case, John Saunders was seen through the magnifying lens. It was well for him that opinion took this course for it enabled him to enjoy himself hugely.

CHAPTER IV.

They arranged their days so as to get the most out of them. In the morning before 5 o'clock they were up and enjoying a row upon the lake, or taking a long walk, or going in swimming. Sometimes after breakfast they would fish a little, or row until the sun got so warm that they took the shade for shelter. Sometimes when the breezes were good and strong, they enjoyed taking the little sail boat out, and coming down the lake with sails set at a good spanking rate. They were not sailors enough to make good progress back with the sail, so they rowed back for the pleasure of the sail down again. During the heat of the day they would loll around, talk, smoke, read, sketch or sometimes take a drive, while in the evening they would probably amuse themselves by another swim or a row, or by waking the startled echoes by wild cries, or sweet melodies, or in visiting their neighbors. Meanwhile their hands were growing hard and their skins tanned, while their animal spirits were always high, save when Seth was in a fitful mood, which was not often. Stanley never enjoyed himself better, and Saunders was having a magnificent time.

As a result of the gossip, whenever they went out for a drive across the country or a row on the lake, they were the center of attraction. Little children stopped in the middle of their play to gaze at them. For a time Saunders was a curiosity. He noticed it all but he was not aware of the true cause. At the store he was accustomed to being eyed by strangers who seemed to think it an odd thing to see colored people in such a place, so he thought now that he was noticed simply because he appeared as the associate of a young rich white man. Rather jokingly he suggested to Stanley that they start a side show, get a hand organ and a monkey, place themselves on exhibition and charge an admission fee of ten cents, thus combining profit with pleasure.

There were two hotels at the lake. The one on the south side had a livery attached and was often patronized by Stanley. He enjoyed an early morning drive over the hills, through Irish town, to Wampler's Lake or to Prospect Hill, from whose eminence an excellent view of the country unfolded itself. This section is famous for the number of its lakes, and from this hill alone, could be seen twelve that glistened like diamonds in green settings. In these excursions they had visited almost all the little villages round about, going as far as Tecumseh.

One day, through Mrs. Tobin, Stanley learned of the popular belief concerning Saunders. He was immensely tickled over it and decided to let that belief have its course, and if possible, keep Saunders from hearing of it. His friendship for that individual every day was growing stronger, and in that was sunk all reference as to color or race. He thought only of the qualities he possessed. People had already dubbed him peculiar and cranky, and he enjoyed the distinction. On the Tuesday of their second week's stay a party was given at —— one of the hotels, and among others a courteous note was sent to Stanley inviting him and his friend to attend. He showed the invitation to Saunders and after a little talk over it they decided to accept, and Stanley sent a message to that effect. Accordingly a little after nine o'clock that evening they wended their way to the hotel. The party or ball was to be held in the hall built for dancing purposes just back of the hotel. Music and dancing had already commenced when they arrived, and quite a number had already collected, the farmers and the vacation sojourners being well mixed. Their entrance caused a slight bustle, as all eyes were immediately turned upon them. One of the managers of the affair, Mr. D——, came up to them, greeted them, and did the "agreeable" by introducing them to all they had not met, and in making them feel at ease. Since he had come Stanley determined to enjoy himself. Besides among the cottagers there were represented many families of wealth and standing from Adrian, Toledo and roundabout. Saunders had been so well received that he left him to take care of himself, and selecting a partner was soon engaged in a waltz. Saunders proceeded more cautiously. He well knew that prejudice was not so rampant in these country gatherings as in the city, but he feared a slight which might mar his own and perhaps rob Stanley of his enjoyment. However, he did not lack company, for many were anxious to get a good look at him and hear what a man of his supposed distinction had to say, and right well did he unconsciously play his part. When partners were called for a quadrille Stanley took him to a rather pretty lady named Miss Andrews, and insisted upon his taking her out and joining in the dance which he did. The ice once broken he had no difficulty in finding partners or in being entertained. Everything went smoothly and pleasure ran on unabated, as it only can in these informal social gatherings in the country, until he made a misstep in a direction of which he was unaware there was any danger.

Squire Andrews, the father of the first young lady he had danced with, was anxious to have a talk with him. He was an old Abolitionist, and was at present the Justice of the Peace in his township. He was a peculiar man in many respects. While he detested human slavery, he did not care for social contact with any of the oppressed save those whom the public courted, because of their high standing in public life. With them he loved to be thought on terms of familiarity. In speaking of them he spoke with that unwarranted freedom little minds indulge in when speaking of the great. Accordingly at his first opportunity he buttonholed Saunders and began to talk of his experience as an Abolitionist.

"S'pose you know Fred Douglass?" he asked, folding one arm across his breast and resting the elbow of the other on it, while he tugged away at his chin.

"Yes, sir. I am quite well acquainted with him."

"A great man is Fred, a great man."

"I am glad to hear you say so."

"I attended the first Abolition meeting in this State where he spoke. I warn't quite a man then."

"Is that so?"

"Yes. Fred is a smart fellow."

"He is one of the few men that we meet that impresses one with the idea of greatness. You cannot be long in his presence without realizing it. You see it sticking out all over him in his movements and actions, and when he opens his mouth the impression is not spoiled, as it so often is, but you are confirmed in your opinion. To my mind he is one of the most important personages in America, by reason of his associations with the past and the breadth of his intellect."

Saunders was getting beyond the squire's depth, who returned to shallow water by saying: "We had warm exciting times in those days in helping runaway slaves on to Canada." Here he branched off and began to talk of the detestation in which he held slavery, and recounted many of his experiences in connection with the underground railroad. When he had finished Saunders said: "You must feel proud now to see the advances some of the race that you helped on to freedom are making."

"I've read that some of them are gettin' on purty well."

"Have you ever been elected to the Legislature?"

The Squire now began his questions. He was full of curiosity to know who and what Saunders really was.

"No, I have not."

"Ever been appointed to a position in the States."

"No."

"S'pose you are a lawyer, eh?"

"No, I thought once of studying for that profession, but gave it up."

"S'pose you are a merchant then, eh?"

"You have missed it again. Although I am engaged in the business, by profession I'm a civil engineer."

"Buyin' and sellin'?"

"No, I am a bookkeeper in Mr. Stanley's store."

If some one had slipped a chunk of ice down the Squire's back he could not have been more astonished and staggered. Finally he managed to ask:

"Own an interest in the business?"

"No."

He thought again as he tugged away at the spare growth of whiskers that adorned his chin. While he was thus meditating Saunders' attention was called elsewhere. Squire Andrews was dumbfounded. The idea that he, Squire Andrews, Justice of the Peace for the township of M——, County of Lenawee, of the State of Michigan, had condescended to take an interest in a common Negro, and had mingled socially with him. He was disgusted, and the more he thought of it the worse he felt. He imagined that the dignity of his person had been imposed upon. He then lost no time in spreading the information that the great somebody was only a common clerk or bookkeeper in Stanley's store. Every now and then he would stand still, his countenance marked with disgust as he took a fresh hold of his chin appendage and muttered, "only a colored bookkeeper, bah!" Saunders was no longer the lion of the occasion. He was still stared at by nearly all present, but not with the look of awe which had hitherto characterized their expressions. The wonder that now occupied the minds of some was how Seth Stanley could so disgrace his family as to make an equal of his father's colored bookkeeper. Others, better informed of the difficulties that surrounded a young colored man in attaining a living, thought that he must be smart and intelligent above the average to secure such a position.

Nevertheless he was treated civilly for they saw that he acted like a gentleman and was excellent company. Beside those who had formally made advances could not so quickly change front, although they might cut him afterward.

Squire Andrews was determined to let Stanley know that he was fully aware of the relation between him and Saunders, and of the false position in which he had been placed. Siding over to where Stanley stood talking with a young lady, while still tugging and stroking his whiskers, he waited his chance. As soon as Stanley was at leisure he stepped up to him saying, "Quite a smart fellow, your friend, Mr. Stanley; everybody thought he was a merchant from down East."

"So!" said Stanley, with a merry twinkle in his eyes.

"Or the son of some distinguished person."

"He is a smart man, who is as good as he is intelligent."

"Only a clerk in your father's store," with a sneer.

"Yet he is a trusted one, and he is my friend," said Stanley with warmth, for he noticed the sneer in the Squire's tone and on his countenance, and he intended to resent any remark that might belittle his companion.

The Squire saw danger ahead and beat a retreat saying, "Oh, I see!" and went away still tugging his whiskers, and muttering, "only a colored bookkeeper."

Stanley was sorry the truth was out for Saunders' sake, but he noticed that during the rest of the ball, very much to his gratification, that only a few seemed to shun his society.

On their way home that night, Stanley told Saunders of the speculations that had been going the rounds concerning him and his greatness, and they had a good hearty laugh over it.

"I was a king then for a part of the evening, if only a merchant king. I thought that Squire Andrews' face fell when I told him I was not a member of the legislature, never had been appointed to an honorary position, was not a lawyer, or a merchant, but was only a bookkeeper in your father's store." He laughed heartily.

"Then you gave it away yourself."

"I wasn't then aware of the joke. Yes, the old Squire had been entertaining me with reminiscences."

"He was bound to let me know he had found out the truth. Poor fellow he almost pulled his crop of whiskers out. That face of his was a study. Ha! ha! ha!"

CHAPTER V.

_____

Only three more days left of their vacation which had been spent so pleasantly that Stanley was thinking of having it extended. He did not care to return so soon to Detroit because of the almost irresistible desire that he had to see Marjorie Stone again, when his mind reverted to her, which was frequent. His attachment to Saunders grew each day and his admiration for his qualities of mind and heart was increased accordingly, while Saunders, in many quiet ways, showed the devotion he felt toward him.

Their reading and talks about different books and topics was one of their indispensable routines of the day and the interest they awakened in him brought Saunders into high favor with Stanley.

The afternoon of the day following the party over at Jones' they had swung their hammocks amongst a clump of trees to the west of the lake for a few hours' reading and sleeping. They had not as yet touched the magazines they had brought.

Stanley picked up the _Forum_ and went through the index. He noticed an article entitled the "Negro Problem" by Senator Eustis, of Louisiana. "Here is something that will interest John," he thought, as he turned to it. Before calling his attention to it he started to read it, but before he had gone far he thought he would read aloud.[67]

"Here is an article by Senator Eustis on the Negro problem, in the _Forum_, John. It may interest you. Let me read you a part of it."

"All right," said John, "fire away," and he assumed a listening attitude. Stanley proceeded and as he got into the article his surprise at the picture presented therein of the incapacity and shiftlessness of the Southern Negro grew as he turned each page. Finally, in disgust, he handed the magazine to Saunders to finish the article. When Saunders concluded it Stanley remarked, "I would not have believed that such a state of things existed in the South. The colored people down there must be different from what they are up here."

"There is but little difference except as to numbers," replied Saunders, "and for that reason it appears the more noticeable. There are Afro-Americans there who are as progressive and intelligent as you will find in the world, and there are those who, if they had the opportunity, would command the attention of civilization. As it is, despite prejudice, deep-dyed and monstrous in the South, and despite the lack of interest in the North, we have men, who have forced themselves above their fellows and became prominent citizens."

"Of course I would expect you to stand by your race, right or wrong, that is pardonable, but Senator Eustis ought to be conversant with the facts. Beside, you should not accuse the North of apathy when they have poured millions of dollars into the South for the education of your people."

"You mistake me. I give all honor to the men who have made noble sacrifices of both time and money in the interests of humanity and education. But of what benefit is education without opportunity. Idle hands are quick to commit the sins that idle minds devise. In Detroit there are about two stores outside of yours that give us employment, and Detroit is a sample of the Northwest in many respects. The men of business say they wish us well, tell us to save our money, but had we the capacity of an Edison in inventing, of a Stewart in planning, coupled with the integrity of a Regulus and the devotion of a Pythias, they would not open to us the opportunities accorded to other youths.[68] I have myself went to men, who pose as professed friends, to solicit work for myself and friends, and have invariably been met with, 'Well, we don't need any one just now. If I do I will let you know.' I have never been informed when they needed help, though I left my address and they have been discharging and hiring all the time."

"You put me in mind of Monte Christo, one of Dumas' characters, when he came home rich to revenge himself upon his enemies.[69] As he dispatched them he numbered them. Your grievance suggests the reference. You are shut out from society and from business; what will be next?"

"I can't say, but I have not lost hope. I believe in time other business men will follow your father's examples. Reports from elsewhere are encouraging. As to society, that does not bother me, we have it among ourselves, as pure and intelligent as it can be found anywhere. But you do not know much about the condition of things in the South, do you?"

"I will confess my ignorance on the subject."

"I thought that you did not from your comments on Senator Eustis' article. His statements are false in many particulars and are most undoubtedly made for the purpose of influencing Northern opinion. I can tell you something of his own state. In the City of New Orleans, the Afro-Americans pay taxes on fifteen millions of dollars and throughout the state on thirty millions of dollars. One of the largest dry goods houses in their metropolis is owned by an Afro-American. T. T. Allain, whose color would prevent him from being mistaken for white, is one of the state's most prominent contractors and sugar planters. Everybody knows of Pinchback.[70] These men are only instances. There are many others I might recall to mind who are by no means considered shiftless or lacking in capacity. In the matter of education, the *Times-Democrat* of New Orleans is authority for the statement that the school accommodations are inadequate, and that in the remote parishes schools are not open two months in a year. Do you know where that State gets its school fund?"

"I suppose from the general tax on property, real and personal."

"Not by any means. You have heard of the Louisiana State Lottery, have you not?"

"Well, I should say that I have."

"That institution furnishes the State with by far the largest part of the school fund, for legalizing it."

"A gambling institution the patron of education. Well, that's rich."

"Well, do you wonder now that there are so many lazy and shiftless people there. To judge from Senator Eustis it is only the Afro-American who is lazy, but investigation will find the ratio between black and white about equal. If it were not so Senator Eustis does not come from a State that would entitle him to be an authority about anything except intimidation and lawlessness, for which that State has become a synonym."

"You seem to be quite an encyclopedia of facts."

Saunders smiled, assumed a more comfortable position in his hammock and continued. "There are so many misstatements made about us that we have to go around armed with facts to contradict them. I have spoken of the tax paid in the State of Louisiana on property, the race pays throughout the South a tax on $200,000,000 in realty. Rather a good record is it not for a race that has hardly had twenty-five years of freedom?"

"It certainly is not a bad showing."

"It would be more were it not for the systems extant throughout the South, of which the reading world is familiar. Systems aimed expressly at keeping Afro-Americans dependent, and from acquiring property, of which the principal ones are the false land contracts and the present store order system. In Louisiana there is a law purported to be aimed at vagabonds and tramps, but directed chiefly at the Afro-American, which is operated quite extensively in some of the parishes of that State. Under this law all persons who live by their labor, whose services are not contracted for by January 1st, for the coming season, are termed vagabonds and their services sold to the highest bidder, for the benefit of the State."

"That is monstrous."

"Monstrous!" exclaimed Saunders with curling lip and flashing eyes. "It is practical slavery. The wrongs of which the Afro-Americans complain are enough to set on fire the blood of age, and make the blood of youth leap in torrents to avenge them. But we are like the Jews, in that 'patience is the badge of all our tribes,' and we hope for peaceful settlements despite the fact that the American world seems to be against us.[71] Some justify these practices, some pity us, and some condemn them, while the majority look on with listless indifference at the crimes against that race which produced the first martyr to American liberty."

Stanley watched him closely and noted the flashing eyes, the dilated nostrils, and the firmly curved sensitive lip that twitched nervously. He would have turned the subject but he was interested and inquired. "Can they not band together to protect themselves?"

"Your question is one that has often been asked. So vigilant are the violators of the law that anything that looks suspicious on the part of the blacks is heralded by the whites at once as a 'Negro Uprising.' Then some dark night a leader among the people disappears. The next day his body is found hanging to a tree. No one knows who committed the cowardly deed. No attempt is made to find the murderers. The law is silent, the criminals are unpunished, the end sought for gained, and the blacks are cowed by these secret assassinations. In South Carolina recently a white man named Hoover was forced to flee for his life for inciting, so the dispatch read, 'the Negroes to riot,' while the truth of the whole matter was that he was engaged in establishing Knights of Labor assemblies among them. The outrage was caused by the fear that these assemblies would breed discontent. There was a strike on the sugar plantations of Louisiana last fall. Some of the strikers were Knights of Labor, and among them were a considerable number of Afro-Americans. Governor McEnery sent troops to that point and as a result there was a useless and uncalled for sacrifice of lives.[72] It was the usual Louisiana method of intimidating the blacks before an election. There are cases where some determined men have banded themselves together for mutual protection, and conquered a peace in their localities, but these cases are isolated. A great drawback against the organization of any kind, whether to check outrages, or to better their industrial condition, is this fact, which was stated by an Afro-American journal of Jacksonville, Fla., that 65 per cent of the race are incapable at the present of such action. You see it is too much to expect a whole race to throw off at once all the influences of two centuries of degradation and a thousand years of superstitions. It seems to be even impossible in the North for the masses of the whites, with their years of freedom and opportunity, to successfully band together to resist the encroachment of capital."

Stanley laughed at this sally.

"Another serious impediment is that any attempt at resistance would bring down upon them the military of the State, they would be hunted down, as is often the case, and shot like dogs. The military is in sympathy with public sentiment, and that is down on the race as competitors only, not as meek laborers. The Federal Government is powerless to protect the rights of the citizens of the Republic. That power devolves upon the State, and they who execute the laws are hostile. But there is a brighter shade to the picture; a great educational work is going on. Schools are increasing. The per cent of illiteracy is decreasing, and habits of thrift are being cultivated. These agencies must in time check the evils complained of and win for us that respect which is now denied."

While Saunders was talking Stanley had been thinking and revolving the subject in his mind, and the resolution was half formed to go South and see for himself. When Saunders had finished he said, "While we have been talking I have half made up my mind to go South, as I have never been there, and see if these things are true, and to judge for myself."

"Then let me give you a word of warning. Don't let them show you the bad side of our case without pointing out to you those who are striving for success. Don't look around among the slums then visit saloons and form a judgment until you have visited our schools and colleges that dot the Southland. When they show you a lazy, shiftless and ignorant man, inquire for an intelligent progressive one. They can be found since the race represents so much wealth."

"You need not fear for that for you will go with me."

"I shall be glad to if you do not put off the trip until too late in the fall. I want to be home about two or three weeks before Christmas."

"What's going to happen then?"

"Only a little private event of mine."

"Something that can't be told."

"No. Something that isn't to be told."

"A love affair! I'll bet a nickel."

"That is the usual charge where a mystery is involved."

"Were you ever in love, John? Tell the truth now and shame the devil."

"I might return your exorcism and ask you the same question."

"You know it, you scamp, and have ever since you posted those letters for me last summer."

"I did suspect it then, but my suspicions were confined to my thoughts. I noticed that you commenced to get better the day she came and all that. I compliment you on your taste and judgment."

Thoughts of Marjorie at once made Stanley serious. He lay back in his hammock a moment before he spoke, and then said with some bitterness: "Yes I have loved and I love her with all my heart. There are many who have sued with less ardor, whose hearts have not been stirred with the deep emotions that have moved mine, who have won without a sacrifice."

"Waiting has its own reward," said John soothingly.

"Each particular case has its own history, John. There are points in mine that keep doubts hanging close upon my hopes. Distrusted and loved. The thought of it has placed my soul and my love in a crucible heated with the flames of doubt, unstability and excesses. So far I have stood the test."

"And will continue to," said Saunders. This sudden burst of passion showed him the mental strain under which Stanley labored at times, and furnished him with the key to his melancholy.

After a few moments' silence Stanley told him of his courtship and probation. "Now that I have unbosomed myself to you as I have not done to one of my dearest white friends, I want you to confide in me. There may be a vein of fellow-experience in which I may give some consolation. I feel relieved since my confession, and I know that I have your sincere sympathy."

"There is no reason why I should withhold anything from you, since you have made such a confidant of me. I am to be married at Christmas."

"I envy you. What is her name?"

"Edith Darrow. We have known each other a long time and she possesses those qualities I like in women. They won my love at any rate. The attachment was reciprocated and the day is set. I have bought a lot in the northeastern part of the city on —— Street. I have plans already drawn for our house and have let the contract. It will be well under way when I return. The reason why I said I desired to return from the South two or three weeks before Christmas is to have everything arranged and ready to receive her."

"I thought so the minute you spoke. Is she pretty?"

"I think so, others might not," answered Saunders modestly. "Her complexion is fair and she has dark hair and eyes. If she had been born in a white family she would have passed for a brunette. Do you know that there are a number of octoroons passing for white all over this country? They have left their former homes and lost their past identity. At once they realized a liberty unknown before, and like the Hessian, who considered discretion the better part of valor, they have deserted from the race in which they are classed, because they thought it better to do so than to wage such an uneven fight as the Afro-American must, no matter what his color. Edith is rather slight in form, but with no inherent delicacy, for her family are all robust and healthy."

"Is she as good and as intelligent as you are? Of course she must be, or you wouldn't have lost your head."

"When I tell you that she is as refined and intelligent as anyone you ever met and more accomplished than the majority, you may think that my love has overdrawn the picture."

"I must see her if I have to go with you to call upon her."

"And I shall be happy to take you, for I know that she will be pleased to meet one who has been so kind a friend to me."

Their talk was interrupted by one of Mr. Tobin's boys coming to summon them to dinner. Frequent reference was made after this to the proposed trip South and to Saunders' future prospects in regard to which Stanley resolved to brighten.

Two days later they packed up and returned to Detroit.

CHAPTER VI.

Before we resume the thread of our story we will digress a little to look into John Saunders' surroundings. In so doing we dig into a field of which the average American reader knows less about than he does of Russian life—its incidents, pleasures and perils. This field is rich in romance, and in the story of the lives of many are incidents, perils, obstacles, despair and triumphs, success and failures, joys, sorrows and pathos, that might command the pens of the most gifted minds to depict in glowing colors.

John Saunders' parents were born slaves, who, fleeing from that "relic of barbarism," had taken refuge in the State of Illinois, where they resided until compelled to flee because of the odious black laws, when they came to Michigan and settled in Detroit where John was born.[73] Realizing what they lacked from the need of education they used every effort to have their children educated. They possessed that thirst for education which has made their race's progress one of the wonders of the age. That progress illustrates this universal rule: If a man is deprived of a common right or a common opportunity his desires increase with his realization of the difference between himself and other men. Deprivation breeds discontent. If the man is ambitious discontent spurs him on to be the equal of his neighbor.

Next to the promises contained in Holy writ, education was the hope of the Afro-American. The desire had descended as a fixed feature in the character of succeeding generations, and the burst of liberty, opening up new opportunities that hitherto had seemed but a dream, met with an unprecedented response by both parent and child.

During the earlier years of their children they were sent to the "colored" school and later to the public schools, when they were subsequently opened to receive Afro-American children. John graduated from the Detroit High School, went to college at Ann Arbor where he took up civil engineering and graduated with honor. It was during his high school days that he first met Seth Stanley, who was attracted to him by reason of his close application to study, and his serious

Appointed

and sad demeanor which was in such striking contrast to his own easy-going manner. After his graduation he wandered from place to place seeking employment, but his color was against him, and all his efforts to attain a position in keeping with his abilities were failures. He was at last forced, much against his wishes, to turn waiter in a hotel because of his limited means. This compulsion made him feel rather bitter against the world, and he began to doubt if he was any better off for the time, money and labor spent in getting an education. He was engaged at this work when he met Seth Stanley on the street one day, who stopped him and inquired about his affairs. Stanley was disgusted when John told him what he was doing, and declared that it was shameful that a man of his ability should be compelled to do such work. He promised to speak to his father in John's behalf, and was successful enough to obtain for him the position of assistant bookkeeper in his father's store.

The self-sacrifices of Saunders' parents to educate their children can never be known or appreciated except by those who have passed through similar experiences. Both toiled from morn till night to provide for their family, and after the children had gone to bed, clothes were mended, and the housework, which circumstances prevented being done during the day, was done. Poets have sung in verse, and historians have recounted for generations, the heroic deeds of devotion of the mothers of Sparta.[74] The early struggles of the pioneers in our own country have been made the subject of eulogy, but they did not exceed in self-denial or loftier purpose the devotion of the thousands of Afro-American mothers who have suffered and endured so much to educate their children, and to give them opportunities far beyond any they ever had. The horrors of war have not been pictured too vividly; but they pale before the horrors of slavery, and its influence. The blighting effect of the desolation it spread upon a whole race, still exists in our Republic. When of an evening the parents would gather the children about them around their humble fireside, and they would recount the tales of cruelties and indignities through which they had once passed and had been subjected to without redress, John's eyes would blaze with indignation and wrath, and his whole being would become agitated. Sometimes, with clinched fists, he breathed inward threats as he listened.

One day the Destroyer—Death—came into their household, and took from it its chief pillar. Over-exertion and exposure had proved too much for the mother. She took a heavy cold, and pneumonia set in. The doctor was called in but he could give no hope, "for her system was too weak." The hour came when she felt that death was near, and the family was gathered around her bedside, bowed down with grief, to receive the parting injunctions and benedictions of

141

the wife and mother they loved so well. To each she gave a charge before her eyes closed in that last sleep. To John her admonition was to complete his education and be what she had desired him to be. He was then attending the High School.

There was more than a vacant chair when her form was taken to its last resting place, for she was their advisor and counselor. She buoyed up their hopes when their trials were most severe or when they were smarting under the wounds caused by some of their schoolmates. When even hope seemed to have ebbed away she instilled into them new ardor and courage. This event was what caused that sadness that had attracted Stanley. The real struggle to carry out his mother's wishes now came to John. His father's earnings were not more than enough to take care of the smaller members of the family, and he had to work out his destiny alone. During vacations he did whatever he could find to do, waiting at tables in hotels or on steamboats, or doing an odd job here and there. During the terms he attended to furnaces, cleaned sidewalks and waited on private families for his board. It was a hard struggle but nerve and pluck won. The one lesson to be learned by the millions, which Saunders learned, who yearly read of Napoleon's determined will, that carried him and his victorious army across the Alps, is the firm determination that brooks no obstacles. Thousands before and since, unknown to fame, have lived and died, and a lonely tombstone in a country churchyard is the sole monument that they have ever lived, who have possessed the will of a Napoleon but not the opportunity. They have struggled at the bottom but could not rise, yet they in their sphere have triumphed. None of us are what we would be, but we can all be the best of what we are.

In all of Saunders' hardships there was one person who watched his progress eagerly, and was very much interested in his welfare. This was Edith Darrow, who afterwards became his betrothed. From the first she had manifested a kindly interest in him, for which he was thankful, and he set her interest and little kindnesses down in his heart to her account. He was restrained then from giving his feelings wider range because of his poverty. In time his position became a more lucrative one, and he became able to save a little and aid his father. His brothers and sisters, all but one, became self-sustaining, and it did not require so much from each to keep the household intact, and to support that one. Finding that his financial prospects would warrant it, he indulged more in society and naturally enough, turned to Edith Darrow, for whom he already cherished an affection. Shortly before Stanley's accident, and subsequent illness, he offered himself, was accepted and the appointed time set for Christmas.

Edith Darrow was a fine appearing woman, and most people would have called her beautiful. Her face was round and intellectual, her form was graceful and trim. These charms, added to laughing dark eyes, made her a mark at which many an aspirant had aimed his cupid darts hitherto, but without success.

The Darrows were one of the most prominent Afro-American families in Detroit, and each individual member of the family was energetic and unusually successful in whatever he undertook. Her father was a mason and contractor and had, by dint of economy and thrift, amassed considerable property and surrounded his family with many luxuries. An instance in his business life is worthy of mention, since it illustrates the feelings which exists in the minds of many, who do not like to see any of this race advance beyond the condition of dependent workmen. One evening a gentlemen called at his house to have him figure on a contract. He was asked into their parlor where Edith sat playing a piano. The furnishing was neat, tasty, even rich. Mr. Darrow came in, the plans were submitted, but though he was the lowest bidder, the builder refused him the contract because he said, "you do not need the work; your family lives as well as mine." Notwithstanding many such rebuffs he was a fairly successful businessman.

The relation between Stanley and Saunders had become so intimate since their vacation in the country, that Saunders really wished to have him meet his betrothed, and only wanted an excuse to make them acquainted. Stanley had also expressed a desire to see her. He had often said to him, "I know she must be a desirable girl or you would not love her. I almost envy you your bright prospects."

Saunders knew that his desire was animated only by a genuine interest for himself, but he feared that a visit from his employer might be construed by her as a matter of curiosity despite what he had said about him. The opportunity came in an unexpected way in the early part of September, about a month before they had decided to start on their Southern trip. A company of Fisk Jubilee singers came to the city, some of whom were quite distinguished, and had sung before many of the crowned heads of Europe.[75] A few of them were known personally by Edith, and as, during their engagement, they had one evening off, she had them to a tea, and invited a few friends to meet them. Saunders begged leave to invite Stanley, as he had heard them sing and had expressed a wish to meet them and compare voices; and as the reader knows he was no mere novice. Edith assented, and Saunders and Stanley came together. When Stanley was introduced he made himself just as affable and entertaining as he would have done in his own circles. At tea he was completely nonplussed at the readiness and range of the conversation. Here were a people, whom he believed incapable of such refined development and ready wit, exhibiting every quality of mind and deportment that he had considered excellent. He had looked upon Saunders as something far above the ordinary, even a prodigy, but here was a whole nest of them in which Saunders did not shine more brilliantly than the rest. He was forced to think how different from those of the same race he had usually come in contact with. During the evening the members of the troupe sang a number of solos and jubilee songs, and Stanley sang once. Altogether, he spent a very pleasant evening, for in conversation with some of the company he compared notes on countries, scenes, and costumes abroad, and thoroughly enjoyed himself. With Edith Darrow he was very favorably impressed. In his judgment, he thought that Saunders had made an excellent choice and told him so.

CHAPTER VII.

Stanley's intimacy with the "colored bookkeeper" had been made the subject of remark. This fact in itself would not have drawn out so much criticism had it not been for the fact that the haunts of society knew him no more, and that he for the time forsook his former friends for that rest and peace of mind which he seemed to obtain in Saunders' company. When it became known that he had attended a reception among these people, and had mingled with them with all his old time vivacity, gossip had a theme worthy of its ability. Stanley's idiosyncrasies came in for a general lashing. Some said he had developed Negrophobia, and some that he was trying to wean himself away from Marjorie Stone, and had chosen this peculiar way to do it.[76] These people reminded others of their prophecy that he would soon tire of her, for said they, "since his recovery he has neither visited her nor been seen in her company." There were some who said he was "going to the dogs," but few were charitable enough to view his position in a favorable light. That the bookkeeper had qualities of manhood that could command a man's admiration suggested itself to but few, or that his presence at the reception may have been for the purpose of finding out whether the general opinion of these people was true or false, society did not dream of. Why should it? Had not society placed a ban upon them. Society is a kingdom. It has its kings, princes, dukes, marquises, earls, lords, savants, and all the paraphernalia of a court which it rigorously obeys, and which sways it at will. This court has deemed them incapable of advancement in its wisdom, and unfit as associates. Its savants are learned and have declared them but a degree above the apes. The judgments of the court are inflexible and society is contented, for are not these judgments entrenched in deepest wisdom and learning? What need has it for personal contact to prove their truths? "Let them not enter into our sacred precincts lest we breathe contamination," is the decree to which society holds rigidly. It departs not from its laws and customs until, perchance, it goes to some foreign country, and there, remarkable to relate, the further it gets away from home the less rigid it becomes, until in the effete capitols of the Old World it meets on equal grounds those whom it scorned while at home, for there it is with difficulty that it holds its own. Bow down and pay homage, oh ye people, to the wisdom of American society—to that wisdom which enables it to discriminate so easily between the customs at home and abroad, and which accepts the dicta of the Old World as easily as it accepts the decree of its own courts in the new.

It is not conscience alone that makes "cowards of us all," but opinions also. We cannot, or will not, withstand its current whims. Conscience and conviction alike go down before it, and one soon becomes the victim of the popular notion. Many of Stanley's acquaintances who knew John Saunders, knew him to be an extraordinary man in many parts. They also recognized the reasons for Stanley's interest and acknowledged it in private, yet they either railed at it or maintained a discreet silence in public. Stanley's latest imprudence came to the Stones through the medium of Mrs. Brooks, who had hitherto received but little encouragement from them for the pains she was taking in bringing and carrying news. She had been treated so coolly that she felt slighted and indignant, and although formerly she had been a constant visitor, she had not called there for over a month. She had viewed this escapade of Stanley's with horror and amazement. Now she had a sensation in store, and thinking that they might view it in her light, expected to derive some revenge. She knew that Marjorie loved Stanley, for she had read it in her eyes, but she had been unable to decide upon any one of the reasons set forth by rumor as to the rightful cause of their estrangement. Now that Stanley had been consorting with "Negroes," she would crush her heart at one blow and so be revenged for her own injured feelings. In her conceit she exulted.

Having viewed this society bird of prey let us return to the victim. Marjorie had not been carrying a light heart all this time by any means. Her lot was made pleasanter, however, by the memory of that visit to Stanley when he was sick, but too often her thoughts would worry her. She was, however, learning to view their relations more philosophically, and each day convinced her more assuredly that Stanley's course was honorable. She also realized that they must remain apart if they abided by her decision until they could meet as lovers.

When Mrs. Brooks came in both Marjorie and her mother apprehended mischief, albeit her face was wreathed in smiles and she manifested that same easy air that characterized her at all times, as she took a chair by the open window to enjoy the cool autumnal breezes. Danger lurks behind the smiles of some persons, who, like the serpents, charm before they strike.

Detailing at first a few choice tid-bits of gossip and descanting on the excellent weather they had been having, she plunged at once into her mission by saying to Marjorie.

"My dear, you do not look well lately. What can be the matter with you?"

"My looks then belie my feelings," answered Marjorie, "for I have not been ill."

"I am glad to hear it. But your appearance is too listless, you should mix more in society. Have you heard the latest sensation?"

"Probably not the particular one you have reference to."

"Why, my dear, it is the talk of the town!"

"Then it must be something serious," said Mrs. Stone.

"It is, indeed. Seth Stanley has neglected his white associates altogether and associates with colored people. He seems to have fallen in love with that bookkeeper of his, and the other evening he attended a reception given in honor of the Jubilee singers that were here last week. What do you think of that?" she asked triumphantly, laying emphasis on each word and directing a meaning look at Marjorie.

"I don't see why that should cause such a social flurry, I am sure," said Marjorie.

"You think it is right then for a young man to mix up with colored people?"

"I think a man has a right to do as he pleases so long as he acts honorably and keeps honorable company. I am acquainted with Mr. Saunders, the bookkeeper you refer to, and I consider him in every respect a gentleman and I don't believe Mr. Stanley will be contaminated by his company. You need not fear for him in that direction."

"What is the world coming to," exclaimed Mrs. Brooks, throwing up both hands in protest, "when a young lady will stand up and defend such things?"

She was disappointed that Marjorie did not take the matter seriously, and her revenge was rudely robbed of all its sweetness. Marjorie was no less than a heroine in giving expression to sentiments that she knew when uttered would be repeated to her disparagement. She now turned Mrs. Brooks' disappointment into consternation by saying:

"I heard that troupe sing, and had I been invited I should have attended the reception given them myself. I remember when I was a little girl, when prejudice against colored people was much stronger than it is now, that the Hon. Frederick Douglass was an honored guest at my uncle Durham's table."

"That is different," gasped Mrs. Brooks, "There is a difference between receiving the great and consorting with the herd."

"The difference is only in degree," said Marjorie, calmly.

Thoroughly put to rout and robbed of her revenge, Mrs. Brooks, disgusted at the unexpected turn of the conversation, had but little else to say before she shook the dust from off her feet and departed from that house. When she had gone Marjorie turned to her mother and said, "Mother, have I not told you that Mrs. Brooks was an evil minded woman?"

"Don't be too hard on her, Marjorie. She usually means well. Don't you think you were a little harsh with her?"

"Not when I consider that what she said, she said in order to wound my feelings."

They were silent a while, then Marjorie said: "I saw Imogene yesterday and she told me that Seth was going South with John Saunders this fall. I hope that they will not meet with any mishaps."

"I am glad of it," replied Mrs. Stone. "Seth's name will then get a rest, but I think your apprehensions are groundless about mishaps. Mishaps, pshaw! From whence?" This was said by her to scout any forebodings of Marjorie as she left the room.

Mishaps! Our Southern country is full of them. Mishaps that have cut short the careers of many brilliant, gifted men; that places a stain upon that part of our country which was intended by nature to be its fairest gem. Mishaps engendered by intolerance that causes a ruthless disregard of life and law. That same intolerance which is the bane of civilization, the cause of strife and war's gloomy horrors, of persecutions and of murder, the twin brother of barbarity, and the consort of envy and jealousy. Intolerance that permits no opinion to clash with its own. Well may Marjorie Stone fear mishaps, for having read a great deal, she knew that a man of Seth Stanley's impulsive temperament, having with him a young man whose race was proscribed, would be apt to meet with difficulties if he attempted to carry out Northern opinions.

If she only knew, but how many heart aches would have been spared, how much less of pain there would be, how much evil averted, how much good been done, how different would have been the policies of governments, of nations, of individuals, if they had only known. Empires that have moulded away and have been forgotten would still have a place on the map of history, and the face of the world how different. Napoleon, instead of the Iron Duke, would have conquered at Waterloo.[77] The South might still have possessed its slaves, or received for them recompense. In social life many ill-fated and ill-assorted matches would have been averted, and more real happiness and peace would exist. If we only knew—it might have been. Fit companions of speculative philosophy. Alas for the frailties of human joys. We seldom know all we might, because of the persistent stunting of desirable faculties. In a conflict between reason and passion, reason too often goes to the wall. In the struggle between conscience and the desire to be popular, conscience often succumbs too easily.

CHAPTER VIII.

Mr. Stanley was at first opposed to his son's proposed trip South, for several reasons. The most important was, that it would occur during the busy season, and deprive him of the services of both his son and John Saunders, when most needed. His business reasons were soon overcome when the question of his son's health was in the balance, for he noted the fact that Seth did not yet appear strong, and he feared that the germs of his recent illness still lurked in his body. When he consented to let his son go, he still thought it was folly for Saunders to leave his work at this time, but Seth was determined that if he went Saunders should go with him, and finally Mr. Stanley reluctantly consented. In this he was influenced, too, by the consideration of his son's health, for he reasoned with himself, "if Seth should be taken sick John is just the fellow to be with him." He had also made recent business investments at Birmingham, Ala., which he thought he should like to have looked into, and he made his son promise to give them attention while in that section.

Time sped rapidly with both the young men, and the day for their departure, which was set for an early date in October, was at hand, and Saunders went to bid his betrothed good-bye. He had first broken the news of their trip South to Edith shortly after the return from Sand Lake, when the lovers were enjoying themselves rowing through the canals at Belle Isle Park. The announcement made her sad and marred the hitherto unbroken pleasure of their evening's outing. She opposed it by many arguments. "The uncertain state of political affairs owing to the approaching elections, and the danger that beset a young Afro-American of spirit unaccustomed to the spiteful discriminations practiced in all public places." He combated her arguments, by stating that going as he was, with a man of wealth and standing, he would be hardly subjected to the indignities common to Afro-American travelers, when alone. "Besides, it will give me an excellent opportunity to see the country and I also consider it my duty to go. One of the objects of Mr. Stanley's visit is to determine for himself questions that have arisen in little arguments we have had. I want to see that he has a favorable opportunity of seeing the South as I have represented it, and not as the Southerners he may meet with, will show it to him. What is the risk I run compared with that of obtaining a probably earnest and capable friend of our cause?"

"I agree with you that far, John. We need more men among us willing to make sacrifices. I suppose many lives must be given unselfishly to the intolerance of Southern thought, but I am too selfish to allow you to offer yourself among the first. It would destroy my brightest anticipations of the future."

"Which cannot be brighter than mine, or looked forward to with greater pleasure. I have conjured up the prospects that our engagement brings to me, since I was a school boy. It has been the dream of my youth, and has nerved me in hours of severe despondency and trial. Now that the dreams of these years are about to be realized, you can imagine with what joy I look forward to them. You say that there must be martyrs. You are right. Every great cause has its martyrs, from whose blood there wells up an incense, that permeating all things, strengthens its cause and finally secures its accomplishment. In this cause of the New Crusade for the realization of liberty who ever may be its martyrs, there will be found ties broken. No one with courage and devotion enough to give his life for his race, comes of a scion of a meaner order of beings."

"But suppose you should be murdered before you had accomplished anything," almost sobbed Edith.

"You forget," replied Saunders, "that there is a destiny that shapes our ends. We do the best we can and leave the rest to the inexorable ordaining of things, from which there is no appeal. Sometimes we think our road rough and unpurposable, but on looking back, we see in all the zig-zag way a common trend to an end, probably the outlines of which have not yet been revealed to us."

"You believe then that we are ever standing with what we have been behind us and what we may be before us, and whatever changes may transpire, this relation remains. It may be so and yet I cannot tell why these gloomy forebodings recur to me, probably they are the result of a disordered mind."

Saunders scoffed at her fears and in time succeeded in allaying them to the extent of seeing the smiles again chase each other over her countenance. He was careful not to return to the subject again. He had a pleasing voice, not very strong, but remarkable for its taste and the execution with which he sang. This evening as there were but few others out rowing he sang for her a baccarol, oft sang by Venetian gondoliers, called "Hearest Thou."[78] He intended by the song to show Edith, that his dangers and those of the boatman, were somewhat analogous, and that he reposed the same trust in God that the boatman did in the Holy Mother.

Human troubles are short when those, who have so won the temper of our natures, as to become sweet consolers, are nigh, and almost before we are aware of it our troubles steal away, and the glistening tears give way to looks of happiness and content. It was so now with Edith, for in his presence, she lost sight of the imaginary evils she had called up in the anticipations she pictured of his return and the consummation of their perfect union.

It is true in life that we enjoy ourselves more in the anticipation than in the realization of things. Castle building, based on some slight fruition of hopes always in the future, gives fortitude to the spirit. Hope is the staff of our soul, and in our hours of distress we lean heavily upon it. The sentiment, beautiful in thought and idea, is at variance with experience. In fact sentiments are derived from the romances of life, yet alone they lift one above himself and make him oblivious of his surroundings.

After parting from Saunders, and when in the solitude of her own chamber, all Edith's fears returned, doubly charged with apprehensions, and seemed to strike a chill to her heart. For a while she was almost dazed, and finally she knelt and committed herself to the same God in whom Marjorie Stone had found consolation.

There is a strange continuity of aspiration and dependence that pervades all human existence. Is it not the result of like feelings innate and acquired?

From that time Edith kept her doubts and fears to herself, telling them to none, but she could not hide the sadness of her looks when anyone alluded to his going. Saunders often noticed it and wished his trip over. When he saw the eloquent pleadings of her eyes he hesitated at times between his love and what he thought was his duty.

Silent, however, as she had been, she endeavored to dissuade him, on his last visit, from going at this particular time as the presidential campaign had opened, the minds of the people were naturally excited, that prejudice ran high, and outrageous deeds were being committed. Saunders admitted that the time was not the best, but such an opportunity might not again present itself soon, and he promised to avoid, as much as possible, any excitement.

"But, John, I feel as if something may happen to you."

"It is only nervousness, Edith."

"Have you read, John, that most of the colored men from the South who took part in the National Convention at Chicago this year, have on various pretexts been driven from home, and that political outrages are becoming frequent," and she pointed to Wahalak, Mississippi; New Iberia, Louisiana; Barnwell, South Carolina, and other places.[79]

"Yes, and when I think of it my blood boils with indignation, and I feel myself wondering when is this to end."

"Oh, John, if anything should happen to you what would I do?"

"Always remember that I was actuated by duty. It will be a pleasant thought. But, come, let us not borrow trouble, Edith, and let us try to spend this last evening as pleasantly as possible."

Like all engaged lovers that aspire to be all in all to each other, their conversation drifted to the time when their aims and aspirations would be more perfectly united. With light hearts and with a sort of rapture they conversed of the new house being built, of the furnishings of the rooms and how much they would enjoy them. There is nothing as sweet as love's young dream save, perhaps, the wedded bliss derived from perfect union. Alas! That their dreams should be so rudely broken.

It was very hard, nevertheless, for Edith at parting, for as he kissed her good-bye she could hardly restrain a sob, and her eyes pleaded so eloquently that with choked voice he said, "Don't look so, Edith, dear, I will not be long," and he hurried away lest his love and inclination overcome him. When he had gone Edith felt as if something had gone out of her life.

The days sped very slowly to her after his departure, and her life was one of continued anxiety for his safety. With it all, however, she kept up a brave front and the sweetness of her nature still diffused itself about her. Her disposition was naturally a cheerful one; she was accustomed to look at the sunny side of life and to enjoy the beautiful things of the world, the products of nature and of man. Sorrow, grief or care, save as it came through color prejudices directed at the Afro-American, was almost a stranger to her, yet these prejudices, met as they had been in school and since, had greatly aided in developing in her the spirit of self-reliance. This faculty, combined with the sweetness and purity of her nature enabled her to accomplish much good in the various works she undertook among the poorer and less educated of her race. She was very thorough in her work, and to a remarkable degree, succeeded in impregnating those she came in contact with by her own virtues. Persons of character like her have a strong influence in the world which surrounds them. They are the conscience or monitor to whom others look for approbation or dissent. From them there seems to be an invisible stream of strength and purity, which, infusing itself into others, makes the weak strong, the surly sweet tempered, and the vicious pure. Since her graduation from the High School she had taught a few years in Mississippi and with much success. To the boys, who would come sometimes smarting under jibes, she would say: "Though you come from a race that is despised, and people look upon you with scorn and contempt, you have greater incentives to aspire and be something than the whites who would oppress you. The greater credit will be yours for equal heights attained, since obstacles placed by race prejudice are against you. You can be the true pioneers in American freedom, and help to achieve it for every citizen for which this government was founded, and earn the lasting gratitude of a people. Is not such honor worthy to aspire to? Be brave, self-reliant, hold your heads high as becomes those in whose hands, together with others, is the future destiny of the Republic." Under her influence they became manly little fellows, full of generous emulation and anxious to do such things as would find favor with Miss Darrow.

To her girls, she was the ideal which they copied when particularly despondent over their lessons or over some slur or remark passed by some ruffian of the dominant race, of which there are plenty in the South who think it is a fine thing to rob these girls of their virtue, she would encourage them by comforting words to persevere and to cultivate the virtues which make a crown of womanhood. "Every inducement lies before you. You are among the future women of the country and its future mothers. Your influence over husbands, lovers and sons can be irresistible and far reaching. Your virtues, your refinements and your culture will rebuke the wicked slanders circulated by our enemies to our detriment." Such a character as hers could not help but be endearing to a community, and in this small town of J—— she was almost idolized. Such teachers as she do more than go through the routine of assigning and hearing lessons, regardless of the fruit born. She did not teach for her salary alone; her whole nature was in the work of uplifting and refining. What a change and what a blessing it would be to the fair South if in every city, town and village, there were teachers like her. When it was known that she was not to return again the expressions of regret were heartfelt and sincere.

Such a woman could not help being an ideal helpmate and that man truly blest who could call such as her, wife. It is no wonder that John Saunders almost idealized her, and that he eagerly looked forward to the day when he could claim her as his bride. She had entered into his life and her influence, in days that were dark and full of trouble, had sustained him and quickened his resolves. They were well mated—well fitted to enjoy that domestic happiness that comes from a perfect union of temperament and souls, and now that that time was so near, pardon the sorrow he felt upon leaving her for even so short a time.

CHAPTER IX.

On the evening of October 2nd, Stanley and Saunders left Detroit for Chicago. On their arrival at Chicago they took the Illinois Central for New Orleans. They passed without incident down through Illinois into Kentucky and near to the old home of Saunders' parents. Being so close to it awakened in his mind a train of tender recollections of his parents, and incidents of their lives of which he was often the enrapt, and at times, indignant listener. There came the memory of the strange weird lore that has its circulation among the slaves; of the careless and easy times that obtained among them, despite their condition; their sources of pleasure and grief, and the tales of brutal conduct of master and overseer. A sigh escaped him, and Stanley noticing it, inquired of him the reason.

"Here is where my parents were born. This is the second time I have been here and I have a feeling, when I put my feet on the soil of their native state, I cannot express. Tenderness and pleasure is mingled with recollections of horror and sorrow. What cruel fate it was that brought us here, what remorseless curse drove us out, the evil effects of which still linger rob us of our citizenship, and from living in peace, in some localities."

"I thought that with your bitterness towards the South you could not muster up a feeling of tenderness for any part of it."

"The soil and climate of the South is adapted to our natures and temperaments. For two centuries the race has tilled its fields, climbed its hills, roamed through its forests, and crossed its brooks and rivers. A great vast country, beautiful to look upon even in its natural aspects, that has yielded abundant harvest to its labor, cannot fail to have in its associations many tender recollections. It is not the Southland that we loathe but the intolerance of a dominant spirit. The bitterness we have would not exist if with every breath we draw in, if with every step we take, we could feel as free as we do in the North. The sweat of our ancestors fed and clothed those who now claim the honor of having made these states. They planned, our race carried out and executed. Here my father spent his best days toiling for another without recompense, and from here he was sold into

Alabama. All his family ties and associations were severed with as little consideration as if he were a brute. The labor that should have brought him store against age and need, was not his to command, and here, I cannot even now travel and be treated as a man in public places."

"You are borrowing needless trouble, John. Don't get into a despondent humor before the occasion requires. Surely time has softened many of the evils of which you complain. But look we can begin to see signs of the South already."

Stanley said this to divert Saunders' mind with more pleasing thoughts. In his heart, he felt truly sorry, and sympathized with him deeply. The signs of the South were, however, visible. The mule and the cabin, and the increasing luxuriance of vegetation proved the truth of his words. They were far across the Ohio and speeding rapidly towards Tennessee. They took great interest in the changing scenes that now became apparent in plantation and cabin life. It was like travelling in a new country, so different appeared the manners, customs and even dialect. That energy and thrift that has marked the North, as shown in the enterprise of cities, and the well laid out and tidy farms, appeared to be lacking here. But the rich foliage of field and forest was a relief to the dust they had left behind in Illinois. There had been a refreshing rain the night before, and nature appeared to perfection. At home the autumnal tints had appeared on tree and plant adding beauty to the natural effect, while here the natural tints were far more beautiful and in livelier form. On went the train through beautiful green vales watered by myriads of little brooks that flowed from the surrounding hills and ridges. Sometimes from an elevation a bird's-eye view over miles of plains revealed many an old plantation with its farm house and row of white washed cabins in the distance, almost the same now as when that relic of barbarism—slavery—existed. At many of the stations, instead of the double truck and white driver they were accustomed to, appeared the Afro-American and his mule ready with courtly air to "commodate you, sah."

They had purchased unlimited tickets and the journey through this section was so arranged as to give them the best opportunity for sight seeing. Time did not wear wearily on their hands, for the novelty of the surroundings, the change of scenery, the cotton plantations and the different types of the people seen from the Pullman car window, relieved the monotony of their long ride. The cotton plantations were of special interest. The picking season which commences in August, was well advanced. The cotton plants were full of bursting bulbs. The laborers were busy with their various duties, and as the train rushed on they saw enough of the work to give them some idea of the manner in which the cotton was picked, seeded and baled for the market.

"Mississippi is the greatest cotton producing State in the South," replied Saunders, in answer to a question from Stanley.

"I notice quite a number of white people in the fields. I had an idea that by far the greater part of the work was performed by the colored people."

"So it is," replied Saunders. "In this State they raise one hundred per cent more of the cotton than white labor, and such value is set on their services that the planters have succeeded in inducing immigrants to come from North Carolina and other Southeastern States by the thousands.[80] Since 1880 white labor is becoming more extensively used, particularly so is this claimed with reference to the State of Texas which is also a great cotton producing State. In 1880 fifty-six per cent of the total crop, according to Southern statistics, was produced by colored labor. In all of the States, except Texas and Arkansas, colored labor produced the most cotton. There are no authoritative statistics on this subject issued." Saunders took out his wallet, and out of it took a clipping from a newspaper, an article from the *Times-Democrat* of September 1st, 1886, "which gives the percentage of production of 1885 as 50.1 per cent, raised by white labor, and 49.9 per cent, by colored labor, a percentage of two tenths of one per cent, in favor of the whites. The same article reads as follows: 'A half dozen Congressional committees have investigated the labor question in this country, and the newspapers also have made it a question of special inquiry. The great burden of these inquiries has been whether the freed Negro is as valuable a producer as the slave. The majority of those giving testimony, best able to speak on this subject in the last report of the Senate was, that the slave produced more cotton, sugar and corn than the freed man. At the same time it was universally acknowledged that Negro labor has improved, especially during the last ten years, is more reliable, and certainly less disposed to wander from plantation to plantation, more earnest, intelligent and capable.'

"Now there is much that is true in this. The Afro-American is certainly improving as a laborer, and is producing more now than he ever did as a slave. The source from which I have read is prejudiced, it is against the evidence of the people in this State and also Arkansas, in encouraging such labor to come from other States, as well as against the testimony borne by prominent Southerners[81] who aver that the Afro-American is the chief dependence for the labor of the South. The same article goes on to state that 'the average productive value of white labor throughout the South is thirty per cent greater than colored labor.' It claims that this is due to the 'agricultural colleges, farmers clubs and other associations, not to mention the immigration of a large number of small farmers from the West,' and 'that this advantage of white labor over colored labor is man for man in the hottest portions of the South.' It also claims that 'the white agricultural labor in the South is increasing rapidly, due to immigration from Northern States.'"

"I have heard the claims made before as well as the one that the colored people produced more and were more reliable as slaves than as freemen," said Stanley.

"The productive capacity may be easily disposed of. Then they were driven to it by the brutal lash of the overseer. But in regard to what I was reading, I think the argument all nonsense. I do not believe that enough Northern labor has come South to make such a great difference.[82] This paper is an enthusiastic advocate of immigration and makes much of little, presumably with the intention of inducing immigration, and hence to depreciate colored labor. If the statistics are thorough in 1890 we may get some idea of the real facts.[83] There are more ways than by outrage to do us an injustice."

"You do not think then that the colored people are lazy, shiftless, and carelessly bent on living an easy life."

"Not the intelligent at any rate; with the ignorant it would be natural enough if it were so for good reasons. As a slave he was forced by overseers, and the dread of the lash formed a great incentive to labor. They were simply machines over which were appointed men whose sole business it was to produce the greatest amount of labor at a minimum of cost, and the cost consisted of a few scant articles of clothing and cheap food. Many plantations only allowed as a week's rations to a man a peck of corn and two pounds of fat pork. If he were unmarried he had to prepare it himself. Such coarse and scanty finding encouraged peculations from the master's pantry and hen roost. Slavery moved there was a reaction.

"From forced labor to labor as one pleased, was a great novelty, and a privilege deemed sacred. As freemen there was that natural antipathy against labor that is forced among the majority which is common to all people. There was also that natural desire, noticeable among people who have been in like situations, to work when and where they please; in other words, to be independent and have a good time. It cannot be denied, too, that the climate greatly aids laziness and shiftlessness. You have travelled extensively and most undoubtedly noticed in Europe that in the Latin countries there is not that same thrift and energy in the pursuits of labor that you find among the Germans, French, English, Scandinavians and Swiss. The climate is not rigorous enough to require the same effort to keep the body as warmly clothed and to support life as in Northern latitudes, their wants being fewer, not as much energy is required to obtain them. The natural result is a multitude of proud, lazy, ignorant and indigent people who live chiefly through beggary. I do not wish to infer from this that I think that the Afro-Americans of the South will occupy a like position always, although the climate is in many respects similar, but merely use it to show the effect of a climate upon races which have produced the most celebrated masters in art, philosophy, science, statesmanship, war and music. But look to your right—there is another specimen of this country. There is a sample of the poor white. Did you ever see a person whose face expressed such a lack of ambition, and who looked more lazy and shiftless? He is despised by the better classes of the whites and by the blacks. He is the ready scapegoat and tool; the medium through which designing men commit outrages against life and property, that has brought such disgrace upon Mississippi. He is the more willing tool because of his pride. He was considered but a degree above the slave and scarcely tolerated in other days. The slave now free and advancing, and he finding himself descending by reason of his sloth, is moved by jealousy, envy, hatred and prejudice."

Stanley looked in the direction indicated and barely had time while the train rushed along to catch a glimpse of a thatched cabin before which stood a lank, lean specimen of the Southern poor white, clad in patched and faded jeans and upon whose head was a tattered and torn straw hat. His face bore the stamp of the characteristics of his class laziness, sloth and pride, but as regards the nobler qualities, it was expressionless. In front of the house stood a bench on which lay a wash basin, nearby on the ground lay a hoe and rake, which when employed at all, were probably used to cultivate the small patch of ground in front of the cabin, which looked to be in want of care.

"The meanest and lowest of them all have in them a pride," continued Saunders, "which makes them think they are the superiors of the best among the Afro-Americans. They are the natural result of the climate and the system of the old South, and their tribe will increase until that intolerance which exists here against men, white or colored, who are not in accord with the reigning political opinions, ceases. Men who love liberty of thought and expression, cannot be induced to leave sections where such rights exist, for climes even more favorable, where such privileges are in danger."

The numbers of poor whites and shiftless blacks around the station, to whom the coming and going of trains was always of interest, was a source of amusement. The near approach of the Presidential election assisted in bringing out more than usual every type of the country, from the wealthy, polite and imperious planter to the poorest black and white. Most of them intent on saving the country from a return to Republican rule, and predicting dire disaster should such a calamity occur. The Afro-American had learned, however, from experience to keep out of such discussions.

"A little while ago," said Stanley, "you spoke of other reasons, besides the natural one you gave, why the colored people did not produce more, and from what I should infer, did not possess more wealth."

"There are several reasons. After emancipation and enfranchisement many were bent on acquiring land. Large numbers bought lands and homes on contract. That was during the Reconstruction. During the days of the K. K. K. many were killed, many were driven from home, and a large number of others discovered that many of their contracts were false, and had their property taken away from them with no means of redress. This of course had an evil effect, for it discouraged many. There are also a large number of small planters, who, because of the severity of the system of doing business, are unable to make headway, and when the crop is in and sold are probably deeper in debt than when the season opened."

"What do you refer to now?"

"The share system, but it affects the white also. The planters are generally poor. To go through a season he raises money on a prospective crop for which he is charged ten per cent interest. He also has to pay a further charge of ten per cent for all provisions advanced, which are charged up against him at a large profit, and at the end of the season when his debts are paid he is no better off than when he begun. Then there is the crop lien system by which he is to mortgage his crop as security for his rent, purchase his provisions at the company's store and comes out no better than he does by the other plan. There are other systems, equally as bad, whose sole purport is to defraud the small planter. This same article from which I read before says: 'The credit system was universal in the South about six years ago. * * * In 1879–80 it was estimated that nearly three-fifths of the entire crop was raised on credit.' Among the Afro-Americans in the back counties the system is still extensively carried on, and of course such a state of things is hardly calculated to make men thrifty and industrious."

"Quite the reverse I should think. But I have always heard that the South had many rich colored men, consequently there must be many exceptions to the general rule."

"There are. Now there are two brothers in this State who were the property of Jeff Davis who have bought the old plantation and are quite wealthy. Others have withstood the tide of persecution that swept over this State in '76 and are well off. I have seen the advance sheets of a book which states that there are twenty-seven whose combined wealth is more than a $1,000,000. The influence of education upon the young, and the inculcation of sound moral principles is improving the status of the Afro-American rapidly. The next decade will witness marvelous strides in educational and material advancements. But here we are at Tougaloo.[84] That row of buildings over there looks as if it might be a university."

Inquiry from the conductor confirmed his surmise.

"The Tougaloo University is one of three for which this state appropriates $3,000 per year for the use of Afro-Americans. It has an average attendance of about one hundred and fifty. In addition to the regular course of study there is manual training. Most of the buildings about the university were built by the students. Such schools are increasing rapidly, for that system which cultivates the use of the hand as well as the head, is growing in favor all over the country. They are a necessity, and particularly so with the freedman, who has not the same facilities for learning trades accorded the whites."

"The colored people here are eager to get education, are they not?"[85]

"Very, but Mississippi and other Southern states are too poor to furnish the adequate sums to make their school systems the equal of the North, and the matter is rendered worse by keeping separate schools." Saunders again had recourse to his wallet for statistics. "Now, by the census of 1880, the number of school days in Mississippi in the country districts was seventy-four and one-half days; in the cities 177 days: In the report of the U. S. Commission for 1884 and 1885 the average for all parts of the state is given at 78.05 days. The average annual pay for teachers in 1880 was a little less than $120.00 a year. This shows the necessity of National aid, does it not, to aid the state to rid itself of its vast ignorance? The increase in the number of scholars in '81 over '80 was 7,000 whites to 13,000 colored.[86] The average pay of teachers throughout the South in 1880 was $111.82 per year and the average number of school days 87.79, ranging from 62 in North Carolina to 118.4 in Virginia.[87] I have seen no reliable statistics since. There is a great lump of ignorance in the South to leaven. The colored children while fairly well provided for are not nearly as well so as the whites. The first colored school was started at Hilton's Head in 1861, now there are thousands of schools well filled, but the supply is inadequate and the work is marred by such talk as that the whites are taxed and the 'Negroes' get the benefit. Such people seem to forget: First, that the Afro-American is largely responsible for the prosperity of the South, that is, his labor helped greatly to create it. Second, that for years he received no returns for his labor. Third, that the man who labors and pays rent, indirectly at least, pays the tax, his share of it anyway, although he may not directly do so. Taking these things into consideration the Afro-American does not get his full quota, nor are his school houses as good, or his teachers as competent; yet his progress has been so rapid[88] as to put the whites in many places on their mettle. Kentucky has more illiterate whites than blacks. Prominent Southern journals have said that the pay and accommodations are equal, but I do not believe that a single Afro-American teacher, who is well informed and is unhampered, will substantiate it."[89]

The door of the car was opened and through it came to their ears: "By Gahd, sah! The South won't tolerate nigger rule, sah! It will fight." The door was closed again and the rest of the conversation was cut off.

"Of all reasons," continued Saunders, "used by the South to keep the Afro-American intimidated, that pretended fear that the South will pass under the control of the Afro-American, seems most senile. There are about nineteen million people in this section, and only about seven million five hundred thousand are colored. Only in three States—Louisiana, Mississippi and South Carolina—are they in the majority, and in the party they are principally connected with, white men are always appointed to lead and hold the most responsible positions. There can be no excuses for the outrages in Arkansas, Texas, Georgia and Alabama on that score. It is all pure meanness. Revenge, perhaps, taken upon the blacks for their failure in the lost cause.[90] Revenge taken upon them for the part played by the Republican party in those stirring times, and for their work in elevating him. It is not fear, it is solely revenge. They know as well as anyone that kindness and justice would divide the Afro-American vote, and that is all that the Afro-American wants. Given justice, we are willing to abide by the doctrine of the survival of the fittest."

All this time Stanley had been quietly sitting while Saunders rattled off his statistics, and gave his view of the problem of the races, at the same time Stanley found his respect increasing. After a while, he said: "You have given reasons for the general shiftlessness, but have neglected to give any for the claim that man for man, white labor produces more than colored."

"That shiftlessness of which I have spoken, if the claim is true, will account for a great deal. Then the white labor that has chiefly immigrated to this section from the North and European countries may aid it. They come from the hardier races and are more used to toil. The claim cannot be made in reference to native white labor solely, for in many parts, particularly in this belt, it is not as good as colored. If political persecutions would only cease, there would be such a tide of immigration that would make a great improvement in the morale and energy of the working people."

CHAPTER X.

_____

At last they arrived in New Orleans, that New Orleans that Cable has made us acquainted with in his "Dr. Sevier," and "Tales of Acadian Life."[91] They were familiar with these tales of New Orleans life, and on their ride to the Hotel the streets seemed familiar upon recalling the scenes that had been enacted there.

Arriving at the hotel Stanley registered for both and had ordered breakfast before Saunders, who had been giving instructions concerning their baggage, knew it. Saunders came in as Stanley was ready to be assigned to his room and spoke to him. The hotel clerk, noticing him then for the first time, asked of Stanley: "Do you wish a place provided for your servant?"

"What do you suppose I wanted?" asked Stanley, somewhat impatiently. "I want a room for both of us. The same room will do. He is not a servant, but a friend."

"It is evident from your language that you are from the North," replied the clerk, "but we don't allow Negroes in this house except as servants."

"Am I to infer then that I cannot procure accommodations in this hotel for my friend?" asked Stanley, with flashing eyes. What Saunders had told him of southern prejudices then suddenly came to his mind.

"I mean just what I say. It is against the rule of the house to entertain Negroes as guests," answered the clerk calmly and politely. "We are sorry to inconvenience you but we can give him quarters with the servants."

The utter indifference of the man to the feelings of his friend made Stanley angry and he rather hotly said: "You can keep all your rooms. I think your rules are an outrage and a reflection upon the reputed civility and courtesy of the South to treat strangers in this manner. He is as good as you any day."

The clerk now began to get angry.

"Don't carry your insults too far, sir, or you may be sorry for it. Besides, you won't make any friends down here by trying to put niggers on an equality with white people."

"I don't have to put him on an equality with you," retorted Stanley. "He is more of a man than you in any particular, and a gentleman at that."

"You are one of those Northern fools that it would be a sin for a gentleman to quarrel with. But still I tell you," and the clerk, to emphasize his words, brought his fist down energetically, "that you are defying our prejudices against the 'niggers,' and you'll get your fill of it if you keep it up, before you get back home."

Quite a number of spectators had been drawn to the spot by the heated conversation, some of whom looked as if they would liked to have had a word in it.

Stanley made no reply to the clerk's last remark, but turned upon his heel followed by Saunders, who expected this much and left the place. Saunders thought that a little experience on Stanley's part with Southern intolerance and prejudice would be more convincing, and carry with it more weight than any argument he might offer, and on this account did not object to accompanying Stanley to the hotel. He re-secured the trunk checks from the porter and rejoined Stanley, who was somewhat agitated, on the street.

Turning to Saunders, Stanley said: "I wouldn't stay a minute in a place where I am insulted in such a manner. We will go where we can get what we desire to pay for."

"It is useless to look for such a place among the hotels so far as I am concerned," replied Saunders. "There is not a hotel in Louisiana, or for that matter in the entire South, that would receive me as a guest. That question is so strongly settled that it is useless, at the present, to kick against the pricks. No matter how rich I might be or intelligent, it wouldn't make any difference so long as I had African blood in my veins and they knew it. These people see but one way."

"I shall appeal to the law," said Stanley, hotly. "Do you suppose I will submit to such treatment peaceably? If your race would stand up and fight for their rights you wouldn't be kicked and cuffed around in this manner."

"Fight for our rights; that sounds as if fighting might be a remedy, but how? by the law or by a resort to arms? Don't you remember that on the train I read you an editorial clipping from the *Times-Democrat* that acknowledged there was no law for the Afro-American in these states when the contest was between him and a white man. The law is not for him but against him. We cannot appeal to the Federal courts for they have remanded us back to the states for justice. There justice is found to be a mockery. I have before shown you the obstacles that prevent the use of force. But what is the use of arguing with you in this manner? Your mind is not in condition to look at this matter soberly."

"We'll see about that. I shall institute inquiries."

"Very well. You find a place to stay and I will take care of myself. I do not care to be subjected to further insults by applying for accommodations at other hotels. We will not be here very long and it isn't worth the fuss to insist against their customs."

Re-entering a carriage they were driven to the Hotel R— Saunders gave up the checks to Stanley and immediately set out in search of a colored boarding place. On Canal street he met an intelligent looking man of his race whom he took for a letter carrier, and on making known his wants was directed to such a place. He was compelled to go quite a distance to reach it, but when he did he found pleasant rooms in a private family on —— street. In the privacy of his room he began to think of home and Edith, of the misgivings she had of making such a trip on the eve of a National election and he resolved not to take any stand that would make him figure conspicuously against Southern customs, on the contrary he would accept things as he found them.

Stanley did not, however, resolve to accept the customs so easily. On being assigned to his room in the Hotel R—, he went at once to it, and taking off his coat, for the weather was quite warm, he sank into a chair and began to survey the situation. He felt keenly the insult offered to him and his friend at the —— Hotel, and the more he thought of it the keener the pang; his temper rose and the more determined he became to find out if there was no redress. The more we nurse our wrongs, fancied or real, the larger proportions they assume. It was so with Stanley. He grew so excited thinking over it that he arose from his chair and paced the floor to and fro.

"What business is it of theirs," he said aloud, "If I want a colored man for a companion or as an associate. If I am willing to share my room and privileges with him, what business or by what right does a public inn dictate to me whom I shall or shall not have as a companion, and presume to insult me for doing as I like. If there is any justice to be had at law I will have it."

From what Stanley knew of the South through newspapers and information derived from Saunders he might have expected the discrimination. He probably knew that if Saunders had been traveling alone he could not have secured accommodations at a hotel. But the idea that Saunders traveling with him not as a companion, but as a friend, one who had nursed him in sickness, widened the horizon of his understanding concerning men and their relations to each other, and had helped him to bear up under a great disappointment—made him forget everything except the insult to Saunders and through Saunders to himself. His idea of the power of wealth to buy what was purchasable received a check, and the check served only as a means to let loose his pent-up feelings.

Recollecting that he had letters of credit to the —— National Bank on Canal street he resolved to go there at once, and after transacting his business he intended to lay his complaint before its officers for advisement. On his way over he met Saunders who had just come from his boarding place. Stanley told him where he was going, and left him to his own resources until he returned.

Saunders started out for a stroll and the magnificent Custom House that the Government had been so many years in completing caught his eye. As he looked at the immense structure of marble and its great dome he thought of "the hole in the ground" at home, and wondered if it would take as long to complete that still undesigned building as it did this. The Hotel where he had been refused was near to the Custom House and vied with it in beauty and finish.

The sun was now getting very warm so he hired a cab to show him around through the business part of the city and down by the wharves, as he had a great curiosity to see the loading and unloading of cotton, the great warehouses, levees, and the large number of steamers always to be found there.

The principal streets of New Orleans, St. Charles and Canal, are broad thoroughfares two hundred feet wide in the center of which there is a kind of continuous park about twenty feet wide, lined on each side with beautiful shade trees and ornamented by a profusion of rich flowers, the like of which is not to be seen in the parks of our Northern cities. Saunders confessed to himself that New Orleans was a rather handsome city, but not to be compared to Detroit. He was conscious, however, that his sphere was circumscribed, and this oppression of his mind weighed upon the attempted exhilaration of the body. There is no beauty without liberty—that conscious possession of the soul that sees the boundless possibilities of man in all things, though he may never realize his expectations. Nature in her brightest hues is somber to the mind oppressed. The dread possibility of insults and curtailments of the rights of manhood forced themselves upon him, and it required considerable effort to throw off the depression that his reverie had brought upon him.

He found his driver to be quite garrulous and he plied him with many questions. He was an Afro-American, not over intelligent, but possessed of a considerable amount of mother wit. He had the dialect peculiar to his class, and was possessed of quite an extensive fund of information.

Going down Bienville street to the wharves and around the warehouses, Saunders noted large numbers of Afro-Americans lying around idle, and as it was then in the middle of the cotton season and knowing too that they were the chief labor around the wharves, he thought it rather strange, and he asked the driver why they didn't go to work.

"Well, I tell you, boss, how dat is. Sum of 'em don't want ter work, en sum cant get it. Dar's to many poh foks heah. When de regilators gits on de rampage dey runs a lot of des fellers out ob de parishes and dey cum into de city fer purteckshun. When dey get heah mos' of um stays."

"You say that some of them are lazy?"

"Yes sah! powful shiftless, sum of dem is, and den agin dey wuks on de plantashuns all de yar and dey ginrally owes mo when de yar are up den dey did when dey commenced, so dey jists make up der min' dat dey aint gwine ter wuk at all."

"There are large numbers who have accumulated considerable property are there not?"

"Golly, boss, yes we has. I kin name hundreds of men nigh heah on my fingers."

Saunders gained quite a bit of information from him if he didn't possess much "book larnin" and he rather reluctantly cut his drive short in order to meet Stanley as he returned from the bank. While doing so he busily plied the driver with questions relative to the mode of carrying elections, of the manner in which the people were bulldozed in the country parishes, of the trouble in Thiboudaux parish last fall, where the Governor of the State sent the militia and the subsequent useless waste of life. He also questioned him relative to the manner of life led by the Afro-Americans in the city and country and their educational facilities, which information he intended to embody in letters to Edith and to his favorite journal, the *Plaindealer*.[92] He arrived at the hotel just in time to meet Stanley on his return, in a mood apparently as bitter as when he set out for the bank, which led Saunders to infer that he had failed in getting satisfaction.

CHAPTER XI.

Upon leaving the hotel, Stanley went directly to the bank, and presented his letters to Mr. George Arnold, the cashier, who received him very cordially, and expressed the hope that he intended to locate in the South. He assured him that Northern capital was always welcomed by the rising institutions in that section, and that large dividends attended its ventures. Stanley explained that he was only on a visit to this particular section of the South and had been led to make it through curiosity, but that his father had interests in Birmingham, Ala., which he expected to look after. He thanked him for his cordial welcome, and then he told him of his experience at the hotel that morning.

Mr. Arnold listened attentively until he had finished, then he said: "I am sorry that your first visit to the South should be thus marred by a disagreeable incident, but if you are at all acquainted with our customs, I cannot commend your desire to force Negro equality. We, of the South, are unalterably opposed to it, and would stand by our convictions, if by so doing we had to shed our life's blood, as we did once before to support our opinions. This question is a prevalent issue with us that we must meet; with you, it is a sentimental theory."

Stanley was inclined to get angry, but Mr. Arnold was so gentle and courteous in his manner, and spoke so dispassionately, that he refrained from showing any signs of irritation and asked: "Do you call a demand for the ordinary civilities of life forcing equality."

"That depends on the circumstance. The Negroes are an inferior race, and the very first idea of the fitness of things demands that he should live apart from a superior race. We, of the South are the best friends they have, and if the North would leave us alone, we would work out his destiny all right."

"Mr. Arnold, our views are diametrically opposed to each other, and it is probably useless for you and me to discuss the question. Your position to me, seems like this: You wish the North to give up its interests in humanity because it interferes with your plans to work out the destiny of eight millions of people without regard to their wishes, and in a manner contrary to the principles that uphold the Republic."

Mr. Arnold was as polished in argument and evasion as the most skillful lawyer. He employed all their casuistry, and did not allow a ruffle of discontent to pass over his countenance, or work a change in his manner. He was as suave as Disraeli's Cardinal Grandison, and did not allow even a change in the inflection in his voice.[93] He replied, smilingly:

"Not at all, Mr. Stanley. We only want the Negro to know and keep his place until he becomes civilized as we are, and in the meantime we will furnish him with schools, and the means to educate himself. We are taxing ourselves every day for his benefit."

"If you are doing all that you claim, what need is there for the large number of educational institutions all over the country established by Northern philanthropy such as Fisk, Tuskegee, Atlanta, and many others. If the South is poor, why burden itself with two systems of schools when the same energies applied to one would complete and perfect it.[94] Then too, I should like to know what you do with the tax you receive from them? Half of the accumulated prosperity of Louisiana is the result of their labor."

"Let me give you a little advice as an old man. If you expect to get along in the South and have a pleasant visit —for the Southerners are as hospitable and as chivalrous a people as can be found anywhere—you ship that Negro friend of yours back North, or make the servant of him that he should be, and stop all such nonsense and sentimental talk as you have now indulged in."

"I thank you kindly for your advice, but I will not avail myself of it, if I am to gain favor by becoming an ingrate and at the price of my convictions also. We have trifling colored people at home, but we discriminate between the intelligent and honorable as against the ignorant and vicious, the same as we do among the white people. You condemn all and confound social with civil privileges. However, I don't intend to go back on a friend to whom I owe as much as I do to John Saunders."

"I see you will not accept reason nor reconcile yourself to our customs, but since we meet as friends let us part friends, and we will be pleased to accommodate you at the bank any time. But as I said before, you Northerners are more sentimental than reasonable. You worship an abstract idea. When you see more of the South with its hordes of ignorant, vicious Negroes you will go back a changed man on this moonshine idea of right."

"A part of my mission South is to see things as they are. I am open to impressions. If we of the North are wrong I am willing to acknowledge it in the most public manner. If we are not," he paused, "You are not willing to acknowledge we are right. There is no sentiment about the esteem in which I hold my colored friend. He would be an exception, no matter to what race he belonged. He is learned to a degree and a gentleman besides. The fact that there are hundreds such as he goes to prove what surroundings will do for a race, despite your claims of viciousness and inferiority. A long train of circumstances, which it would take me too long to relate, threw us together and my friendship for him has grown from the first."

"He may have some strange influence over you that you are not aware of. The Negroes are tricky. We have to use every vigilance to keep them down and the better educated they become the worse they are."

"I should think it would make them better. Education broadens one's ideas and their aspirations become higher. Perhaps this is why you think them worse."

"It unfits them for laborers and makes them dissatisfied with their lot. These educated Negroes are always dreaming about social equality. We have to be a little severe in our repressive measures to protect our homes. No one wants a nigger in his family, you agree with me in that do you not?"

"As far as I am concerned I cannot, but I am a step even in advance of the masses of the North in my idea of one's liberty of thought and action. Still I know of cases where black and white have intermarried with the consent of friends. I don't see how your daughters could ever marry a colored man with the opinions you hold concerning them, and yet I have read of numerous cases of elopements in the South where white women have run away with colored men. Perhaps it may be due to that inexplicable influence you claim my colored friend has over me, or it may be the case of the willful girl and the coachman as is the case North, though rare. None of our families are invaded in the North by any objectionable people, be they black or white. In many public places in receptions given by societies in which there are colored members I have met Saunders and others. They have always deported themselves well, and those who knew them treated them well as far as I have ever noticed."

"But we can't do that down here Mr. Stanley. We have too many of them, we wouldn't think of it either. We believe them inferior and treat them accordingly."

"If you are the superior and the stronger race then your duty to the weaker is to be inflexibly just.[95] And you are not that. It is nonsense to my mind to say you cannot distinguish between the educated and the ignorant among the colored people the same as you do among the white. To say that you wouldn't think of it is nearer the truth and forms the key to the situation. You of the South accuse us of being a slave to an abstract sentiment while you are slaves to a prejudice that keeps the country in dread of a future awakening of terror and which sometimes startle us with the news of some horrible massacre." Stanley arose to go; as he reached the door Mr. Arnold called after him : "Do you expect to remain long in the South?"

"Not in this city," replied Stanley, sharply.

"You will find before you get home how useless it is to try and introduce your Northern sentimentality into the South. I warn you in time."

"I call it Northern justice," said Stanley, walking back to where the banker sat. "The Southern people are wont to look upon Northern ideas and customs, our love of liberty and ideas of the right of citizenship with disdain. You trample upon the very principles of a Republic and seek to create a caste by means which if persisted in, will be ruinous.

"'Ill fares the land to hastening ills a prey.'[96] Where such misdeeds are done and rights frittered away for customs which we regard as more senseless than you, our ideas of right. Your Southern problem is not as intricate as ours. You have a race born to the soil to whom only kind and equitable treatment is necessary to win regard and respect, while we have the ignorant and depraved, with all the pernicious isms that prevail among the slums of Europe. Yet with our ideas of justice we will solve our problem more quickly. However, I did not come down here to argue or convince anybody, but your prejudices inconvenienced me. I suppose if I had not brought Saunders with me we should have fallen in with one another and would have had a good time with those I chanced to meet."

"Exactly, and you would have been entertained royally, but to have invited you to one's house and have you express yourself as you do about the rights of Negroes, would be like letting loose a cyclone about one's ears." Mr. Arnold laughed heartily. "If you want to meet the best people of the South, don't meddle with the Negroes, or you will be ostracised."

Stanley sat down and told him what he had at first intimated. How it was that he had been influenced to visit the South, of his sickness, Saunders' devotion to him, his position at the store and of his superior intelligence. "Now then, you know I did not come to seek social recognition, and I will not be disappointed if no one notices me. With all Saunders has done for me, if he isn't quite as white as I am, I couldn't look him in the face again if I treated him less than as a man. He is here by my invitation and we can keep our own company. I have been in the same position before and have been well entertained."

"We have servants who have done as much for us, would lay down their lives for us, and we care for them, would do all in our power for them, but we teach them to keep their place at the same time, or they would soon get 'sassy' and commence to talk about their rights, I suppose, about the way your friend does. I advise you to take the same course and you will find, my dear fellow, that experience and years will cure you of all sentimentality."

"Not if I know it," replied Stanley, as he bade him adieu and started for his hotel.

On his way there he thought over his experience and tried to forecast what he might expect. Meeting Saunders at the door of the hotel they both entered. He secured some writing paper in the lobby and then they went up to his room by the stairway.

He told Saunders of his conversation with the banker and said that he meant to leave New Orleans as soon as he had taken a run down to the gulf. Saunders protested and said that he did not wish to prove a burden. He even offered to return home at once and leave him unhampered, but Stanley would not consent to it and said: "If I can afford to stick to you, you can afford to stay with me," and they sealed this decision by grasping each other's hands.

Saunders then left the hotel to go to dinner and Stanley proceeded to write to his father in detail about his experiences. He would have liked to have written to Marjorie, and had he done so his mind perhaps would have been relieved in transcribing his thoughts to one so dear to him. If he could have only known how gladly she would have welcomed them. He wrote a cheery letter to Imogene, omitting the disagreeable incidents. As he wrote he recollected a promise he had made her. "I promised to take her with me the next time I went away. It is perhaps as well that I did not."

CHAPTER XII.

————————

Despite the conclusions arrived at between the two concerning the length of their stay in New Orleans, they remained there several days. The life it presented, the peculiar types of character it displayed, were to them sources of study, thought and amusement. Its various parks, and places of interest and pleasure had to be visited —some of which were of peculiar interest to Saunders because they were connected with the educational interests of the Afro-American, such as the St. Charles and Straight Universities.[97] In the common schools he found discrimination he did not expect in such a large city. Some years ago a wealthy man named MacDonogh died and left a large sum of money for educational purposes. His will provided that the benefactions should be equally shared by the colored and the white people. With the money left for the purpose twenty-six school buildings had been built, and of that number the colored people have the use of only one.[98] Their numbers entitled them to at least five of these schools, "but the school board refuses them to us," said an intelligent Afro-American in response to a query from Stanley.

Of the public parks and pleasure grounds to which they would resort for a study of the different types which the city afforded, they were pleased with the Spanish Port, which was situated way out at the upper end of the city by Lake Pontchartrain, and at the mouth of Bayou St. John; also with the West End and Carrollton gardens. Of this latter place, George W. Cable, in "Au Large," grows enthusiastic, and from that work we take the following: "If I might have but one small part of New Orleans to take with me wherever I go or may wander in this earthly pilgrimage, I should ask for Carrollton gardens. They lie near the farthest upper limit of the expanded city. I should want, of course, to include the levee under which runs one side of the garden's fence, also the opposite shore of the Mississippi, with its just discernible plantation houses behind their levee; and the great bend of the river itself, with the sun setting in unutterable gorgeousness behind the distant low-lying pecan groves of Nine Mile Point, and the bronzed and purpled waters kissing the very crown of the great turfed levee, down under whose land side the gardens blossom, and give forth their hundred perfumes and bird songs to the children and lovers that haunt their winding alleys of oleander, jessamine, haurustine, orange, aloe and rose, the grove of magnolias and oaks and come out upon the levee's top as the sun sinks to catch the gentle breeze and the twilight change to moonlight on the waters."[99]

From Cable's delightful romances had they formed their conception of some of the types which they came hither to see. Nor were they disappointed, for many a gallant Narcisse, shy Claudes and bashful Marguerites did they see.

They took a trip to Shell Beach and down to the gulf through the jetties— that marvel of scientific engineering which has rendered certain the channel of the Mississippi at the Delta. The idea originated in the mind of, and was pushed through and finished by, the indomitable Eads.[100]

There was a vast difference between the Mississippi River with its floating wharves and dark stevedores passing to and fro, echoing and re-echoing their songs as they went, and the scenes they were accustomed to on the Detroit docks. The river, too, was muddier and their boats different. There was a waiting-room for the colored people and a part of the boat set aside for their use, although the rule is not always strictly adhered to. By keeping close to Stanley, Saunders passed without challenge to the upper decks, from which they had an excellent view of shore and country in the ride down the Mississippi past Forts Jackson and Phillips and out through the jetties into the gulf where Saunders caught his first sniff of salt water, and saw ocean steamships for the first time. The experience was novel and exciting. He sniffed the sea breezes, drew it in by great breathfulls, and felt his chest expand and his spirits rise with its bracing effect. "This is magnificent," he remarked to Stanley, and out came his note book.

Being a civil engineer by profession he was very much interested in the jetties. He was familiar with its scientific principles in gathering, by means of its aprons, the water as it came out of the river and forcing it through a narrow channel into the sea. Gradually the channel deepened until its least depth in 1885 was 31.3 feet. The engineering instinct was in him and he looked with pride upon the work that had done so much for New Orleans, and wondered if ever the time would come when such as he would be able to so overcome customs, as to secure the confidence that would enable him to undertake such tasks.

The weather was simply delightful and the trip a most pleasant one. Neither had aught to say to their fellow passengers, finding abundant entertainment in their surroundings and in each other, but they were objects of considerable speculation. By a sort of tacit agreement, however, they avoided everything in which the least sign of prejudice, to their mind, could manifest itself.

Saunders, however, was getting nervous from sheer apprehension. He would have felt much better traveling alone, for Stanley's persistent efforts to secure for him the same privileges he enjoyed made matters appear worse. Owing to the state of excitement incident to the election he would have been willing for the short time he expected to remain in the South to accept the situation rather than fight at such a time against such unequal odds. He did not care to become a martyr to his ideas of justice, although if danger unforeseen had overtaken him he would have met it like a hero. At last he persuaded Stanley to leave New Orleans and not to make a lengthy Southern trip. He desired that they proceed at once from there to Birmingham, Ala., transact their business and return to God's country, as he termed the North.

CHAPTER XIII.

The following afternoon at four o'clock found them seated on the promenade deck of the steamer Louisiana, bound for Vicksburg. All the arrangements thereto had been made by Stanley, who, much against his desire, forced himself, in order to satisfy Saunders, to consider the relations between the races. Being somewhat in advance of the time for the boat to leave for the upriver ports, they ascended to the promenade deck to have a better view of the bustle going on along the levee. As Saunders attempted to go above he was approached by an officer of the boat who rather forcibly told him that he had no business there. The blood mounted to his face in anger, a quick hot reply was on his lips, but he remembered his promise and with difficulty restrained himself. Stanley remonstrated and went to the captain of the steamer to ask the privilege of having "his servant with him on deck." It was a bitter pill to swallow for one of his principles, but he saw or rather knew it was useless for one to struggle against so many. His request was granted and for the balance of their time on the steamer they had no further trouble in that direction.

The scene along the wharves was a busy one and gave them a striking example of New Orleans business and thrift. There was a large number of steamers along the levee whose crews were busily loading and unloading their cargoes. The celerity with which the cotton bales were unloaded and assigned to their proper places, was to those ignorant of the system employed, astonishing. There were dock loungers, both black and white. There was the imperious mate, and his squad of stevedores, hustling freight and cursing like a trooper. There was the typical old black aunty with her red bandanna—one of the last relics of slavery—and basket, and the equally ancient relic of Bourbon aristocracy—the broken-down colonel of the late unpleasantness; broken down in physique and fortune.

Stanley noticed one of these standing near the levee talking to an attentive group. His long beard, broad hat and thin features proclaimed him a type of the Southern politician. From a word that reached him now and then Stanley concluded that he was talking politics. Desiring to become better acquainted with the species he left Saunders, went below and stepped ashore to join the group and hear what the man had to say about his subject.

He was expatiating on the beauties of Bourbon principles and the rule of the "superior" race. He was also urging a vigorous and aggressive campaign to keep down the Afro-American and to maintain a white man's government. He had the broad dialect peculiar to the Southeastern coast, and after talking a while, after Stanley joined the group, began to answer questions that were asked him. He was uniformly addressed as Colonel and Stanley wishing to ask a few questions, addressed him in the same style.

"Excuse me, Colonel, I am a stranger here. What's the drift of politics down here, and who do the people think will be the next president?"

"Befoh I answer your question, sah, may I ask you from what part of the country you are from?"

"From Michigan, Colonel."

"I thought you were a Yank the first time I sot my eyes on yer. I didn't spose yo'd care how politics was getting on down heah."

"You are mistaken, Colonel. I take a great interest in the South."

"You're not one of 'em Sunday School fanatics as thinks the niggahs ought to rule we'uns, are you?" chimed in an old fellow who looked the worse for wear.

"I don't think I should be called a fanatic," said Stanley, smiling.

"Well, you'uns up North whipped we'uns once, and freed our niggahs, and I didn't know but what you mout aide with the rest of 'em up North."

"Sah!" said the Colonel proudly, "I was in de wah. I raised a company in the State of Georgia, Gahd bless her. She's the peah of any State in the Union today, sah. At Manassah, sah, our company made the Yanks run like sheep. I was with Lee at Richmond, and with Pickett at Gettysburg, but you war too much for us, and we had to lay down our arms, but, sah, we haven't laid down our principles, and now we, sah, we who was whipped, now make the laws and control Federal legislation."

"That is all over now, and the Union is stronger than ever," said Stanley ignoring the last part of his speech.

"Sah! the fightin' is stopped, but de North has dun the South a great wrong, sah, a great wrong in teaching the niggahs that they're as good as white folks, sah, and we have to use severe measures to keep them down, sah. Not mor'n two weeks ago one of their sassy coon teachers had the boldness, sah, the boldness to get on a white folks coach and take a seat in front of me, sah, and my wife. Me, Kunnel Jackson, of the 5th Georgia, who owned slaves befoh de wah!

I called the brakeman and ordered him removed, but he wouldn't go, sah, and had the impudence to say he was as good as a white man, that he had paid for his seat and was goin' to stay thar. The idea of a niggah talking back to me riled me, sah, but I kept cool, sah, did you heah me? I kept cool. We passed the word ahead to the next station and when we got there, some of the boys as war with me in the army, came on, and yanked that darkey out of thar and taught him a lesson that he won't soon forget. You folks up North think us hahd on the niggahs, but you've got to live with 'em to know 'em. If we didn't keep 'em down they'd get so sassy, we white folks would have to move. Now, sah, I'll answer your question. Everything heah, sah, is Democratic, and we think without doubt that Cleveland will be re-elected. The safety of the State, sah, demands it. This is a white man's government, sah, (Heah! heah! from bystanders), and by the eternal, white men's going to rule. (Great applause from same source). Republican supremacy—" But Stanley had heard enough. He left the crowd and went on board the steamer while the Colonel went off into another long speech on the dangers of Afro-American supremacy and misrule, on the superiority of the whites and the growing impertinences of the blacks. To which harangue all of his listeners applauded. Each one looked as if he might have been a good "after taking" sign on a patent medicine bottle, warranted to make a man poor. Yet they were so thoroughly impressed with the idea of superiority, and as there were none except the Afro-American whom they could lord it over, they clung with pertinacity to this last straw that enabled them to look down on something in human creation as inferior to themselves.

The Louisiana soon got under way and New Orleans was left behind, much to Saunders' comfort. That evening he was compelled to eat with the servants. "The next time," said Stanley, "we attempt anything like this we'll carry our provisions with us." Afterwards as they sat on the deck enjoying the beautiful moonlit scene and smoking their cigars, Saunders said: "The more liberal-minded people of the South are not responsible for the outrages committed against Afro-Americans, but prejudice is so prevalent that everyone had to accede to its demands, and many rash people have overstepped all rules of decency to do what they conceived to be popular. My observation and experience assure me of this fact, that the poorer and more ignorant the people—North or South—the deeper rooted are their prejudices."

"I don't blame you for not wanting to live South after what I have seen," said Stanley. "I wonder if they would allow you in their churches. We will see when we get to Birmingham."

The rooms were so warm within that they sat quite late out on the deck enjoying the night breeze and viewing the lights along the shore. Occasionally the steamer would stop to take on a few bales of cotton to save time on the down trip when loaded.

Stanley had fallen into a reverie over his cigar and was musing over their experiences in New Orleans. His generous, impulsive spirit could not view the customs of the South as anything else but artificial, as a something that was contrary to all natural law or reason, which must at some time have a rude awakening. For a long time not a word passed between them. At last Stanley broke the silence.

"John, I have been thinking what a monster prejudice is. It is hideous in every particular, and when a man becomes possessed of it he has a disease which biases his reason, blights his judgment, warps his conscience and withers all his charitable impulses. He becomes more intolerant than a Pharisee, and narrower than the man who scoffs at the revelations of science. What to some men would be considered the dark lurking of a sinister imagination, to the prejudiced soul would be considered the beau ideal of manly qualities. Since we have entered this country that should resound with songs of happiness and content, should even be filled with 'milk and honey', be rich in agricultural and mineral wealth, where harmonious nature is so complete, like an unhappy stroke of fate, prejudice has followed us at every step and turn, until I have no words strong enough to express the disgust I feel."

"And yet you have only felt it in its mildest forms. When you have felt it as I have your tongue will be unhinged, for if out of the 'fullness of the heart the mouth speaketh,' your words would flow without the effort of utterance.[101] Twixt rebellion and despair we have nursed these man-imposed curses, and been patient when Job would have carried his resentment to the point of fury. Mercy is twice blessed, but prejudice is thrice cursed. It curses him who practices it, him at whom it is aimed, and is cursed of God who made all men and nations of one blood and redeemed them through His Son. Prejudice is conscienceless and relentless. Conscienceless because that lever of the soul which lifts it unto Heaven, once warped, moves it to deeds of hell that gives sanction to its conceptions. Relentless because shorn of its attendant quality, charity, it is conscious of no wrong. See how it blights our prospects by circumscribing the avenues of our usefulness and associations; how it dwarfs the sphere of our thought by the narrowness that prejudice imposes on the mind. See how it permits outrages and murders that are contrary to every sense of justice and right. See how, because of it, the virtue and integrity of our homes are laid an open prey to vicious men.

This is all a natural outgrowth of this fixed idea of race superiority, and the evidences of it is attested by the bleaching of the original African stock."

"My own observations of it have made me the more determined to use every endeavor to make my colored fellow citizens feel that in my presence they are men in so far as they are fitted by education and integrity to be so considered. Hitherto I have lived without a purpose; this shall now be my purpose, and you shall be my advisor in the matter. I believe that justice is growing in the South, however. The number of liberal-minded people will be in the majority in another decade, and public sentiment will cry down many of the disabilities under which your race now labors. You must furnish men of capital and business who can meet these men, who are swallowed up in their bigoted idea of superiority, on terms of business equality. Such competition never fails in winning respect. I could not have believed that you would have been treated as a criminal when there is no excuse for it. Your eloquent protest but deepens my admiration for you."

"If we are to confess our mutual admiration, my esteem for you approaches to love, for you have treated me as a man from the first, showing not the slightest taint of prejudice and you are a friend now."

"Hush! Do not pollute the name of love by coupling it with prejudice. Love is a sacred and consoling thought to me now that I am in this despondent state. How I have loved, you may not know, yet I should not imagine to myself that I love better, that it is stronger, or purer than others, but I cannot define the depths and heights of the love my heart contains. This brief separation, although self-imposed, has refined and sweetened the anticipation of its final consummation."

"I cannot concede that your love is stronger than mine, for with me my love is my chief hope. Still there are many incapable of the strong passions of either love or hate. Adversity smothers their love, and the power of money purchases either. But why do you choose to lacerate your heart by enduring a separation when you are convinced that you are beloved in return?"

"Because I cannot bear to be considered so weak when the limit of our separation is set. Should I allow myself the pleasure of her society I might someday forfeit my claim to reason and endurance by renewing what I have sworn to let be at rest. I know though that she longs for me even as I long for her."

"I shall be glad to see you two united."

"We will be, John, we will be. I feel it in every heart beat."

"You are more sanguine than I am then, although I am engaged, for I have a presentiment that I shall never see Edith again."

"Fiddlesticks! Apprehension has called up latent superstitions which you should not encourage. Fight it, if you wish for peace. Why, I have always thought you very sanguine. I cannot understand your melancholy presentiment."

"I confess that melancholy has seized me since I have been here. The odds have been so against me, greater than I have ever known before. That makes me apprehensive and I cannot escape the melancholy."

"I will admit that such a marked change in one's condition would have its influence on his feeling. I never experienced such a strange longing, mixed with hope and anxiety, in all my life before. If I had been sent away rejected, I might have nursed my wounds and made a cure, but this suspense unnerves me. I have wondered often, judging from my experience, what a man who has committed a crime must feel if he has the least spark of conscience. The dread apprehension of punishment here and the still fearful uncertainty of the scourge of the hereafter."

Before he could finish there rose on the night air a cry, so distinct that no doubt was left as to its intent, so clear and strong that it penetrated through the boat to either bank, across the levees, waking up the echoes, so dreadful, that it struck a chill to their hearts, blanched their cheeks, filled them with terror and made them look at each other with stupefaction and dismay.

CHAPTER XIV.

———————

The Louisiana was one of the largest and most elegantly equipped of all the steamers that left New Orleans for upriver ports. She was a very popular steamer and had usually a large number of cabin passengers. She was built chiefly, however, as nearly all these steamers are that ply the lower Mississippi, for the cotton carrying trade.

On her way up the river she had stopped at a few unimportant points to take on a few passengers and some cotton bales which her officers thought best to take on now and save time on the down trip when the steamer would be heavily loaded. She had a large crew of roustabouts, and on this trip carried a large number of deck passengers, most of whom were Afro-Americans.

As the nights were still warm these passengers lay carelessly around among the cotton bales looking, talking and some sleeping. The moon, which was yet young, cast a bright silvery light over the water, but was beginning to descend behind the trees on the left which lay beyond the swamps back of the levee.

A few hours later everything was still save the beatings and the pulsations of the engine and the splash of the steamer's great, stern paddle wheels. The still monotony was at times relieved by the tread of the watch, the voice of the pilot or by the sound of firing up. The night was now dark and it was relieved only by the glimmer of the stars above or a solitary light here and there along the shore that pierced through the thick darkness that seemed to envelop it. There was then no sign of danger to warn "the people on board of the peril they were in. Everything about them was so calm and peaceful.

It may have been a spark from the smokestack that alighted among the cotton bales, or it may have been a spark from the pipe of a deck passenger who had fallen asleep among them. Certain it was that the cotton became ignited, and being very inflammable, the fire sped with great rapidity, and the first note of warning came to the officers through a colored woman, who, terrified with fright and horror, rushed forward frantically shouting, "De cotton's a blazin' and we'se all dead." [102]

181

Then arose that dreadful cry that so startled Stanley, and Saunders. A cry that fills the sailors' hearts, and all others when at sea, with terror, deprives men of reason, and makes them rush hither and thither like mad objects bent only upon the pursuit of safety.

"Fire! Fire!" rang out the cry, followed by the roar of the steamer's whistles, as the alarm was given, that awoke the startled echoes along the shore, causing pandemonium to reign on board, while the startled inhabitants here and there along the shore rushed out of doors, ran to and fro upon the levees where a sight grand and terrible in its every aspect met their gaze.

What spectacle is more horrible and heart-rending, grand even in its horror and agony than a steamer wrapped in a lurid flame from stem to stern, of fire rushing like a screaming, living thing in torture through the dark water? In appearance a monster from whose entrails is heard far above the crackling of the flames, the hoarse roaring of the whistles, and the escaping steam, the shrieks of human beings in mortal agony and fear. The piteous appeals for help that were heart-rending to the souls of the onlookers, made their flesh creep and almost impelled them to flee away from such a scene of distress, or close their ears to the shrieks of agony. But their feet seemed rooted, their eyes set and they felt compelled to gaze by some strange fascination on the sickening horror and gather in its minutest details.

In the ghastly lights of the flames they could see human forms rushing madly hither and thither over the decks, fleeing wildly from hot scorching tongues of fire. They saw forms, as if vomited forth from the crater of a volcano, leaping and falling into the waters lit up by the flames, whose swells engulfed them and where a death more merciful, because less painful awaited them.

As the boat drew nearer they could distinguish the features of the people on board. Some were marked by terror and despair, some transfixed by fright, others by a calm resignation, and a few by hope as they saw the steamer nearing the shore. They could see brave men doing their utmost to calm, cheer and save. They could see pilot, calm and undaunted, grasping the wheel, while the flames almost lapped him. They could see men leaping with impromptu rafts, or pushing overboard a cotton bale, and vainly endeavoring to float upon it safely to the shore. Under the glow of the flames, upon the surface of the water here and there they could see a face whose owner was making a brave struggle for life.

Nearer still came the steamer and the watchers on shore shook off the strange fascination that bound them, and stood ready to render all the aid in their power. At last the steamer's bow struck the bank, and obeying her helm she swung around broadside to the levee. The great stage plank was swung out but ere it could secure a support on the bank, the people rushed panic stricken upon it. The strain was too much for the men holding the guy ropes, they loosed their hold and the plank with a splash fell down under the steamer's guard and the people upon it were cast into the water and mired in the mud. Confusion heaped upon confusion. The stage plank rendered helpless, and the pilot having left his post the boat swung round and began to drift down stream and new horrors were added to a scene already made horrible.

CHAPTER XV.

Stanley and Saunders, looking into each other's eyes, read the same thoughts that agitated each, and each was asking himself, is it destiny? While thus they sat, for the moment their muscles paralyzed, the dread cry rose again on the air and the roar of the whistles aroused them from their stupor.

Saunders was the first to recover and exclaimed: "Save yourself, Seth, while I awake the passengers."

"Remember your presentiment, John, and be careful. I will go with you and if the worst happens we will die together."

"You shall not go. You shall not die and you must not think of it, for you have too much to live for."

"When the lives of others are at stake and may be saved from a horrible death, shall future prospects occupy the mind to the detriment of our duty. Move on and be quick."

"I say you shall not go," said Saunders with a look of determination. "What if I should die so that you survive. Now that there is time, Seth, prepare to escape by the river." Saunders' voice at the last became one of entreaty.

"And I say that you shall run no risks that I dare not share," said Stanley, proudly. His form seemed to expand with the thought of the work before him and Saunders seeing that it was of no use to argue when every minute meant lives sacrificed to the fury of the flames, said: "Come on then!"

They started for the door leading to the cabin, but too late, already the flames coming up from below were lapping the passage ways in such a manner that it made progress impossible. The cotton bales were burning like tinder and the draft that swept through the boat, caused by its flight through the water, fanned the flames which like furies leaped from point to point igniting whatever they touched that was inflammable. In but a short space of time after the alarm was given the Louisiana was wrapped in a pitiless embrace of flames whose touch blighted, seared and devoured everything it came in contact with.

Finding this means closed to them they saw at once that the cabin passengers must escape through their cabin windows to the deck, and they went to work breaking in the windows and helping those who were almost stupefied with terror to escape therefrom.

Then came a dreadful struggle for life, a struggle which to many had in it only the choice of the manner of death.

There is a something so terrible about fire that even on land and in our homes when awakened from sleep by the dread cry and with only a door or a window between us and safety, it benumbs our faculties, robs our reason and brings to the front only the prevailing instinct of self-preservation. How much more terrible is it when on ship board, when the action and the means of safety are limited. Between Scylla and Charybdis, the raging flames or the deep sea, they know not which way to turn or whither to fly.[103]

Some of the startled and half-crazed passengers rushed to and fro from place to place seeking an exit from the cabin which was nearly filled with smoke. Some, rendered desperate by fear, ran the gauntlet of the flames in the passage-way and blinded by pain, leaped over the steamer's sides. Some were shrieking and crying for help and others crying aloud to God for mercy. The sounds of the roaring flames and cracking timbers, the escaping steam and the cries of the passengers continued to make a horrible babel that made Stanley's heart thump with anxiety and excitement and his hair to almost stand on end. A few made their way through the windows forward, bruised and bleeding, to where Stanley and Saunders stood. Others pushed through side entrances. Still others, bruised and burned, frantically leaped with shrieks into the water. Some to sink into its depths with but a struggle or groan, others to make a struggle to reach the shore. Still others sank overcome by the smoke and fear and their bodies became prey to the flames.

To watch the struggles of some and be unable to help or give relief was a source of great anguish to the two young men.

The Louisiana was headed for the shore and was going at a fair rate of speed, but so fiercely did the fire rage that in their excitement it seemed as if the steamer would never reach the shore, and that all of them would be compelled to risk their chances by water, where if they died they would meet a more merciful death.

Every minute seemed an hour in length as the great tongues of flame came reaching out to them. It is already so hot that to protect their faces and bodies from the scorching glare, they must leap overboard or burn to death.

At last the boat with a thud touches the shore. The flames, now unfed by the draft, shoot straight upward and some relief is given. The great plank is pushed out, but before a landing could be secured, mad with excitement and fear, the people rush upon it. The guy ropes give way, the plank swings around under the steamer's guard and becomes useless. Those upon it are precipitated into the water and become mired in mud. To increase the horror the boat swings around and out by the force of the current and drifts down the stream. The pilot had, despite the heat and his great danger stuck to his post, until the steamer had struck the bank when he too, made a rush for safety.

Afloat on a burning steamer with no pilot to guide and safety so near. The situation seemed appalling. The cries of anguish and agony, and appeals for help to those on shore were redoubled. Made desperate many leaped overboard. Some escaped with the aid of those on shore, but a few were held fast in the mud and were nearly roasted to death by the intense heat from the burning steamer as it slowly drifted past. The rest on board began to get ready to trust their chances to the waters when the boat again acted as if under control, and looking up to the pilot house they saw there at the wheel, shading his face with one hand as if protecting it from the intense heat and lapping flames, a black man. His black face was red from the glowing heat for he was fringed in with fire. His deed of heroism challenged the admiration of the crowd, and despite their terror and danger there arose a cheer for that indifference that could so calmly brave certain death. Slowly the steamer swung around again and made for the shore, and again passing those who had become mired in the mud or were climbing upon the steep levee banks, the intense heat, finished with some, the work of death, and with others fairly cooked parts of their flesh. Their shrieks and piteous appeals were fearful.

Again the boat with a thud struck the shore, and those on board lost no time in getting ashore. Bruised, bleeding, burned, and scarred by their fight with fire they presented a pitiable appearance. With the aid of those on the levee, however, they soon crawled to a place of safety. Stanley and Saunders among them.

Again the steamer swung out, but all on board have now left it save the black pilot, who had stuck to his volunteer post until all the people who had been able left it.

Like a statue carved in ebony, but woefully disfigured and burned, he now stood near the rail of the steamer's deck either calculating the effects of a leap into the water or benumbed by pain, while the tongues of flame played about him, burnt his clothes and licked his body. A black nameless hero he stood, whose voluntary self-sacrifice made him fit to rank among those whom Nations delight to honor as the saviors of men. He was no less a hero because his skin was black or that he came of a despised race, or from the nameless poor.

He looked up and in the red glare of the blaze could be seen the traces of great pain.

Admiration for his courage took possession of the onlookers and from the crowd a dozen voices cried: "Leap! man, leap! or you are lost."

He moved with effort, gathered himself together and made a feeble jump into the water below, where his feet became embedded in the soft mud, from which he was rescued while dying, with a countenance so disfigured by burns as to be beyond recognition.

The steamer drifting down the stream, still continued in its work of destruction. It passed so close to the brave captain of the Louisiana, who had jumped overboard when the steamer first drifted away from the levee and had become bogged, as to literally roast him to death despite the heroic efforts that had been made to rescue him.

In those trying hours race was for the moment forgotten. There were Afro-Americans among both passengers and crew. They numbered among the dead and dying and were among the rescuers. Misfortune and disaster had for a time abolished racial lines, and that condition which knew no racial distinction existed.

Kind hearts and willing hands did all that could be done to alleviate suffering. Captain Jameson and the nameless black hero lay side by side upon the levee. The two brave loyal souls found rest, white and black, after dreadful moments of agony and distress, in the bosom of Father Abraham. There is no separate place or prejudice there where their two souls, together, went.

Down the river a loud report told of the bursting of the boiler or steam valves, while here and there could be seen burning bales of cotton blazing like beacons in the darkness. The next morning the Louisiana was found burned to the water's edge and stuck in the soft mud—a few miles below where the survivors had landed, a useless wreck.

The scene of human beings crying for help in mortal agony and leaping to destruction to escape a more cruel death while those on shore were powerless to aid, had stirred every heart to its depth, and the measure of human kindness heaped to the full, was spent on the survivors. Sore and bedraggled with blood and mud they were cared for throughout the night, and the next morning such as were able to go were sent to the nearest station. Here Stanley telegraphed home for money, and when it came, he purchased, as far as the place could supply, another outfit for himself and his companion. They had saved nothing from the missing steamer, except what they had on their persons. All their notes, clothing and trinkets had become a prey to the devouring flames, and they, sore and bruised, with bandages upon their persons, rejoiced that they were yet alive.

CHAPTER XVI.

"I thank God," said Seth Stanley, "to be again on terra firma. No more of your presentiments, John; you have half made me a believer in the divination of the future. Yet I am constrained to think that your feelings and the subsequent accident with its perils, was but a strange coincidence."

"My mind," replied Saunders, "has been so full of the scenes of that fire, and its horrid pictures of human beings struggling in the throes of death, that I am in no condition to think. It seems as if I can even now hear their shrieks as the flames enveloped them and they fell, to grope for an instant, and then die with their eyes turned toward Heaven, with a staring, appealing look. Then the gurgling moans of the unfortunates who preferred death by drowning to that by fire, and who went down in the sight of help that was powerless to aid. I have but to close my eyes and the picture is before me with all its details vividly depicted."

"I shall never forget that scene myself. I hid my face from it once. I could not stand it or I should have been impelled to rush into the flames myself, and have met the same death. Never shall I forget the heroism of those brave men who met such a horrible death through their efforts to save others. Brave Captain Jameson, blistered and burning, saying: 'Don't mind me; save the others,' and that nameless black hero martyr, who looked death in the face so intrepidly, in its form of raging flames, whose fiery tongues licked and scorched him while he remained at his self-imposed station until the boat ran ashore. We owe our lives to him." Greater love hath no man than this, to give up himself to such a horrible doom to save others. When the Captain and he were laid on the shore together, the color of his skin did not prevent the recognition of his heroism or keep him from sharing the full sympathy of those present. Hearts and hands were wrung as they lay writhing in their death agony. It may be some such great sorrow, afflicting both black and white, that will chasten and refine this section, that the two people will be finally brought closer together and live in greater harmony. Misery and trouble, like God, are no respecters of persons and are great levelers.

They were on a railway train which was speeding rapidly through the State of Mississippi to Birmingham, Ala. A word here and there of their conversation was caught up by their neighbors, and soon it became noised through the cars that there were two people on the train that had been passengers on the ill-fated Louisiana. They became the center of an interested and enquiring group, were plied with questions and on request, went over the scenes they had passed through.

"Your experience must have been horrible," said one.

"Horrible does not describe my feelings," said Stanley.

The dispatches relating to the accident had preceded them and at every station where the train stopped, there were people on the lookout for more complete details, and over and over again they repeated to the curious the details of the disaster.

Exhausted and almost sick from excitement, loss of appetite and sleep, and from exposure they were compelled to stop off at —— for rest. They remained there for a day before proceeding on to Birmingham.

"Birmingham is one of the worst places in the South, I have heard, for Afro-Americans," said Saunders.

Stanley looked at him questioningly.

"One of the hotels here recently refused to a delegation of Afro-Americans permission to visit Senator Sherman when he was here, either in his room or in the parlors."[104]

"Oh," said Stanley.

But he was willing to profit by his experience at New Orleans, and he did not wish, in his present state of mind, to encounter anything that would add excitement to his already excited brain, so he had not the slightest objection to offer when Saunders proposed seeking for accommodations wherever he could find them, while he went to the —— hotel.

Among Afro-Americans Saunders had no difficulty in finding some who were in good circumstances and had but little trouble in finding those who were willing to accord him every favor. His experience South and his relations North made him of much interest to them.

The following day he felt much better and not wishing to trouble Stanley in his rest, devoted a part of the day to correspondence. Among others he wrote to his sweetheart. In the letter he described their thrilling experience on the Louisiana and said that they soon expected to start for home. The name of home never sounded so sweet to him as it did then. He showed her that her fears for his safety had so far been groundless, and as they were to return now so soon, the probabilities were that no serious trouble would now befall him. He assured her that there was no ground for apprehension, although political feeling was at concert pitch.

"These people down here believe that without a doubt they will elect their president, and are so enthusiastic over it that they think he will be re-elected without much opposition. They seem to judge the whole country by the sentiment of their section, and they have but one doctrine. Just think of it, they expect to carry our own Michigan. The idea of Michigan being a party to the infamous tactics of Southern methods is preposterous, isn't it? Or Ohio, the new mother of presidents either, for that matter. To my mind the observations I have made while in the South, and the conversations that I have had with many of our race here bears me out, it seems as if the old ideas here are getting the upper hand again. Plots and schemes are being laid which connive at the disfranchisement of the Afro-American, in many districts, a return to a condition not far removed from slavery. Worst of all, this state of affairs is sanctioned by those high in state authority. Such a thing, however, cannot be; not though blood be shed and millions of money be spent. I fear, however, that in the event of Harrison's election that their disappointment will be so great that it will find vent in increased outrages against our people. If so, these words of Mr. Harrison which took such deep lodgment in my mind that they have never been uprooted or forgotten, can be used by him to test their efficacy:

'There is a vast power in a protest. Public opinion is the most potent monarch this world knows today. Czars tremble in its presence, for its every breath is pregnant with reforms. It arrests the vicious, arouses the needless and forms the iconoclastic principle in social and civil reforms. We may bring to bear upon this question, by bold and fearless denunciation of it, a public sentiment that will do a great deal in correcting it.'[105] Such opinions, backed by men in high authority, would have great weight.

"The time may come, I hope never, when the Afro-American will be compelled to take that position that all races, in all times, have taken to secure the rights and liberties that belong to citizens, which are denied them. I say may come, for I have some confidence that the wisdom, patriotism and statesmanship of the country, backed by a strong public sentiment, may arrive at some peaceful solution. Nations used to war with one another for trivial matters, now affairs of great importance are settled by arbitration. Once it took years of warfare to overthrow a system, now instances occur when a system is overthrown quietly, quickly and peaceably, but none the less surely. This is why I have at times confidence that without the usual resort to arms to obtain privileges and complete freedom, the Afro-American may drift somehow, some way, peacefully, quietly, but none the less surely, into the harbor of full citizenship.

"Today I met a brawny laborer, with hands hardened by toil, with muscles of iron, pleasing countenance and honest eyes, of whom I asked directions. When he found out I was from the North he plied me with questions. He gave me quite an insight into affairs (he did not tell her that the man said that Birmingham was one of the worst places in the South, for fear of arousing her apprehension). Speaking of their employment in the mines and furnaces around in the district, he said, with homely but poetic language: 'We's risin', sah, down heah, and soon we's gwine to brake de crust dat obscures our sun, and kum out in de full day of manhood.' Considering their position there is more fortitude and hope among these people than I expected to find.

"In the past I have been much indebted to Mr. Stanley for kindness, but all of the past has been eclipsed by the interest in, and the position taken by him in his relations with me down here. As you know, one of his chief objects in coming South was to find out if the representations he had heard were true. He is now of the opinion that the full extent of the wrongs committed against the Afro-American and white Republicans have never been made public at the North. Many Northern people have come down here, but they have simply skimmed over the South. Being wined and dined they saw it in its brightest or took for granted the representations of their hosts. The curtain was not drawn aside for them to see how hideous and unreasonable are the forms and practices of prejudice. They did not feel or experience it as we have. Others coming here and falling into social life have out-Heroded Herod by their false representations.[106] Our experiences have been such as to thoroughly disgust Seth with the customs here, and has made him a staunch friend of the race in all that the term friend implied. With his unselfish interests, his undaunted spirit, and fixedness of purpose, such a friend can be of inestimable value in presenting our cause to the people. We have reached an era in the history of our advancement when we need staunch friends who will give us positions of responsibility, that our worth and capabilities may be seen. As it is now the wealthy and refined whites see too little of the best elements amongst us, and there can, as a result, be but one consequence, a low estimate of what we are capable of doing and being.

"Stanley's Christian name, Seth, is from the Hebrew, and its meaning is Appointed. Who can tell but what he may be Appointed of God to help bring this fearful race question to a peaceful and successful solution. If I were asked why this idea occurs to me I would say because he has the material in him that distinguishes the great man. There are men who act only when the world applauds;

they are creatures of sentiment and observers of opinion, which they follow. But the great man acts without thought of whether the world will condemn or applaud. He cares nothing for the popular clamor, but he acts according to his preconceived ideas of right and justice, and if the world does not appreciate them at first, it does afterwards. Such men were Garrison, Phillips, Sumner, John Brown, Lovejoy, and others whose memories are dear to us. Such are the convictions that sway Stanley, and he has the requisite courage to obey his ideas of right and justice.[107] Such a man, or rather hero, deserves success in life and in affairs of love. We will soon be home now, and I feel sorry to know that he cannot at once repair to Miss Stone with the same anticipation of a happy future with which I will return to you. I only wish you could know her as I do him. She is so pleasing in manner and address, that she would win almost any one's respect, if not their love. She has often joined with him in making me feel that I am a man, and by no word or gesture has she made me feel that she considered me an inferior, or unworthy of friendship. When they are married no harsh requirements of prejudice, or conformity to the opinions and customs of society, shall keep you from knowing one whom you will find to be a kindred spirit.

"Give yourself no further concern as to my safety. I am all right and cautious. I shall soon be at home to you and dear old father, in ten days at least. May God give his angels charge concerning thee.

Yours affectionately,

John."

CHAPTER XVII.

_____

Edith Darrow had not heard from John Saunders for what seemed to her a long time, and she had begun to feel quite despondent over it. Her active imagination, aided by her love and fears, conjured up difficulties that increased in size and became more numerous as each succeeding day passed with no tidings of the absent one. She was familiar, from constant watching, with the time the postman made his appearance, and if away from home she usually managed to return shortly after he was due.

One afternoon a few days after Saunders wrote his letter, she was out shopping. Timing herself, as usual, she hastened home rather despondently. As soon as she entered the door she put the usual anxious query.

"Any mail?"

"Yes, a letter from John."

A great change came over her in an instant. She forgot that she was tired; gone was the despondent feeling of a few moments before; with eyes dancing and with a smiling countenance, she gave a hop and a skip to her mother's side as she asked with all eagerness.

"Where is it, mother?" looking from table to sideboard and taking all the articles upon them in at a glance.

"If it had been a snake it would have bitten you," answered her mother. "I put it up in the window so it would be the first thing you might see when you entered the house."

Edith clasped her mother's cheeks between her hands and kissed them first on one side and then on the other.

"Now for my letter," she said, as she tripped over to the window. "I see that it is a good fat one. I guess he must be trying to atone for waiting so long," breaking the seals of the letter. "He's going to get a scolding, nevertheless, unless he has a good excuse."

She sat down and began to read. Before she had read a couple of lines her mother asked her smilingly, "Hadn't you better take off your hat? The contents of the letter won't spoil by waiting a minute."

"I had forgotten all about my hat," replied Edith, laying the letter in her lap while she took it off and laid it on the table. Then pointing her finger at her mother she said. "Don't say another word to me until I finish this letter."

"I'm mum," said her mother, resuming her work.

Edith resumed the reading and before she had finished, her face went through various transformations. Frequently she exclaimed, "Oh, how dreadful!" Once her pent up feelings gave expression in a little low whistle of surprise. Excitement over the steamboat disaster, anger at the treatment accorded them at New Orleans, grief over his losses, joy that he escaped without serious injury from the burning steamer, admiration at the heroic conduct of the black hero martyr, and seriousness over the picture he drew of the Southern problem, in turn, held the mastery over her.

When she had finished it she rather excitedly said to her mother, "I must take this over to John's father and read it to him. John and Mr. Stanley have had a narrow escape from death through fire. They were on that steamboat that burnt under such horrible circumstances."

"You don't say!" exclaimed her mother, throwing up one hand, "read it to me."

Edith re-read the letter for her mother's benefit, then put on her hat to go and see Mr. Saunders.

"To use a slang phrase, mother, Mr. Stanley is a brick, and I hope that John's estimate of his character and surmise of his future will prove true."

"He seemed to be a nice fellow when he was here. I have often wondered why he took such a liking to John."

"For the same reason I did. I understand it perfectly."

Before her mother could reply Edith had gone.

Mr. Saunders was now living with a married daughter on W—— street, not far from the Darrows. John made his home with her also. Thither Edith went to find the old gentleman sitting out enjoying the autumn sunshine. He was now too old to engage in the active duties of life, and in his old age depended upon John for support. When he saw Edith, her face flushed and radiant, he accosted her with, "God bless you, honey, I know you've got good news from John. I see it in your face."

"Yes, and I have brought the letter with me to read it to you. He expects to be home in at least ten days."

"He's a good boy, honey, but jest wait till I gets you a chair. We'll sit right out here and enjoy that letter all by ourselves."

The way Mr. Saunders bobbed up and hurried around, getting his future daughter-in-law a seat would have made one believe that he was the suitor instead of the son. He soon appeared with a chair, and after seeing Edith comfortably seated, took his own chair and sat in front of her, and inclining his head to one side, he placed a hand behind one ear so that no word could escape his eager hearing. "Now we's ready," said he.

As she read in her rich voice that fell like sweet music upon his ears, ever and anon he put in an ejaculation of surprise or approval, disgust or anger, according as he was moved by what he heard, sometimes he would stop her to make a comment on what had been read.

"I am glad the boy is comin' home so soon," he said when she had finished. "I have felt kinder uneasy since he's been down there. You see my chile, he don't know how to take them white folks as use ter own slaves. He growed up different from what we did. I thank God often that our children do not have to go through what we did."

"I think it's a shame that he has to be insulted the way that he is. He is just as good as any of them. There isn't anything about him, either in manner or person, that could be offensive to the most fastidious, and yet he is treated as if he had no more feeling than a brute."

"He is a great deal better than lots of them, but its going ter take them white people down there a long time to find it out. A good many of 'em will die before they ever know it, or knowing it, to own it. You see the trouble is, honey, old Joe and Uncle Sam who don't know nuthen' and don't want much is better to them than these fellows that know as much as they do. They have always got the old heads, like me, who don't know much under 'em, and they keep 'em so. When we gets so we know better, we are no use to 'em."

"But, Father Saunders, they get around facts, and it is a fact that the thousands of colored children graduating year after year from our public schools, with the same test applied to them as to others, are almost, if not quite, as intelligent as their classmates."

"That's jest it, Edith, the trouble is that one-half the world is trying to devise means to escape facts. A man seldom accepts anything agin his in trust till he's forced to."

"Well, it isn't right, just nor fair for ambitious, capable people to be forced to the bottom and kept there, because others not connected with you in any way, except by race and hardly that in this country, are ignorant. We are willing to be subjected to any test that civilization and enlightenment may apply, so that the test be applied to all alike, and will be willing to abide by the tests."

"You may live to see such a time Edith; God grant that you may. I know I won't. If only I could, I would say, like Simeon, Now Lord lettest thy servant depart in peace."

"I trust I may see a better day for my people; if I thought not I would want to die now."

"There now, honey, don't you get to feeling so miserable, I didn't mean to make you sad. When John comes home life will appear like itself again."

Edith arose to go, but upon being urged by Mr. Saunders, went in to "visit awhile."

CHAPTER XVIII.

Buried in thought, and enjoying the ease that comes to those who have passed through severe trials, when in safety, or through a period of restless activity, Stanley sat in an elegant suite of rooms in the —— hotel.

Presently he pressed the call and upon the appearance of the bell boy, ordered writing materials, and then he resumed his former easy position. Intent in the same deep train of thought that seemed to carry his mind far away, he did not hear the boy as he entered the room with paper and ink. From his manner, and the expression of deep perplexity that now and then crossed over his face, it was evident that he was engrossed with some weighty subject. He arose from his chair shortly after and paced up and down the room several times, then a light broke over his countenance as if some revelation had suddenly burst upon him. Whatever he had been thinking about was settled to his own satisfaction. Then, noticing the writing materials he had ordered, he sat down and wrote:

"Dear Father:—I am at last in Birmingham, and have received enough rest to now supplement the meager information imparted by my telegram from ——, La. You have doubtless eagerly scanned the papers for all information concerning the burning of the Louisiana, but you can scarcely form a conception of its horrors from newspaper reports. When I think of it I become completely unnerved, so I shall reserve a description of the fire with its perils, for a time when I can look back upon it with calmer feelings. John and I lost everything—clothing, curiosities, and different memoranda which we had jotted down for future use.

"We will probably remain here for several days, so if you have not confidence enough in my memory to think it has retained all the instructions given to me relative to the investments made, and which you desire to make, you will have time to write them down and forward the same to me here. Owing to the outrageous customs here I am domiciled at the hotel, while John is somewhere else. Where, I do not know, as he left me but a few hours ago. We are very much inconvenienced by having to remain apart, but I cannot have him near me and justify my conscience, for neither at the hotel, or traveling on the steamer is it possible to have him near me, except in the capacity of a servant. I had fully made up my mind to resist such insults to my friend, but for his sake I suffer it, and the position is a bitter one to me.

"Everything down here runs to politics at present. Political excitement is very high, and the relation between the races is rendered more dangerous. This is one reason why, for John's sake, I have refrained from insisting on those rights due him as a man. In a few of the country districts a reign of terror prevails, whose embers are kept alive and fanned by the ignorant poor whites, who seem to be as low down in the scale of ignorance and degradation as the lower order of the Negroes, or as John calls them, and I shall do likewise, Afro-Americans. In my short time around the hotels here I have heard a strange terrible story, but it illustrates the depravity, and intense political hatred, borne to the blacks and to white Republicans. It happened in a small town in Mississippi. The story is as follows:

"Three traveling men sat on the piazza of a hotel; their talk had been on trade and finally drifted to politics. A party of whites came along and catching enough of their conversation to think that they were Republicans, began to insult and abuse them. A few colored men came along and took their part. The white men were armed. There was a jostle and a short scuffle, a few shots, and the colored men had yielded up their lives. When the traveling men saw their defenders thus disposed of, they looked at each other with pale faces. The same thought that the dead must not go unavenged passed through their minds. Each to the other, with his eyes, said farewell, and they made a rush at their assailants. But what chance have unarmed men against the armed? Instead of conflict there is murder and massacre—relics of brute savagery and man's unhumanity. In less time than it takes to tell it, these men were also murdered, and without fear of justice or retribution, because public sentiment was with them, they rode off perhaps exulting in the death of the 'niggers' and the infernal Yankees. Thus to satisfy insensate hatred six human beings had been murdered. I have heard of no such cold-blooded barbarity enacted this side of the Fiji Islands, or by Russian despotism, and yet it is only one instance of many that occur with increasing regularity if reports be true.

"I fancy I hear you say, 'Horrible! Where are the authorities?' There is no justice for the Afro-American or his sympathizers in the country or in the towns, and but a little in the larger cities. Before coming down here I refused to credit the stories of race troubles, and rather attributed them to political partisanship to serve party purposes, but my own experience goes to confirm a great many of them, and I fear for the peace of a country which permits such things. True, there are liberal men here who denounce these outrages, but they seem powerless to prevent them.

"I have used my eyes while here and have observed a great deal. I have watched the different classes in the cities and for the life of me, I cannot see that the ignorant black is more vicious than the ignorant classes in the large cities of the North, nor can I account for the bitter feeling manifested against him. His greatest fault seems to be that his ancestors were torn from their native country, worked for centuries in the fields of the South, contributing to its great material growth for which he received no compensation. Then permitting himself, through the strange vicissitude of events, to become a free man and the political equal of his late master.

"An impartial mind, brought to bear upon the problem of this section, would consider all these fears of black domination or extravagance to be chimeras, which are used to perpetuate a wholly unjust and pernicious system. I have examined into the past carefully with an unbiased mind, and I find that in extravagance, the Afro-American has not been more so than many whites in the North, nor have his peculations been so large as those of white men in this section. The corruption of the Tweed ring and others, brought into prominent notice in the Empire State, far exceed anything committed by the Afro-American under Reconstruction, and yet there is no talk concerning the unfitness, or rather, no measures to forcibly preclude such men from governing.[108] There is something about this Reconstruction period which the country hears but little of, but which redounds to the credit of this persecuted race, who were hardly a decade out of slavery. Their conception of government, their ideas of the basic principles of the Republic, their generous treatment of their late masters, are in striking contrast to the government of the 'superior race' now. Of course the carpet-bagger, who has also been so roundly and unjustly abused, deserves no little credit for the part taken by them in leading these people to adopt such measures. The constitutions of the States, adopted in 1868, were models of a Republican form of government. They established the public school system of this section, and first made it a part of the fundamental law of the State. They instituted a uniformity of taxation and overthrew the barbarous penal system, which, now reinstated, is barbarously used against them. They also inaugurated the municipal system of self-government and abolished the property qualifications; and with generous motives, removed the bars that had excluded those, who had taken part in the war, from citizenship. Still this is the same people of which we hear so much as to their inferiority, by those who have received from them benefits and whose return to power, it is claimed, would be attended by such dire consequences. What awful return has been his for his generosity? Since '76, thousands have been murdered, and our civilization disgraced by wanton and inhuman butcheries from the hands of the very men who owed to him their citizenship. What would you or I do under like circumstances?

"During my convalescence and since, from words that have passed between John and myself, I have thought a great deal about this subject, and have concluded that even in the North, much as it appears to be shocked by the barbarity of the South, justice is not done to the Afro-American. True, he has liberty of person and free use of the ballot, but employment, save as, a menial, he finds it difficult to obtain, no matter how intelligent or well fitted he may be to fill the position for which he applies. The laboring elements keep him out of workshops and stores by their exhibitions of prejudice, and the American people, despite the fact that he is a loyal citizen, who has done his share in upholding the national flag and preserving the Union intact, by a shameful silence, acquiesces in their dicta.

"I learn from John that his race does not ask for particular favors. It simply wants the same chance to earn a living that is given to others, and it is willing to submit to the same tests of intelligence and fitness. Ought not their simple request be granted. (By the way I forgot to say that John has informed me, and he is corroborated in his statements by others, that the Afro-American does not desire to rule, but they do desire that the Constitution should be supreme). Of all the people I have come in contact with, only our own seem to have an improper idea of social and equal rights. It seems to be granted that if you are at all familiar with a man in a business way, he is to have a free entry into the family, and this is probably one reason why the Afro-American has so much trouble. Such an idea is, however, absurd, and in no other country than ours is it expected. The Afro-American does not want it or expect it, John says. He is satisfied with his own home relations, and being of a sensitive nature (particularly the more intelligent) would not obtrude where he was not invited or wanted.

"I am glad that the house of Stanley has taken an advanced step, and particularly so that it was taken before I owed to John a debt of gratitude. You know his fitness for the position he occupies, and you are satisfied with his work. I have found him to be unusually bright and intelligent, well informed, and with a capacity for hard work in business beyond the average. I now wish to apply the standard of fitness and ability to him, and with your consent will promote him, on our return, to the position to be made vacant by Morley, who leaves us in November to embark in an enterprise out West. The increase in salary will also be a handsome wedding present. You will excuse me for dwelling almost entirely upon this one subject, but almost every circumstance since coming South has forced the question on my mind.

"You can rest assured that I will do my best in reference to the business to be done here.

"Give my love to Imogene. Don't let her worry over what I may have suffered on the burning steamer. Barring my shattered nerves, Richard is almost himself again. We'll return to Detroit as soon as possible without extending the trip further. I have seen and experienced enough. Good-bye.

Your affectionate son,

Seth."

Birmingham, Ala., Oct. 14th, 1888.

CHAPTER XIX.

Several days were required by Stanley to attend to business, and the time when he was not engaged thus he and Saunders spent doing the city and visiting the mines and great furnaces in the district. The growth of Birmingham has been simply wonderful, and it has rightly been called the Magic City. Northern capital, in the last decade, has invaded the section and out of almost a howling wilderness, there sprang forth towns with marvelous growth. Immense iron works and furnaces were started, and entering the bowels of the earth, workmen began to rob it of its coal and iron. Now, Birmingham and Chattanooga are beginning to rival Pittsburg, and the miners of Pennsylvania find new competitors in those of Alabama and Tennessee. The labor problem becomes more complicated because of the antagonisms of the whites to the blacks, and the refusal of the former to take the latter as equals into their organizations of labor.

As common laborers, the blacks are preferred here, and are considered better than cheap white labor. Some prefer them as skilled laborers.

When not with Stanley helping him with his negotiations or visiting points of interest with him, Saunders spent a great deal of time among the works that employed Afro-Americans. He was a great searcher after facts and was on the continual lookout for items that would interest the race North. He was also very methodical, and whatever he learned he jotted down. "It will come in handy when I get home," he said to Seth.

He abstained altogether from the discussion of politics, save when alone with the family he was boarding with, or among a group of Afro-Americans. They manifested much interest in the general outcome, and his opinions as to the result of the canvass in the North were gladly heard, and caused many a look of satisfaction to pass over their ebony features.

It was late in the week when Stanley finished his business, which was to result in the establishment of new works, so he concluded to remain over Sunday, and as they had not attended church since leaving home, to visit one of Birmingham's churches.

When he proposed this to Saunders and suggested that they go together, he objected and said, "That he would rather go with the family with whom he was boarding, as they had invited him; besides, he might not be wanted where Stanley wanted to go."

"Nonsense!" said Stanley, "You don't suppose that anyone would object to your attending church. That is what churches are for. Their mission and purpose—the saving of souls—as the bride of Christ, is to invite and make welcome all who will come to Him. Besides this is one of the most distinguished divines of the South. You would miss a treat not to hear him. Rev. Randolph Rucker is celebrated for his logic and oratory all over the country. Such a man must be pious, and as good as he is able."

"I have often told you," replied Saunders, "that you don't view these things like the people down here, and because you don't you can't conceive of their views or their interpretations of the Scriptures. Prejudice makes the teachings of Christ a vehicle to carry out its own purposes. It is the same old story of using the livery of Heaven to serve the devil in. For they see in every clause of holy writ a squinting construction, which is so interpreted as to suit their preconceived ideas. Men who are earnestly desiring to be right, form their views from what they learn, but there are others who form an opinion, and make all things else conform to it, even in the face of plainest facts. There is but one way with them, and that is their own way. By nursing certain fancies, whole communities become infected with the disease. You know the bible has been interpreted in many one-sided ways, hence the number of sects and creeds. I'll wager you that if the white man's bible in the South does not recognize race superiority in fact, it does in fancy, which suits their purposes as well. Don't you remember that slavery found its justification in the leaves of the same book. I can remember how my father said the white ministers were wont to preach to the slaves. It was after this manner: 'Be good niggers now. Don't run away. Don't steal. Don't lie, and bye and bye when your master and mistress get high up in heaven you'll be there in the kitchen.' Even the old slaves, who were wont to exhort, had to use practically the same argument. Do you suppose the preachers of today are less subtle in their interpretations, or less ironclad in their ways?

"Beside what is not openly or tacitly excused, like Pilate, they wash their hands of. How many professed Christians, like him, will go into eternity, their only record consisting in what they have not done of what they might have done. You asked me once what part I thought the Negro would play in American civilization. My answer is that he is to give to our Christianity, that chiefest of graces, which is now its lacking element, charity. I thought so often of the race in connection with the thirteenth chapter of First Corinthians that I can repeat every word of it. Let me give you a few verses that you may measure the sermon by what we are to hear. St. Paul says in such a masterly way: 'Though I speak with the tongues of men and of angels, and have not charity, I am become as sounding brass, or a tinkling cymbal. And though I have the gift of prophecy, and understand all mysteries, and all knowledge; and though I have all faith, so that I could remove mountains, and have not charity, I am nothing. And though I bestow all my goods to feed the poor, and though I give my body to be burned, and have not charity, it profiteth me nothing. Charity suffereth long, and is kind; charity envieth not, charity vauniteth not itself, is not puffed up.' Show me a church that practices these principles toward me and I will say that the South is a paradise. Such an one has not been here before to my knowledge."

"Those days have all gone by, John. With the new dawn of humanity, Christianity took a forward step, and put in the rear the old ill-conceived ideas of servitude without compensation, or even of distinctions such as you have mentioned in the future world. The Rev. Rucker is celebrated, and surely up to the most enlightened ideas of Christianity."

"If my interests in his subject would cause me to lose self-consciousness, that would keep constantly before me, the fact that he and the larger part of his audience would despise my fellowship, then I might enjoy it. It is not always the real violence and insult that cowers me, it is the constant apprehension of it."

"Self-consciousness is good enough in its place, but you have seen so much to condemn down here, that I want to show you something you can commend."

"Then I will lend to my feet wings, and go with you without farther protest. I should like to say once when I get home, that I thoroughly enjoyed myself while exercising the rights of a man. But mind, now, there must be no rumpus should my appearance be objected to except in the corner, which I have heard has been set off for the colored people."

Sunday morning was all that one could wish. The sun was just enough obscured by a thin fleece of clouds to cut off the intensity of its heat, and to those who could see God in nature, every surrounding seemed to say, "Today is the Lord's. He has set it apart unto Himself. The heavens offer testimony to his glory, and all the earth responds in unison to the chant of harmony." 'Twas such a day when man having cast aside the turmoil of life, the task of breadwinning, and the seditions that make discontent rebel against its fate,

Could steal away from themselves, and care,
And give their souls to thoughts of Him, and prayer.

Stanley had arisen early, and immediately after breakfast went to Saunders' boarding house, and together they walked around the streets of Birmingham, until the ringing of the church bells announced the hour of worship. The divine, of whom Seth had spoken—Rev. Randolph Rucker —was in charge of one of the fashionable churches. His name and fame had spread beyond the limit of city and state, as a man of eloquence and much learning, and towards his church they directed their way, as the bells began to chime.

The church itself was not imposing, yet of ample structure and architecture, to make a fine appearance and have a comfortable seating capacity.

They ascended the broad stone steps together and entered the vestibule, and waited there for an usher to come and seat them. One presently came towards Stanley and with a pleasant voice and manner said: "This way, sir," and started down one of the aisles.

Stanley and Saunders started to follow, but had not proceeded far when Saunders was tapped on the shoulder by a man in the audience. As he turned around the man said, "You will find a place in the gallery," at the same time pointing to it, and to a section forming a part of it, which was separated from the main gallery by a partition about the height of an ordinary man.

Saunders looked at him as if he would like to have withered him with a glance and asked, "Am I not to be allowed to sit with my friend?"

The man did not answer his question directly, but said, "Here, the usher will show you. You ought to know better, sir."

By this time Stanley had been attracted to the spot by Saunders stopping, and the sound of voices. Hearing the last remark of the man who had stopped Saunders, his ire was aroused at once. "Do you mean to insult us in church?" he asked, trying to suppress his indignation.

"Are you a nigger, too?"

"I cannot comprehend such an epithet in a house of God. If you mean by it, am I colored, I answer, No! But color or the absence of it does not make a man one whit less a gentleman."

"Come, come," said the usher. "We can't have a scene in the church. Step out into the vestibule and I will explain to you! I did not know that he," indicating John by a gesture, "was with you."

The whole congregation was by this time staring in their direction, and Stanley, fearing that he had made a mistake, followed the usher.

When they reached the vestibule, the usher turned and said: "You are evidently from the North, my friend, and of course not acquainted with our customs. There is a place fitted up for colored people to worship in when they visit here, and it is nice and comfortable. We don't think of such a thing as inviting them down where our wives and daughters sit."

"You mean then," replied Stanley, "that my friend must go up into that little fenced coop all by himself, or he cannot hear the gospel preached here."

"You don't look at it in the right light. We invite them to come, but we expect that they will keep in their place."

"I see. It is an exclusive gospel you preach. We will have none of it. Come on, John. I will go to church with you," and they left the church.

"What did I tell you?" said Saunders.

"I wouldn't have believed it," replied Stanley, as he stopped suddenly. "I am going back and have it out."

"Not for me; it isn't worth raising a fuss about, and you know I have determined not to get into any trouble down here."

"I am not going to make a fuss. I'm only going to see the Rev. Rucker and lay the matter before him."

"I wouldn't go back with you now, even if for your sake he should reverse a common practice of the church. I would think more of the insincerity of the proceedings than of the sermon, if I did."

"Well, I am going to see for my own satisfaction what his views are on the matter. He is a minister of the Gospel."

"All right. Do as you please. I am going where I am certain I shall be welcome."

They parted. Saunders to go with friends to a colored church, and Stanley to the one they had just left. The same usher met him, and Seth imagined he saw a triumphant look in his eyes as he again offered to show him a seat.

After taking the proffered seat Stanley wrote a note to the Rev. Rucker, giving briefly their experience and asking for an interview. He sent in his note by another usher—a younger man—and in a little while the answer came, short but to the point:

"I have not the time to be interviewed before services, but I am in entire accord with the action of the ushers in this matter.

RANDOLPH RUCKER."

Stanley felt chagrined at this curt reply, but concluded to sit and hear the style of gospel that was preached.

Soon the notes from the organ began to peal the doxology. Shortly after in came the pastor and took his seat in the pulpit. He was rather tall, with dark complexion, heavy eyes, and features somewhat irregular. A critical eye might have thought it discerned a trace of the obnoxious blood in his veins. When he arose to speak, his voice, deep and sonorous, gave Stanley the impression that he was an orator of uncommon power. He read as the preliminary lesson the thirteenth chapter of the First Corinthians, also the chapter from which he afterwards took his text. This reading of the chapters with singing and prayer, concluded the opening services, and he arose to preach.

CHAPTER XX.

———————

"The spirit and the bride say, come; and let him that heareth say, come. And let him that is athirst come, and whosoever will let him take of the waters of life freely."

—Revelations xxii., 17.

Stanley was now all attention.

"I wish," began the minister, "to call your attention to the latter part of the verse read, from which I take my text this morning, 'whosoever will, let him take of the water of life freely,' to illustrate the charity of God. Look wherever we will, in whatever condition we find ourselves, we cannot escape the conclusion that God has dealt with a generous lavish hand with his people. Every jot and tittle of nature bespeaks His unbounded love to man. Moreover, he counted it not loss, but sent His only begotten Son that we, who had forfeited our claim on an eternal inheritance, might be again restored to our estate. From the eternity of existence redemption was planned for us. The word that was in the 'beginning,' which afterwards became flesh to dwell among men, is a part of the great plan of salvation of the God who had all to give, and yet who requires so little in return. The whole history of His chosen people from the selection of Abraham to the destruction of Jerusalem is a constant series of man's rebellious acts, and of the charitable dealings of God with their weaknesses; of the loving Father, of the stern Parent, who made them pass through great vicissitudes of fortune, captivity and perils, only that they might be brought back to bear testimony to His goodness and love, and enable them to reject the false gods and teachings which had borne them astray. The unspeakable love of God culminated in the gift of His blessed Son. He left His estate in glory to save such as you and I. Moreover, He came among men to feel as they had felt and to teach them an example by contact. Did He come to those in authority, the leaders among men? Did He identify himself with the conceited Pharisee with his holier than thou assumption, His long phylacteries and public ablutions and prayers? No. He appeared among those with whom the struggle of life was hard, among the poor and lowly. He despised not the Publican nor the Samaritan. He healed the sick and preached the gospel to the poor. If Christ, the Son of God, condescended to sup and commune with the lowliest, shall we despise the least of His creatures?

"Not only was the veil of the temple rent at His death, by which each human soul became its own altar unto God, but the fountain of charity was opened wide and human hearts touched with its flow. As a consequence the hospital, the asylum, the house of the unfortunate, are institutions wherever Christian civilization has obtained a foothold. Noble men and women have consecrated their fortunes and their lives to the work; and those whose hearts do not find an awakening chord of love in this abundant profusion of God's providence are out of tune with Christianity, out of tune with the irresistible charitable spirit that is moving the universe, and which finds its eternal spring in God himself.

"God's love has restored to us all things lost by sin. When the wickedness of disobedience after the flood led Noah's descendants to defy God's power and with a self-conceit unparalleled said: 'We will build a temple unto heaven,' He sent the confusion of tongues and the people were dispersed abroad over the land, but with chastisement came the promise of one who should restore all things. He came, He spake as never man spake. He suffered in Gethsemane under the weight of the sins of the world which were heaped upon His head for our sakes until he sweat great drops of blood. He was crucified for us, died and arose again, bringing captivity captive in that those who died in Christ shall be raised again at the last day and shall stand with Him. He is now our advocate and mediator with God. And lo, when the promised comforter came on the day of Pentecost the tongues were for a time restored and every man of the vast throng that had come to the feast had the gospel preached to him in his own tongue. This is the charity that suffereth long and is patient. This is the universal love that saved to the utter most. The glad cry went forth that day and has been ringing from thousands of people ever since. 'Whosoever will, let him take of the water of life freely.'

"The Promised One had come, had accomplished His purpose and sent the Comforter at the appointed time. The day of Pentecost was but the beginning of the era of restoration which will be consummated in the last day as spoken of by John in his vision on the Isle of Patmos. He tells us the result. Out of every Nation, and tongue, and people there will be representatives singing the new song, Hallelujah! To the Lamb who is worthy to receive power, and glory, and riches, and wisdom, and strength and honor; and 'Blessings and honor, and glory, and power, be unto Him who sitteth upon the throne and unto the Lamb forever.'

"Already the gospel missionaries are carrying the glad tidings, inviting all nations and people to aspire for salvation. Soon all nations and tongues will have the gospel preached to them in their own land and tongue and all will be brought together in a common worship looking for the end of time. The Jew took a narrow view of Christ's mission in the world. They believed He would re-establish the kingdom of Judea, and that Jerusalem would be restored to its original splendor and precedence, and be the mistress of the world. The good old Simeon, moved by the inspirations of prophesy, saw the grander purposes of God in the Emanuel. He expressed it when He said of Jesus that He was a light of revelation to the Gentiles and the glory of Israel. With prophetic eyes He saw in all the ends of the earth those who should be called the children of Abraham, because they heard and believed.

"Are you poor today? Are you sinful? Are you outcasts? Have you nothing to offer to God? His charitable, loving sacrifice is for you; for the Spirit and the Bride say, come. They who hear His words and have found it precious, say, come. Will you, who are out of Christ, come my friends? Oh, will you come?

"I wish to address myself to the members of my church; those who are Christians. Are you following after Christ as He has pointed out the way in His Holy Book? Are you doing for others what He has done for you? Do you treat the lowly and extend the helping hand to the weak as you yourself would like to be treated were you in their station? If you have not, begin now. There is a continuity of principle in the grand qualities of charity that reaches from God to His chosen people, and from His chosen people to the sympathetic heart everywhere that beats for humanity with its sorrows and woes. No child of God should be isolated. If Christ be our elder brother who shall deny us or whom shall we deny, or who shall say that all are not of the brethren?

"One of the most pathetic scenes in the history of the life of our Lord from the time of His minority to the time when He was scourged and crucified upon the cross, was His weeping over His chosen city, Jerusalem. What words could have better revealed a heart overflowing with anxiety and pity than 'Jerusalem how oft would I have gathered you as a hen gathereth her brood, but ye would not. If you had but known the things that worketh for thy peace?' He wept over Lazarus although poor and despised. He weeps today over the world lying in wickedness, going astray with its thousands of churches and pastors, and its millions of communicants. Are you doing your duty? Are you going into the gutter to rescue the fallen? Are you exerting yourself to relieve the oppressed?

To do these things is charity. Can you take the outcast and the lowly, the dirty and ragged by the hand and tell them of Jesus? This is charity. Can you go into desolate homes and soothe the last moments of the wretched with a word of prayer? This is charity. Such deeds done in seclusions may not be told in the streets of Gath or whispered in Askalon, but they are trumpeted in the streets of the New Jerusalem, for God takes cognizance of them and they are written in the Book of Life. Lo! Christ said: 'Inasmuch as ye have done it unto one of the least of these my children ye have done it unto me.' If we have not done it when the opportunity came we were remiss in our duty, our profession is Pharsaical and is condemned already. These are the sacrifices we must make for the Church if it ever becomes a power for good in the world. If we are followers of Christ we must exercise Christian charity. We should find our duty to our fellowman in an abundance of love and do it with an unstinting charity. If as St. Paul said: 'Though I speak with the tongues of angels, and give my body to be burned, and have not charity, it profiteth me nothing,' shall we gainsay it and move and live and act as if heaven was made for us alone and thus make of non-effect the invitation, 'Whosoever will let him take of the water of life freely.'

"Unto all Nations must the gospel be preached, for so the Savior did command, and to them is the invitation extended. Come! Come! from the ends of the earth, from the isles of the sea, from the inheritance of the heathen, from the hovels of the poor. Salvation is without price. It is as free as the air around us. It is more precious than riches. It is more beautiful than nature in its loveliest garb. It is the inspiration of the noblest thoughts. Come! It is God's bounteous charity. Who will take up the glad strain,

'Confirm the tidings as they roll,
And spread the truth from pole to pole?'[109]

"Charity creates a generous feeling for all mankind, takes away covetousness, ennobles the soul and blesses it. The church must be filled with it. Individual Christians must be imbued with it, else they do not live up to the high standard of Christianity. We can deceive the world by hollow pretenses, but we cannot God. If evil is in your hearts, root it out. God is not mocked. Be not deceived, for whatsoever a man soweth, that shall he also reap."

. . . .

"The water of life; oh! how precious. Without cost and without price. Oh! the beneficence of God. The charity displayed to us poor creatures of the world. Do you thirst for righteousness? Come! Take of it freely and you shall find rest in your souls, and that peace that comes with perfect content and trust in God. There is no doubt of it now. There was a time when the cry went out, 'Who is able?' Since then the Lamb slain from the foundation of the world has prevailed and that cry has been changed to the glad one of whosoever will come and take of its benefits.

"Go out into the world and extend the invitation to come and drink of the fount that continually pours forth the fresh, pure water of salvation. With all charity extend your hand to the lowly, the outcast, the oppressed and the ignorant. Tell them of that which is more precious than rubies. The great goodness of God and the love of Christ, our elder brother. Of the invitation of the Spirit and the Bride, to him that heareth, to him that is athirst to come and take of the water of life freely, for

'The fountain of life is flowing,
Is flowing, freely flowing.
The fountain of life is flowing,
Is flowing for you and for me.' "[110]

CHAPTER XXI.

With a feeling akin to wonder as to the kind of gospel that would be preached, Stanley had sat and listened while, with a well-modulated voice, the minister read St. Paul's masterly commentary on charity. But while the minister, with an almost divine eloquence, delivered his sermon on the invitation of the Spirit and the Bride, he could not help but think, "Either his lips and heart are at variance, or his moral judgment is sadly warped." Of what avail are their grand eloquent words about taking the ragged, dirty and drunken from the gutter, when they shut out those worthy and anxious to come for no other reason than that they are as white as themselves? Their acts are not in accord with these words: "Inasmuch as you have done it unto one of the least of these, my children, ye have not done it unto me." While the minister was in the very height of his eloquence, Stanley looked around to catch a glimpse of the usher and the man who had so discourteously and so unchristianlike refused his companion a seat, to see how they took the words of the preacher. No sign of guilt or shame was there, nothing but a passive calm. While he was almost fascinated by the language of the speaker, his thoughts could not help but dwell on the subject uppermost in his mind. "Are not," thought he, "insults directed at the colored people in these places of divine worship sure to react? After all, was not all the ruin that was brought upon the South, the desolation of its homes, due to the domination of the teachings of the church here in relation to slavery? Will not God's warning, 'Be not deceived; God is not mocked, whatsoever a man sows that shall he also reap,' be heeded?" As the minister finished his sermon by his eloquent peroration, "to him that heareth and to him that is athirst come and drink of the water of life freely," touching and grand in its delivery and effort, he could not help but think of that parable of Jesus in which He speaks of those who at the last day will come and say, "Lord! Lord! Have we not called upon Thee and in Thy Name cast out devils," and the Lord said, "Depart from Me; I never knew you." It was evident that Stanley had profited by the church going

213

that Marjorie had led him into, and many times some favorite passage of hers flitted over his mind. He liked to recall them as memories of her.

After the services, with brows knit in thought, he went back to the hotel. In vain he tried to frame an excuse for their customs, that would harmonize with them. His religion, although confined to no particular creed or tenet could find no excuse for such treatment, for any kind or manner of men. "The children of Ethiopia shall stretch forth their hands to the Most High God. (A favorite text of Saunders'.)

Is not that enough for these people?"[111]

Looking back upon his life, when his youth was gayest, when his thoughts were lightest, when his ambition was least troubled about the future he could not recall ever being so biased towards others, although blind to his own interests. If he had done himself an irreparable injury, he was conscious of no wrong to anyone save probably her, and he was now willing to devote his life to correct the wrong impressions she might once have entertained concerning him. Since he had known her how changed he had become. Her gentle influence over him had been incalculable for good. His views of life had wholly changed. His passion had reformed his aims, and purified his thought and intellect. He comprehended more clearly what was expected of man, and saw that rightly his duty should be more in the pursuit of those things that make mankind better and happier, instead of being engaged chiefly in selfish pursuits of pleasure. The things that satisfy for the moment, but which in parting leave a greater vacancy than they had filled. Marjorie's influence was the leaven that had wrought the change, that still working, was to make him the devout Christian, the man whose sole aim and purpose was in making others happy and lightening the burdens of those around him. His contact with Saunders had helped to widen his understanding, as contacts with such minds will. Free from such prejudices as sway the narrow minded, he could not conceive why its influence should be so blighting upon intelligent men and women of color, or why it should be more malignant when emanating from the lower orders of the people, than among the more refined and intelligent classes. "I wonder if public opinion can be so moulded as to change this order of things, and if so what would be the best way to go at it." So abstracted had be become in his reverie that he did not notice the time. When he turned from gazing at the curling smoke of his cigar to look at his watch he gave a bound from his chair and began to move around lively. He had almost forgotten an engagement.

Mr. Warner, his father's representative at Birmingham, had invited him to dinner, after which they were to take a drive. He profited by his former experiences, and at this dinner he refrained from mentioning the episode of the morning, because he thought it would not be likely that he would find in this part of the country any one whose views would be near as liberal as his own. He had come across many whose views were liberal but they were passive in asserting them for fear of social ostracism, and hence they allowed the ultra-minded to shape all sentiment.

The dinner party was such an enjoyable one and the people made it so pleasant for him that he concluded to extend his stay a few days longer. Among his new acquaintances was the mayor of the city, who became quite interested in him when he discovered that his father had investments in that section. He also insisted that Stanley should remain a few days longer. He afterwards dined him, at which time Stanley enjoyed himself hugely. He was now in the social swim and in no hurry to return home. He was in the way of creating pleasant memories of the South and the time passed swiftly and pleasantly.

Mr. Warner gave a reception for him at his elegant home on —— street, where he had the opportunity of meeting many Southern beauties, none of whom he thought compared with Marjorie. During the arrival of the guests he occupied a place between Mr. Warner and Mayor Gregory, and was introduced by the latter to the guests as they came. He exerted himself to please with great success. His good spirits overflowed; his wit sparkled; he became a great favorite, and made many friends and admirers. He had many invitations to call, and hospitalities were offered him in case he should again return to the city.

After the reception he thanked heaven that all Southerners were not made of the same stuff. In this he was mistaken. The people here shared the same views in common with others he had come in contact. Birmingham is more radical than New Orleans. Had he not been so persistent while at New Orleans, in asserting the rights of the individual, he would have been made a social lion there, and would have come in contact with older and more aristocratic families than he had met in Birmingham. Had he acted in Birmingham as he had in New Orleans he would have been left to enjoy the society of Saunders, and perhaps with not the freedom he had exercised in New Orleans.[112] The pleasures of the moment had blinded him and too soon he was to be rudely awakened from his dream.

For several days he had not seen much of Saunders who was enjoying himself among the friends he had made, and spending much of his time in about the same way as he had the week before, in making tours of observations about the mines, furnaces and factories and wherever Afro-Americans were employed.

One night at a church lyceum when he was surrounded by some of his new friends he said to them: "Your employments seem more varied than ours in the North, but I think that that is due to your large numbers, but I do not think that in the proportion of numbers, you have as many successful business men, nor do you begin to have near as many in positions of trust as we do. With your wide field in the commoner branches of labor, your privileges are limited. You have a fine country down here. I like it; but its worst feature is man. Man narrowed by prejudices and customs, circumscribing the privileges and limits of man. I would rather live in a country less favored by nature, where the avenues of employment are less wide and be able to walk the streets a free man, going whither I please; to places of public entertainment, churches, opera houses, concerts and other places of a public nature which are educators, as a man among men. I had rather live where I can travel when I please, unrestrained by obnoxious customs, and be able to find a room at a public inn when I stop; where I can obtain justice when my rights are transgressed, and where I can stand no chance of being lynched or murdered for exercising the rights of manhood."

"But our home is here," interposed one, "here were we born, and around here are memories sacred and dear to us. We cannot leave them. We bide our time. It will come someday, some way. How? I don't know. Perhaps misfortune may unite us. Perhaps wrongs drive us into one united revolt against the task masters. Perhaps the government may in some way interfere. But here most of us will stay until the time of our deliverance comes."

"In the great Northwest," said Saunders, "are several territories of vast extent, preparing for statehood. In their borders are large tracts of unoccupied land belonging to the government and to different railroads, that are open for settlement. These places offer excellent opportunities for all to come and take up these lands. What is required by the government to make your claim good on its land and entitle you to a deed is that you work it for a short term of years. Railroad land is to be had cheap; for from about two to six dollars per acre. Beyond the mountains the climate is excellent. Two crops are had per year. It is never very cold and the temperature is about that of Tennessee. All of the fruits grow there and the soil is very fertile. Show the disposition to go there and you will not lack friends to find the means to carry you thither. The race in the North will make sacrifices. The friends of the oppressed will give their aid. This side of the mountains, in Montana, Idaho and Dakota, the climate is more severe. In many of the states of the North there is room for thousands. Wisconsin, Minnesota, Iowa, Nebraska, Colorado and the northern part of Illinois, Indiana and Ohio could absorb thousands. Michigan could absorb and scatter throughout its vast extent over 50,000 without attracting notice. The farmers of the New England states are leaving their farms and going west, and, as a result, there are hundreds of good farms with no tenants and some of these states are talking of offering extra inducements in the way of loaning money to industrious people to come and settle upon these farms.[113] In the Northern countries the climate may be hard upon you at first, but with such privations as come from cold, comes the fact that you are free to enjoy the rights and privileges of freemen, and that the qualities of manhood will secure something like its proper recognition. You will find good mixed schools for your children, and new homes whose sanctity will not be invaded. I have heard people say, 'get money and education and these conditions down here will change.' When this becomes universal, they may, but now intelligence and wealth, and refinements count for nothing. They who possess these things are subject to the same treatment as others. I read the other day of a rich intelligent woman who was forced to enter the Jim Crow car, with its dirt and filth, upon a railroad of which she held bonds. If they are self-assertive or interest themselves in politics actively they are warned. If they are forcible in proclaiming their rights as citizens for their life's sake, they must leave the country."

His hearers were silent for his logic was irresistible. To those that wished he promised when he returned home information as to what requirements were necessary to take up the land, the best season to emigrate, etc.

"I don't presume that the old would leave long associated ties, but the young, those in the full bloom of health and youth, whose sinews are lusty, whose ties are yet unformed, who are unemployed and desire the liberty that should be as free as the air, limited only by the laws of God and man, who are willing to work hard, sacrifice a few conveniences, there is an excellent opening."

Saunders did not suffer from lack of entertainment. His new friends were as active, according to their limited means, in making it pleasant for him as Stanley's friends were for him. When it became known under what conditions he was traveling in the South; that he was traveling as a companion; that he was not stopping at the hotel because he would not be received except as a servant, there was an interest added to his presence which made him more than an ordinary personage. They had heard that up in "de Norf" some folks were getting along nicely, but to see one in such a relation was something they had not calculated upon, and among them, the lower classes particularly, he was a curiosity. "Laws, chile," said an old Aunty to her son, "Up Norf de folks can be sumfin. When yous' old go Norf or Wes."

No potentate was ever the object of greater admiration or received greater homage from his subjects than that accorded him by the simple and honest colored folk. He was honored. He received great attentions. There were little receptions and numerous teas. Still the time passed heavily with him. He longed to leave the country. The eyes of hate that now and then were directed at him from the poorer whites, who knew he was from the North and thought he might be "teachin' our Niggers" his Northern equality notions, made him feel nervous. He also feared an outbreak at any moment because of the political excitement. Home and Edith, twin thoughts, were uppermost in his mind. No lover loved more devotedly. None looked with greater eagerness to the time when Church and State would set its seal upon their loves, and unite their lives and fortunes. The nearer the day the longer it seemed. He had now commenced to count the time by weeks where before he had counted by months. He sighed to think how far off it seemed, and how far away he was from her and home. Tender recollections filled his mind. Love works alike in the hearts of all people, no matter what the race, color of skin, or condition in life.

CHAPTER XXII.

The day following the reception at Mr. Warner's, Stanley, who had seen but little of Saunders the past few days, sought him out. Having found him, he said: "I have neglected you, John, but I fell in with a lot of the cleverest people I have met so far on our trip, and I've been having a royal time."

"I'm glad to hear it," replied Saunders. "Don't you worry about me, I have been busy. Still I only await your pleasure to start homeward."

"Tomorrow night, then, sure. I promised to go out this evening, but tomorrow we will surely start."

"I am very glad of that, for the time is beginning to hang heavily upon me."

"Come with me. I will cheer you up a little. There is a beautiful little suburban park I visited yesterday that I would like you to see. You have a streak of the blues which I think I can dispel with a little recreation."

Saunders assented willingly, and they took a street car and soon arrived at their destination—a beautiful park, rich in plants and flowers, that the autumn season had not yet affected. It had numerous drives and walks, and seats arranged in convenient places. They went through the park examining with deep interest its flowers, plants, shrubs and other attractions, and compared them with those of the North. Many differences were noticeable. The petals were richer in hue and larger, the odor stronger and sweeter. The green of the leaves seemed to be deeper perhaps from contrast with the rich and varied color of the flower itself.

"I know that you feel better already," said Stanley, as he noticed his companion's keen interest in his surroundings.

"I certainly do. I think that I could live here."

After sauntering around awhile, they began to feel quite tired and warm, for the sun's rays were very warm, and they started for a shady spot near the entrance of the park to rest. While going there Saunders' attention was for a moment attracted in another direction to a beautiful bed of roses. Intent upon this he did not observe a middle-aged man, who walked with a cane, approaching him from an opposite direction. Being similarly engaged, and before either had turned or noticed the other, they collided. Not only was the collision a forcible one, but Saunders stepped upon the other's pet corn. The result was surprising. Colonel Grub, as he was called, whether from services rendered or from the usual custom of bestowing titles promiscuously throughout the South, is not known, jumped about two feet into the air, and gave vent to words that would certainly not improve the English language. He was very fluent, and angry with pain he turned upon Saunders, who was busy trying to apologize, with—

"You sassy niggah," he yelled, "I'll whale the life outer you. How dare you run agin me?"

"You must really excuse me, sir, it was unin—"

"Shut up! You black rascal. Don't dare to talk back to me."

He advanced on Saunders with uplifted cane. Before Stanley could interfere, he had struck. Saunders warded off the blow as best he could, and being a little angry at the imperious manner and conduct of the Colonel, struck him in return with his light rattan. Several people noticing the affray rushed to the scene and soon had the combatants apart. One of those who came up after they were parted did not stop for a moment until he had struck Saunders full in the face, felling him to the ground, so unexpected and forcible was the blow. As he struck, the man exclaimed: "You'll hit a white man, will you?"

Saunders' blood was now thoroughly aroused, and gone were his resolutions to abstain from scenes in which his life might be endangered. As he fell his hand came in contact with the colonel's cane which he had dropped in the fracas, and although a little dazed, he picked it up and used it industriously on his assailant and others who interfered, until Stanley reached him and took it away from him. By that time the collecting crowd had attracted the attention of a policeman who came over, and at the instigation of John's assailant, handcuffed him, Stanley's protest being in vain. When Saunders was secured threats began to be uttered in a low voice that increased in volume as the crowd grew larger, and as others catching them up repeated them, "Kill him! Lynch him!" was repeated louder and oftener. As Stanley heard the cry the terrible truth began to dawn upon him of the dangerous position of his friend. He was in a strait betwixt two opinions. He did not know whether to fly for help to Mr. Warner and seek thus the interference of Mayor Gregory, or stay to protect Saunders until he was safely confined.

On their way the crowd grew larger, the cries to lynch and hang more ominous. Some a little bolder than others approached so close that they struck him in his defenseless position. Some spat on him and most of them acted like the mean, mangy curs that they were. The officer made no remonstrance. It would have been useless against such a crowd with its now large proportions. Soon after, another policeman joined the one that had John in charge, and they succeeded in keeping the crowd back.

Stanley was doing all that he could to help them in their efforts. He expostulated with the crowd and finding this of no avail he called them cowards and curs for their efforts to strike a defenseless man, but his words only seemed to urge them on.

One overgrown boy threw a stone which hit Saunders on the side of the face and cut it so that the blood spurted out. In a frenzy of anger and pain he cried out, "If I had my hands free, you cowards, I would teach you a lesson."

"We'll teach you a lesson before morning," came back an answer from the crowd.

"Ther'll be a nice lynching bee, tonight," said a bystander, as the noisy procession passed.

Each moment the danger became more imminent, and Stanley, now puffing and blowing, pushed his way along with the crowd and kept as close to Saunders as possible to shield him as much as he could from threatened violence.

It was past noon and they were still a long distance from a police station, and Stanley began to quarrel with the officers for not using a conveyance which he offered to pay for, so as not to expose Saunders to so much danger and abuse. But they paid no heed to his requests.

Some one in the crowd, who had seen Saunders before in his tour of the mines, and had seen him talking to some of the colored laborers had found out that he was from the North, imparted his intelligence to others. The information lent fuel to flames already fanned to white heat. "He's a Northern nigger, been petted by the Yankees, down with him," was the cry, and the mob—a howling, roaring, senseless, hating mob—made extra efforts to get nearer to him.

The mob itself was a motley one. It seemed as if the riff-raff of the town had suddenly blown together to whirl and twist around a moving center and vent its fury in loud curses and threatenings as it surged along, with each individual part of it endeavoring to get nearer to the center. Here and there was a respectable appearing person who was urging on the others, and who were the most industrious in keeping up the passions of the mob by their loud and persistent crying of "Hang him! String him up to the nearest lamp post! Where's a rope? D— the nigger!" They acted like party whips in keeping their members in line and ready for action, or rather like devils urging on their imps to malicious acts and tortures.

Everyone seemed to be saying something. One was telling how Col. Grub had been insulted and then beaten by this Northern darkey. Another was crying, "its teachin' our niggers to be sassy!" Still another yelled, "He'll never insult another white man," while a lot of small boys, omnipresent; were adding their shrill trebles to the babel of noise and confusion. Stanley was almost breathless, besides choked with dust, and suffering from the heat and jam. It was only excitement and the danger of his friend that kept him up; while Saunders, manacled and bleeding, was hurried along, dodging blows and missiles, now and then casting a look at Stanley that savored of despair. Nevertheless, he still retained a spark of dogged determination that would not quail in the face of the mob, nor did his face or bearing betray any signs of fear. The presentiment of which Saunders had spoken of on board the ill-fated Louisiana flashed across Stanley's mind. Saunders' peril was so imminent that it looked as if he would never see home and Edith again, and from the fury of the mob it seemed that his body would be so mutilated as to be beyond recognition. How could he face Edith again with the story of John's murder on his lips. The thought was agonizing. If they could only reach shelter, he would visit Mayor Gregory and have him use his influence in saving him and putting him in safety. They would leave the South with its damnable customs and prejudices forever. All the good impressions made at the reception last night were lost, and there was in his heart great bitterness. He would pay a large sum if necessary to secure Saunders' life. His anxiety over it was now aroused to its highest tension.

They were making some headway, and every step nearer to the goal aroused new hope in his breast. Suddenly a shout arose louder than the rest from the intersection of the street which they had just passed, and looking in that direction he saw some men running up with a rope. Hope fled. Saunders saw them also, and for the first time the danger of his death by lynching at the hands of a Southern mob flashed upon him. Was he, after all, to be a martyr to their accursed prejudices? He regretted that he had not used his revolver when he had the opportunity. Edith's misgivings rushed upon him. Her appeals for him not to go at this time; he almost wished that he had heeded. But, he glanced at Stanley, saw the despair on his face, the race will gain a friend who will leave no stone unturned in demanding justice for it.

The rope was passed from hand to hand, and with eager grasp and shout the noose was passed along. "On with it! Lasso him!" was the cry, and Saunders, unable to ward off his danger, with a grim determined countenance, watched the instrument of cruel death approach. The mob goaded on by its frenzy of excitement, passion and prejudices, acted like tigers thirsting for human blood. Soon the rope was near, then the officers remonstrated. "Down with them, then," came an angry cry from the outer edge of the circle. The mob, quick to obey in its frenzy, attacked the police and in the melee the rope was slipped over Saunders' neck. "We've got him now," yelled those nearest to him and as many as could grasped hold of the rope and began to pull. Again Saunders turned to Stanley with a look that said a mute good-bye, as the rope tightened about his neck, and the crowd began to sway and pull away. But there was no sign of reproach or fear on his countenance. Stanley realized that something must be done quickly or Saunders would be beyond all hope. Making a superhuman effort he sprang to Saunders' side, pulled out his knife and cut the rope in two, but not until its cruel threads had cut deep into Saunders' neck, tore his flesh, almost choked him, and pulled him backward to the ground. He was helped to his feet. His face and neck were bloody, and the increased flow from his wounds made his appearance look ghastly. His clothes were torn and begrimed with dust and blood.

The police had been obliged to defend themselves and had beaten back the crowd and were reforming. So also was the mob. The cut rope was again being brought forward with a new noose in it. To Stanley's despair was now added exhaustion. He could not stand much longer between Saunders and his assailants. Besides his efforts to protect him, had drawn upon himself the attention of the crowd, and he too, became the object of cries and missiles. His own life was in danger. He saw his own peril and thoughts of home, friends and Marjorie came to him. He vowed if ever he came out of that affair his energies should be devoted to doing something that would correct this state of things that annually costs so many hundreds of lives. He would try to create an opinion that would grow so strong as to demand the enforcement of justice.

CHAPTER XXIII.

Stanley had no sooner made his vow when, upon looking up, he saw Mayor Gregory who had been attracted by the noise and confusion making his way towards them.

"Thank God," he cried; "there is hope yet, John. Save him for my sake," he appealed to the mayor, pointing towards Saunders, then he fainted away from extreme excitement, exhaustion, heat and anxiety.

The crowd hardly noticed him in its onward rush, trampled him in the dust, and but for the timely arrival of an acquaintance, he might have been seriously injured.

The presence of the mayor and his words of command had their effect upon the crowd, and for the time they refrained from further effort on Saunders' life. What was left of him was safely taken away to jail while a cab was called and Stanley was taken to Mr. Warner's, the mayor accompanying him.

His first inquiry, on regaining his senses, was concerning the safety of his friend, and on being assured that he was safe he gave a sigh of relief and rested easier. Soon after he attempted to get up, but he was not permitted to. The mayor then informed him that he had directed the sheriff to place a strong posse on guard and that tomorrow Saunders would be placed out of the reach of danger. Stanley had heard, however, so many threats of what the mob would do at night that the mayor's assurances did not wholly allay his fears.

"I am surprised," said he, "that such lawlessness should exist in such a flourishing town as this."

"Well, you see," replied the mayor, "it doesn't take much to arouse the intense anti-Negro feeling here because of prejudices and opinions long nourished and an idea that the result of the war, with the equality it created, was a great wrong. In the turbulent days, when the South was shaking off the iniquities of carpet bag rule the best of our citizens encouraged this lawlessness against the Negro to cower them into submission. Now that many of us would discourage it, we find ourselves almost powerless, for these men's passions only require a spark to light up decaying embers and fan into white heat, old animosities. There are many of our oldest and most respected people who are still rigorously intolerant at the expense of the younger progressive element, who wish to rid our section of such lawlessness and to invite that increase of capital and immigration which these acts deter. Then, in almost any city you can always find a howling company, drawn from the dregs of life, ready to do the bidding of those who desire to revenge wrongs, actual or imaginary, outside the course of the law."

"Why don't you hang some of them, then, or shoot them down like the howling wolves they are?" asked Stanley, in an excited but decided manner.

"I confess," added the mayor, "that it is hard to secure a jury who will convict a white man for an injury done on a Negro, when the race issue is raised. One in the twelve at least, is sure to balk justice and in many cases the sympathy of the judge is with the jury and the man on trial. Whatever a white man desires against a Negro here is often law. This is something that we must reform, or take the consequences of an uneasy community and stagnant trade."

Stanley rose quickly, and grasping his hand earnestly said: "I am proud to see and talk with a man in this section who possesses thoughts contrary to the general opinion, and who realizes the effects such acts will lead to. If you can only save my friend, who has been more faithful to me than a brother, I shall never be able to repay you. You cannot tell what feelings of apprehension and grief are now gnawing at my heart, caused by seeing the objects of my affection and regard torn from me one by one. First, by the inexorable fate of a disordered life, but that being caused by my own action must be borne patiently." His voice fell as he spoke the last words, and he paused for a moment as in reflection. "Now by the relentless, fury of a mob I have seen with my own eyes a constant friend, who would have laid down his life for me, torn and mercilessly lacerated by all manner of violence, and I powerless to help him. When the helpless victims of that steamboat disaster went down in the fire-lit waters of the Mississippi, and their last despairing cry of help went up as they sank to rise no more, those on the bank, standing impotent to render aid, felt a poignant grief that could not find utterance. So stand I now with my heart wrung by so great anxiety and grief that I cannot give it utterance. But theirs was a more merciful fate than that which threatens Saunders. I would a thousand times rather have seen him engulfed in the waters of the Mississippi than to be lynched by this brutal rabble and be a helpless spectator. The dark waters, swallowing up the objects of our affections, is unconscious of its deeds. In its onward flow it leaves no bitterness against itself. It even returns again in refreshing showers to nourish the flowers that tender memories have planted. Cruel fires may blast and burn the house, but it cheers and warms it in its turn. But what of the irreparable wrongs of men when they wantonly take away what they cannot give? Is there power in human nature to forgive it?"

Mayor Gregory was moved by his touching and eloquent appeal. "Don't take on so," he said. "You are beside yourself. But one outburst of such anguish is certainly worth a life. Your friend is safe, and tomorrow— it would not be safe now—I shall escort him to the train myself and see him put safely out of harm's way. Come, now, don't grieve so."

But Stanley still doubted Saunders' safety. The influence which the dreadful and infuriated cries of the mob created was still upon him. "Tonight, we'll teach you a lesson," seemed ever ringing in his ears.

"Will you order me a carriage, Mr. Warner?" he asked, turning to that gentleman.

"Mine is at your disposal and I with it," replied Mr. Warner.

"Will you please order it for me, then. I have some duties to perform and I wish to go alone. I will call for you presently."

Mr. Warner bowed in reply, went out of the room and ordered the carriage put in readiness.

Getting into the carriage Stanley directed the coach man to drive in all haste to Saunders' boarding place.

The house, which was situated in a respectable quarter of the city, presented a cleanly appearance without, and was neatly furnished within.

He asked at once for Mr. Fulton, the landlord, and a stout man, rather dark, and with a fairly intelligent look made his appearance.

Stanley made himself known, and at once entered upon the object of his mission by detailing the events of the morning, the general facts of which Mr. Fulton was conversant with, Stanley wanted to know what could be done towards saving his friend by getting him out of the city, and on the way to the North.

"Nothing short of a miracle can save him now, Mr. Stanley, for the thirst for blood has been aroused in the fiends."

"But he is one of your race," protested Stanley, "and a worthy one too. I want you to arouse your people and guard the jail tonight. I will be one of you."

"We are powerless to do it. But few of us have arms, and money could not buy them for us tonight. God help the colored man that the mob finds abroad when it began its work. If we went we would be shot down like dogs. The excuse would be a Negro uprising. Should we strike back the chain gang would await us with all its fearful horrors, while the law would set free the originators of the trouble."

"You should be prepared for such an emergency. You might as well die fighting like men as to be lynched like craven cowards."

"Cowards, do you say. Ask the men who were with us at the 'Crater,' or at Fort Wagner, or Nashville, when the bullets flew like hail, if we were cowards.[114] The odds are now too heavy against us. But give us arms and the assurance that the forces of the State and Nation will not be brought against us, and we will stand guard tonight with you, and fight the mob, and man to man, we will take their vaunted boasting out of them. But you might search from now until night, and you will be unable to find ten men with arms to stand guard with you, and yet there are colored men as brave and desperate here as can be found in any city."

Stanley saw that it was wasting time to argue, that it was beginning to get late and that if he found help he must find it in another quarter. Driving back to Mr. Warner's, together with that gentleman and Mayor Gregory, he drove to the jail to see what security had been made for Saunders' safety.

A few men and a crowd of boys still lingered about the jail and in its vicinity, many bearing arms openly. Some were acting as spies, whose duty it was to observe all persons coming and going, and to give an alarm, if, perchance, the prisoner should be removed to another place for better security. As the carriage containing Stanley and his friends drew up, and they made ready to enter the jail, the small crowd seemed to grow larger by reason of its concentration.

After entering the jail, upon the order of the mayor, the turnkey brought Saunders into the reception room.

Pale, haggard and bruised, his clothes still bespattered with blood and dust, which had been but half washed away; his neck and face swollen, he came down the corridor, though weak, with a firm step. He knew who had called for him, and knowing his generous impulses, knew that he was heaping all sorts of self-reproaches upon himself for not having left the city before. He felt that he must be brave and exhibit no sign of the fear that he felt, nor look too despondent over the trials through which he had passed. So by a strong effort of the will he put on a brave front.

"Poor fellow. Poor fellow," said Stanley, as he saw him approach with the turnkey. Then rushing quickly to his side, he grasped both hands, and shook them again and again, while his eyes expressed the sympathy he felt at his sorry appearance. "When we get out of this, John, we will never return to such an accursed place."

"If we get out, is that the question now? If I had only known that my life had to pay the forfeit for defending myself, I would have sold it dearly. I only regret, that when I had the opportunity, I did not use my revolver and have given the cowardly hounds some excuse for running me down like a wild beast."

"You'll be all right now, my boy," said the mayor. "I have given my word to Mr. Stanley that you would not be further disturbed."

Saunders felt more hopeful at these words of the mayor, and said: "I do not care so much for myself, but I was just getting something to live for; besides my poor old father in his declining years looks to me for support and a home."

As thoughts of Edith and home, mingled with the threats of the mob, and his imminent danger, the prospect that he perhaps might never see them again, so completely unnerved him, that despite his resolution to show no signs of fear, he burst into tears—the first he had shed.

Stanley, seeing them, could not repress his own feelings and the tears rolled down his cheeks as with quivering voice he exclaimed: "My God, is there no way out of this?" Then his strong mind came to his relief, he checked his tears and standing erect in his young manhood said: "Something must be done, and now."

"Don't get agitated, Mr. Stanley. You are overestimating the danger. I tell you that your friend is all right. He is safe here. Let him stop his blubbering."

Stanley, however, did not consider these offers of aid and protestations of safety, sufficient reparation for the cruelties inflicted upon Saunders; as he thought how his head had almost been jerked from his shoulders before he had cut the rope, he considered them unnecessarily cold and cruel.

"I am extremely thankful, Mayor Gregory," he said, moved by his consideration for his companion, "not so much for your proffers of aid now, but for the kindnesses which you have shown me and your timely rescue today. Your appearance was as glad a welcome as ever a sail was to famishing souls at sea. But I cannot help sympathizing with my friend, and exhibiting my surprise and disgust that the good people here don't arise in their strength and put an end to such outbursts of outlawry that bring disgrace upon them. If father ever invests another cent here in the South, he will do it against my advice."

"Be careful, Mr. Stanley," said Mr. Warner, "don't say in an extremity of feeling what you will be sorry for when this danger is averted. Besides we are talking of that which is of the least importance in this issue. This boy should at once have the doctor's care, and we must get him out of the city before night, sure, to avoid your anxiety."

Stanley saw the wisdom of these remarks and refrained from further comment. A doctor was sent for who dressed Saunders' wounds. The bloody clothes were exchanged for clean ones and he was prepared for flight. A number of people whom Stanley had met during his stay, hearing of his misfortune, had interested themselves in his behalf. A few came and offered their services which were accepted. Together they formed a plan. A closed carriage was to be driven to the rear of the jail, while Stanley, Mr. Warner and Mayor Gregory went to the front where the crowd, which was all the time increasing in numbers, would be sure to congregate. Then Saunders was to be slipped out of the back door and driven to a small station on the Louisville and Nashville road, where he could take the train to Nashville. There he was to wait until Stanley joined him. Mr. James, a business partner of Mr. Warner's, and an admirer of Stanley's, volunteered to accompany him a safe distance. The plan seemed to be a simple one, and likely to be successful in getting Saunders safely out of the city without further trouble. It was now dusk and they proceeded at once to carry their plan into action. Stanley and his friends lingered in front, in their attempt to divert the attention of the crowd, while the cab which had been secured drove up to the rear entrance, where Mr. James and Saunders entered it. They drove slowly at first for fear that their rapid driving would arouse suspicion. When Stanley and his friends were assured that all was carried out according to the plan agreed upon, they entered Mr. Warner's carriage and drove to his home. Ere they had entered the house they heard such yells and shouting in the direction of the jail that the fears of Stanley again arose and he proposed that they drive back.

"Nonsense," replied the mayor, "you are full of alarms. Your servant is now probably far away, and they are howling because they have learned of his escape. Nothing serious has happened, and if the mob is again formed, I have left orders that I should be notified at once. If necessary the militia will be ordered out, as I have left word for them to prepare for trouble. I think I made a mistake in not calling them out at first and having them patrol around the jail."

The confusion and the babel of voices in the distance grew more ominous as he spoke which caused him to listen. Before any one spoke again the clatter of horses' hoofs were heard as if running at great speed, and the form of a horse and rider, barely visible by reason of the distance and dust, told them that some news of importance was at hand.

"I knew it! I knew it!" exclaimed Stanley. "Those hounds are at it again."

The rider gave them startling information. The flight had been discovered and they were being hotly pursued and perhaps overtaken by now.

"For God's sake," cried Stanley, "let us hurry." The team had been almost unhitched, but the hostler was required to re-gear it with all possible haste. Stanley, however, impatient of delay, had started to run on foot to where the sounds came from, and was only restrained by force, until the carriage could be again got ready.

CHAPTER XXIV.

During the periodic outbreaks that occurred in Paris and other cities in France, after the beginning of the French revolution, the class that always created the greatest consternation was the *canaille*.[115] At their appearance abroad, shopkeepers closed their doors, put up their blinds, and sat during the long nights with arms guarding their stores; all respectable people put out their lights, and virtue kept within. The *canaille* comprised all the lower orders of the people— the vulgar, the debauched, the vicious, thieves, murderers, the social fungi and the pariahs of French civilization. This off-scouring of society was indispensable to these outbreaks. They were used as tools. They built and defended barricades. In defying the law they were in their element. They were the representatives of chaos as opposed to system. They sprang up from everywhere, quickly, suddenly, as if emptied from the earth's surface; their work done, they as rapidly disappeared. Their appearance was always a signal for a reign of terror. Vice stalked abroad. During the terrible reign of the commune in Paris in '71 they controlled.[116] They hung upon the skirts of the honest revolutionists, and in their name committed excesses that shamed civilization.

In the large cities of our own Republic this class, from various causes, is growing numerous, and it is always ready when opportunity offers to come forth and destroy; to mingle in mob and riot and ply their trade; to steal honor and to take life. Among just such a rabble had Col. Grub and his friends been all that afternoon, inflaming their passions and sowing the seed of murder. It was easy work to do this for the Afro-American, especially an aspiring one, was an eyesore to them. Counted as being low in the social scale, they feared the Afro-American would rise above them, and they were quick to proclaim the white man's superiority, no matter how ignorant and depraved he might be, or intelligent and refined the Afro-American. Here was to be found the seat of the deepest prejudices, and here could be found the tools to wreak vengeance for fancied or real injuries. Now these people were alive; they scented blood in the air. From everywhere there issued pariahs of society; men under the ban of the law, came forth from their concealment and mingled in the crowds, being sure of their safety while the excitement lasted. The chief topic was of the assault on the life of Col. Grub, and the account had been so contorted and twisted as to scarcely be recognizable.

"The niggers must be taught to know their places." "The niggers will be running the town pretty soon." "White men must hang together, if they don't want to see niggers rulin'," were expressions to be frequently heard on all sides. These inflammatory phrases were repeated so often that some began to think the "niggahs" were really contemplating an uprising. It was even telegraphed abroad that such was the case. Some in the crowd were poor, hungry, and ignorant creatures, who actually thought they were commissioned to right a great wrong perpetrated upon one of the superior class by a "sassy Northern niggah," that, to let go unpunished, would be the beginning of a great evil. They became fanatics. Some were controlled by pure fiendishness, and sought only to satisfy their human thirst for blood as they had done before. "Dere's no penalty fur killin' a niggah," said one fellow as he marched through the street with a Winchester slung across his shoulder, while busily engaged in enlisting others to join him.

They proceeded about their business in true military style. They sent out spies to watch the jail at all points. Here and there scattered in concealment, laymen ready to pounce upon any vehicle coming from the jail with prisoners. It had been completely shadowed before Stanley and his friends arrived. They little dreamed that the small group of men that they saw were spies watching the main entrance, who immediately communicated with others by means of signals. They little dreamed that the carriage containing Saunders and Mr. James was observed and shadowed as they were driving back to Mr. Warner's. In fact Mr. James and Saunders had proceeded but a little distance when they were attacked by the mob with cries that were terrible to hear. This was what first attracted the attention of Stanley. It was already dark, and the howling mob in mad pursuit, rushed after the cab as it rattled up streets and lanes. The members of the crowd carried all kinds of arms—rifles, revolvers, old army muskets, clubs, sledge hammers and picks, in case it became necessary to assault the jail.

Alarmed by the cries one of the sheriff's deputies, who was on the watch, immediately rushed away to notify the police. Another rushed to summon the military company that had been ordered to hold itself in readiness.

Mr. James quickly saw the danger that they were in and instructed the driver to push ahead with all possible speed. He did not need much urging for he feared the mob's vengeance, if, perchance, it might think that he was interested in the prisoner's escape. He laid the whip vigorously on his horse and had obtained quite a start on those in the rear, but the streets were being crowded, the deafening yells drew others from their homes out of curiosity, and fresh dangers thus arose before them. The mad designs of the *canaille* were soon made manifest. The cries of the pursuers were soon answered by those in front. Reckless of danger they attempted to stay the course of the cab. Horse, like master, was frightened and fear lent him a speed that was not easily checked. Several men were knocked down and one or two severely hurt. This, however, only seemed to incense the mob, arouse it to greater fury and make it redouble its efforts to stop the fleeing fugitives. No sooner was it successful than it stripped the cab bare of its covering. Mr. James was overawed and powerless, and Saunders, having no means of defense, sat almost dazed with bewilderment, until he was seized and hurled violently to the ground. Then he grappled with his assailants, but he was like a reed in a tempest. He was soon bound hand and foot and nearly killed by the effects of a blow upon his head with a club. A rope was passed around his body under his arms and, with fiendish glee, the crowd shouted as it made for some vacant lots about two blocks distant in which were a few large oak trees, dragging his almost lifeless body after them. As his limp body jostled and bumped over the rough cobble pavement some of the crowd gratified their desire of torture and their hatred of the Afro-American by kicking and beating him all the way, others by thrusting their knives into his quivering flesh.

Before they could arrive at their destination Mr. James, who had escaped and hurried away, met the police who now came hurrying to the scene. By making a rapid detour they faced the lynchers before they could carry out their designs. Then the mob showed its generalship, for while some opposed, with a show of force, the police, others, with Saunders, escaped in another direction. Many of them had now become wild and reckless and began firing in an indiscriminate manner as they ran on. Saunders was nearly dead when the mob's leaders halted under a large tree and stopped a moment for consultation. But there was only a little delay, then taking the rope from his body they threw it across a limb of the tree, then adjusting the loop around his neck—yelling, shouting and firing—they started to pull on it. He had scarcely been raised from the ground when the rapid measured tread of feet was heard and a horseman wildly dashed into their midst and cut the rope from about his neck. This act was followed by a command from Mayor Gregory to the mob to disperse. It was stubborn, however, and showed fight, but upon the command to fix and charge bayonets it turned tail, but not before one of its leaders had turned and emptied part of the contents of a revolver into Saunders' body while he lay in Stanley's arms.

Shrieking and uttering cat-calls the mob fled. The streets were cleared by the military company. The better classes had already retired indoors, particularly the timid and the Afro-Americans of the city. The few prisoners at the jail, most of whom were Afro-Americans, alarmed at the cries and fearing an assault upon the jail, crawled in terror under the cots in their cells. Dark were the houses and cabins where that race resided and more than one heart beat with anxious terror when the mob was at its height, and when cursing and yelling at being balked of the final consummation intended for its prey, it sought for other objects to destroy.

CHAPTER XXV.

Rapidly Stanley and his friends hurried to the scene with the rider. On the way they overtook the military company going with rapid strides to the same scene of action. Stanley was wild with excitement, and chafed at what he thought was their slow progress. A messenger notified them of the conflict with the police and the escape of the mob with their prisoner. However, the yells, constant and unceasing, like the cries of wild beasts bent on prey, betrayed their course, and with redoubled efforts they started in pursuit. At Stanley's urgent solicitation his friends allowed him to exchange places with the rider. No sooner done than he urged the horse to its fullest speed and coming upon the mob, dashed into it, and severed the rope as it was prepared to launch Saunders in mid-air. Then dismounting he endeavored to find if there was still life in his limp body. He found that there was still a faint action at the heart, and he began to rub his hands, arms and body, in an effort to bring him back to consciousness. Then it was that one of the mob shot Saunders, and strange as it may appear, it seemed to arouse him to consciousness. He opened his eyes, looked around in a scared and bewildered manner and whispered: "Where are they? This is terrible."

"They have gone," exclaimed Stanley, "John! John! It is I, Seth, who is holding you."

"Thank God! Thank God! But you are too late to save me. I have such pains here," and he tried to lift his hand to indicate, but was too feeble. "I have but a few more minutes to live, I am dying." He saw the look of pain that flashed over Stanley's countenance, and fearing that he might blame himself for the accidents of the day, continued: "Don't blame yourself for this. You could not foresee the incidents of this terrible day. Either blame the customs and prejudices of this people under which they have been raised." Then the soul of this sincere patriot flashed forth in "Oh, my country! What scenes of carnage and strife, of woe and sorrow, will take place if these unworthy ideas and wild passions are allowed to hold such full sway. Dear friend, I leave you with a mission which by temperament, and by your ideas of justice, you are eminently fitted to fulfill. Stir up and create a public opinion and cease not, until it is so aroused that justice, waking from her long sleep, will demand equal protection and liberty, for all citizens of the Republic. God will be with you. In naming you Seth, Hebrew for appointed, your parents must have been inspired, for you are APPOINTED by God, through me—the dying—to aid in clearing our country from its false ideas. You accept the trust?"

"Yes, yes. I accept and will labor earnestly."

"Then may good come of my death," said Saunders feebly. "Such pain is here." He stopped, groaned, closed his eyes, but to Stanley's infinite relief, he opened them again and whispered, "When you return, seek out Miss Stone, such a heart as yours should have its recompense."

Stanley's grief was beyond the outward manifestation of tears and visible emotions. Grief was gnawing at his heart and the fever in his body parched up the tears. His eyes showed the tenderness he felt for his friend, and the great pain at his sudden and violent taking off. Saunders was rapidly failing. His breathing was difficult. He commenced to gasp for breath.

"Seth," he whispered, "are you near? We were friends in life, and I want you to be near me as I pass over to the other side."

"Yes, John, I am here," and Stanley bent lower.

"Have my remains taken home, and let me lay alongside my mother in beautiful Elmwood. You will come there sometimes and bring her with you, won't you? I was father's chief support; how he will miss me."

"I will look after him," said Stanley. "You must not die, John, for their sakes, for mine, live. We cannot spare you." But the warm blood that had now found the way to his knee, and which had already formed a puddle at Saunders' feet, told him that the inevitable could not be staid. Saunders made a feeble effort to move, but could not. For a moment his mind seemed to wander, then he whispered:

"Oh, Edith, what happiness had I dreamed of with you. Poor heart, how she will suffer. Try to comfort her, Seth. Tell her I thought of her to the last and breathed a blessing for her. Tell her not to grieve; to forgive those who have caused my death, as I do. Their own sins will have their fitting retribution." He then became silent, his breathing more difficult. The sands of life were fast ebbing away. A noble soul was preparing to leave the earth to dwell with Him who said: "In my Father's house are many mansions. I go to prepare a place for you."[117] His life had been one of unselfish devotion to family and friends, and all his plans teemed with noble thoughts and grand ideas for the uplifting of his race.

Once again he opened his eyes. The film of death had already commenced to cover them. "Seth, don't blame yourself; good-bye," was uttered in a feeble whisper. Then his spirit fled.

Stanley knew that he was dead, but still held his body while he looked straight ahead in the direction taken by the mob. But not of them was he thinking. He saw the home that would see his friend no more, saw its desolation and its grief, saw Edith coming and demanding of him the life that was lost to her. Oblivious to surroundings, to friends, he sat in silent thought until Mr. Warner, noticing his abstraction, with uncovered head, approached and touching him on the shoulder, aroused him and said:

"Mr. Stanley, I am deeply grieved at what has happened and at the wild license of the mob, and the terrible manner in which your friend has met his death. But this is no place to stay; come, let us go home where you can have rest and quiet."

"Not until his remains are placed in charge of an embalmer," replied Stanley. "Although dead he is mine yet; mine while life remains to honor and to cherish his memory. Here on bended knees in the presence of God and the sacred dead, I swear it."

Those who clustered about were moved by the touching scene and all removed their hats, some turning away as they could not bear to witness his distress.

Tenderly he stroked the features of the dead and with his handkerchief he wiped away the dirt and blood that covered his bruised face. Then he stood up and by a great effort mastered his feelings and spoke to those around him. His voice was calm, oh, so calm, that it struck a chill to their very hearts.

"Here lies another victim to your section's violence. This body possessed a soul, untainted by baser metals. A soul so noble, that in its last breath here, it did not curse this country and pray for revenge upon his murderers, and it is not for me, much as I loved him to do that which he was too noble to do. Dying, his last words were an admonition against these fell customs, which, if continued, will bring in their wake, carnage, strife, desolation, woe and sorrow. He leaves it to you, if you love your country, and would avert coming evils, and for me, and for all who love peace, and hate war and strife, those who desire contentment, and who wish to see our country, glorious and prosperous, march on to a successful and great career, to labor earnestly, patriotically to create a condition when the black and white, the rich and poor, can live together in peace. Oh, your land is wet with the blood of the innocent, which has been made to flow in defiance of law and decency. Is it not shameful that this is so? Is it not shameful that no law can reach the offenders, and that your public opinion winks at such frightful occurrences and moreover screens the offenders? Man cannot always thus sin against God with impunity. Retributive justice is sure to follow such wild scenes of disorder. Can you not, will you not endeavor to create among yourselves a public opinion that will condemn these mobs, and try to see that your laws are made equitable and just and have them enforced? I go with his lifeless body to render an account to his aged father who once wore the chains of slavery in this State. The curse that enchained him has left an evil in its train that has killed the son for defending himself against assault. I go to render an account to the sweetheart, who, in her Northern home, awaits the coming of her lover and her wedding day. How can I face them with the horrible evidence of their blighted future hopes? What shall I say to assuage their grief?" The silence around him was as quiet as that of the grave. Hearts were touched. All regretted this terrible ending of a noble life, and many wondered that a person of his race possessed qualities so noble. It was wonderful and almost past their belief. "This morning I arose with a light heart, and a higher opinion of the people here than I have hitherto held. My hopes and spirits were high. Now those hopes are blasted. What misery has been caused, what grief has been felt, will be still felt by others in the events of this day. If your hearts be not of stone they will be touched with pity, and you will be moved to sorrow, to action that this fair land should be tainted with 'man's inhumanity to man.'" Here he broke down. Nature came to his relief, and kneeling over the prostrate form of his friend he burst into a flood of tears.

His listeners were moved by his appeal. None essayed to stop his reproaches or to check this outburst of his feeling. And for fear of the return of the mob, to mutilate the body of the dead they waited and watched while Stanley gave vent to his emotions, until the undertaker came and took the dead body away to be embalmed, and to prepare it for shipment to its Northern resting place.

CHAPTER XXVI.

When the baser passions of men are aroused, despite their God-given attributes, they descend to the level of the brute creation. In their ferocity and gloating over their fallen victims they exceed even it. Ascending to the highest scale of intelligence and virtue, they also reach the lowest depths of depravity.

The death of John Saunders had by no means appeased the base passions of the mob. True, they had killed him, but they had not been allowed the opportunity of gloating over his dead body; of giving vent to their curses and of leaving his lifeless body hanging as a warning to all "sassy niggahs." Driven away the most determined and blood thirsty formed again to consult as to what further crime should be committed. A few days before one of the self-constituted leaders of the mob had been worsted in an altercation with an Afro-American, and at his suggestion a considerable body of the mob started for the intended victim's cabin, which was located quite a distance from the center of the city in what was known as the "Negro quarters."

Arriving at his place they surrounded the house and called him out. But his knowledge of what had been transpiring, and the noise made by the mob on the street, caused him in terror to look for a hiding place. No thought of resistance crossed his mind as he quickly crawled under his bed. After waiting for a few moments the mob repeated their calls, then as their intended victim did not appear they broke in the door, finding him, hauled him out from under the bed and placing a rope around his neck pulled him out into the street.

In this manner he was dragged several blocks, his tongue hanging out and his eyes almost starting from their sockets, until they halted by a sign lamp-post. His hands were then pinioned behind him and a rope placed in position. "Hang him," came the cry from all sides. The few people on the street, not of the mob, viewed the proceedings with silence. It was only a nigger. Humanity did not appeal to their hearts or inspire them to protest against the outrage. The victim begged for time to pray. "Let him pray if he wants to," said one. "Pray be d—d," cried several. "Hang him before the police interfere." The instigator of this additional crime to the night's terrible work stepped forward and said: "The police will not interfere with this case. The Northern darkey had a white man interested in him who was rich, and who intended to make some investments down here. They had a motive for interference." Then he turned to the victim and said: "In two minutes you will be in eternity. Make your prayer short and be lively."

The doomed man dropped to his knees and began aloud a rambling petition, partly to his Maker and partly to the mob, while his executioners stood by and called off the half minutes. An ashy pallor covered his face as he crawled on the ground and made piteous appeals for mercy, for life. Two minutes seemed a long time to some of his tormentors, one of whom kicked him brutally in the side as he lay groveling and warned him to hurry up.

Pain and terror overcame the victim's reason as he cried aloud for mercy. Cries of "Hang him! Hang him!" again went up. The word was given and in an instant he was gasping and struggling for breath. Then commenced a wild carnival. Some of the inhuman wretches emptied the contents of their arms into his body as betwixt heaven and earth it struggled. Some yelled and cursed in their mad fury, and others as they watched his struggles subside into convulsive twitchings, becoming awed at their own wanton work, silently stole away.

The victim dead, the crowd made the rope fast, leaving the body for the friends of the dead man to find. Then they departed and dispersed to their homes.

The superiority of the white race had been shown. The majesty of the law had been defied. To keep the "niggah" down and "make him know his place" two souls had been sent into eternity.

CHAPTER XXVII.

Alone in his chamber Stanley paced the floor until nearly daybreak. So appalling and fearful had been the events of the day that they appeared unreal. It seemed to him as if they might be tricks of the imagination, or that he had passed through a horrible nightmare. But when he looked at his clothes, that were soiled and bloody; at the tear stained face upon which were written the evidences of the great conflict of emotions through which he had passed, he was convinced that all the horrible events were true. His faithful friend was indeed dead—killed by means that were a disgrace to civilization. The fact that the murderers could not be brought to justice made the matter worse. Towards morning, exhausted by his long vigils, mental anguish and his experiences of the day, he threw himself across the bed and fell into a disturbed sleep. His mind traveled over the events of the day. In his dreams, the mob took upon itself horrible shapes— "monstrous and prodigious things, abominable in shape and to sight," reared themselves before him, unlike anything ever yet conceived by the imagination, except when wrought upon by fear. Huge serpents lashed their tails in frenzy. "Gorgons, hydras and chimeras dire," pursuing and raising aloft their hideous heads, or darting out their forked tongues, surrounded and trampled upon the form of his friend until his life was extinguished and he was powerless to render aid. Then the monstrous shapes turned threateningly upon him and prepared to strike, when, with a cry he awoke to find himself in a cold, clammy sweat. "What a hideous dream," he said to himself, as he got up and walked the room in the effort to shake off the effects of the dreadful feeling that had seized upon him.[118] Again he lay down and tried to sleep; this time there rose up before him the forms of John's father, his brother, sisters, and his sweetheart Edith, all demanding of him an account for the life of the murdered man. The looks of reproach they cast upon him, more severe than words of denunciation, pierced him to the heart. "No! No! No! Not that," he cried. "My burden is heavy enough already, but do not look so reproachfully." Then a mist seemed to arise between them that gradually assumed the shape of Saunders, and he exclaimed: "There!

He is not dead after all. See! I have brought him back to you." The great stress that he was under in this dream again awoke him, and so until morning his sleep was disturbed and haunted. In the morning he presented a haggard appearance when some of his new made friends called upon him to deplore the action of the previous night, and to extend sympathy and help. They hoped that he would not lay the disgraceful scenes of yesterday to the better class of the people South, as they were using every effort to stamp out such disorder.

Said Mayor Gregory in extenuation: "We had at one time to adopt severe measures to make the Negroes know their place; the spirit we encouraged then has become emboldened, is at times even beyond our control, and conspires to bring disgrace upon us."

Said another: "The Negroes are ignorant, incapable of education and most of them are vicious. I assure you we were justified in cowing them, although I am sorry for the occurrence of yesterday."

These condolences and explanations did not right Stanley's outraged feelings, nor lessen one whit the pangs of grief and sorrow. He turned sharply upon them and said: "Could you scare up a more vicious crowd among the Negroes in all Birmingham than the one that made a hell of your city? Are you anxious to stamp out these disorders? You know those who commenced the assault, who inspired the mob and excited it to a frenzy. Bring these men to punishment, and I will have faith in your professions."

"You are not in a mood to discuss such topics," replied the mayor, evading the question, as is usual with the apologists for crime in the South, "besides you come from a place where a large number of cranks preach social equality."

Stanley looked at him and replied sharply, "Mayor Gregory, I have received at your hands kindnesses, hence courtesy now forbids that I should answer you as your insinuations demand. This much I will say: Each individual is sole arbiter of the company he keeps, and upon his privacy no one has a right to intrude unless invited. When I leave this city this evening, my absence forever afterward will show the contempt I feel for it."

Stanley's remarks nettled a few present, but they were excused on the ground of his excitement.

"I had no intention of making my remarks personal," explained the mayor, blushing furiously, then turning abruptly he bade him adieu, and with the others left the room.

That morning Stanley arranged for the shipment of the body. Then he returned to his room to write a few letters —one to his own father, one to Saunders', one to Edith Darrow and one to Marjorie Stone.

He had seen the account of the lynching in the morning papers—a garbled report like all others in which black and whites are engaged, which made Saunders the aggressor. A sassy nigger who grossly insulted an old soldier, and that his life paid the forfeit at the hands of a large number of our best citizens who were enraged at his insults. Thinking that perhaps the Associated Press report might be likewise garbled he gave a clear concise record of the events that finally cost the life of his friend. Because of the kindly interest Marjorie Stone had taken in his friend's welfare, he considered the circumstance of his death sufficiently strong enough to break the silence between them. The letters written, he settled back in his chair to think more calmly of his affairs and plan his future action. As he recalled the mayor's efforts in Saunders' behalf, he felt half remorseful that he had answered him so sharply at the morning interview. Despite the views held by him, he felt that he owed him an apology. He commenced to write one, thinking as he did so of a quotation that Saunders and he had often read during his own sickness: "Common souls pay with what they do. Nobler souls with what they are." So he thanked all concerned for their kindly interests.

CHAPTER XXVIII.

————————

Homeward bound, on a train speeding rapidly northward through East Tennessee, sat Stanley, with a heavy heart, as he thought of the trial that awaited him at his journey's end; of the grief that he must witness; of the sad and sorrowful countenances, and still sadder proofs that he bore with him.

Usually, when returning home from a long journey the heart beats faster, the pulses quicken at the bright anticipations of being again at home with the old familiar faces, and as fast as we may travel, the speed attained seems tame with that of our desires. To him altogether too swiftly speeded the rushing train. The nearer home, the greater anxiety he felt. He could not help but contrast his present feelings with that of a little over one year ago when returning home from the North on a pleasure trip. Then overflowing with life and good spirits, browned and full of health, he and his gay companions chafed each other with good natured raillery. The expectations then and now were vastly different. Then, all eagerness, he hastened with the springy step of youth to one whom he had learned to love. Since then reverses in love, health somewhat impaired, his new relation with Saunders, that brought in their wake his new ideas of life, the grand thoughts that began to teem through his brain, and gave face and form a manlier appearance, the fair prospects of a return of affection that brought back much of the old fire, passed before him. Now careworn and sorrowful with heavy heart he dreaded the coming and sometimes he sighed

"For a long, long sleep, with never a dream,
Nor even one passing thought
Of life with its care and sadness."[119]

until the trials were over and the things he so dreaded had passed.

The letters sent home by him containing the news of the sad misfortune fell like heavy blow upon Saunders' family. The aged father was grief stricken and wailed over the loss of his son. When Edith knew of it she went to him and when they met, heart-broken, the old man exclaimed: "Edith! Edith! It is true;

it is true." She fell upon his neck, and they wept together over their mutual loss. Tears are a relief to overburdened souls. Bewailing their misfortunes we will leave them, for the pen of man cannot portray the deep emotions and strong affections of the heart; the severe pangs and heartaches, beside, their grief is sacred. Their different friends came to condole with them when they heard the sad news, for the relation that Saunders and Edith bore to one another was well known.

Quite a number of the friends of Stanley and of the deceased awaited the train as it came in. There was a tone of sadness in their anxious inquiries, as with a warm grasp they shook Stanley's hand and inquired about his own injuries. His father, too, was there with a heart full of pity, indignation and sorrow, at the manner in which a faithful employee had come to an untimely end. Saunders' remains were taken to his home, where his heart-broken father fell upon the bier and refused to be moved or comforted. His sobs of anguish that shook his whole frame caused the tears to stand in more eyes than one. Seeing that protest and persuasion were of no avail in relieving his sorrow they left him alone with his dead. When the watchers returned, he, too, was dead, and had fallen beside the coffin, having died of a broken heart.

Together in a common grave they were laid in Elmwood. Among the mourners at the funeral were Stanley, his father and Imogene. In Imogene's eyes Saunders had been elevated to the rank of a hero. He had told her stories, drawn pictures for her, helped her in her lessons and she had often consulted with him. Under the heavy stress of sadness that pervaded all things in connection with the last sad obsequies, she joined with others in weeping, while many a tear coursed down the cheek of father and son.

Afterward Edith Darrow said to her friends: "Call me no more Edith, but Mara, for, as with Naomi, the Lord has dealt bitterly with me."[120]

. . . .

After Stanley had gone South and Marjorie Stone could see no more of him or hear but little, save through Imogene, her misgivings and loneliness returned with double force to harass her. As she recalled his many acts of kindness to her since their acquaintance she felt a strong yearning for the absent one, while his struggle with himself seemed to render him more of an ideal than ever. Under such circumstances Maxwell's attentions which were becoming pointed, were a little disagreeable. His defects stood out in striking contrast to the perfection that she had clothed Stanley in, although as a gentleman she highly esteemed him. Everything that a lady might do, without being rude, to discourage his attentions, she resorted to, but he still persisted in his regular visits, and was as far off in declaring his passion as ever.

While in this mood Stanley's letter came and was received as a welcome boon, despite the fearful tiding it bore. She was indeed sorry to hear of the horrible treatment and death of Saunders, for she knew how much Seth was indebted to him for care during his sickness, and then she liked him for Seth's sake. She reread the letter again and again; not a word of love or reference to the past, not a word of self, but full of tenderness and grief for his dead friend. He could have done nothing better to elevate himself in her estimation. She answered his letter and expressed her deep regret at Mr. Saunders' untimely end, "for I think he was a man in every respect, and I am sorry that his color, which is no crime and for which he is not responsible, should have placed him in a position subject to such indignities and the loss of his life without cause. He surely must have been above the ordinary in temperament and intelligence, when one in your station bestowed such friendship upon him. I should like to hear the whole story, both of his death and your escape from the steamboat accident on the Mississippi." The gentle hint conveyed in this request she thought he surely could not refuse.

She was present at the last services paid to the dead.

. . . .

Upon his arrival home Stanley found this letter, and after some reflection he decided to call upon her and comply with her request.

Imogene plied him with questions fast and thick about their experiences, and he spent several evenings with her and his father in going over and over in detail the moving and perilous incidents of his Southern trip. The third evening he called upon Miss Stone. The warm and gracious manner in which he was received, the welcome light in her eyes made him think that he was expected. There was a natural reserve at first of which each was conscious, and traced to its proper source. Another drawback was the presence of Maxwell, who was surprised to see Stanley and that she lavished so much attention upon him. With that keen perception possessed by those that love, and find that their love is not returned, he could read in every look, in every expression of her countenance, the assurance that she loved, aye, almost idolized Stanley. He would have given all that he was worth to have been the recipient of those looks. So well had their own council been kept that he never was able to find out what had kept them apart.

Until the conversation drifted to Stanley's experiences South, it was somewhat tame and spiritless. Before he commenced to recount them, Mr. and Mrs. Stone, who were as curious as their daughter, entered the parlors. Commencing with the first rebuff at New Orleans to the lynching of Saunders, he told his story in a simple way. Unconsciously as he proceeded his eyes gleamed, and his cheeks reddened with the excitement of going again through the terrible ordeals. Never did an Othello charm a Desdemona more completely than did he with his fervid simplicity, charm Marjorie.[121] She watched every gesture, drank in every word, and allowed full rein to her feelings, rejoicing or sorrowing as he depicted his feelings in the course of his story.

Mr. Stone was deeply interested in his recital and his opinion of Stanley was somewhat elevated. He was so agreeably disappointed to see his earnestness that he thought: "He is a far nobler fellow than I thought he was." When Stanley concluded, he said, "I don't see how some people can go South, and come back and speak so of their royal treatment. If you and Saunders had been two dogs you could not have been treated worse."

"I would have been treated royally myself, if I had treated him as a servant. Notwithstanding the fact, that in our service he earned his living, a warmer and a more honest heart never beat in the breast of man. I owe him much. He saved my life; he has been a faithful servant, and when I was sad, a consoling friend. I could not sacrifice him to their whims. He would not have complained, but his looks would have haunted me. I shall never forget the look of despair he gave me when the rope fell over his neck and the shout of triumph went up from the mob like the infuriated delight of demons. What I maintained at home I stood up for in the South."

"A man's principles are his fortress," said Mr. Stone, "the same as his home. Once taken, his manhood is surrendered."

"There will be a change in sentiment before I visit that section again. Although had I gone alone my impressions would doubtless have been different."

Maxwell was much interested and now he aroused himself to say, "Remarkable how people with so much intercourse should hold such widely different views."

"It is the old story of the bent sapling," said Mrs. Stone, who had been silently and quietly watching her daughter.

"The world is full of injustice and false conceptions," said Stanley, "that must disappear with time. The age is developing and destroying ideas that once were thought fixed and permanent. Time is yet to destroy what might be called racial superiority. Intellect is not confined to race or color. All men have like emotions, like sensibilities, are moved by like impulses and feelings. Under like conditions who can say who would lead or who would lag. The end of the civil war completed a cycle in our national growth. It witnessed the freedom of the individual.

We are now in another cycle that will be completed only when our national life is free to all its citizens in all its various branches."

Your conquest is won Seth Stanley. You need never more doubt the result of waiting. Do you see that fair girl? How eagerly she hangs on every word, and how her eyes sparkle? The man freed from his follies has conquered. Nobility of soul has won.

The rest of the evening passed quickly and pleasantly. When he rose to go Marjorie escorted him to the door, and as he bade her goodnight she said: "I am so glad you called. I have enjoyed the evening more than I have since—" here she paused to think. He was looking at her steadily, and she, catching his eyes, with some confusion, cast hers to the ground. "Come, again," said she, after a pause, and gave him such a look that all the old passion that had partly lay dormant since their forced estrangement returned with redoubled force, and he was no weakly creature that moved and felt by halves. The touch of the hand that lay in his sent the blood rushing furiously through his veins. The time was not now he thought to himself to open up the question of love again, so bidding her good night and promising to call again he departed, his whole soul being filled with ecstasy.

His calls were oft repeated.

He had not been home long before his friends, Parker, Morgan and Fox called upon him and soon everything was going along in the same old way, save that the earnest God-fearing man had taken the place of the frivolous youth.

. . . .

A year has passed. The fears entertained by Saunders, of which he wrote to Edith Darrow from B——, have been verified. The election of '88 seemed to embitter old antagonisms, and the outrages and crimes against Afro-Americans and white men who dare run counter to the popular feeling have increased.[122] Hundreds have died and their blood is calling for justice. Housed at last the Afro-American is about to take steps looking for relief. Popular sentiment among all true Americans is taking up their cause, and no little part of it is due to Seth Stanley. Not so strong has it been, in favor of justice, agitated over the Southern race question since the few years before the war, when it so strongly condemned slavery.

Edith Darrow still wears her badge of mourning, and like a ministering angel is ever to be found doing good, and exerting all her power to raise the standard among the masses of the poorer classes of the Afro-Americans, and in inculcating in them the virtue of self-reliance. It is said that she contemplates going to Alabama to teach, where her influence and gentle manners, glowing from her person like an invisible stream, will have greater opportunity and wider scope.

She will never marry, she was too strongly attached to John Saunders and loved him too deeply to ever give to another the love that should accompany plighted faith. With the Stanleys, for Seth and Marjorie were married in the Spring, she is on intimate terms of friendship and is ably seconded by them in all her work.

Morgan has not yet entered business. Fox is preparing to enter the ministry. Parker is still the same kind hearted pun-loving, frivolous fellow, and it is rumored that he is engaged to Miss Downing.

Stanley has not forgotten the promise he made to Saunders, for in the house of Stanley & Son room has been made for two or three bright Afro-American youths, whose future with them, depends upon their own ability. They will have every opportunity to rise accorded to their fellow laborers. To mark Saunders' grave he has had ordered a handsome monolith.

Happy is the home where he and Marjorie reside. We will give one glimpse to the reader. There he sits in a huge arm chair in the library of his elegant and tasty home, on an ottoman sits Marjorie with an arm resting on his knee, looking up into his face and thinking how good, brave and handsome he is. They have been talking about Saunders.

"I have never told you, Marjorie, that among his last words he bid me repair to you, for said he, 'Such hearts as yours deserve recompense.' He was a noble soul far superior in all things that go to make life good and noble than those who insulted and destroyed him."

"Pity it is that such as he are so debarred from recognition."

"But the dawn breaks for them, darling. You know that at Harvard and Cornell the students appointed one of them their class orator, and that high honors are being won by them in other colleges, and that individuals all over our country are having their merits recognized.[123] Public opinion is being agitated on their side as it never has been done since the last days of the anti-slavery agitation. Among even the severer of our Northern papers, is a healthy sentiment pervading, that says: 'Not from the race as a whole, but to individuals must we look, and we must accord to them the same chance that we give to others.' That is all he ever desired. So our age goes on destroying false teachings and creating new and more useful conditions. So our crusade for justice is gaining ground, and the present cycle of our National growth bids fair to prove more glorious than the first."

"And you will have aided in it, my husband."

"I have been so APPOINTED by the dead, and I am but an instrument in the hands of God."

THE END.

Appendix A: Reviews of *Appointed*

The publication of *Appointed* went more or less unremarked in the white press, but the book was at least mentioned in several Black newspapers including the *Leavenworth* (KS) *Herald*, the *Parsons* (KS) *Weekly Blade*, and the *Indianapolis Freeman*. The advertisement in the *Cleveland Gazette* suggests that the book garnered attention in several other papers as well, and it also received notice from luminaries like Frederick Douglass and David Augustus Straker. Albion Tourgee reviewed *Appointed* in his weekly Bystander's Notes column for the *Chicago Inter Ocean*, which was reprinted in, among other sources, an even longer review in the *Cleveland Gazette*.

Cleveland Gazette, October 20, 1894

APPOINTED:
AN AMERICAN NOVEL,

—BY—

SANDA.

Appointed is a novel that introduces new types of the Afro-American into American literature and deals with the race question from new standpoints.

OPINIONS:

Hon. Frederick Douglass: "This is not a bad book: on the contrary it is a good book, and a very good and timely book. It comes just when most needed. I am proud of the book, excellent as it is and for what it is."

Judge A. W. Tourgee: "Appointed presents in a peculiarly dignified and philosophical manner the view which the colored man of culture, aspiration and self-respect must take of race prejudice among the American people, in the American republic, and in American Christianity."

New York Churchman: "We scarcely consider Appointed the great

American novel, but there is earnestness in it and an honest desire to better an undoubtedly shameful condition of things."

New York Independent: "We sympathize with the aim of the author and the moral tone of the book."

Detroit News-Tribune: "The novel is cleverly written, and is of absorbing interest."

Richmond Planet: "We perused the pages of this work with a steadily increasing interest."

Hon. D. A. Straker: "APPOINTED is the complement to Uncle Tom's Cabin."

Copies can be had at THE GAZETTE office, or by addressing Wm. H. Anderson, 19 ½ Woodward Avenue, Detroit, Mich.

PRICE $1.00, POSTPAID.

Chicago Inter Ocean, AUGUST 2, 1894

FROM BYSTANDER'S NOTES

Two other colored men of Michigan have lately made another and quite different appeal to the brain and conscience of a people—not the colored people this time, but the white Christian people of the United States.

"Appointed" is a novel based on the friendly relations of an intelligent young colored man to an educated young white man. Written by Mr. William H. Anderson, late editor of the Plaindealer, of Detroit, and Mr. Walter H. Stowers, it presents in a peculiarly dignified and philosophical manner the view which the colored man of culture, aspiration, and self-respect must take of race prejudice among the American people, in the American Republic, and in American Christianity.

To those who wish to know the other side of that separatism which underlies the "Jim Crow" car, a "Jim Crow" government, and a "Jim Crow" church, the Bystander most earnestly commends the perusal of this work. It is a glass in which we may all see the condemnation of our neighbor's sins, though few will find their own virtues exemplified therein. The book may be obtained by addressing William H. Anderson, care Endicott & Co., Detroit, Mich.

In these days when the colored man is being made a monstrosity, even in the house of God, because his soul has been encased in a darker integument than ours, it may be well to note what the calmest, most hopeful and self-respecting of the people we are insisting upon thrusting to one side, and giving only the crumbs that fall from the table of civilization, thinks of the manhood and Christianity which thus openly flexes the golden rule and counts the truths uttered by Jesus of Nazareth mere sentimental whimsicalities.

ALBION W. TOURGEE
Aug. 2, 1894.

———

Cleveland Gazette, DECEMBER 29, 1894

"APPOINTED."

Of comparative recent publication is "Appointed," a novel by Messrs. W. H. Anderson and W. H. Stowers of Detroit, which will be classed with Judge Tourgee's splendid works, "Bricks Without Straw," "Paetolus Prime" and others of a like nature.

The scene is mainly laid in Detroit, and the principal characters are Seth Stanley, a wealthy young man, a sort of leader for some time, a rather wild, careless and pleasure-seeking coterie of young men of means; John Saunders, an Afro-American employee servant, then friend, who had been a classmate of Stanley; Marjorie Stone, a lovable young lady; a dude by the name of Maxwell, and Mrs. Maxwell, and Mrs. Brooks, a gossip. There are several other minor characters. The most interesting portion of the last half tells of Stanley and Saunders' visit to the south, the former desiring to know more of the great southern problem, their experiences there resulting in the latter's terrible death, and Stanley's return to Detroit. The description of the lynching of Saunders is indeed thrilling and appeals strongly to the reader. In our opinion it is, with the closing paragraphs of "Appointed," one of the strongest efforts of the kind favoring our side of the great lynch questions. Stanley took the body of his friend to Detroit. When the aged father of the deceased stood by the lifeless form he dropped upon his knees as if to pray, and Edith Darrow, Saunders' affianced, and others left the room. When they returned the old gentleman was also dead. His bereavement had killed him. Edith Darrow went to the south and devoted her life to the education of our people. In the grave of John Saunders was buried her hope of earthly happiness. Seth Stanley and Marjorie Stone become man and wife and never forget John Saunders. A year after, as they sat around their fireside, the former said:

"Our age goes on destroying false teachings and creating new and more useful conditions. So our crusade for justice is gaining ground, and the present cycle of our National growth bids fair to prove more glorious than the first."

"And you will have aided in it, my husband."

"I have been so appointed by the dead, and I am but an instrument in the hands of God."

A grand character indeed is furnished in John Saunders. More Stanleys would leaven the lump if well distributed through the country, principally in the south. . . .

[The *Gazette* review closes by attributing and reprinting the text of Tourgee's review.]

APPENDIX B: WRITINGS FROM THE *Plaindealer*

With the exception of the first editorial below—which is cited as written by William H. Anderson in I. Garland Penn's *The Afro-American Press and Its Editors* (1891)—we cannot identify the authors of the following *Plaindealer* editorials since, like most of the content on the editor's pages of the paper, they were unsigned.[1] Even though it is impossible to attribute the editorials to specific *Plaindealer* staff, these texts reveal some of the concerns that animated the editors more generally and Anderson and Stowers specifically: labor relations, education, southern "outrages," political representation, economic opportunity, and the value of race-based organizations like the National Afro-American League.

OUR RELATION TO LABOR

(REPRINTED IN THE HUNTSVILLE LEDGER, APRIL 10, 1886)

The Plaindealer believes that the first step of the Afro-American to better his condition as a wage worker, and to obliterate all feelings of prejudice, and disburse the idea of his inferiority from the minds of the white laborer[,] lies with the Afro American, in making the common cause of the wage workers his own; and in accomplishing this, no better opportunity is to be had than by connecting himself with such labor organizations, as show a disposition to take him in, and who, perhaps influenced by self-interest, more than anything else, are willing in the general improvement for the emancipation of the wage-worker to include him. It is therefore meet that all such overtures of friendship on their part should be met half way and a unit made for a common cause.

The agitation on this subject by the Plaindealer has not been without effect. It has set the race to thinking, and we doubt not but what it will result in something tangible. In all parts of the country it has attention of the most powerful of the labor organizations, the Knights of Labor, and in the city has resulted in this order making the first public attempt it has made to gather the Afro-American into its ranks.

Among the communications published in this issue under "Our Labor Status" will be found one from Judge Grenell, a prominent man in Knights of Labor circles, and one especially noted for the breadth of his views and "Common Sense" opinions, which merits our consideration, coming as it does from the representative of the Knights of Labor, and the frequent expressions it bewars to the Afro-American.[2] Mr. Grenell at the outset recognizes the fact that the Afro-American has not been accorded fair treatment, and that he possesses qualities, which, if he was properly treated, would place him before the world in a far better light. He also asserts that to make effective the work of the humanitarian in the behalf of the Afro-American, that there must be on his part "an inward yearning for grander opportunities and better environments," and then he asks: Do we see this? "Are not the masses of the Afro-American satisfied with their present condition? Do they seek by agitation and organization to place themselves in a position to demand their social political rights?" In the brief space of an editorial article we cannot answer these questions as fully as we should like to.

I.   Do we see this? That is, do we recognize the fact that back of better environments there is "an inward yearning" or desire. To this we answer, Yes. We will go still further to ask ourselves. "Do we possess this inward yearning?" The cry for better opportunities constantly rising from the masses, answer Yes.

II. Are not the masses of the Afro-Americans satisfied with their present condition? No. It was the discontent of the masses at their status which created the necessity for race journals, of which there are now a large number. The journals are mediums by which the race seeks to bring before the public the full knowledge and extent of their wrongs and through which they voice their demands for justice. They are taking the place of men who propose as leaders of the race yet do nothing but look for political honor. That there is dissatisfaction even in certain sections of our country where ignorance is as dense as it is in the wilds of Africa where educational influences have scarcely permeated; and where the Afro-American is found in the greatest numbers, is evidenced by their pleas for education and light; by their efforts in becoming land owners—which shows that they are awake to the need of the race, and by establishing industrial schools where the hand and heart as well as the head can be trained. The Afro-American by no means occupies an inferior position willingly. Neither should the capabilities and desires of the race, as too often happens, be judged by the idle and the shiftless, nor will the mission of the race journal be fulfilled until the race stands on an equal plane with the other citizens of the country.

III. Do they seek by agitation and organization, to place themselves in a position to demand their social, political and economic rights? The process of
evolution is slow. It must be remembered that a score of years has hardly
intervened since every noble aspiration or ambition of the Afro-American
was crushed, and everything that was degrading encouraged. It must be
remembered too that it took centuries for the white wage worker to bring
himself to his present condition, and that his labor organizations are yet
raw and undisciplined, and unable as yet to carry on a successful warfare
against organized capital. Under these circumstances it is not to be wondered at that the Afro-American has no perfected national organization
looking to the social, political, and economic rights. Their agitation in the
Northern states has secured repeals of black laws and passage of civil right
bills. Their agitation has secured to them positions of trust in public places.
An organization, which is designed to be national, is being organized,
whose object it is to see that the Afro-American all over the county is protected in his civil and political rights, and is now preparing [to] assert his
rights—against those who should be his friends and have opposed him—to
be employed in the trades and mechanical pursuits of life.

The reason why the Knights of Labor have received no accessions from the
Afro-Americans in Detroit is that the same effort to enlist the white mechanic
or tradesman in their order was not made to enlist the colored wage worker, and
this organization was looked upon as something kindred to trades unions in
objecting to him as a member of their organization, and as he has known to his
cost both as to pocket and personal feeling, in refusing to work with him. Such
experience has no tendency to make a rush blindfolded into the meeting insult
and prejudice. Are you answered, Mr. Grenell?

With respect to the invitation made to the Afro-American to become
connected with the Knights of Labor, either by joining the older or forming a
separate assembly, the Plaindealer would advise the race to have nothing to do
with separate assemblies, but to connect themselves with the older, and strive
by becoming useful members to do away with the prejudicial feeling which has
acted against their better judgement. Isolate themselves by forming separate assemblies, and they will foster and encourage the idea of inferiority and thus delay
their emancipation, and the stride forward will be more [less?] rapid. There is in
this movement of labor much that is to be commended. Its object is a glorious
one. Accomplishment is not far off, and the Afro-American should take a hand
in the fight and be in at the finish.

OCTOBER 11, 1889

From the condition of affairs growing out of slavery, the popular idea obtains that there is a natural antipathy resting among the white and dark races. This assumed truth has been urged with all the force, persistence and sophistry the south could master. Having peculiar and exclusive ideas they have tried to impress them upon the world. They have succeeded so far that the social atmosphere of America is generally tainted with exclusive ideas of radical race tendencies, not unmixed often with the idea of superiority. In opposition to this erroneous narrow doctrine is the tendency of the times to a more liberal plan of thought and action, and the lovers of truth, the more progressive people of America, are outgrowing narrowness in every avenue of thought. The mind is too lofty to dwell on such trifles to the exclusion of nobler things. The Waterbury *American* told the whole truth when it said, "the measure of prejudice against the Negro is in proportion to the ignorance and vice of the people."[3] This question has recently been vividly brought to mind by petty acts of discrimination in Northern cities that are annoying and humiliating. In every case it has been practiced by and at the behest of narrow-minded, bigoted people, and condemned by the better classes. People joined inseparable to error have, in all ages, been the ignorant. And in all ages conspicuous and uncompromising champions of right, justice and truth have stood out in bold prominence against the narrowness and prejudice of their times. Many have lived to see a transformation of sentiment hardly creditable. They constitute the other factor of which we have spoken that has combatted caste and wrong.

The South is particularly active at this time in disseminating its doctrine of "superiority and natural antipathy," and in proportion to this activity in the direction of error is the spirit of justice aroused in the North. It is a natural consequence of cause and effect. It was so just preceding the war, when slavery became most cruel the abolition movement became most aggressive. To those intrepid champions of right, GEORGE W. CABLE and ALBION W. TOURGEE, have been added many more. REV. JOHN SNYDER in the *Forum* for October shows conclusively that race animosities are due to a false education, showing that it is unknown outside of America. But it remained for the REV. CHARLES STANLEY LESTER of Milwaukee to put his views into practice—as well as in a finely woven magazine article. The manager of the Bijou theatre of that city discriminated against its Afro-American patrons, claiming that it was obnoxious to his white patrons. This is the same ground taken by all who strive to draw the color line. Although we have published the facts once we reproduce them to show that the alleged prejudice was from the lower order of Milwaukee society, if at all, as in the case all over the United States. The following clipping from our news columns is substantially what Rev. LESTER and his congregation did:

> To a large congregation composed of wealthy business and professional men the clergyman from the text, "God is no Respecter of Persons," delivered a strong arraignment of Manager LITT for his action in excluding colored people from certain parts of the Bijou. While tickets were not refused to gamblers, drunkards, thieves, and prostitutes, provided their skin were white, there should be no denial of the same privilege to a black man simply for the reason of his color. 'It is evident,' said the preacher, 'that the theatre in question expects to draw its patrons only from the ill-bred classes, but that there are not enough people in Milwaukee to resent and punish this contemptible barbarism is sad to chronicle. The Christian church, in so far as it is Christian, will fight against this American iniquity.' The sermon has been printed in pamphlet form for circulation. Mr. LESTER is very much in earnest in his crusade and is said to have his congregation behind him.

We need just such ministers as this in every community, who will make the church in spirit what it is in profession. Men who will not pander to the false doctrines of ignorance to become popular with the rabble or make elastic the immutable principles of the Bible. It is better to be decried by BARRABAS than to be extolled by him.[4]

JANUARY 24, 1890

During the past two weeks, in the National Congress, Southern Senators have been airing their views in regard to the Afro-American of the South. The "Appeal to Pharaoh," which was issued but a few months ago, seems now to have been published with the express purpose of creating a sentiment in favor of just such legislation as is now attempted.[5] This book with its ideas of justice fell flat in the North, and if anything, the remedies it favored met with condemnation. The same result will attend these bills of Southern Senators. The Afro-American nowhere in this country, wants special legislation. There are laws enough on our statute books to suit the most fastidious. What is most desirous is a public sentiment that will demand the enforcement of the law. Laws under the present jury system are useless if public sentiment is against them. Justice for all men of different political creeds or races will never be obtained so long as an intolerant bigotry prevails.

It almost makes the angels weep to hear Senator BUTLER, he who led the mob at Hamburg and disgraced civilization by a horrid butchery, pleading in favor of his bill to provide for the deportation of Afro-Americans, because there were no 'Negro' banks, bank presidents, cashiers, or tellers, no 'Negro' corporations, etc.[6] The question that most naturally arises, after reading such a plea is why are there none? Investigation shows that it is due in a great measure to the intolerant opinions of such men as Butler, Morgan, et al. The American people are not to be fooled by specious reasoning or a mock hypocritical interest such as is displayed by these senators. When the Afro-American wants to go to Africa or elsewhere and requires aid, he will get it from others besides his worst enemies.

The Afro-American as a race, has not been free or enjoyed educational facilities long enough to have many banks, rich corporations, statesmen, and a large number of men, eminent in scientific pursuits. But there *are* Afro-American banks, [and] consequently, bank presidents, cashiers, tellers and bookkeepers. There are statesmen and politicians, unfortunately the Southern mode of butchery has dwarfed their genius. There are men who are gaining eminence in scientific pursuits. All other things that combine to make races great will follow with opportunities.

The Afro-American has gone beyond the period of asking for special legislation, and now demands, by virtue of his loyalty and services rendered to the Republic, only justice and equal opportunities of the American people. The Afro-American, hardly twenty-five years a freeman, with 50 per cent of his race illiterate, throws down the gage of competition to the rest of the American nation and announces that, given justice and equal opportunities he is content to abide by the decision of the survival of the fittest. The superior (?) race of the South dares not accept the challenge.

———

JUNE 20, 1890

At this time of year the very air is filled with college oratory. The work of the institution is lauded, and the brilliant prospect of the graduate pictured. The Plaindealer does not wish to discourage anything that would add to the enthusiasm with which the student enters the active business duties that are required of him. But hopes are easily brought to despair and what seemed so full of promise often suddenly blasted. The more we come in contact with the stern requirements the more is it shorn of romance. Things may be what they seem, but are seldom what they are pictured. Numbers of Afro-American graduates with the best of college records are to-day occupying menial positions. To say that their college hopes have been shattered inadequately expresses it. Whereas then all promising, now the dull routine of circumscribed usefulness is enervating. The danger to our students lies in the limited opportunities open to them. They become disappointed, then lethargic and sometimes lose all ambition. Every Afro-American collegiate should begin the active duties of bread winning fully comprehending what he is to meet, and with a firm determination to conquer, else his education [is] in vain.

OCTOBER 31, 1890

The SOUTHERNER may cry out, "Lynch him" every time an Afro-American advocates blow for blow in consideration of the outrages perpetrated on him. Lynching will not always avail to corner us, the Afro-American of today is not the one of twenty-five years ago, and the bourbon will someday be rudely awakened to that fact. Someday, and that soon, we are going to return blow for blow, openly if possible, secretly if necessary. If the Southern conscience will not heed our appeals for fair play they shall fear our vengeance. We trust the day will speedily come even though a few lives be sacrificed. No more will be lost in a manly defense of our rights, than in tamely submitting to outrages.

JANUARY 9, 1891

In the varied discussions of the Afro-American much of the buncombe and dogmatic ignorance that has characterized the treatment of this subject has been eliminated. There were a class of men writing who did not care for facts as long as they could be heard and another class who knew the truth, yet maliciously and purposely misstated it. Now there are few of either of these classes who essay to speak advisedly on the much discussed "Negro Problem." Many Anglo-Saxon writers are now seeing the disadvantages and hindrances to our race progress in the very factors that have been set forth by our leading men and journals for several years. Rev. A. D. Mayo in the *Forum*, points out very concisely one of these hurtful drawbacks. He sees in the opposition of organized labor in the North to Afro-American workmen, a serious hindrance to the latter's advancement. His conclusions are true in this regard for there are few employers courageous enough to stand against the prejudices of their employees. As a result, with us the training in business that comes from contact with business men and business methods is wanting. This partly explains the few co-operative business firms established among Afro-Americans in which the Rev. A. D. Mayo discovers a weakness which he attributes to a want of confidence in one another.[7] Trusted clerks and agents make the future men of business.

———

SEPTEMBER 18, 1891

It seems strange that the Plaindealer at this date should have to explain its attitude relative to the position the Afro-American must take to secure what really belongs to him as a citizen, yet the idea the New South seem to have formed, caused by an editorial in our issue of August 28th, which ended: "Activity is life; stagnation is death. Resistance to oppression means liberty, and indicates manhood. Submission indicates servility, and means debasement. Between the two, there is for the Afro-American, no middle ground. He must organize to resist oppression and to secure the rights belonging to him."

The Plaindealer is not so ignorant of the state of affairs throughout the South as to advocate an uprising to try to secure by force of arms his rights, for it knows that such an attempt under present conditions would be foolhardy, and result in partial, if not complete, extermination, and it sees with regret that the great number of lynchings and outrages against life and property of the race is rapidly trending toward such a condition when a box of lucifers in the hands of desperate men may prove more terrible, and inflict greater loss than an armed conflict. It is because it fears this that the Plaindealer has been so constant in advising the organization of the League to secure through the methods of peace their rights. The world has advanced in thought, and greater victories are won in time of peace than ever were gained as the result of disastrous warfare. Public sentiment is the great factor of our times, and compels kings to bow to its mandate, and nations to agree to its will. But public sentiment is not to be gained by servility, nor freedom to be won by the cringing words of debased natures. Suits are not to be won against railroads, for unequal accommodation, without legal fights, nor will class laws be declared unconstitutional unless a fight is made in the

Supreme Court of the United States, where the most brilliant talent, and the strongest argument will have to be made to gain the victory. The abuses of the convict camps cannot be overcome by fawning or even sporadic attempts, but the enormities have to be held up constantly before the people, their consciences are to be lashed, caucuses are to be won, legislatures carried, and all this requires a courage as great, a persistency as strong, as ever influenced soldiers on the field of battle. The same can be said with reference to other abuses of the South, and the Afro-American must try to win his fight by such means, rather than wait to be driven to more desperate ones for there are extremes to every nature which revolt at a given point and the victim turns upon his tormentors.

Acquisition of wealth alone will not give freedom. Southern intolerance is more fierce and severe than Russian despotism, and there the accumulations of the Jews are fast disappearing in the face of the persecutions they are subject to. The Plaindealer would rather have freedom, and be just able to eke out a bare existence, than to have wealth and not have the privilege of using it as a man, and be denied the common rights that the most debased and ignorant whites have. The Afro-American cannot afford to be quiet. He must be active by the very force of circumstances, or sink lower in the scale, for, as the Plaindealer said in the beginning, "Activity is life; stagnation is death. Resistance to oppressions means liberty and indicates manhood, while submission means debasement and indicates servility."

NOVEMBER 20, 1891

INVADING NEW FIELDS

THE COLOR QUESTION IN THE REALMS OF FICTION

The prominence which the color question is assuming in the Republic is causing a number of books to be written bearing on the subject in the light of fiction and from a scientific standpoint.

Howells, perhaps the most celebrated of American novelists, has made a venture into this field. It might be called a venture for it did not go deep into the question. In tracing the agony of mind of a beautiful girl, who suddenly found out that she had African blood in her veins, and who, because of this, felt it to be her duty to identify herself then and impel her to reject her white lover he displays a keen insight of character and feeling. Howells's character analysis is always interesting. His stories are natural and seem commonplace, so in his "An Imperative Duty," one is not so surprised to find that the girl's love overcomes her objection, that they marry, and go at once to Italy, where her small part of African blood even if it were known would make no difference.[8]

Then there is Dr. Huguet, as full of life, action and movement, as the other is devoid of it, going deeper into the problem, and even essaying a solution. These books go to show the interest that is being awakened.[9] It makes the Afro-American talked about. It creates an interest in him, that can be used to his advantage. These works of fiction reach a class of readers too, that scientific, or economic works fail to reach, whose influence is just as needful to be used before this vexatious question will be settled right.

It is not at all surprising that in view of the prominence the question is taking that the enemies of the Afro-American should also write books in antagonism to his desires to be recognized as a man and brother. The "Noted Men of the South" is an instance, save that it was written and published and issued as a book, and added one more to the "writing of books of which there is no end," it is hard to find what reason it had for existence. There is another more recently issued called Anthropology for the People by "Caucasian," in which the African is hardly recognized as a human being at all . . . [10]

Appendix C:
"A Strange Freak of Fate"

Several years after they had written *Appointed* but soon after the *Plaindealer* stopped publishing, Anderson and Stowers collaborated on the short story "A Strange Freak of Fate." The two men sent it to their friend and fellow author Albion Tourgee's magazine, the *Basis*, knowing that Tourgee was both an admirer of their novel and a political fellow traveler. Indeed, Anderson and Stowers had regularly reprinted Tourgee's Bystander's Notes from the *Chicago Inter Ocean* in the *Plaindealer*. Tourgee's *Basis* only lasted for one year, though, and the story never appeared in print, so the two men sent it to the *A. M. E. Church Review*, the long-running literary magazine published by the African Methodist Episcopal Church Book Concern in Philadelphia. The story appeared in Volume 13 (1897).

"A Strange Freak of Fate" resonates with *Appointed* but also takes readers in new directions. As is the case in *Appointed*, the male protagonist, Edwin, is college educated and highly capable; unlike John Saunders, his own racial identity (which he discovers during the story) seems not to impede either his social or his economic prospects. In fact, by revealing his identity in the middle of the story, the authors establish his character traits without regard to his race and then lead readers to accept those traits even after his race becomes known. In this way, the authors establish a hierarchy rooted in character, intelligence, and achievement and demonstrate its operation within a particular geographic context. At the same time, and just as they did in *Appointed*, Anderson and Stowers take aim at both the customs and attitudes of southerners, especially as those customs and attitudes lead to the creation of race-based hierarchies. As was the case with the Stanley/Saunders relationship, too, the character Mrs. Jones changes her mind about those race-based hierarchies when she is able to consider them in a personal context.

These various similarities to the novel aside, "A Strange Freak of Fate" also brings to mind the fictions of the color line that the authors mention in their 1891 editorial "Invading New Fields," particularly Howells's novel *An Imperative Duty* (1891). The story also recalls several of the tales in Charles Chesnutt's short story collection *The Wife of His Youth* (1900). In both the titular story of that collection as well as "Her Virginia Mammy," Chesnutt highlights the tangled genealogies of southern men and women and the confused (or unknown) racial identities that complicated relationships in the wake of the Civil War and Reconstruction. Though there is no evidence that Chesnutt read this specific story, he was an admirer of Anderson and Stowers's work and he drew on other African Americans' writings as he formulated his own fiction, so it would come as no surprise if Chesnutt found inspiration for his own stories in this one.

Miscellaneous.

VIII.

A STRANGE FREAK OF FATE.

CHAPTER I.

IT ALL CAME ABOUT through the nerves of Mrs. Jones. Little Mary was really in no great danger; for Silver Lake, although one mile wide by two miles long, was not a danger-

Walter H. Stowers

William H. Anderson

ous lake. The wind sometimes swept over it with great force and lashed its waters into a miniature fury; but fatalities, except such as came through carelessness, were unknown. Little Mary had been playing upon the beach and seeing the row boat that some one had carelessly left, only about half-beached, got into it and was soon busily engaged playing in the water. There was a good wind blowing at the time, and the boat was soon after cast adrift. Little Mary unmindful of danger was still busy at play when she was suddenly aroused by hearing her mother's wild scream, as, she coming down from the house, saw the boat with its four year old occupant, drifting out into the lake, and a storm coming up. Mrs. Jones was an extremely nervous little woman, and imagining the danger to be greater than it really was, uttered scream after scream. The little girl would have been perfectly safe until another boat could

A STRANGE FREAK OF FATE

CHAPTER I.

IT ALL CAME ABOUT through the nerves of Mrs. Jones. Little Mary was really in no great danger; for Silver Lake, although one mile wide by two miles long, was not a dangerous lake.[1] The wind sometimes swept over it with great force and lashed its waters into a miniature fury; but fatalities, except such as came through carelessness, were unknown. Little Mary had been playing upon the beach[,] and seeing the row boat that some one had carelessly left, only about half-beached, got into it and was soon busily engaged playing in the water. There was a good wind blowing at the time, and the boat was soon after cast adrift. Little Mary unmindful of danger was still busy at play when she was suddenly aroused by hearing her mother's wild scream, as, she coming down from the house, saw the boat with its four year old occupant, drifting out into the lake, and a storm coming up. Mrs. Jones was an extremely nervous little woman, and imagining the danger to be greater than it really was, uttered scream after scream. The little girl would have been perfectly safe until another boat could have been sent to her rescue had it not been for her mother's nervousness. Mrs. Jones' cries, however, alarmed Edwin Barden who happened to be nearby at the slaughter-house of his father; he came rushing up and seeing Mrs. Jones' agonized face and Little Mary's danger, hastily doffed his coat and shoes and plunged into the lake; he was an expert swimmer but could not make rapid headway because of his clothes. Little Mary, very much frightened by the clamor and the wind, started to meet him and toppled overboard. Mrs. Jones then gave one long, piercing cry and fainted. A number of people from the house and village had heard the screams and came hurrying to the scene; among them Mrs. Jones' step daughter, Ida, who rushed to her mother's side before she realized the danger her little sister was in.

Little Mary's clothes kept her afloat for a few short moments; but the scare and tumult set her to screaming and kicking lustily, despite Edwin's cherry[2] voice as he called to her, telling her to keep quiet as he would soon be with her. He had almost reached her, when to his consternation, and of those also on the beach, she suddenly sank from view. He redoubled his efforts to reach the spot at which she disappeared, and then dived for her. It seemed a long time to the onlookers before he reappeared on the surface with the child, then what a shout of encouragement and approval went up from the small crowd. On coming to the surface, Edwin looked first for the boat, but seeing that it had drifted too far out, he struck out for the shore with the child. He was an expert swimmer under ordinary circumstances, but his clothes were now water-sogged, little Mary a dead weight and his strength seemed to be leaving him. The situation became apparent to the observers, and there was some rustling in the crowd. A few waded out into the lake as far as they could with boards, but he was too far out to take advantage of such aid.

Among the crowd was Edwin's little brother, George, a lad about twelve years of age, but a good swimmer. Seeing his brother's need, he retired a little way and quickly taking off his clothing went at once to his rescue. He was only a little fellow, but he had a stout heart and his love for his brother amounted almost to worship. The wind was strong and Edwin had to come in the face of it. He was puffing laboriously. He felt that if aid did not soon come he would never reach the shore. The thought had hardly passed through his mind before he felt he was being drawn down by the weight of the child and his clothes. The mother seeing this swooned away and was borne with gentle hands to the house. But George was rapidly nearing the endangered pair, and when Edwin with a supreme effort reappeared with little Mary, George was there to relieve him of the little girl, and soon all were in reach of help.

Edwin was the hero of the hour, and little George came in for no small share of glory. Among the first to rush to Edwin to thank him was Ida, who threw her arms about his neck and kissed him before all the people. At this the blood rushed to his face, and he became as shy and backward as any school girl.

CHAPTER II.

———

The village of J—— lies in the northeastern part of the State of Ohio. It is a cozy little place nestling on a slope, and near the foot of a beautiful hill, lying at the foot of which was Silver Lake, the pride of that section, and which fairly glistened under the rays of the sun. The lake seemed a synonym of perfect peace and restfulness. On the village side of the lake several persons had houses whose grounds ran down to it; elsewhere it was skirted by woods and fields. On a clear night when the moon shone down upon it, casting its silvery light over all, it was a perfect paradise for lovers, who were not slow to take advantage of it.

J—— had a share in the rapid growth and new conditions of the country that followed after the war of the rebellion. What with the returned soldiers, new families coming in from various parts and the energy shown in taking advantage of the promising conditions of the times, the village bid fair to start anew its stunted growth. It had fair railroad facilities, hence had a fair outlet for the product of its few enterprises and of the farms.

At the time of the opening of this story there were two families who had come in early after the war—the Bardens and Jones. During that stage of the growth of the village, no one stopped to inquire from whence one came. Yet through such gossip as is usually to be found in such places, whether true or false, it was learned that they had come from the South. The heads of these families were enterprising men and soon had a place in the conduct of affairs.

George Barden was originally from Kentucky, but had removed to J—— from one of the great growing cities of the West, where he had married Mrs. Barden. He had two sons—Edwin, the elder, twenty-four years of age, and George, a young lad just entering his teens. Mr. Barden was the principal butcher of the town, and a man of considerable property. As Edwin had a leaning toward medicine he had attended college at C——, was recently graduated and had opened up an office. The Joneses (as they were called in village parlance) came from Virginia and were five in number. Mr. John Jones, his daughter Ida by a former marriage, now a very pretty young lady with all the graces that attend budding womanhood, Mrs. Jones and Henry and Mary, their two children. Mr. Jones with Mr. Thorp, his partner, were the leading bankers of the town. He lived on the outskirts of the village at the foot of the hill, and his spacious grounds bordered on the lake.

He was a good father and husband and took advantage of every opportunity afforded by his money, his beautiful home and the lake, to make it pleasant for his family.

The rescue of Little Mary by Edwin Barden had cemented the bond between the two families. When Mr. Jones heard of it, in the exuberance of his feelings and joy he promised her rescuer anything in his possession that he desired. Mrs. Jones, although in a high fever and exceedingly nervous, had insisted on his coming to her bedside, to receive her thanks. Thus Edwin and Ida were thrown more closely together, and he became her devoted and constant attendant. They were regarded throughout the village as accepted lovers and were considered as one of the best matches the village had ever furnished. From almost every standpoint they seemed fitted for each other. Edwin was tall, dark and muscular, like his father, while Ida was of medium height, graceful and inclining to the blonde type.

There was but one point of difference between the families and each knowing the others views on the subject, it was never brought up. The Jones were essentially Southern in sympathies, especially Mrs. Jones, who was a thorough Southerner, and regretted the defeat and present conditions of the South. On the other hand, Mr. Barden had accepted the results of the war and was an enthusiastic Republican. The Grant and Greeley campaign was on.[3] Mrs. Jones was for Greeley and the Democracy forever, and was very assertive in her opinions. These questions were not troubling either Edwin or Ida at this time, for each to the other contained all that there was in this life worth living for. Each filled the heart and eye of the other and no such humdrum affairs, like politics, were considered important beside the love they felt for each other, and which spoke out of their eyes and in the numerous ways lovers show their affection to one another. Life to them was one sweet day dream, overflowing with ineffable sweetness. Summer was in its full bloom, and the young couple spent many evenings on the lake, in drives or strolls among the hills that undulate that section, and which make it so picturesque. Sometimes they talked of the future at others, they were silent for a long time, enjoying that silent communion that exists between two souls that are all in all to each other. One moonlight evening, while out on the lake, reveling in the beauty around them, and feeling that quiet peace that seemed to rest on the bosom of the lake, Edwin ceased rowing, and each seemed to be engaged in the silence of their thoughts, when Edwin spoke out:

"How calm and placid the lake is, and how beautiful. Scarcely a ripple disturbs its surface. How like unto it seems the course of our love: hardly a ripple has disturbed its surface, and yet, they say true love never runs smoothly. I trust that there will never be any storms or squalls to mar ours."

"I trust so, too," she answered musingly. "These are glad, blissful days to me, almost like a dreamland. The skies seem so bright, the song of the birds so sweet, the flowers so beautiful, and music in everything. No thoughts of storms should be allowed to mar our happiness."

"They shall not," exclaimed Edwin, impulsively. "We will live in the pleasure of the moment, for does not happiness lie in the present rather than in the future? And yet, three months intervene before you will come to me as my wife. I cannot help but think of the happiness and good fortune that awaits me. The days and weeks seem to pass so slowly, when you are not present time drags on a weary march. Ah! we will be so happy, dear."

They were sitting facing each other, and Ida, leaning forward, stroked his hand caressingly, as she soothingly said: "There are no stern parents to withhold their blessings, for mother dotes on you, Edwin. She would never forgive me if I should do anything to mar your happiness."

Then silence again fell between them; but they were so happy, and such harmony filled their souls. Neither had any thought of the events, so soon to happen, that would mar their peace and try their love.

CHAPTER III.

———

It was one of those rare June days when heaven and earth seemed in perfect harmony; when every sound fell on the ear like music, and there was not one note of discord to mar the beauty of the day. To one at ease the brightness of the day, the abundant foliage and the beautiful scenery gave inspiration; but to those forced to plod many weary miles over dusty roads, it was hot and sultry enough, except, when taking advantage of some cool, shady spot, one could draw strength and inspiration from the beauty and harmony of the scenery. About four o'clock in the afternoon of the day in question, a weary traveler with a little bundle at the end of a stick swung over his shoulder, approached J——. He was dusty and weary from the effects of a long journey. There was that about his appearance somewhat unusual to what the people of J—— had been accustomed to seeing; as he passed along the main street, the little children stopped in their play and gave expression to their amazement. It was a rare sight and they watched him until he passed out of their view. He saw that he was attracting attention and almost hesitated to inquire for whom he was seeking. At last approaching an old gentleman, he asked: "Does George Barden live here?"

"Yes, sir," came back the reply. "He keeps a meat market over there on Main street, and that large brick residence you see near the lake is his home."

The traveler thanked him and moved on toward George Barden's home. The old man turned around once to look after him; there was a queer expression on his face and he was evidently wondering where that fellow came from.

The vicissitudes of slavery with its attendant looseness of morals, had created for the South, men and women of all colors and gradations of features. While all bearing any infusion of Negro blood were classed as Negroes, still there were names classifying them according to their degree of mixture. It was evident that the traveler was either a quadroon or an octoroon. As he neared the Barden's he hesitated as if uncertain whether he should enter; yet, at the same time he was taking a careful look over the surroundings. Deciding at last, he went up to the door and rapped on the screen; Mrs. Barden answered and was met with the same inquiry that greeted the old gentleman.

"Does George Barden live here?"

"Yes, sir."

"Are you his wife?"

"Yes, sir."

"Are you from Kentucky?"

"No, I'm not. My husband was."

"Has he a scar over his left eye?"

"Yes, sir."

The stranger nodded his head in a satisfied manner and said: "It must be that he's my brother. I haven't seen him in thirty years."

"Your brother!" exclaimed Mrs. Barden in surprise. "How can that be? Why, you're a colored man and my husband is white. There isn't a colored man in this town." Then noting the despairing look in the man's eyes, her sympathies were aroused and she said, "I'm sorry for you, my poor fellow."

"All these weary miles travelled for nothing," said the stranger, dejectedly. "Well, I must commence all over again. I must find him. He's my only brother— younger than I am. I was sold away South, and we became separated while young lads." He picked up his bundle and was about to go when Mrs. Barden said kindly, "Don't go yet, my man. We never turn a stranger from our door in distress. Mr. Barden will be home soon; as he is from Kentucky, he may be able to help you find your brother; besides, you look tired and hungry, and I would not see you go away without having something to eat."

The stranger was given water to bathe his dusty hands and face, while Mrs. Barden went down to the gate to watch for her husband.

When she saw him coming she went out to meet him, and catching him by the arm, she said laughingly,

"George, I've a good joke on you. There's a colored man in the house who thought that you were his long-lost brother. Come now, own up. Have you any colored relations?" and she laughed heartily.

Receiving no reply, she looked up and saw signs of distress on his face. Her sympathies were all aroused, and with great tenderness she asked, "Why, George, what is the matter?"

The decisive moment had come in the life of George Barden. He was fully aware of his position; but never for a moment did he ever intend to deny the truth should it be brought home to him. Since coming to the North he had passed current for his worth as a man, and had taken advantage of such opportunities as were offered to him. Even now the thought did not occur to him to deny his blood mixture, but the way in which his wife would receive it, troubled him. There was a tremor in his voice, a serious look on his face, but his lips were firm as he passed his arm about her and said: "Addie, there is something to explain now that I at one time thought need never be known. My mother was a quadroon, and I did have a brother, Tom, who was darker than I, and older. When I was very young he was sold away by his master and father, to help meet financial reverses. It broke my mother's heart and she died. When father saw the consequences of his act, he was very sorry. He died shortly afterwards, but before his death I was made a freeman and came to the North. It is possible that this man is my brother."

"Oh, George, what will the neighbors say? Can't you send him away? No one knows that you are colored."

"Disown my brother! I would not do that." They passed around to the rear of the house in silence, and then with a voice that grieved, but which left no doubt of his purpose and honest convictions, he continued: "Addie, I will not ask you to make any sacrifice to public sentiment. I will leave you free, and bear it all alone. The love that has bound us and made us constant and true for these thirty years may by this revelation be shorn of its constancy should you ever upbraid or nag me because of this. I couldn't bear that." There were tears in the strong man's eyes, and an appeal in his voice that went straight to her heart.

"Addie, my wife, in all of our joys and sorrows, in all our hopes and reverses, in all our castle-building for the future of our children, you have always thought of me and them as white, when lo, I possess in part, the blood of the despised. Is the picture marred by it? If so—"

"No, no, no, my husband!" she cried. "For you are still my husband and the father of my children. You are and have been a hero. And if because of this, the world regards you and ours differently, yet will I cleave to you and love you, my dear, forever, and no word of complaint or regret shall ever pass my lips." Then she flung her arms about his neck and kissed him.

The tears were still in his eyes, but as he pressed her to his bosom he said in a choking voice, "You have made me very happy, my wife. Let us go in and see this stranger."

Together they went into the house. The traveler proved to be his brother, Tom.

CHAPTER IV.

When it became known throughout J—— that the stranger was a colored man and brother to George Barden, it created for a time some talk. It is true that some thought he had committed a crime against the community for sailing under false colors; but George Barden was a man of such sterling worth, and so well thought of that there was no difference in the treatment accorded him. There is a rugged sort of independence in these small towns, not so easily found in the large centers of population, which does not consider the mere fact of race, or the color of the skin, essentials of manhood. Worth is considered as the standard of the man and this spirit existed in J—— to a large degree.

When Edwin parted from Ida that evening he little dreamed of the surprise for him at home, or the reception that Mrs. Jones would greet him with when next he called. All of her hot Southern blood, and contempt for Negroes, arose to the surface when she heard the news. It changed her entire feelings towards the Bardens, and particularly towards Edwin. She developed a case of hysterics and had to be put to bed. When she recovered, Ida was summoned to her bedside, and rather forcibly told that Edwin was a Negro, no better than one of the slaves her father had owned; that the engagement must end at once, and Edwin was never to darken their doors again. Ida was stunned at first by the news; but recovering, protested against such a hasty decision. She claimed that Edwin was all that she desired in a husband: that he was noble in character, gentlemanly and kind, and that she saw no reason why she should give him up. Then overwrought by the news and her feelings she burst into tears.

"You act like a silly little girl," said Mrs. Jones, angrily. "Would you marry beneath you and then repent of your rashness all your life. You will see the day that you will thank me for my decision and firmness. Now go to your room, you foolish girl, and never let any one know that you were soft enough to shed tears over a nigger." The last sentence was delivered with biting sarcasm.

Without a word Ida left her mother and went to her room, where she wept bitterly. Such love as hers was no ephemeral fancy; but had taken deep root in her soul. During the long hours she spent alone, the prey of emotions that almost overwhelmed her, buffeted between her love for Edwin and her duty to her mother, she became the woman she had not been before. She decided to have a talk with her father, and if he shared her mother's views, then love should be sacrificed to duty. When morning came she feared the meeting and was thoroughly miserable. It was a great struggle for her to calm her feelings so as to meet the ordeal she expected that awaited her downstairs. It was a relief to find that her father had gone. Fate seemed kind to her, for even her step-mother said nothing of the event of the night before. Not that she had abated one jot or tittle in her decision, but having planted the seed, she was for the while content to see it grow and bear fruit in its own way. While Mrs. Jones was only step-mother to Ida, she had never before used harsh words towards her, and Ida had never thought of her save as her own mother, as she had known no other.

After breakfast Ida strolled towards a little grove at the other end of the village, a favorite spot of hers. While on her way she met Jack Flanders, a former suitor, who was mean and brutal enough to suggest that she had his sympathy for wasting her love on a Negro. This was a light blow to what she had borne, and it fell harmless. Reaching her favorite spot she gave herself up to contemplation of the swift series of events that had carried her almost beyond her depth. This thing she had never dreamed of—it was so wild and improbable. She could not think. She could only dream and give herself up to the witchery of the beautiful June morning. For the rustling leaves, the chirping birds, the rolling wheels, the distant halloes, the clanking cow bells, and all nature's sounds seemed to cry "Edwin!" "Edwin!" She reveled in the harmony of these melodies, that were so in accord with the love in her heart and seemed to find as did Byron:

> "Pleasure in the pathless woods
> And society where none intrudes."[4]

The dreamy echo of these impressions helped her through the next few days.

CHAPTER V.

When Edwin went home that evening and met his uncle he was greatly surprised; but in the presence of the family he mastered his feelings and gave no hint of the struggle that was going on within him. The full significance of the revelation, however, presented itself before him. When he went to his room and allowed his thoughts full sway he paced it like some furious captive, and again like one flogged and made submissive. It was not because of the taint of Negro blood, for he knew that blood-mixture had but little to do with the making of a man, but because of what he knew would be the effect on others. When away from J—— in the city of C—— attending college he had learned something of what the world—the American world—thinks, and how such people are regarded. He found that no white man, however mean his station in life, would care to exchange places with the most brilliant and educated of them. He knew then that the thought was wrong; that the soul only reflected the true man, and that character was more than race or the color of the skin. But the knowledge of what the world thinks and says, like a knife cut deep to the bone and he groaned in an agony of spirit. He could see the lines of his usefulness being narrowed, the avenues of success closed, the respect of men to a large degree withheld, and more than all, his virgin love withered. Despair, like a white hoar frost seemed to fall about him and blight all his hopes. How could he break the news to her and release her from her vows if she wished him to do so. The tempter whispered, "Fly, fly away from J—— and her, to some new section and commence life over again where your blood-mixture is unknown." Open came the lid of his trunk and into it went his clothes and souvenirs. Her picture stood upon his dresser, that too, must go. He picked it up, gazed at it for a moment, pressed it to his lips and put it back with the remark, "She must not think me a coward." The reaction set in. He put back his things to their proper places and sat down holding his throbbing head between his hands arguing with himself. "Am I not Edwin Barden? Have I not been for twenty-four years in and out among my neighbors with not one word of reproach? Surely my identity is not lost, my record will not cast me out, nor will she."

As it has been said, he had recently graduated from college, had opened up his office, and his prospects were fair, and he could not see why this thing should interfere with his success and happiness. "Yet if I am a Negro," he said to himself, "my duty is to fight and suffer with that people until they, like others, are measured by what they are. No one can tell what the virgin soil of Negro intellect may yet accomplish. Like the virgin soil of mother earth its growth must be luxuriant, though sometimes rank, hard to cultivate, yet paying for the care. They have but just started towards zenith in their career, and, like promising lives cut off in their growth, no one can tell what this race may produce."

Far into the night and early in the morning, until after the family had risen, he sat and thought and resolved, but the sum of it all was because of her. He would give Ida time to hear of his family connections, so that her mind could be fully made up when he should offer her back the hand and heart she had so freely given him some months before.

It required an effort on his part to go about his way the next two or three days as if nothing had happened, in meeting his friends and attending to his business. But outside of a stolen stare that now and then he intercepted, everything seemed to remain as before. But even then the thought that to meet one friendly and politely in a business way, is not carrying one's feelings so far as to give one's daughter away to him, was a heavy load for him to carry. He did not now care for the opinion of the world if she were but true. His love was the dearest thing in the world for him, and he had too high a conception of God to think that he had anything to do with the evil wrought by men. His God and his love still were sacred. He expected that Mrs. Jones would interpose serious objections, for he had often talked with her on Southern questions, and out of gallantry had given way to her impetuous feelings against the Negro. Thus he had unwittingly plead guilty, by a silent acquiescence to the truth of her assertions. Now her two-edged tongue would be pointed at him, but he could stand all that if Ida were true.

CHAPTER VI.

————

Several evenings later Edwin set out, with any misgivings, to call on Ida. His heart beat more rapidly, and there was a great lump in his throat as he neared her home. He hoped to be able to find her alone so that he might learn his fate before he met the other members of the family. His wish was gratified for he saw her in the garden among the flowers just as he was entering the gate. He went up to her quickly and noiselessly, and was by her side almost before she was aware of his presence.

"Why, Edwin," she said, jumping back as if startled. "How you frightened me. I have a notion to chastise you for it."

"I have come almost expecting to be chastised," he replied, seriously. And she, looking at him, knew what was in his mind.

"I suppose you have heard what has happened in our family, and knowing your mother as I do, I cannot hope longer that you will become my wife. I have come to offer you an honorable release from our engagement. I only ask one boon in return, that you may say from your heart that you do not love me less for that which is not my fault."

She looked at him steadily for a moment, her love shining in her eyes. "I will say more than that, Edwin. I loved you, dear, for what you have been to me. I love you more deeply now because you need it. Your willingness to sacrifice yourself for me I will return. Nothing, Edwin, nothing but death or yourself shall separate us.

"But your mother?"

"As Ruth said to Naomi, so say I to you." [5]

He needed no more. All his burdens were lifted from him as if airy nothings. He was superlatively happy. He clasped her in his arms and kissed her repeatedly, and she too was very happy.

As her head lay confidingly on his shoulder she said, "This will come out all right, Edwin, I know it will," and then burst into tears.

This was almost too much for him. He clasped her more closely while saying:

"Ida, I appreciate the sacrifice you would make for me, and I have no adequate return to make for it, except a heart overflowing with love."

"Leave it all with me, Edwin. You can trust me, can't you? I am a woman now."

"Yes, dear."

"Then leave me for the present, and do nothing until you hear from me. I have not talked with father, and now that I have seen you, I want to see him. Will you do it?"

"I will." He kissed her and was gone.

．．．．

While Ida was talking with Edwin in the garden, an entirely different scene was going on within. Mrs. Jones had grown restless over the apparent indifference of Mr. Jones and was taking him to task for it.

"John," she said, somewhat impatiently, "John, you don't seem to care if your daughter does marry a nigger. She's your child, and it's your duty to keep her from going to ruin."

"Why, Madge, don't get so excited. You ought not to talk in such a way. For Ida to marry Edwin Barden is no crime. He is neither better nor worse than he [had] been, and ever since he rescued Mary, you have doted on him as a magnificent ideal of young and true manhood."

"But I didn't know he was a nigger," she replied spitefully, "and that alters things. But if you want her to marry him she can do it for all of me. I wash my hands of the whole matter. I will tell you though, and I intend to tell her, if she marries him she shall not come near me with him."

"Tush, tush! Madge. Would you cast her off because she couldn't reconcile her love with your views? If you had been young, you would have been in love with Edwin yourself and might have married him."

"John Jones! Are you crazy?"

"No, Madge. But you can't make me believe that tincture of Negro blood destroys manhood. There is no one in J— more respected than George Barden and his family, even though this great bug-bear is known. Besides, nowadays, one cannot tell who may have a little of this blood in their veins."

"Well, they ought to pass a law prohibiting any Negro passing off for a white man. If there had been we never would have come to this, but you men are so pokey. If Ida's mother were living today, what would she say to such a match?"

"That is the question: What would she say?" Mr. Jones was getting excited now. "She would approve of it."

"Don't you tell me that, John Jones. She would be false and untrue to the South and its traditions."

"Untrue to the South and its traditions! There is much about the South that is false and untrue. The time has come when we should not look upon its peculiar prejudices with the palliating eyes that we did years ago. Conditions change and we should change with them. Besides, Madge, I could tell you many of its falsities—marital vows were not held so sacred. Why do you suppose that laws were passed in State compelling the child to follow the conditions of mother? Surely not merely to keep enslaved the child born of a woman slave, however white it might be, no law was needed for that, it was Southern tradition, and it was chivalrous too, was it not? Ah, you suspect the reason. Let us not mar this epoch by practices that should be buried with the past and forgotten. Oh, God," cried Mr. Jones, springing to his feet, wringing his hands and pacing rapidly up and down the room. "Help me to forget. I would not make this revelation but for Ida's sake; but it would do no good to reveal it to her, and you must not; Madge, her mother was as dark as Edwin's uncle. Has fate cut out any stranger freak than that?"

"Ida a Negress! Oh, my God!" cried Mrs. Jones, and she fainted just as Ida entered.

. . . .

Mrs. Jones made no further objection to the marriage. The secret of Ida's birth was not revealed to her. Mrs. Jones knew that so far as she and Edwin were concerned it would make no difference and would make matters worse and so kept her own counsel. She never had cause to regret Ida's marriage to Edwin, for after the panic of '73 Mr. Jones failed in business and shortly afterward died leaving her penniless.[6] No son ever proved more dutiful than Edwin, and again she grew to love him as she did before. Edwin remained in J—— and achieved success and distinction in his profession, and no one in that section is more respected or in greater demand than he. Ida and he have been very happy in their love for each other and in the children who have blessed their union.

(NOTE [in the original publication]:— This story was written for the Short Story Prize competition instituted by the *Basis* nearly two years ago. That journal suspended before any awards were made and the MMS. [manuscript] returned to the authors. The incidents of the story are founded on real life, and they were much more intense and dramatic as they happened than the authors have been enabled to write them.)

Notes

Introduction

1. Indeed, in an ironic twist of fate, Stowers's daughter Marjorie, who shares her first name with Seth Stanley's love, would marry a man named Nelson M. Saunders two decades after the novel's publication, and their son would be named for his father and maternal grandfather, Nelson Walter Saunders.
2. Extant records offer several alternate spellings (including Bowdree and Boudrey) for this surname; among other siblings, Lucy also had a brother who would carry her father's full name.
3. Stowers would be admitted to the Michigan State Bar the year after *Appointed* was published. Mayhew's, sometimes listed as Mayhew's Business College and sometimes simply as Mayhew's School, was the brainchild of Ira Mayhew (1814–1894), author of *Mayhew's Practical Book-keeping*, and was more of a business and vocational school than a traditional college. Mayhew sold his school in 1883, and it became Spencerian Business College and then merged with Goldsmith Business College (a similar institution) to become the Detroit Business University in 1887. At least one source suggests that Stowers's studies there focused on stenography; see I. Garland Penn, *The Afro-American Press and Its Editors* (Springfield, MA: Wiley and Co., 1891).
4. This concern is evident in the 20 June 1890 editorial reprinted in appendix B.
5. A 1 January 1898 *Cleveland Gazette* biography of Anderson, for example, said that Anderson was "a mathematician of recognized ability" and that "there are few better-read or better-posted men in Detroit of any race."
6. Early studies of the Black press tended to focus on the decades before the *Plaindealer*. Martin Dann's collection of commentary and documents titled *The Black Press*, for example, even carries the subtitle "1827–1890." While new generations of scholars have begun the work demanded by the subject's amazing richness and complexity—see, for example, Eric Gardner, *Black Print Unbound: The Christian Recorder, African American Literature, and Periodical Culture* (New York: Oxford University Press, 2015), and Benjamin Fagan, *The Black Newspaper and the Chosen Nation* (Athens: University of Georgia Press, 2016)—they have also attended primarily to periodicals published before the 1890s, even though, in addition to the *Plaindealer*, these years saw the development of the *Indianapolis Freeman*, among other key papers.
7. While rare Black printers made key contributions to earlier Black publications—one thinks especially of New York's Hamilton family, who produced, among other texts, the *Anglo-African Magazine* and the *Weekly Anglo-African*—the printing trades often remained closed to African Americans, a fact embodied, for example, in the battles of Lewis Henry Douglass (a Civil War veteran and one of Frederick Douglass's sons) to secure membership in the Columbia Typographical Union and the National

Typographical Union in 1869. The *Christian Recorder* relied on contracted white printers until the late 1870s, when they were able to hire enough Black printers to move publication in-house.

8. The date is supplied by coverage in the 9 June 1883 *New York Globe*.
9. The *Post-Tribune* went through a variety of changes in title and ownership during the period. *Chronicling America* marks its founding in 1877 in a merger of the *Detroit Daily Post* and the *Detroit Advertiser and Tribune*. In 1884, it became simply the *Detroit Post*; in 1885, the *Detroit Daily Tribune*; and, in 1886, began morphing into the *Detroit Tribune*. It was white-run throughout.
10. The Colored Conventions digital project (coloredconventions.org) has made landmark contributions to recovering senses of these amazing sites of early Black activism.
11. Penn, *Afro-American Press*, 158, 161.
12. Penn, *Afro-American Press*, 163.
13. Eventually Robert Pelham Jr. would move to Washington, DC, and work for decades for the Census Bureau; his brother Benjamin would serve for over forty years in Wayne County government.
14. The novel's failure to mention the National Afro-American League (in which Anderson became deeply active during the 1890s) buttresses the suggestion that the novel was mostly composed in the mid to late 1880s.
15. See, for example, the 24 November 1894 *Leavenworth* (KS) *Herald*, the 8 December 1894 *Parsons* (KS) *Weekly Blade*, the 29 December 1894 *Cleveland Gazette*, and the 26 January 1895 *Indianapolis Freeman*.
16. Novels published in serial form during the period include the *Weekly Anglo-African's* serialization of William Wells Brown's *Miralda* (1860–1861, a variation of his *Clotel*) and Martin Delany's *Blake* (1861–1862), as well as the *Christian Recorder's* serialization of Julia C. Collins's *The Curse of Caste* (1865) and Frances Ellen Watkins Harper's *Minnie's Sacrifice* (1869), *Sowing and Reaping* (1876–1877), and *Trial and Triumph* (1888–1889).
17. Some of the novels printed in the *Plaindealer* include Jules Verne's *A Two Years' Vacation* (1888), Wilkie Collins's *Royal Love* (*Mr. Medhurst and the Princess*, 1884), and William Clark Russell's *A Marriage at Sea* (1891).
18. Until somewhat recently, scholarly attention to African American literature after the Civil War and before the Harlem Renaissance has been fairly thin. For two comparative examples, see Dickson D. Bruce's focused *Black American Writing from the Nadir: The Evolution of a Literary Tradition, 1877–1915* (Baton Rouge: Louisiana State University Press, 1989) and Bernard W. Bell's more general *The Afro-American Novel and Its Tradition* (Amherst: University of Massachusetts Press, 1987). Barbara McCaskill and Caroline Gebhard's edited collection *Post-Bellum, Pre-Harlem: African American Literature and Culture, 1877–1919* (New York: New York University Press, 2006) arguably inaugurated a new phase of much greater attention, which has yielded significant new scholarship on figures like Charles Chesnutt and Pauline Hopkins. However, there is still much work to do. The scholarship on self- and subsidized publication in early African American literature is similarly thin, and we do not know

whether Anderson and Stowers sought a "mainstream"/white publisher before making their publication decisions.

19. In addition to Frances E. W. Harper's *Iola Leroy* (1892), work by white authors like William Dean Howells sometimes moved beyond the "plantation school." This was the complex landscape that Charles Chesnutt would negotiate when and after he published "The Goophered Grapevine" in the *Atlantic* in 1888, and that Paul Laurence Dunbar, who published five books of poetry and three novels—all with major commercial presses that helped him access a wide audience—would engage with most famously in *The Sport of the Gods* (1902).

20. Review of *Appointed*, *Churchman*, July 14, 1894, 47.

21. Review of *Appointed*, *Cleveland Gazette*, December 29, 1894, 2. Tourgee's review first appeared in his 2 August 1894 Bystander's Notes column in the *Chicago Daily Inter Ocean*. It is reprinted in the *Indianapolis Freeman*, August 25, 1894, 3. See appendix A.

22. "Books, Periodicals, etc.," *Indianapolis Freeman*, January 26, 1895, 4.

23. Advertisement for *Appointed*, *Cleveland Gazette*, October 20, 1894, 3.

24. In his letter to a woman from Kansas asking for help with a speech titled "What Has the Negro Done in Science and Literature?", Chesnutt noted that there were few African Americans writing literature and mentioned—almost in passing—that "a couple of young men in Detroit one of whom is named Anderson, have recently published a novel." It would have been easy enough for Chesnutt to obtain the novel in Cleveland since it sold at the *Gazette* office. See Chesnutt to S. Alice Haldeman, February 1, 1896, in *"To Be an Author": Letters of Charles W. Chesnutt, 1889–1905*, ed. Joseph McElrath Jr. and Robert C. Leitz III (Princeton: Princeton University Press, 2014), 88. It is also notable that, among the few extant copies of the novel's 1894 publication, there are copies that show that it reached leaders in African American journalism as well as prominent local African Americans. The copy now housed at Yale University belonged to *New York Globe* writer and later *New York Age* coeditor and activist Jerome Peterson (1859–1943); the copy now housed at the University of Michigan's Bentley Historical Library belonged to John A. Loomis (1862–1914), an "expert stenographer" and one of the first African Americans to teach stenography, per a description in the *Michigan Manual of Freedmen's Progress* (Detroit: [State of Michigan], 1915).

25. Daylanne K. English, *Each Hour Redeem: Time and Justice in African American Literature* (Minneapolis: University of Minnesota Press, 2013), 49.

26. See W. E. B. Du Bois, "The Talented Tenth," in *The Negro Problem: A Series of Articles by Representative Negroes of To-day* (New York: James Pott, 1903).

27. See appendix C for "A Strange Freak of Fate." In his early study of African American novels, Robert Bone links *Appointed* to other "middle-class" novels of the 1890s. See Bone, *The Negro Novel in America* (New Haven: Yale University Press, 1958). Few other critics have written about *Appointed* beyond passing mention. Two exceptions are Bruce's *Black American Writing* and David Katzman, *Beyond the Ghetto: Black Detroit in the Nineteenth Century* (Urbana: University of Illinois Press, 1973).

28. Some African American novels of the period held back from marking the race of their

characters—as in Harper's *Sowing and Reaping* and *Trial and Triumph* and Amelia E. Johnson's *Clarence and Corinne* (1890) and *The Hazeley Family* (1894).

29. The *Forum* was a leading white journal of opinion and politics published between 1886 and 1930. In the late nineteenth century, it regularly printed essays by senators, congressmen, authors, and scientists and received a great deal of attention. James B. Eustis was a Harvard Law graduate, a former Confederate judge advocate, former state representative and senator, and a United States senator from Louisiana between 1876 and 1879 and again from 1885 to 1891. His essay generated a number of responses (both favorable and unfavorable) from around the country. The *Independent* sponsored a forum to discuss the article in its 21 February 1889 issue, and replies to Eustis appeared in Black newspapers including the *Cleveland Gazette* (December 1, 1888), the *New Orleans Weekly Pelican* (February 16, 1889), and the Leavenworth (KS) *Advocate* (March 23, 1889) as well as at least one white Republican paper, the *Chicago Daily Inter Ocean* (November 28, 1888).

30. James B. Eustis, "Race Antagonism in the South," the *Forum* 6, no. 2 (October 1888): 147, 153.

31. The evidence in many of the passages from John's speech is drawn directly from "The Colored Race," *Cleveland Gazette*, October 23, 1886, 1.

32. In addition to the *Appeal*, Anderson and Stowers cite the *Times-Democrat* and Henry W. Grady's *Atlanta Constitution*.

33. See "Free Speech in the South," *New York Freeman*, July 9, 1887, 2. The authors also use the *Topeka* (KS) *American Citizen* as an (uncredited) source.

34. Continuing to emphasize material in and from periodicals, the authors seem to have based their description of the steamboat disaster on the story of the *Kate Adams*, which exploded in flames on December 23, 1888. The sinking of the *Kate Adams* was widely reported in newspapers from Boston to San Diego, and a particularly lengthy story appeared in the *Chicago Inter Ocean* on December 25, 1888.

35. In choosing this as a precipitating event in the novel, the authors might be alluding to the "caning" of Massachusetts Senator Charles Sumner by South Carolina Senator Preston Brooks. On May 26, 1856, two days after Sumner made a speech condemning slavery, Brooks beat Sumner while the latter was sitting at his desk on the floor of the US Senate. Sumner nearly died, and the event came to symbolize the breakdown of legislative solutions in the run-up to the Civil War.

36. In *Living with Lynching: African American Lynching Plays, Performance, and Citizenship, 1890–1930* (Champaign: University of Illinois Press, 2011), Koritha Mitchell highlights the early twentieth-century rise of African American dramas concerning the southern lynching epidemic, a demonstration of the multigeneric response to the scourge of lynching that built from and included books like Charles Chesnutt's *Marrow of Tradition* (1901), Paul Laurence Dunbar's "The Haunted Oak" (1900), Pauline Hopkins's *Contending Forces* (1900), and James Weldon Johnson's *The Autobiography of an Ex-Colored Man* (1912)—novels which were themselves preceded by antilynching speeches, journalism, and pamphlets by Frederick Douglass, Albion Tourgee, Booker T. Washington, and Wells, among others.

37. Mitchell, *Living with Lynching*, 7.
38. Mitchell, *Living with Lynching*, 9.
39. Bruce, *Black American Writing*, 41.
40. See *Parmalee v. Morris* (218 Michigan 625, 1922) and *Schulte v. Starks* (238 Michigan 102, 1927). Michele Ronnick's entry on Anderson in the *African American National Biography* is perhaps the best place to begin further exploration of Anderson and Stowers's lives, though Stowers is not yet included in this resource. Francesco Nepa's entry on Benjamin Pelham in the *African American National Biography* is also useful, though Robert Pelham is not yet included in this resource.

APPOINTED

1. The university at Ann Arbor is the University of Michigan, founded in 1817.
2. The Michigan Military Academy was a military prep school in Orchard Lake, a small town in Oakland County, Michigan. It was founded in 1877 and went bankrupt in 1908. Its most famous alumnus is probably Edgar Rice Burroughs (class of 1895).
3. In the nineteenth century, a "dude" was a man who seemed overly fastidious and overly concerned with fashion. Thus "dudishness" can be taken as a synonym for foppishness or dandiness.
4. Universalism is both a theological stance that emphasizes universal reconciliation with God and a broad label for a set of more liberal Protestant denominations in the nineteenth-century United States.
5. Bayreuth is a town in southeastern Germany and is the home of the famed composer Richard Wagner.
6. Richard III (1452–1485) was king of England between 1483 and 1485. In his well-known history play, Shakespeare portrayed Richard III as a scheming hunchback, which explains the allusion here.
7. Ecclesiastes 12:8.
8. Hypatia (415–355 BCE) was an astronomer and mathematician who lived in ancient Alexandria; she lectured widely and was well known for rejecting both the institution of marriage and the polytheism of her contemporaries.
9. "Hoyster" is a purposeful mispronunciation of "oyster" designed to mock Maxwell.
10. *The Gypsy Baron* is an 1885 operetta by Johann Strauss II.
11. "True to the Last" is a nineteenth-century song written by Stephen Adams and Charles Rowe.
12. [Authors' note] This race name has been recently adopted by large numbers of colored people in the United States to show, 1st, their origin, and 2d, their present race standing. So far as long residence, a century or more of living, by one's ancestors, and an active participation in a country's affairs can change a race, they claim to have changed and that no other class of people in the country have a better right to be called American. The term *Negro*, while it may have been aptly applied to their ancestors, they hold, as to themselves, it is, 1st a misnomer, and 2d, is un-American and alien. In *Appointed* this term, *Afro-American*, will be used when the author has

occasion to speak of them out of dialogue. In dialogue the terms generally in use will be used.

13. Detroit and Windsor are on the American and Canadian side (respectively) of the Detroit River.

14. Formerly "Hog Island" and rechristened in 1845, this Detroit River island became a city-owned park in 1879. Partially designed by Frederick Law Olmstead and connected by bridge to Detroit, it was long a popular destination for area residents because of its lush landscapes and, after 1895, its zoo.

15. Lord Byron, or George Gordon Byron, (1788–1824) was a British author well known for both his dashing persona and his enduring contributions to Romantic poetry.

16. Hull's surrender refers to the siege of Detroit during the War of 1812. The American general William Hull surrendered Fort Detroit to the British general Isaac Brock. Pontiac's Conspiracy refers to a 1763 rebellion against the British led by the Ottawa leader Pontiac; the rebellion lasted only a year, but it forced the British to modify some of their policies toward Native American tribes.

17. This is a play on James Russell Lowell's line "And what is so rare as a day in June?" in "The Vision of Sir Launfal" (1848).

18. Matthew 6:34.

19. Lake St. Clair sits between Ontario and Michigan, just north of Detroit. The Flats are on the east bank of the lake, right next to the Canadian border.

20. The *Century* magazine was an influential literary and news magazine with a wide circulation in the late nineteenth century.

21. "Mackinac" refers to the straits separating the lower peninsula of Michigan from the upper peninsula. It is the site where Lake Huron meets Lake Michigan and is home to Mackinac Island, where the British maintained a fort during the American Revolution. The fort was later taken over and manned by the American army.

22. Sand Beach is in northern Huron County; Sault Ste. Marie, a city at the far northeastern edge of Michigan's Upper Peninsula built around Fort Brady, is separated from its Ontario twin by the St. Mary's River. The locks there allow water traffic from Lake Superior to enter the lower Great Lakes.

23. Lakeside towns in northern Michigan.

24. This paragraph describes several of the natural wonders of Mackinac Island.

25. The men refer to Henry Wadsworth Longfellow's famous poem "The Song of Hiawatha," which is set on and around Lake Superior, in Michigan's Upper Peninsula.

26. Palissy (meaning Bernard Palissy) and Sèvres (a French manufacturer) refer to fashionable French pottery and porcelain of the nineteenth century.

27. *Ben Hur: A Tale of the Christ* (1880) was the bestselling novel of the nineteenth century in the United States; it was written by the American soldier, writer, and politician Lew Wallace (1827–1905).

28. William Dean Howells (1837–1920) and Henry James (1843–1916) were two of the most famous American novelists of the late nineteenth century. In both their novels and in several essays published throughout the 1880s and 1890s, the two men advocated for a realist aesthetic in fiction. Book clubs like the one mentioned here

became widespread at the end of the nineteenth century. Elizabeth McHenry's *Forgotten Readers: Recovering the Lost History of African American Literary Societies* (Durham: Duke University Press, 2002) explores such clubs among African Americans.

29. Neither this line (nor any like it) appear in the published works or the correspondence of Alexander Pope. Perhaps the authors found the misattributed quotation in a newspaper and included it in their novel, or perhaps they simply made it up.

30. Formerly enslaved activist Frederick Douglass (1817–1895) was widely recognized as one of the nineteenth century's greatest orators.

31. Phillis Wheatley (1753–1784) was a pioneering African American poet best known for *Poems on Various Subjects* (1773).

32. This line is from the song "Here's a How-De-Do!" from Gilbert and Sullivan's musical *The Mikado* (1885).

33. The authors use this paragraph to describe various features of Detroit and environs, including Woodward Avenue (a major north-south thoroughfare), Grosse Pointe (tony suburbs east of the city that border Lake St. Clair), and the Log Cabin Farm (a cabin built in what is now Palmer Park, in north-central Detroit).

34. Here Marjorie alludes to Matthew 7:16.

35. Here the authors allude to Benjamin Franklin's famous *Poor Richard's Almanack*.

36. The Mohawk River is a tributary of the Hudson River and runs just north of Albany, New York.

37. "Madame Grundy" is a name used to describe a conventional and sanctimonious woman. See, for example, Mrs. Grundy in Frances Ellen Watkins Harper's 1876–1877 serialized *Christian Recorder* novel *Sowing and Reaping*.

38. Orson Squire Fowler was the author of *Practical Phrenology* (1843) and an influential "scientist" in the nineteenth century.

39. This is a line from the song "The Love Chase," which was published in R. E. Egerton Warburton's *Hunting Songs and Miscellaneous Verses*, first published in 1859. This may also be an allusion to Luke 22.

40. A saying adapted from the 1786 poem "To a Mouse," by the Scottish author Robert Burns.

41. From Alfred, Lord Tennyson's 1835 poem "Locksley Hall."

42. Often attributed to John Keats, this is from Maria Lovell's 1854 translation of Friedrich Halm's *Der Sohn der Wildnis*.

43. Matthew 11:28.

44. An allusion to one of Puck's lines in *A Midsummer Night's Dream* (act 3, scene 2): "What fools these mortals be."

45. Coined by Lord Byron to describe a bridge in Venice that was often part of the last view prisoners saw before entering the Prigioni Nuove.

46. This rhyme is unattributed but appears in a number of quotation books and folklore treasuries published in the late nineteenth and early twentieth centuries.

47. *Les Misérables* by Victor Hugo (1802–1885) was published in 1862 and translated into English soon thereafter. Jean Valjean is the main character, who serves nearly

twenty years in prison for stealing a loaf of bread with which he hopes to feed his sister's starving children.

48. Henry Wadsworth Longfellow, "The Old Clock on the Stairs" (1845).

49. These lyrics come from the hymn "Abide with Me" by Henry Francis Lyte.

50. A trick-taking card game.

51. "Doubting Castle" and "Giant Despair" are allusions to John Bunyan's *Pilgrim's Progress* (1678), an allegory of the journey of a faithful Christian.

52. A county in southeastern Michigan that borders Ohio on the south; Adrian is the county seat.

53. Charles Dickens (1812–1870), Thomas Mayne Reid (1818–1883), James Fenimore Cooper (1789–1851), Edward Bulwer-Lytton (1803–1873), and George Eliot [Mary Anne Evans] (1819–1880) were well-known nineteenth-century authors.

54. This comes from canto 1 of Byron's "Don Juan" (1818).

55. Herodotus (ca. 485–ca. 424 BCE) and Plutarch (46–120) were ancient historians. George Rawlinson (1812–1902) was a British historian who wrote about ancient civilizations and translated Herodotus into English. Max Muller (1823–1900) was a German historian who wrote definitive works on Indian culture and religion and Indo-European relationships. Johann Friedrich Blumenbach (1752–1840) was a German scientist who promoted the idea that Africans were a "degenerate" race, though only in terms of their physical appearance. Though Blumenbach denied any differences between Africans and Caucasians in terms of intellect or ability, his ideas were used to justify scientific racism in the nineteenth century.

56. Gaius Marius (157–86 BCE) served as a praetor, senior legate, and—ultimately—six-time consul in ancient Rome. He was celebrated by Plutarch for his various political reforms and for his battlefield heroics.

57. The "gall of bitterness" comes from Acts 8:23.

58. Scottish poet Robert Burns (1759–1796).

59. L'Ouverture (1743–1803) was a former slave who led an uprising against the French in Saint-Domingue. In the wake of that successful rebellion, L'Ouverture became a well-known military leader whose battlefield exploits helped to secure independence for Haiti.

60. Crispus Attucks (1723–1770) was an African American sailor killed during the Boston Massacre on March 5, 1770.

61. These are all battles fought (in part) by African American troops during the American Civil War.

62. William Sanders Scarborough's *First Lessons in Greek* was first published in 1881 and was widely used in classrooms for several years after.

63. The Hydra was a serpent that grew new heads whenever one head was cut off; Hercules ultimately destroyed the Hydra.

64. The Thousand Islands is an archipelago of over 1,800 islands that dot the St. Lawrence River between Canada and New York.

65. Buffalo, New York, is on the eastern edge of Lake Erie, while Detroit sits on the Detroit River on the northwestern edge of the same lake.

66. All of these were leading American magazines of the late nineteenth century.

67. James B. Eustis (1834–1899) was a Democratic senator from 1876 to 1879 and again from 1885 to 1891. His article was titled "Race Antagonism in the South" and was published in the *Forum* 6, no. 2 (October 1888): 144–54.

68. Famed inventor Thomas Edison (1847–1931) was a scientific and business leader in the late nineteenth century. Alexander T. Stewart (1803–1876) was a businessman who built the largest and most profitable department store in the United States. Regulus is one of the brightest stars in the sky and is part of the Leo constellation, hence the association with kingliness. In Greek mythology, Pythias is notable for his willingness to sacrifice himself for his friend Damon.

69. In Alexander Dumas's novel *The Count of Monte Cristo* (1844), the main character is a man named Edmond Dantès who is wrongly imprisoned, escapes, acquires a great fortune, and then takes on the name "The Count of Monte Cristo" while he seeks revenge upon his enemies. One might note the similarities between Valjean and Dantès as men who were unfairly bound by the state.

70. Pinckney Benton Stewart Pinchback (1837–1921) was the governor of Louisiana from 1872 to 1873. Pinchback was the first African American governor in the United States (and the last until Douglas Wilder was elected governor of Virginia in 1990).

71. "All our tribes" comes from *The Merchant of Venice* (act 1, scene 3).

72. In 1887, a white mob attacked striking sugar workers in Thibodaux, Louisiana. The strike had been organized by the Knights of Labor (an organization both Stowers and Anderson supported) and was timed to interfere with the harvest on sugar plantations. The mob killed over thirty Black laborers and thereby ended the strike.

73. The antebellum "Black Laws" were restrictions placed on free African Americans in "free" states like Illinois that often limited mobility, property ownership, voting rights, testimony rights, and a host of basic civil liberties.

74. According to Plutarch, Spartan women demanded that male soldiers adhere to a standard of "victory or death."

75. The Fisk Jubilee Singers are a highly regarded African American a cappella group founded in 1871. They are well known for their renditions of African American spirituals and hymns, and they have performed to enthusiastic audiences around the world.

76. The authors seem to mean "Negrophilia" rather than "Negrophobia" here.

77. Napoleon Bonaparte (1769–1821) was emperor of France from 1798 to 1814. He was exiled to Elba in 1814, but he returned to France soon thereafter to reclaim his position and lead the French Army in battle. He was defeated by the Duke of Wellington at the Battle of Waterloo (June 18, 1815). Waterloo was a great victory for the "Iron Duke," and it effectively marked the end of Napoleon's reign; by late 1815, Napoleon had been exiled to St. Helena, where he died six years later.

78. Probably "Hearest Thou? Odi Tu?" by Italian composer Tito Mattei (1841–1914).

79. This is perhaps a bit of anachronism in the novel since the authors seem to be referring to the national convention of the African American League that was held in Chicago in 1890, two years after the events narrated in the novel. Even so, their

mention of retributive threats and of lynchings and riots would have been accurate in 1888 as well as 1890. The towns listed in the paragraph were sites of lynchings and riotous uprisings against African Americans, many of which were reported in the *Plaindealer* and by Ida B. Wells, the well-known chronicler of southern "outrages" who wrote for the Memphis *Free Speech*.

80. [Authors' note] During the National Editorial convention that met in Detroit in the summer of 1889, the Author had occasion to converse with several representatives from the Yazoo District on this subject. These men, while they believe in keeping the Afro-American subjected politically, confessed that they were glad that slavery was destroyed; and that the labor of these people was very valuable. Mention being made of immigration, they said that 40,000 Afro-Americans had recently come to that district (the Yazoo), and that despite what was said of the desirability of getting rid of that class, it was indispensable to the South.

　　The immigration of such large numbers from the Southeastern States, has also led to the introduction and passage of immigration laws in the States of Georgia and South Carolina. These laws were the outgrowth of public sentiment in these states, which was aroused by the departure of their laboring element. The sentiment against the agents became so intense that they were compelled to leave the States, and were not allowed to stand upon the order of their going.

81. [Authors' note] We give to the World this year a crop of 7,500,000 bales of cotton worth $450,000,000, and its cash equivalent in grain, grasses and fruit. This enormous crop could not have come from the hands of sullen, discontented labor. I present the tax-books of Georgia which show that the negro in Georgia has about $10,000,000 of assessed property worth twice as much. Can it be seriously mentioned that we are terrorizing the people from whose hands come every year $1,000,000,000 of farm products.—Henry Grady, December, 1889.

82. [Authors' note] Recent statistics show that the percentage of white Northern emigrants are decreasing, and that throughout the whole South during the last decade there were only 150,000, and only 200,000 foreign emigrants.

83. [Authors' note] In 1888 more cotton was produced by 1,000,000 bales than ever before in the South, largely due to the increased intelligence of the negro.—Col. J. M. Keating of *Memphis Appeal*.

84. Tougaloo College is one of the oldest of the many historically Black colleges and universities in the United States. Tougaloo sits just north of Jackson, Mississippi, and was founded in 1869 by the American Missionary Association and functioned as a normal school and teacher training institute until 1892, when (contrary to the article Saunders cites) the state of Mississippi stopped supporting Tougaloo. Soon thereafter, the school began offering a more academic curriculum and has been granting bachelor's degrees for over one hundred years.

85. [Authors' note] Since 1861 the Negro has decreased his illiteracy 50 per cent. Col. J. M. Keating.—*Memphis Appeal*.

86. [Authors' note] The *Times-Democrat*, Sept. 1, 1889, gives the total scholastic

population of the South as 5,966,142, of whom 2,057,990 are colored and 3,908,152 are white, with a total enrollment of 3,220,955 of whom 985,022 are colored. The different Commissioners of Education in the states all concur in saying that the Afro-American ratio in attendance is on the increase and that the per cent of ignorance is decreasing.

87. [Authors' note] The same authority quoted above gives the average days of school in the South as 98.25 and the average pay of teachers as $29.80 per month in 1889.

88. [Authors' note] The *Times-Democrat*, September 1, 1889, gives the exclusive colored schools as follows:

	SCHOOLS.	TEACHERS.	PUPILS.
Public Schools	19,550	20,000	985,022
Normal Schools	16	119	1,771
Secondary Instruction	31	247	6,655
College Arts and Science	12	79	922
Schools of Theology	16	77	933
Schools of Science	2	29	840
Schools of Law	4	15	1,991
Schools of Medicine	3	48	165
Schools of Deaf and Dumb			255
Schools of Blind			91
Schools of Feeble Minded			136
Schools of Reform Farms			1,699
Totals	19,634	20,615	1,000,580

Increase since 1882, 34 per cent.

Contributions of Southern States by taxation since the war	$37,377,673
Contributions from Societies and Missions	$15,767,746
Total	$53,145,419

The authority quoted above. Sept. 1, 1890, says: There are now in the South 15,254 colored schools with 17,160 teachers and 1,986,492 pupils enrolled, and 84 colleges or high schools with 509 teachers and 15,412 pupils.

Contributions of Southern States by taxation	$39,746,850
Contributions from Societies, Missions and other sources	$16,434,520
Total	$56,181,370

If the solution of the Southern problem is in the education of the Negro, it is rapidly being reached.

89. [Authors' note] In the State of Georgia a Negro school teacher is paid about $30 per month while white teachers get from $75 to $150, and the whites get about $200,000 for higher education, and the Negro gets nothing, yet it is said we get half the money for educational purposes.—Atlanta, Ga. News, December, 1889.

While the Southern States for year ending June 1, 1890, raised $14,767,397 for school purposes, only $2,369,397 was given toward colored schools, and yet they represent over one-third of the whole population.—Author.

90. The US Civil War.
91. George Washington Cable (1844–1925) was a New Orleans–born author best known for his novel *The Grandissimes* (1880).
92. Anderson and Stowers's own newspaper.
93. Cardinal Grandison is a villainous and duplicitous character in Benjamin Disraeli's novel *Lothair* (1870).
94. [Authors' note] This argument is used by Lewis H. Blair, of Richmond, Va., in his book entitled: "The Prosperity of the South Dependent upon the Elevation of the Negro."
95. [Authors' note] If we assert our rights to guide the destinies of a Nation claiming that we are the stronger race, then we must be inflexibly just to the weaker. The new South must be a South of law and order, a South in which full and equal justice shall be done only through the machinery of the tribunals of the law. On this basis alone can be raised the edifice of enduring prosperity and power.—Weekly *Times-Democrat*, Dec. 27th, 1889.
96. This line is from Oliver Goldsmith's poem "The Deserted Village" (1770).
97. Straight University (1869–1934) was an early Black college in New Orleans; Leland University (1870–1960) was situated on St. Charles Avenue in the same city.
98. [Authors' note] This building they have occupied for fifteen years. From this they have been driven out by the police, by the order of the school board. It is but just to say that a pretty good building is being erected in Carrollton for the colored children, and another tolerably fair building now occupied by them in MacDonoghville, but apart from these the only respectable public building occupied by them was that in the sixth district from which nearly five hundred of them have been driven into a worthless, uncomfortable and dilapidated building to make room for about fifty white children. Another piece of injustice rests in the fact that third rate white teachers, having no sympathy with the colored children, are placed in charge of nearly all their schools, while worthy and competent colored teachers are turned off.—*S. W. Christian Advocate*, November, 1889.
99. The authors seem to have been great fans of George Washington Cable, who—like Albion Tourgee—was deeply engaged with post-Reconstruction politics in the South. Cable's novel *Au Large* was serialized in the *Century* starting with vol. 35, no. 1 (Nov. 1887) and running through vol. 35, no. 5 (March 1888).
100. James Buchanan Eads was a civil engineer who devised a system to keep the Mississippi River from silting in and blocking the port of New Orleans. Eads's 1876 innovation saved the port.
101. Luke 6:45.
102. [Authors' note] When the steamer Kate Adams was burned, Dec. 23, 1888, the first alarm was given by a colored woman in the manner as described.
103. In Greek mythology, Scylla was a monster that lived on one side of a channel while Charybdis was a whirlpool on the other side. Ships passing through the channel had to navigate between Scylla and Charybdis with peril on both sides; Odysseus traverses this narrow passage in *The Odyssey*.
104. John Sherman (1823–1900) was a Republican senator from Ohio between 1861 and

1877 and from 1881 to 1897. Sherman, the brother of the well-known Union general William T. Sherman, was a career politician and strong advocate of civil rights.

105. These words from President Benjamin Harrison were spoken before he was elected. They come from a speech he delivered at the Michigan Club in Detroit on February 22, 1888. The speech appears in Thomas Knox, *The Republican Party and Its Leaders* (New York: Collier, 1892), 461–68.

106. Herod the Great was the king of Judea from 37 BCE to 3 CE.

107. William Lloyd Garrison (1805–1879), Wendell Phillips (1811–1884), Charles Sumner (1811–1874), John Brown (1800–1859), and Elijah Lovejoy (1802–1837) were nineteenth-century American abolitionists.

108. William "Boss" Tweed was a New York legislator and, eventually, the mayor of New York City. Tweed was the leader of a corrupt group of politicians who enriched themselves by controlling judges, police, and balloting in the city. Tweed was imprisoned in 1872 and again in 1876; he died in prison in 1878. By invoking Tweed's name here, the authors are highlighting the corruption of white government officials.

109. From Joseph Addison's ode to Psalm 19, which was widely reprinted under various titles and integrated into hymns.

110. From Fanny Crosby's popular 1867 hymn "The Water of Life."

111. Psalms 68:31.

112. [Authors' note] Recently an Englishman in Birmingham was arrested and kept in jail for two days for speaking to an Afro-American woman. The only excuse given for it was that he had violated their customs.

113. [Authors' note] A company has been formed in Massachusetts whose object is to induce Afro-American families to come to that state.

114. See also Book II, chapter 2, note 61.

115. The "canaille" are the common people. The French word comes from "canine," suggesting an association between commoners and dogs.

116. A radical socialist government deposed Napoleon III and took over France for six months in 1871.

117. From John 14:2.

118. The language of this dream alludes heavily to John Milton's *Paradise Lost* (1667).

119. From a poem titled "Rest" and signed "W. L. E." that was written for the San Francisco periodical *The Wasp* (January 26, 1889, page 5).

120. As explained in the Book of Ruth, Naomi means "pleasant," but she changes so greatly over years of hard labor that she asks her former friends to call her Mara, meaning "bitter."

121. Othello, the "moor of Venice," charms and marries Desdemona, who is white. It is interesting to note that Seth is aligned with the Black character in this metaphor.

122. In 1888, Benjamin Harrison, a Republican from Indiana, won election to the presidency. Political parties and their orientations were very different in the nineteenth century than they are today, and Harrison won the presidency without

any support from the southern states. Though Harrison's election dismayed the white supremacists in the South who favored the Democrat Grover Cleveland, Harrison was unable to pass any civil rights legislation due to Democratic intransigence, and Harrison's one-term presidency is not regarded as a particularly influential one.

123. In 1890, Clement Garrett Morgan delivered the commencement address at Harvard, and Morgan's speech was printed in full in the 4 July 1890 issue of the *Plaindealer*. Charles C. Cook was elected class orator at Cornell for 1890, but he declined the honor. See "Will Not Accept," the *Plaindealer*, November 1, 1889, 1.

Appendix B

1. The editorials, unless otherwise indicated, are also untitled.
2. Judson Grenell copublished the socialist *Detroit Times* from 1881 and remained a leading voice for labor in the 1880s. On labor and labor newspapers in Detroit, see Carlotta R. Anderson, *All-American Anarchist: Joseph A. Labadie and the Labor Movement* (Detroit: Wayne State University Press, 1998).
3. The Waterbury (CT) *American* began publishing in 1844 and continued publishing until the 1930s.
4. At the time of Jesus's trial and conviction, Barabbas was held by the Roman authorities, but—according to a Passover tradition—his sentence was commuted by Pontius Pilate. According to the gospels, when Pilate asked the crowd whether he should release Jesus or Barabbas, the crowd asked that Barabbas be freed and that Jesus be sent to death.
5. *An Appeal to Pharaoh: The Negro Problem, and Its Radical Solution* was authored by Carlyle McKinley and published in 1890. In the book, McKinley ultimately argues that "the forcible removal of the whole black and colored population of the United States could be accomplished and should be accomplished" (205).
6. Here the editors refer to Matthew Calbraith Butler (1836–1909), a former Confederate general and a US senator from South Carolina between 1877 and 1895.
7. Amory Dwight Mayo (1823–1907) was a Unitarian minister from Boston who traveled to the South in the 1880s in support of public education.
8. William Dean Howells's short novel *An Imperative Duty* (1891) features protagonist Rhoda Aldgate, the "beautiful girl" referred to in the editorial. For a very different treatment of some of these issues, see Frances Ellen Watkins Harper's novel *Iola Leroy* (1892).
9. *Dr. Huguet* (1891), by Ignatius Donnelly, is a work of speculative fiction in which the titular character (a southern doctor) exchanges bodies with a lower-class Black man.
10. *Anthropology for the People: A Refutation of the Theory of the Adamic Origins of All Races* was authored by "Caucasian" and published by the Everett Waddey Company in 1891.

Appendix C

1. There is a Silver Lake in Summit County, Ohio, about five miles north of Akron and forty miles south of Cleveland and Lake Erie.
2. Perhaps a typographical error for "cheery."
3. In 1872, Ulysses S. Grant, a Republican, ran against the Democrat Horace Greeley, who died after the votes were cast and before the Electoral College cast its ballots. Even before Greeley's death, Grant had prevailed decisively in the popular vote and had secured more electoral votes. He would go on to serve his second term (1873–1877), during which he continued Republican Reconstruction policies.
4. This comes from canto 4 of Byron's poem "Childe Harold's Pilgrimage."
5. Ruth 1:16 reads in part, "For wherever you go, I will go; And wherever you lodge, I will lodge; Your people shall be my people."
6. Set off by a range of factors in Europe and North America, the Panic of 1873 led the United States into what, until the 1930s, was described as the "Great Depression"—dire economic conditions including bank closures and a temporary shutdown of the New York Stock Exchange. Its effects were still being felt into the 1880s.

Bibliography of Related Works

Late Nineteenth-Century African American Literature and History

Alexander, Shawn Leigh. *An Army of Lions: The Civil Rights Struggle Before the NAACP* (Philadelphia: University of Pennsylvania Press, 2012).

Bell, Bernard W. *The Afro-American Novel and Its Tradition* (Amherst: University of Massachusetts Press, 1987).

Bone, Robert. *The Negro Novel in America* (New Haven: Yale University Press, 1958).

Bruce, D. Dixon. *Black American Writing from the Nadir: The Evolution of a Literary Tradition, 1877–1915* (Baton Rouge: Louisiana State University Press, 1989).

Ernest, John. *Chaotic Justice: Rethinking African American Literary History* (Chapel Hill: University of North Carolina Press, 2009).

Gardner, Eric. *Unexpected Places: Relocating Nineteenth-Century African American Literature* (Jackson: University Press of Mississippi, 2009).

Jackson, Blyden. *A History of Afro-American Literature.* Vol 1, *The Long Beginning, 1746–1895* (Baton Rouge: Louisiana State University Press, 1989).

Katzman, David. *Before the Ghetto: Black Detroit in the Nineteenth Century* (Urbana: University of Illinois Press, 1973).

McCaskill, Barbara, and Caroline Gebhard, eds. *Post-Bellum, Pre-Harlem: African American Literature and Culture, 1877–1919* (New York: New York University Press, 2006).

McHenry, Elizabeth. *Forgotten Readers: Recovering the Lost History of African American Literary Societies* (Durham: Duke University Press, 2002).

Meier, August. *Negro Thought in America, 1880–1915* (Ann Arbor: University of Michigan Press, 1963).

Miles, Tiya. *The Dawn of Detroit: A Chronicle of Slavery and Freedom in the City of the Straits* (New York: New Press, 2017).

Richardson, Heather Cox. *The Death of Reconstruction: Race, Labor, and Politics in the Post-Civil War North, 1865–1901* (Cambridge: Harvard University Press, 2001).

Suggs, Jon-Christian. *Whispered Consolations: Law and Narrative in African American Life* (Ann Arbor: University of Michigan Press, 2000).

Williams, Heather Andrea. *Self-Taught: African American Education in Slavery and Freedom* (Chapel Hill: University of North Carolina Press, 2005).

The Black Press in the Late Nineteenth Century

Alexander, Ann Field. *Race Man: The Rise and Fall of the "Fighting Editor," John Mitchell Jr.* (Charlottesville: University of Virginia Press, 2002).

Bullock, Penelope L. *The Afro-American Periodical Press, 1838–1909* (Baton Rouge: Louisiana State University Press, 1981).

Danky, James, and Maureen Hady. *African-American Newspapers and Periodicals: A National Bibliography* (Cambridge: Harvard University Press, 1998).

Gardner, Eric. *Black Print Unbound: The* Christian Recorder, *African American Literature, and Periodical Culture* (New York: Oxford University Press, 2015).

Giddings, Paula J. *Ida: A Sword Among Lions* (New York: Amistad, 2008).

Penn, I. Garland. *The Afro-American Press and Its Editors* (Springfield, MA: Willey and Co., 1891).

Suggs, Henry, ed. *The Black Press in the Middle West, 1865–1985* (Westport, CT: Greenwood Press, 1996).

Thornbrough, Emma Lou. "American Negro Newspapers, 1880–1914," *Business History Review* 40 (1966): 467–90.

Vogel, Todd, ed. *The Black Press: New Literary and Historical Essays* (New Brunswick: Rutgers University Press, 2001).

Washburn, Patrick S. *The African American Newspaper: Voice of Freedom* (Evanston, IL: Northwestern University Press, 2006).

CPSIA information can be obtained
at www.ICGtesting.com
Printed in the USA
LVHW091449221019
634987LV00001B/4/P

9 781946 684394